FROM

Florence

With Love

With Love
COLLECTION

February 2017

February 2017

February 2017

March 2017

March 2017

March 2017

FROM
Florence
With Love

CAROLINE   **CATHERINE**   **LUCY**
ANDERSON   **GEORGE**   **GORDON**

& MILLS BOON

First Published in Great Britain 2017
By Mills & Boon, an imprint of HarperCollins*Publishers*
1 London Bridge Street, London, SE1 9GF

FROM FLORENCE WITH LOVE © 2017 Harlequin Books S.A.

Valtieri's Bride © 2012 Caroline Anderson
Lorenzo's Reward © 2000 Catherine George
The Secret That Changed Everything © Harlequin Books S.A. 2012
*(Special thanks and acknowledgement are given to Lucy Gordon
for her contribution to THE LARKVILLE LEGACY series.)*

ISBN: 978-0-263-92792-4

09-0317

Our policy is to use papers that are natural, renewable and recyclable products and made from wood grown in sustainable forests.
The logging and manufacturing processes conform to the legal environmental regulations of the country of origin.

Printed and bound in Spain
by CPI, Barcelona

VALTIERI'S BRIDE

CAROLINE ANDERSON

Caroline Anderson has the mind of a butterfly. She's been a nurse, a secretary, a teacher, run her own soft furnishing business, and now she's settled on writing. She says, 'I was looking for that elusive something. I finally realised it was variety, and now I have it in abundance. Every book brings new horizons and new friends, and in between books I have learned to be a juggler. My teacher husband John and I have two beautiful and talented daughters, Sarah and Hannah, umpteen pets and several acres of Suffolk that nature tries to reclaim every time we turn our backs!' Caroline also writes for the Mills & Boon Medical Romance series.

CHAPTER ONE

WHAT *on earth* was she doing?

As the taxi pulled up in front of the Jet Centre at London City Airport, he paused, wallet in hand, and stared spellbound across the drop-off point.

Wow. She was *gorgeous*.

Even in the crazy fancy-dress outfit, her beauty shone out like a beacon. Her curves—soft, feminine curves—were in all the right places, and her face was alight with laughter, the skin pale and clear, her cheeks tinged pink by the long blonde curls whipping round her face in the cutting wind. She looked bright and alive and impossibly lovely, and he felt something squeeze in his chest.

Something that had been dormant for a very long time.

As he watched she anchored the curls absently with one hand, the other gesturing expressively as she smiled and talked to the man she'd stopped at the entrance. She was obviously selling something. Goodness knows what, he couldn't read the piece of card she was brandishing from this distance, but the man laughed and raised a hand in refusal and backed away, entering the building with a chuckle.

Her smile fading, she turned to her companion, more sensibly dressed in jeans and a little jacket. Massimo flicked his eyes over her, but she didn't hold his attention. Not like the blonde, and he found his eyes drawn back to her against his will.

Dio, she was exquisite. By rights she should have looked an utter tramp but somehow, even in the tacky low-cut dress and a gaudy plastic tiara, she was, quite simply, riveting. There was something about her that transcended all of that, and he felt himself inexplicably drawn to her.

He paid the taxi driver, hoisted his flight bag over his shoulder and headed for the entrance. She was busy again, talking to another man, and as the doors opened he caught her eye and she flashed a hopeful smile at him.

He didn't have time to pause, whatever she was selling, he thought regretfully, but the smile hit him in the solar plexus, and he set his bag down on the floor by the desk once he was inside, momentarily winded.

'Morning, Mr Valtieri. Welcome back to the Jet Centre. The rest of your party have arrived.'

'Thank you.' He cleared his throat and glanced over his shoulder at the woman. 'Is that some kind of publicity stunt?'

The official gave a quiet, mildly exasperated sigh and smiled wryly.

'No, sir. I understand she's trying to get a flight to Italy.'

Massimo felt his right eyebrow hike. 'In a *wedding dress*?'

He gave a slight chuckle. 'Apparently so. Some competition to win a wedding.'

He felt a curious sense of disappointment. Not that it made the slightest bit of difference that she was getting married; she was nothing to him and never would be, but nevertheless…

'We asked her to leave the building, but short of escorting her right back to the main road, there's little more we can do to get rid of her and she seems harmless enough. Our clients seem to be finding her quite entertaining, anyway.'

He could understand that. He was entertained himself— mesmerised, if he was honest. And intrigued—

'Whereabouts in Italy?' he asked casually, although the tightness in his gut was far from casual.

'I think I heard her mention Siena—but, Mr Valtieri, you really don't want to get involved,' he warned, looking troubled. 'I think she's a little…'

'Crazy?' he said drily, and the man's mouth twitched.

'Your word, sir, not mine.'

As they watched, the other man walked away and she gave her companion a wry little smile. She said something, shrugged her slender shoulders in that ridiculous meringue of a dress, then rubbed her arms briskly. She must be freezing! September was a strange month, and today there wasn't a trace of sunshine and a biting wind was whipping up the Thames estuary.

No! It was none of his business if she hadn't had the sense to dress for the weather, he told himself firmly, but then he saw another man approach the doors, saw the woman straighten her spine and go up to him, her face wreathed in smiles as she launched into a fresh charm offensive, and he felt his gut clench.

He knew the man slightly, more by reputation than anything else, and he was absolutely the last person this enchanting and slightly eccentric young woman needed to get involved with. And he would be flying to his private airfield, about an hour's drive from Siena. Close enough, if you were desperate…

He couldn't let it happen. He had more than enough on his conscience.

The doors parted with a hiss as he strode up to them, and he gave the other man a look he had no trouble reading. He told him—in Italian, and succinctly—to back off, and Nico shrugged and took his advice, smiling regretfully at the woman before moving away from her, and Massimo gave him a curt nod and turned to the woman, meeting her eyes again—vivid, startling blue eyes that didn't look at all happy with what he'd just done. There was no smile this time, just those eyes like blue ice-chips skewering him as he stood there.

Stunning eyes, framed by long, dark lashes. Her mouth, even without the smile, was soft and full and kissable— No! He sucked in a breath, and found himself drawing a delicate and haunting fragrance into his lungs.

It rocked him for a second, took away his senses, and when they came back they *all* came back, slamming into him with the force of an express train and leaving him wanting in a way he hadn't wanted for years. Maybe ever—

'What did you *say* to him?' Lydia asked furiously, hardly able to believe the way he'd dismissed that man with a few choice words—not that she'd understood one of them, of course, but there was more to language than vocabulary and he'd been pretty explicit, she was sure. But she'd been so close to success and she was really, really cross and frustrated now. 'He'd just offered me a seat in his plane!'

'Believe me, you don't want to go on his plane.'

'Believe me, I do!' she retorted, but he shook his head.

'No. I'm sorry, I can't let you do it, it just isn't safe,' he said, a little crisply, and she dropped her head back and gave a sharp sigh.

Damn. He must be airport security, and a higher authority than the nice young man who'd shifted them outside. She sensed there'd be no arguing with him. There was a quiet implacability about him that reminded her of her father, and she knew when she was beaten. She met his eyes again, and tried not to notice that they were the colour of dark, bitter chocolate, warm and rich and really rather gorgeous.

And unyielding.

She gave up.

'I would have been perfectly safe, I've got a minder and I'm no threat to anyone and nobody's complained, as far as I know, but you can call the dogs off, I'm going.'

To her surprise he smiled, those amazing eyes softening and turning her bones to mush.

'Relax, I'm nothing to do with Security, I just have a social conscience. I believe you need to go to Siena?'

Siena? Nobody, she'd discovered, was flying to Siena but it seemed, incredibly, that he might be, or else why would he be asking? She stifled the little flicker of hope. 'I thought you said it wasn't safe?'

'It wasn't safe with *Nico*.'

'And it's safe with you?'

'Safer. My pilot won't have been drinking, and I—' He broke off, and watched her eyes widen as her mind filled in the blanks.

'And you?' she prompted a little warily, when he left it hanging there.

He sighed sharply and raked a hand through his hair, rumpling the dark strands threaded with silver at the temples. He seemed impatient, as if he was helping her against his better judgement.

'He has a—reputation,' he said finally.

She dragged her eyes off his hair. It had flopped forwards, and her fingers itched to smooth it back, to feel the texture…

'And you don't?'

'Let's just say that I respect women.' His mouth flickered in a wry smile. 'If you want a reference, my lawyer and doctor brothers would probably vouch for me, as would my three sisters—failing that, you could phone Carlotta. She's worked for the family for hundreds of years, and she delivered me and looks after my children.'

He had children? She glanced down and clocked the wedding ring on his finger, and with a sigh of relief, she thrust a laminated sheet at him and dug out her smile again. This time, it was far easier, and she felt a flicker of excitement burst into life.

'It's a competition to win a wedding at a hotel near Siena. There are two of us in the final leg, and I have to get to the hotel first to win the prize. This is Claire, she's from the radio station doing the publicity.'

Massimo gave Claire a cursory smile. He wasn't in the least interested in Claire. She was obviously the minder, and pretty enough, but this woman with the crazy outfit and sassy mouth...

He scanned the sheet, scanned it again, shook his head in disbelief and handed it back, frankly appalled. 'You must be mad. You have only a hundred pounds, a wedding dress and a passport, and you have to race to Siena to win this wedding? What on *earth* is your fiancé thinking of to let you do it?'

'Not my fiancé. I don't have a fiancé, and if I did, I wouldn't need his permission,' she said crisply, those eyes turning to ice again. 'It's for my sister. She had an accident, and they'd planned—oh, it doesn't matter. Either you can help me or you can't, and if you can't, the clock's ticking and I really have to get on.'

She didn't have a fiancé? 'I can help you,' he said before he could let himself think about it, and he thrust out his hand. 'Massimo Valtieri. If you're ready to go, I can give you a lift to Siena now.'

He pronounced it Mah-*see*-mo, long and slow and drawn out, his Italian accent coming over loud and clear as he said his name, and she felt a shiver of something primeval down her spine. Or maybe it was just the cold. She smiled at her self-appointed knight in shining armour and held out her hand.

'I'm Lydia Fletcher—and if you can get us there before the others, I'll love you forever.'

His warm, strong and surprisingly slightly calloused fingers closed firmly round hers, and she felt the world shift a little under her feet. And not just hers, apparently. She saw the shockwave hit his eyes, felt the recognition of something momentous passing between them, and in that crazy and insane instant she wondered if anything would ever be the same again.

The plane was small but, as the saying goes, perfectly formed.

Very perfectly, as far as she was concerned. It had comfortable seats, lots of legroom, a sober pilot and a flight plan that without doubt would win her sister the wedding of her dreams.

Lydia could hardly believe her luck.

She buckled herself in, grabbed Claire's hand and hung on tight as the plane taxied to the end of the runway. 'We did it. We got a flight straight there!' she whispered, and Claire's face lit up with her smile, her eyes sparkling.

'I know. Amazing! We're going to do it. We can't fail. I just know you're going to win!'

The engines roared, the small plane shuddering, and then it was off like a slingshot, the force of their acceleration pushing her back hard into the leather seat as the jet tipped and climbed. The Thames was flying past, dropping rapidly below them as they rose into the air over London, and then they were heading out over the Thames estuary towards France, levelling off, and the seat belt light went out.

'Oh, this is so exciting! I'm going to update the diary,' Claire said, pulling out her little notebook computer, and Lydia turned her head and met Massimo's eyes across the narrow aisle.

He unclipped his seat belt and shifted his body so he was

facing her, his eyes scanning her face. His mouth tipped into a smile, and her stomach turned over—from the steep ascent, or from the warmth of that liquid-chocolate gaze?

'All right?'

'Amazing.' She smiled back, her mouth curving involuntarily in response to his, then turning down as she pulled a face. 'I don't know how to thank you. I'm so sorry I was rude.'

His mouth twitched. 'Don't worry. You weren't nearly as rude to me as I was to Nico.'

'What *did* you say to him?' she asked curiously, and he gave a soft laugh.

'I'm not sure it would translate. Certainly not in mixed company.'

'I think I got the gist—'

'I hope not!'

She gave a little laugh. 'Probably not. I don't know any street Italian—well, no Italian at all, really. And I feel awful now for biting your head off, but…well, it means a lot to me, to win this wedding.'

'Yes, I gather. You were telling me about your sister?' he said.

'Jennifer. She had an accident a few months ago and she was in a wheelchair, but she's getting better, she's on crutches now, but her fiancé had to give up his job to help look after her. They're living with my parents and Andy's working with Dad at the moment for their keep. My parents have got a farm—well, not really a farm, more of a smallholding, really, but they get by, and they could always have the wedding there. There's a vegetable packing barn they could dress up for the wedding reception, but—well, my grandmother lived in Italy for a while and Jen's always dreamed of getting married there, and now they haven't got enough money even for a glass of cheap bubbly and a few sandwiches. So when I heard about this competition I just jumped at it, but I never in my wildest dreams imagined we'd get this far, never mind get a flight to exactly the right place. I'm just so grateful I don't know where to start.'

She was gabbling. She stopped, snapped her mouth shut and gave him a rueful grin. 'Sorry. I always talk a lot when the adrenaline's running.'

He smiled and leant back, utterly charmed by her. More than charmed…

'Relax. I have three sisters and two daughters, so I'm quite used to it, I've had a lot of practice.'

'Gosh, it sounds like it. And you've got two brothers as well?'

'*Si*. Luca's the doctor and he's married to an English girl called Isabelle, and Gio's the lawyer. I also have a son, and two parents, and a million aunts and uncles and cousins.'

'So what do you do?' she asked, irresistibly curious, and he gave her a slightly lopsided grin.

'You could say I'm a farmer, too. We grow grapes and olives and we make cheese.'

She glanced around at the plane. 'You must make a heck of a lot of cheese,' she said drily, and he chuckled, soft and low under his breath, just loud enough for her to hear.

The slight huff of his breath made an errant curl drift against her cheek, and it was almost as if his fingertips had brushed lightly against her skin.

'Not that much,' he said, his eyes still smiling. 'Mostly we concentrate on our wine and olive oil—Tuscan olive oil is sharper, tangier than the oil from southern Italy because we harvest the olives younger to avoid the frosts, and it gives it a distinctive and rich peppery flavour. But again, we don't make a huge amount, we concentrate on quality and aim for the boutique market with limited editions of certified, artisan products. That's what I was doing in England—I've been at a trade fair pushing our oil and wine to restaurateurs and gourmet delicatessens.'

She sat up straighter. 'Really? Did you take samples with you?'

He laughed. 'Of course. How else can I convince people that our products are the best? But the timing was bad, because we're about to harvest the grapes and I'm needed at home. That's why we chartered the plane, to save time.'

Chartered. So it wasn't his. That made him more approachable, somehow and, if it was possible, even more attractive. As did the fact that he was a farmer. She knew about farming, about aiming for a niche market and going for quality rather than quantity. It was how she'd been brought up. She relaxed, hitched one foot up under her and hugged her knee under the voluminous skirt.

'So, these samples—do you have any on the plane that I could try?'

'Sorry, we're out of wine,' he said, but then she laughed and shook her head.

'That's not what I meant, although I'm sure it's very good. I was talking about the olive oil. Professional interest.'

'You grow olives on your farm in England?' he asked incredulously, and she laughed again, tightening his gut and sending need arrowing south. It shocked him slightly, and he forced himself to concentrate.

'No. Of course not. I've been living in a flat with a pot of basil on the window sill until recently! But I love food.'

'You mentioned a professional interest.'

She nodded. 'I'm a—' She was going to say chef, but could you be a chef if you didn't have a restaurant? If your kitchen had been taken away from you and you had nothing left of your promising career? 'I cook,' she said, and he got up and went to the rear of the plane and returned with a bottle of oil.

'Here.'

He opened it and held it out to her, and she sniffed it slowly, drawing the sharp, fruity scent down into her lungs. 'Oh, that's gorgeous. May I?'

And taking it from him, she tipped a tiny pool into her hand and dipped her finger into it, sucking the tip and making an appreciative noise. Heat slammed through him, and he recorked the bottle and put it away to give him something to do while he reassembled his brain.

He never, *never* reacted to a woman like this! What on earth was he thinking of? Apart from the obvious, but he didn't want to think about that. He hadn't looked at a woman in that way for years, hadn't thought about sex in he didn't know how long. So why now, why this woman?

She wiped up the last drop, sucking her finger again and then licking her palm, leaving a fine sheen of oil on her lips that he really, really badly want to kiss away.

'Oh, that is so good,' she said, rubbing her hands together to remove the last trace. 'It's a shame we don't have any bread or balsamic vinegar for dunking.'

He pulled a business card out of his top pocket and handed it to her, pulling his mind back into order and his eyes out of her cleavage. 'Email me your address when you get home, I'll send you some of our wine and oil, and also a traditional *aceto balsamico* made by my cousin in Modena. They only make a little, but it's the best I've ever tasted. We took some with us, but I haven't got any of that left, either.'

'Wow. Well, if it's as good as the olive oil, it must be fabulous!'

'It is. We're really proud of it in the family. It's nearly as good as our olive oil and wine.'

She laughed, as she was meant to, tucking the card into her bag, then she tipped her head on one side. 'Is it a family business?'

He nodded. 'Yes, most definitely. We've been there for

more than three hundred years. We're very lucky. The soil is perfect, the slopes are all in the right direction, and if we can't grow one thing on any particular slope, we grow another, or use it for pasture. And then there are the chestnut woods. We export a lot of canned chestnuts, both whole and puréed.'

'And your wife?' she asked, her curiosity getting the better of her. 'Does she help with the business, or do you keep her too busy producing children for you?'

There was a heartbeat of silence before his eyes clouded, and his smile twisted a little as he looked away. 'Angelina died five years ago,' he said softly, and she felt a wave of regret that she'd blundered in and brought his grief to life when they'd been having a sensible and intelligent conversation about something she was genuinely interested in.

She reached across the aisle and touched his arm gently. 'I'm so sorry. I wouldn't have brought it up if...'

'Don't apologise. It's not your fault. Anyway, five years is a long time.'

Long enough that, when confronted by a vivacious, dynamic and delightful woman with beautiful, generous curves and a low-cut dress that gave him a more than adequate view of those curves, he'd almost forgotten his wife...

Guilt lanced through him, and he pulled out his wallet and showed her the photos—him and Angelina on their wedding day, and one with the girls clustered around her and the baby in her arms, all of them laughing. He loved that one. It was the last photograph he had of her, and one of the best. He carried it everywhere.

She looked at them, her lips slightly parted, and he could see the sheen of tears in her eyes.

'You must miss her so much. Your poor children.'

'It's not so bad now, but they missed her at first,' he said gruffly. And he'd missed her. He'd missed her every single day, but missing her didn't bring her back, and he'd buried himself in work.

He was still burying himself in work.

Wasn't he?

Not effectively. Not any more, apparently, because suddenly he was beginning to think about things he hadn't thought about for years, and he wasn't ready for that. He couldn't deal with it, couldn't think about it. Not now. He had work to do, work that couldn't wait. Work he should be doing now.

He put the wallet away and excused himself, moving to sit with the others and discuss how to follow up the contacts they'd made and where they went from here with their marketing strategy, with his back firmly to Lydia and that ridiculous wedding dress that was threatening to tip him over the brink.

Lydia stared at his back, regret forming a lump in her throat.

She'd done it again. Opened her mouth and jumped in with both feet. She was good at that, gifted almost. And now he'd pulled away from her, and must be regretting the impulse that had made him offer her and Claire a lift to Italy.

She wanted to apologise, to take back her stupid and trite and intrusive question about his wife—Angelina, she thought, remembering the way he'd said her name, the way he'd almost tasted it as he said it, no doubt savouring the precious memories. But life didn't work like that.

Like feathers from a burst cushion, it simply wasn't possible to gather the words up and stuff them back in without trace. She just needed to move on from the embarrassing lapse, to keep out of his personal life and take his offer of a lift at face value.

And stop thinking about those incredible, warm chocolate eyes...

'I can't believe he's taking us right to Siena!' Claire said quietly, her eyes sparkling with delight. 'Jo will be so miffed when we get there first, she was so confident!'

Lydia dredged up her smile again, not hard when she thought about Jen and how deliriously happy she'd be to have her Tuscan wedding. 'I can't believe it, either. Amazing.'

Claire tilted her head on one side. 'What was he showing you? He looked sort of sad.'

She felt her smile slip. 'Photos of his wife. She died five years ago. They've got three little children—ten, seven and five, I think he said. Something like that.'

'Gosh. So the little one must have been tiny—did she die giving birth?'

'No. No, she can't have done. There was a photo of her with two little girls and a baby in her arms, so no. But it must have been soon after.'

'How awful. Fancy never knowing your mother. I'd die if I didn't have my mum to ring up and tell about stuff.'

Lydia nodded. She adored her mother, phoned her all the time, shared everything with her and Jen. What would it have been like never to have known her?

Tears welled in her eyes again, and she brushed them away crossly, but then she felt a light touch on her arm and looked up, and he was staring down at her, his face concerned.

He frowned and reached out a hand, touching the moisture on her cheek with a gentle fingertip.

'Lydia?'

She shook her head. 'I'm fine. Ignore me, I'm a sentimental idiot.'

He dropped to his haunches and took her hand, and she had a sudden and overwhelming urge to cry in earnest. 'I'm sorry. I didn't mean to distress you. You don't need to cry for us.'

She shook her head and sniffed again. 'I'm not. Not really.

I was thinking about my mother—about how I'd miss her—and I'm twenty-eight, not five.'

He nodded. 'Yes. It's very hard.' His mouth quirked in a fleeting smile. 'I'm sorry, I've neglected you. Can I get you a drink? Tea? Coffee? Water? Something stronger?'

'It's a bit early for stronger,' she said, trying for a light note, and he smiled again, more warmly this time, and straightened up.

'Nico would have been on the second bottle of champagne by now,' he said, and she felt a wave of relief that he'd saved her from what sounded more and more like a dangerous mistake.

'Fizzy water would be nice, if you have any?' she said, and he nodded.

'Claire?'

'That would be lovely. Thank you.'

He moved away, and she let her breath out slowly. She hadn't really registered, until he'd crouched beside her, just how big he was. Not bulky, not in any way, but he'd shed his jacket and rolled up his shirtsleeves, and she'd been treated to the broad shoulders and solid chest at close range, and then his narrow hips and lean waist and those long, strong legs as he'd straightened up.

His hands, appearing in her line of sight again, were clamped round two tall glasses beaded with moisture and fizzing gently. Large hands, strong and capable, no-nonsense.

Safe, sure hands that had held hers and warmed her to the core.

Her breasts tingled unexpectedly, and she took the glass from him and tried not to drop it. 'Thank you.'

'*Prego*, you're welcome. Are you hungry? We have fruit and pastries, too.'

'No. No, I'm much too excited to eat now,' she confessed,

sipping the water and hoping the cool liquid would slake the heat rising up inside her.

Crazy! He was totally uninterested in her, and even if he wasn't, she wasn't in the market for any more complications in her life. Her relationship with Russell had been fraught with complications, and the end of it had been a revelation. There was no way she was jumping back into that pond any time soon. The last frog she'd kissed had turned into a king-sized toad.

'How long before we land?' she asked, and he checked his watch, treating her to a bronzed, muscular forearm and strong-boned wrist lightly scattered with dark hair. She stared at it and swallowed. How ridiculous that an arm could be so sexy.

'Just over an hour. Excuse me, we have work to do, but please, if you need anything, just ask.'

He turned back to his colleagues, sitting down and flexing his broad shoulders, and Lydia felt her gut clench. She'd never, *never* felt like that about anyone before, and she couldn't believe she was reacting to him that way. It must just be the adrenaline.

One more hour to get through before they were there and they could thank him and get away—hopefully before she disgraced herself. The poor man was still grieving for his wife. What was she thinking about?

Ridiculous! She'd known him, what, less than two hours altogether? Scarcely more than one. And she'd already put her foot firmly in it.

Vowing not to say another thing, she settled back in her seat and looked out of the window at the mountains.

They must be the Alps, she realised, fascinated by the jagged peaks and plunging valleys, and then the mountains fell away behind them and they were moving over a chequered landscape of forests and small, neat fields. They were curiously ordered and disciplined, serried ranks of what must be olive trees and grape vines, she guessed, planted with geometric precision, the pattern of the fields interlaced with narrow winding roads lined with avenues of tall, slender cypress trees.

Tuscany, she thought with a shiver of excitement.

The seat belt light came on, and Massimo returned to his seat across the aisle from her as the plane started its descent.

'Not long now,' he said, flashing her a smile. And then they were there, a perfect touchdown on Tuscan soil with the prize almost in reach.

Jen was going to get her wedding. Just a few more minutes...

They taxied to a stop outside the airport building, and after a moment the steps were wheeled out to them and the door was opened.

'We're really here!' she said to Claire, and Claire's eyes were sparkling as she got to her feet.

'I know. I can't believe it!'

They were standing at the top of the steps now, and Massimo smiled and gestured to them. 'After you. Do you have the address of the hotel? I'll drive you there.'

'Are you sure?'

'I'd hate you not to win after all this,' he said with a grin.

'Wow, thank you, that's really kind of you!' Lydia said, reaching for her skirts as she took another step.

It happened in slow motion.

One moment she was there beside him, the next the steps had disappeared from under her feet and she was falling, tumbling end over end, hitting what seemed like every step until finally her head reached the tarmac and she crumpled on the ground in a heap.

Her scream was cut off abruptly, and Massimo hurled himself down the steps to her side, his heart racing. No! Please, she couldn't be dead…

She wasn't. He could feel a pulse in her neck, and he let his breath out on a long, ragged sigh and sat back on his heels to assess her.

Stay calm, he told himself. She's alive. She'll be all right.

But he wouldn't really believe it until she stirred, and even then…

'Is she all right?'

He glanced up at Claire, kneeling on the other side of her, her face chalk white with fear.

'I think so,' he said, but he didn't think any such thing. Fear was coursing through him, bringing bile rising to his throat. Why wasn't she moving? This couldn't be happening again.

Lydia moaned. Warm, hard fingers had searched for a pulse in her neck, and as she slowly came to, she heard him snap out something in Italian while she lay there, shocked and a little stunned, wondering if it was a good idea to open her eyes. Maybe not yet.

'Lydia? Lydia, talk to me! Open your eyes.'

Her eyes opened slowly and she tried to sit up, but he pressed a hand to her shoulder.

'Stay still. You might have a neck injury. Where do you hurt?'

Where didn't she? She turned her head and winced. 'Ow… my head, for a start. What happened? Did I trip? Oh, I can't believe I was so stupid!'

'You fell down the steps.'

'I know that—ouch.' She felt her head, and her hand came away bloodied and sticky. She stared at it. 'I've cut myself,' she said, and everything began to swim.

'It's OK, Lydia. You'll be OK,' Claire said, but her face

was worried and suddenly everything began to hurt a whole lot more.

Massimo tucked his jacket gently beside her head to support it, just in case she had a neck injury. He wasn't taking any chances on that, but it was the head injury that was worrying him the most, the graze on her forehead, just under her hair. How hard had she hit it? Hard enough to...

It was bleeding faster now, he realised with a wave of dread, a red streak appearing as she shifted slightly, and he stayed beside her on his knees, holding her hand and talking to her comfortingly in between snapping out instructions.

She heard the words '*ambulanza*' and '*ospedale*', and tried to move, wincing and whimpering with pain, but he held her still.

'Don't move. The ambulance is coming to take you to hospital.'

'I don't need to go to hospital, I'm fine, we need to get to the hotel!'

'No,' Massimo and Claire said in unison.

'But the competition.'

'It doesn't matter,' he said flatly. 'You're hurt. You have to be checked out.'

'I'll go later.'

'No.' His voice was implacable, hard and cold and somehow strange, and Lydia looked at him and saw his skin was colourless and grey, his mouth pinched, his eyes veiled.

He obviously couldn't stand the sight of blood, Lydia realised, and reached out her other hand to Claire.

She took it, then looked at Massimo. 'I'll look after her,' she said. 'You go, you've got lots to do. We'll be all right.'

His eyes never left Lydia's.

'No. I'll stay with you,' he insisted, but he moved out of the way to give her space.

She looked so frail suddenly, lying there streaked with

blood, the puffy layers of the dress rising up around her legs and making her look like a broken china doll.

Dio, he felt sick just looking at her, and her face swam, another face drifting over it. He shut his eyes tight, squeezing out the images of his wife, but they refused to fade.

Lydia tried to struggle up again. 'I want to go to the hotel,' she said to Claire, and his eyes snapped open again.

'No way.'

'He's right. Don't be silly. You just lie there and we'll get you checked out, then we'll go. There's still plenty of time.'

But there might not be, she realised, as she lay there on the tarmac in her ridiculous charity shop wedding dress with blood seeping from her head wound, and as the minutes ticked by her joy slid slowly away...

CHAPTER TWO

THE ambulance came, and Claire went with Lydia.

He wanted to go with her himself, he felt he ought to, felt the weight of guilt and worry like an elephant on his chest, but it wasn't his place to accompany her, so Claire went, and he followed in his car, having sent the rest of the team on with a message to his family that he'd been held up but would be with them as soon as he could.

He rang Luca on the way, in case he was there at the hospital in Siena that day as he sometimes was, and his phone was answered instantly.

'Massimo, welcome home. Good flight?'

He nearly laughed. 'No. Where are you? Which hospital?'

'Siena. Why?'

He did laugh then. Or was it a sob of relief? 'I'm on my way there. I gave two girls a lift in the plane, and one of them fell down the steps as we were disembarking. I'm following the ambulance. Luca, she's got a head injury,' he added, his heart pounding with dread, and he heard his brother suck in his breath.

'I'll meet you in the emergency department. She'll be all right, Massimo. We'll take care of her.'

He grunted agreement, switched off the phone and followed the ambulance, focusing on facts and crushing his fear and guilt down. It couldn't happen again. Lightning didn't strike twice, he told himself, and forced himself to follow the ambulance at a sensible distance while trying desperately to put Angelina firmly out of his mind…

Luca was waiting for him at the entrance.

He took the car away to park it and Massimo hovered by the ambulance as they unloaded Lydia and whisked her inside, Claire holding her hand and reassuring her. It didn't sound as if it was working, because she kept fretting about the competition and insisting she was all right when anyone could see she was far from all right.

She was taken away, Claire with her, and he stayed in the waiting area, pacing restlessly and driving himself mad with his imagination of what was happening beyond the doors. His brother reappeared moments later and handed him the keys, giving him a keen look.

'You all right?'

Hardly. 'I'm fine,' he said, his voice tight.

'So how do you know this woman?' Luca asked, and he filled him in quickly with the bare bones of the accident.

'Oh—she's wearing a wedding dress,' he warned. 'It's a competition, a race to win a wedding.'

A race she'd lost. If only he'd taken her arm, or gone in front, she would have fallen against him, he could have saved her…

'Luca, don't let her die,' he said urgently, fear clawing at him.

'She won't die,' Luca promised, although how he could say that without knowing—well, he couldn't. It was just a platitude, Massimo knew that.

'Let me know how she is.'

Luca nodded and went off to investigate, leaving him there to wait, but he felt bile rise in his throat and got abruptly to his feet, pacing restlessly again. How long could it take?

Hours, apparently, or at least it felt like it.

Luca reappeared with Claire.

'They're taking X-rays of her leg now but it looks like a sprained ankle. She's just a little concussed and bruised from her fall, but the head injury doesn't look serious,' he said.

'Nor did Angelina's,' he said, switching to Italian.

'She's not Angelina, Massimo. She's not going to die of this.'

'Are you sure?'

'Yes. Yes, I'm sure. She's had a scan. She's fine.'

It should have reassured him, but Massimo felt his heart still slamming against his ribs, the memories crowding him again.

'She's all right,' Luca said quietly. 'This isn't the same.'

He nodded, but he just wanted to get out, to be away from the hospital in the fresh air. Not going to happen. He couldn't leave Lydia, no matter how much he wanted to get away. And he could never get away from Angelina...

Luca took him to her.

She was lying on a trolley, and there was blood streaked all over the front of the hideous dress, but at least they'd taken her off the spinal board. 'How are you?' he asked, knowing the answer but having to ask anyway, and she turned her head and met his eyes, her own clouded with worry and pain.

'I'm fine, they just want to watch me for a while. I've got some bumps and bruises, but nothing's broken, I'm just sore and cross with myself and I want to go to the hotel and they won't let me leave yet. I'm so sorry, Massimo, I've got Claire, you don't need to wait here with me. It could be ages.'

'I do.' He didn't explain, didn't tell her what she didn't need to know, what could only worry her. But he hadn't taken Angelina's head injury seriously. He'd assumed it was nothing. He hadn't watched her, sat with her, checked her every few minutes. If he had—well, he hadn't, but he was damned if he was leaving Lydia alone for a moment until he was sure she was all right.

Luca went back to work, and while the doctors checked her over again and strapped her ankle, Massimo found some coffee for him and Claire and they sat and drank it. Not a good idea. The caffeine shot was the last thing his racing pulse needed.

'I need to make a call,' Claire told him. 'If I go just outside, can you come and get me if there's any news?'

He nodded, watching her leave. She was probably phoning the radio station to tell them about Lydia's accident. And she'd been so close to winning…

She came back, a wan smile on her face. 'Jo's there.'

'Jo?'

'The other contestant. Lydia's lost the race. She's going to be so upset. I can't tell her yet.'

'I think you should. She might stop fretting if it's too late, let herself relax and get better.'

Claire gave a tiny, slightly hysterical laugh. 'You don't know her very well, do you?'

He smiled ruefully. 'No. No, I don't.' And it was ridiculous that he minded the fact.

Lydia looked up as they went back in, and she scanned Claire's face.

'Did you ring the radio station?'

'Yes.'

'Has…' She could hardly bring herself to ask the question, but she took another breath and tried again. 'Has Jo got there yet?' she asked, and then held her breath. It was possible she'd been unlucky, that she hadn't managed to get a flight, that any one of a hundred things could have happened.

They hadn't. She could see it in Claire's eyes, she didn't

need to be told that Jo and Kate, her minder, were already there, and she felt the bitter sting of tears scald her eyes.

'She's there, isn't she?' she asked, just because she needed confirmation.

Claire nodded, and Lydia turned her head away, shutting her eyes against the tears. She was so, *so* cross with herself. They'd been so close to winning, and if she'd only been more careful, gathered up the stupid dress so she could see the steps.

She swallowed hard and looked back up at Claire's worried face. 'Tell her well done for me when you see her.'

'I will, but you'll see her, too. We've got rooms in the hotel for the night. I'll ring them now, let them know what's happening. We can go there when they discharge you.'

'No, I could be ages. Why don't you go, have a shower and something to eat, see the others and I'll get them to ring you if there's any change. Or better still, if you give me back my phone and my purse, I can call you and let you know when I'm leaving, and I'll just get a taxi.'

'I can't leave you alone!'

'She won't be alone, I'll stay with her. I'm staying anyway, whether you're here or not,' Massimo said firmly, and Lydia felt a curious sense of relief. Relief, and guilt.

And she could see the same emotions in Claire's face. She was dithering, chewing her lip in hesitation, and Lydia took her hand and squeezed it.

'There, you see? And his brother works here, so he'll be able to pull strings. It's fine, Claire. Just go. I'll see you later.' And she could get rid of Massimo once Claire had gone...

Claire gave in, reluctantly. 'OK, if you insist. Here, your things. I'll put them in your bag. Where is it?'

'I have no idea. Is it under the bed?'

'No. I haven't seen it.'

'It must have been left on the ground at the airport,' Massimo said. 'My men will have picked it up.'

'Can you check? My passport's in it.'

'*Si.*' He left them briefly, and when he came back he confirmed it had been taken by the others. 'I'll make sure you get it tonight,' he promised.

'Thanks. Right, Claire, you go. I'm fine.'

'You will call me and let me know what's going on as soon as you have any news?'

'Yes, I promise.'

Claire gave in, hugging Lydia a little tearfully before she left them.

Lydia swallowed. Damn. She was going to join in.

'Hey, it's all right. You'll be OK.'

His voice was gentle, reassuring, and his touch on her cheek was oddly comforting. Her eyes filled again.

'I'm causing everyone so much trouble.'

'That's life. Don't worry about it. Are you going to tell your family?'

Oh, cripes. She ought to phone Jen, but she couldn't. Not now. She didn't think she could talk to her just yet.

'Maybe later. I just feel so sleepy.'

'So rest. I'll sit with you.'

Sit with her and watch her. Do what he should have done years ago.

She shut her eyes, just for a moment, but when she opened them again he'd moved from her side. She felt a moment of panic, but then she saw him. He was standing a few feet away reading a poster about head injuries, his hands rammed in his pockets, tension radiating off him.

Funny, she'd thought it was because of the blood, but there was no sign of blood now apart from a dried streak on her dress. Maybe it was hospitals generally. Had Angelina been ill for a long time?

Or maybe hospitals just brought him out in hives. She could understand that. After Jen's accident, she felt the same herself, and yet he was still here, still apparently labouring under some misguided sense of obligation.

He turned his head, saw she was awake and came back to her side, his dark eyes searching hers.

'Are you all right?'

She nodded. 'My head's feeling clearer now. I need to ring Jen,' she said quietly, and he sighed and cupped her cheek, his thumb smoothing away a tear she hadn't realised she'd shed.

'I'm sorry, *cara*. I know how much it meant to you to win this for your sister.'

'It doesn't matter,' she said dismissively, although of course it would to Jen. 'It was just a crazy idea. They can get married at home, it's really not an issue. I really didn't think I'd win anyway, so we haven't lost anything.'

'Claire said Jo's been there for ages. She would probably have beaten you to it anyway,' he said. 'She must have got away very fast.'

She didn't believe it. He was only trying to make it better, to take the sting out of it, but before she had time to argue the doctor came back in, checked her over and delivered her verdict.

Massimo translated.

'You're fine, you need to rest for a few days before you fly home, and you need watching overnight, but you're free to go.'

She thanked the doctor, struggled up and swung her legs over the edge of the trolley, and paused for a moment, her head swimming.

'All right?'

'I'm fine. I need to call a taxi to take me to the hotel.'

'I'll give you a lift.'

'I can't take you out of your way! I've put you to enough trouble as it is. I can get a taxi. I'll be fine.'

But as she slid off the edge of the trolley and straightened up, Massimo caught the sheen of tears in her eyes.

Whatever she'd said, the loss of this prize was tearing her apart for her sister, and he felt guilt wash over him yet again. Logically, he knew he had no obligation to her, no duty that extended any further than simply flying her to Siena as he'd promised. But somehow, somewhere along the way, things had changed and he could no more have left her there at the door of the hospital than he could have left one of his children. And they were waiting for him, had been waiting for him far too long, and guilt tugged at him again.

'Ouch!'

'You can't walk on that ankle. Stay here.'

She stayed, wishing her flight bag was still with her instead of having been whisked away by his team. She could have done with changing out of the dress, but her comfy jeans and soft cotton top were in her bag, and she wanted to cry with frustration and disappointment and pain.

'Here.'

He'd brought a wheelchair, and she eyed it doubtfully.

'I don't know if the dress will fit in it. Horrible thing! I'm going to burn it just as soon as I get it off.'

'Good idea,' he said drily, and they exchanged a smile.

He squashed it in around her, and wheeled her towards the exit. Then he stopped the chair by the door and looked down at her.

'Do you really want to go to the hotel?' he asked.

She tipped her head back to look at him, but it hurt, and she let her breath out in a gusty sigh. 'I don't have a choice. I need a bed for the night, and I can't afford anywhere else.'

He moved so she could see him, crouching down beside her. 'You do have a choice. You can't fly for a few days, and you don't want to stay in a strange hotel on your own for all that time. And anyway, you don't have your bag, so why don't you come back with me?' he said, the guilt about his children growing now and the solution to both problems suddenly blindingly obvious.

'I need to get home to see my children, they've been patient long enough, and you can clean up there and change into your own comfortable clothes and have something to eat and a good night's sleep. Carlotta will look after you.'

Carlotta? Lydia scanned their earlier conversations and came up with the name. She was the woman who looked after his children, who'd worked for them for a hundred years, as he'd put it, and had delivered him.

Carlotta sounded good.

'That's such an imposition. Are you sure you don't mind?'

'I'm sure. It's by far the easiest thing for me. The hotel's the other way, and it would save me a lot of time I don't really have, especially by the time I've dropped your bag over there. And you don't honestly want to be there on your own for days, do you?'

Guilt swamped her, heaped on the disappointment and the worry about Jen, and she felt crushed under the weight of it all. She felt her spine sag, and shook her head. 'I'm so sorry. I've wasted your entire day. If you hadn't given me a lift...'

'Don't go there. What ifs are a waste of time. Yes or no?'

'Yes, please,' she said fervently. 'That would be really kind.'

'Don't mention it. I feel it's all my fault anyway.'

'Rubbish. Of course it's not your fault. You've done so much already, and I don't think I've even thanked you.'

'You have. You were doing that when you fell down the steps.'

'Was I?' She gave him a wry grin, and turned to look up

at him as they arrived at the car, resting her hand on his arm lightly to reassure him. 'It's really not your fault, you know.'

'I know. You missed your step. I know this. I still…'

He was still haunted, because of the head injury, images of Angelina crowding in on him. Angelina falling, Angelina with a headache, Angelina slumped over the kitchen table with one side of her face collapsed. Angelina linked up to a life support machine…

'Massimo?'

'I'm all right,' he said gruffly, and pressing the remote, he opened the door for her and settled her in, then returned the wheelchair and slid into the driver's seat beside her. 'Are you OK?'

'I'm fine.'

'Good. Let's go.'

She phoned Claire and told her what was happening, assured her she would be all right and promised to phone her the next day, then put the phone down in her lap and rested her head back.

Under normal circumstances, she thought numbly, she'd be wallowing in the luxury of his butter-soft leather, beautifully supportive car seats, or taking in the picture-postcard countryside of Tuscany as the car wove and swooped along the narrow winding roads.

As it was she gazed blankly at it all, knowing that she'd have to phone Jen, knowing she should have done it sooner, that her sister would be on tenterhooks, but she didn't have the strength to crush her hopes and dreams.

'Have you told your sister yet?' he asked, as if he'd read her mind.

She shook her head. 'No. I don't know what to say. If I hadn't fallen, we would have won. Easily. It was just so stupid, so clumsy.'

He sighed, his hand reaching out and closing over hers briefly, the warmth of it oddly comforting in a disturbing way. 'I'm sorry. Not because I feel it was my fault, because I know it wasn't, really, but because I know how it feels to let someone down, to have everyone's hopes and dreams resting on your shoulders, to have to carry the responsibility for someone else's happiness.'

She turned towards him, inhibited by the awful, scratchy dress that she couldn't wait to get out of, and studied his profile.

Strong. Clean cut, although no longer clean-shaven, the dark stubble that shadowed his jaw making her hand itch to feel the texture of it against her palm. In the dusk of early evening his olive skin was darker, somehow exotic, and with a little shiver she realised she didn't know him at all. He could be taking her anywhere.

She closed her eyes and told herself not to be ridiculous. He'd followed them to the hospital, got his brother in on the act, a brother she'd heard referred to as *il professore*, and now he was taking her to his family home, to his children, his parents, the woman who'd delivered him all those years ago. Forty years? Maybe. Maybe more, maybe less, but give or take.

Someone who'd stayed with the family for all that time, who surely wouldn't still be there if they were nasty people?

'What's wrong?'

She shrugged, too honest to lie. 'I was just thinking, I don't know you. You could be anyone. After all, I was going in the plane with Nico, and you've pointed out in no uncertain terms that that wouldn't have been a good idea, and I just don't think I'm a very good judge of character.'

'Are you saying you don't trust me?'

She found herself smiling. 'Curiously, I do, or I wouldn't be here with you.'

He flashed her a look, and his mouth tipped into a wry grin. 'Well, thanks.'

'Sorry. It wasn't meant to sound patronising. It's just been a bit of a whirlwind today, and I'm not really firing on all cylinders.'

'I'm sure you're not. Don't worry, you're safe with me, I promise, and we're nearly there. You can have a long lazy shower, or lie in the bath, or have a swim. Whatever you choose.'

'So long as I can get out of this horrible dress, I'll be happy.'

He laughed, the sound filling the car and making something deep inside her shift.

'Good. Stand by to be happy very soon.'

He turned off the road onto a curving gravelled track lined by cypress trees, winding away towards what looked like a huge stone fortress. She sat up straighter. 'What's that building?'

'The house.'

'House?' She felt her jaw drop, and shut her mouth quickly. That was their *house*?

'So…is this your land?'

'*Si.*'

She stared around her, but the light was fading and it was hard to tell what she was looking at. But the massive edifice ahead of them was outlined against the sunset, and as they drew closer she could see lights twinkling in the windows.

They climbed the hill, driving through a massive archway and pulling up in front of a set of sweeping steps. Security lights came on as they stopped, and she could see the steps were flanked by huge terracotta pots with what looked like olive trees in them. The steps rose majestically up to the biggest set of double doors she'd ever seen in her life. Strong doors, doors that would keep you safe against all invaders.

She had to catch her jaw again, and for once in her life she was lost for words. She'd thought, foolishly, it seemed, that it might shrink as they got closer, but it hadn't. If anything it had grown, and she realised it truly was a fortress.

An ancient, impressive and no doubt historically significant fortress. And it was his family home?

She thought of their modest farmhouse, the place she called home, and felt the sudden almost overwhelming urge to laugh. What on earth did he think of her, all tarted up in her ludicrous charity shop wedding dress and capering about outside the airport begging a lift from any old stranger?

'Lydia?'

He was standing by her, the door open, and she gathered up the dress and her purse and phone and squirmed off the seat and out of the car, balancing on her good leg and eyeing the steps dubiously.

How on earth—?

No problem, apparently. He shut the car door, and then to her surprise he scooped her up into his arms.

She gave a little shriek and wrapped her arms around his neck, so that her nose was pressed close to his throat in the open neck of his shirt. Oh, God. He smelt of lemons and musk and warm, virile male, and she could feel the beat of his heart against her side.

Or was it her own? She didn't know. It could have been either.

He glanced down at her, concerned that he might be hurting her. There was a little frown creasing the soft skin between her brows, and he had the crazy urge to kiss it away. He almost did, but stopped himself in time.

She was a stranger, nothing more, and he tried to ignore the feel of her against his chest, the fullness of her breasts pressing into his ribs and making his heart pound like a drum. She had her head tucked close to his shoulder, and he could feel the whisper of her breath against his skin. Under the antiseptic her hair smelled of fresh fruit and summer flowers, and he wanted to bury his face in it and breathe in.

He daren't look down again, though. She'd wrapped her arms around his neck and the front of the dress was gaping slightly, the soft swell of those beautiful breasts tempting him almost beyond endurance.

Crazy. Stupid. Whatever was the matter with him? He gritted his teeth, shifted her a little closer and turned towards the steps.

Lydia felt his body tense, saw his jaw tighten and she wondered why. She didn't have time to work it out, though, even if she could, because as he headed towards the house three children came tumbling down the steps and came to a sliding halt in front of them, their mouths open, their faces shocked.

'Pàpa?'

The eldest, a thin, gangly girl with a riot of dark curls and her father's beautiful eyes, stared from one of them to the other, and the look on her face was pure horror.

'I think you'd better explain to your children that I am *not* your new wife,' she said drily, and the girl glanced back at her and then up at her father again.

'Pàpa?'

He was miles away, caught up in a fairy-tale fantasy of carrying this beautiful woman over the threshold and then peeling away the layers of her bridal gown...

'Massimo? I think you need to explain to the children,' Lydia said softly, watching his face at close range. There was a tic in his jaw, the muscle jumping. Had he carried Angelina up these steps?

'It's all right, Francesca,' he said in English, struggling to find his voice. 'This is Miss Fletcher. I met her today at the airport, and she's had an accident and has to rest for a few days, so I've brought her here. Say hello.'

She frowned and asked something in Italian, and he smiled a little grimly and shook his head. 'No. We are *not* married. Say hello to Miss Fletcher, *cara*.'

'Hello, Miss Fletcher,' Francesca said in careful English, her smile wary but her shoulders relaxing a little, and Lydia smiled back at her. She felt a little awkward, gathered up in his arms against that hard, broad chest with the scent of his body doing extraordinary things to her heart, but there was nothing she could do about it except smile and hope his arms didn't break.

'Hello, Francesca. Thank you for speaking English so I can understand you.'

'That's OK. We have to speak English to Auntie Isabelle. This is Lavinia, and this is Antonino. Say hello,' she prompted.

Lydia looked at the other two, clustered round their sister. Lavinia was the next in line, with the same dark, glorious curls but mischief dancing in her eyes, and Antonino, leaning against Francesca and squiggling the toe of his shoe on the gravel, was the youngest. The baby in the photo, the little one who must have lost his mother before he ever really knew her.

Her heart ached for them all, and she felt a welling in her chest and crushed it as she smiled at them.

'Hello, Lavinia, hello, Antonino. It's nice to meet you,' she said, and they replied politely, Lavinia openly studying her, her eyes brimming over with questions.

'And this is Carlotta,' Massimo said, and she lifted her head and met searching, wise eyes in a wizened face. He spoke rapidly to her in Italian, explaining her ridiculous fancy-dress outfit no doubt, and she saw the moment he told her that they'd lost the competition, because Carlotta's face softened and she looked at Lydia and shook her head.

'Sorry,' she said, lifting her hands. 'So sorry for you. Come, I help you change and you will be happier, *si*?'

'*Si,*' she said with a wry chuckle, and Massimo shifted her more firmly against his chest and followed Carlotta puffing and wheezing up the steps.

The children were tugging at him and questioning him in Italian, and he was laughing and answering them as fast as he could. Bless their little hearts, she could see they were hanging on his every word.

He was the centre of their world, and they'd missed him, and she'd kept him away from them all these hours when they must have been desperate to have him back. She felt another shaft of guilt, but Carlotta was leading the way through the big double doors, and she looked away from the children and gasped softly.

They were in a cloistered courtyard, with a broad covered walkway surrounding the open central area that must cast a welcome shade in the heat of the day, but now in the evening it was softly lit and she could see more of the huge pots of olive trees set on the old stone paving in the centre, and on the low wall that divided the courtyard from the cloistered walkway geraniums tumbled over the edge, bringing colour and scent to the evening air.

But that wasn't what had caught her attention. It was the frescoed walls, the ancient faded murals under the shelter of the cloisters that took her breath away.

He didn't pause, though, or give her time to take in the beautiful paintings, but carried her through one of the several doors set in the walls, then along a short hallway and into a bedroom.

He set her gently on the bed, and she felt oddly bereft as he straightened up and moved away.

'I'll be in the kitchen with the children. Carlotta will tell me when you're ready and I'll come and get you.'

'Thank you.'

He smiled fleetingly and went out, the children's clamouring voices receding as he walked away, and Carlotta closed the door.

'Your bath,' she said, pushing open another door, and she saw a room lined with pale travertine marble, the white suite simple and yet luxurious. And the bath—she could stick her bandaged leg up on the side and just wallow. Pure luxury.

'Thank you.' She couldn't wait. All she wanted was to get out of the dress and into water. But the zip...

'I help you,' Carlotta said, and as the zip slid down, she was freed from the scratchy fabric at last. A bit too freed. She clutched at the top as it threatened to drift away and smiled at Carlotta.

'I can manage now,' she said, and Carlotta nodded.

'I get your bag.'

She went out, and Lydia closed the bedroom door behind her, leaning back against it and looking around again.

It was much simpler than the imposing and impressive entrance, she saw with relief. Against expectations it wasn't vast, but it was pristine, the bed made up with sparkling white linen, the rug on the floor soft underfoot, and the view from the French window would be amazing in daylight.

She limped gingerly over to the window and stared out, pressing her face against the glass. The doors opened onto what looked like a terrace, and beyond—gosh, the view must be utterly breathtaking, she imagined, because even at dusk it was extraordinary, the twinkling lights of villages and scattered houses sparkling in the twilight.

Moving away from the window, she glanced around her, taking in her surroundings in more detail. The floor was tiled, the ceiling beamed, with chestnut perhaps? Probably, with terracotta tiles between the beams. Sturdy, simple and homely—which was crazy, considering the scale of the place and the grandeur of the entrance! But it seemed more like a farm now, curiously, less of a fortress, and much less threatening.

And that established, she let go of the awful dress, kicked it away from her legs, bundled it up in a ball and hopped into the bathroom.

The water was calling her. Studying the architecture could wait.

CHAPTER THREE

WHAT was that noise?

Lydia lifted her head, water streaming off her hair as she surfaced to investigate.

'Signorina? Signorina!'

Carlotta's voice was desperate as she rattled the handle on the bathroom door, and Lydia felt a stab of alarm.

'What is it?' she asked, sitting up with a splash and sluicing the water from her hair with her hands.

'Oh, *signorina*! You are all right?'

She closed her eyes and twisted her hair into a rope, squeezing out the rest of the water and suppressing a sigh. 'I'm fine. I'm OK, really. I won't be long.'

'I wait, I help you.'

'No, really, there's no need. I'll be all right.'

'But Massimo say I no leave you!' she protested, clearly worried for some reason, but Lydia assured her again that she was fine.

'OK,' she said after a moment, sounding dubious. 'I leave your bag here. You call me for help?'

'I will. Thank you. *Grazie.*'

'Prego.'

She heard the bedroom door close, and rested her head back down on the bath with a sigh. The woman was kindness itself, but Lydia just wanted to be left alone. Her head

ached, her ankle throbbed, she had a million bruises all over
her body and she still had to phone her sister.

The phone rang, almost as if she'd triggered it with her
thoughts, and she could tell by the ringtone it was Jen.

Oh, rats. She must have heard the news.

There was no getting round it, so she struggled awkwardly
out of the bath and hobbled back to the bed, swathed in the
biggest towel she'd ever seen, and dug out her phone and rang
Jen back.

'What's going on? They said you'd had an accident! I've
been trying to phone you for ages but you haven't been answering! Are you all right? We've been frantic!'

'Sorry, Jen, I was in the bath. I'm fine, really, it was just
a little slip on the steps of a plane and I've twisted my ankle.
Nothing serious.'

Well, she hoped it wasn't. She crossed her fingers, just to
be on the safe side, and filled in a few more details. She didn't
tell her the truth, just that Jo had got there first.

'I'm so sorry, we really tried, but we probably wouldn't
have made it even without the accident.'

There was a heartbeat of hesitation, then Jen said, 'Don't
worry, it really doesn't matter and it's not important. I just
need you to be all right. And don't go blaming yourself, it's
not your fault.'

Why did *everyone* say that? It *was* her fault. If she'd looked
where she was going, taken a bit more care, Jen and Andy
would have been having the wedding of their dreams in a
few months' time. As it was, well, as it was they wouldn't,
but she wasn't going to give Jen anything to beat herself up
about, so she told her she was fine, just a little twinge—and
nothing at all about the head injury.

'Actually, since I'm over here, I thought I'd stay on for a
few days. I've found a farm where I can get bed and breakfast, and I'm going to have a little holiday.'

Well, it wasn't entirely a lie. It *was* a farm, she had a bed, and she was sure they wouldn't make her starve while she recovered.

'You do that. It sounds lovely,' Jen said wistfully, and Lydia screwed her face up and bit her lip.

Damn. She'd been so close, and the disappointment that Jen was trying so hard to disguise was ripping Lydia apart.

Ending the call with a promise to ring when she was coming home, she dug her clean clothes out of the flight bag and pulled her jeans on carefully over her swollen, throbbing ankle. The soft, worn fabric of the jeans and the T-shirt were comforting against her skin, chafed from her fall as well as the boning and beading in the dress, and she looked around for the offending article. It was gone. Taken away by Carlotta? She hoped she hadn't thrown it out. She wanted the pleasure of that for herself.

She put her trainers on, managing to squeeze her bandaged foot in with care, and hobbled out of her room in search of the others, but the corridor outside didn't seem to lead anywhere except her room, a little sitting room and a room that looked like an office, so she went back through the door to the beautiful cloistered courtyard and looked around for any clues.

There were none.

So now what? She couldn't just stand there and yell, nor could she go round the courtyard systematically opening all the doors. Not that there were that many, but even so.

She was sitting there on the low wall around the central courtyard, studying the beautiful frescoes and trying to work out what to do if nobody showed up, when the door nearest to her opened and Massimo appeared. He'd showered and changed out of the suit into jeans and a soft white linen shirt stark against his olive skin, the cuffs rolled back to reveal

those tanned forearms which had nearly been her undoing
on the plane, and her heart gave a tiny lurch.

Stupid.

He caught sight of her and smiled, and her heart did another little jiggle as he walked towards her.

'Lydia, I was just coming to see if you were all right. I'm
sorry, I should have come back quicker. How are you? How's
the head?'

'Fine,' she said with a rueful smile. 'I'm just a bit lost. I
didn't want to go round opening all the doors, it seemed rude.'

'You should have shouted. I would have heard you.'

'I'm not in the habit of yelling for help,' she said drily, and
he chuckled and came over to her side.

'Let me help you now,' he said, and offered her his arm.
'It's not far, hang on and hop, or would you rather I carried
you?'

'I'll hop,' she said hastily, not sure she could cope with
being snuggled up to that broad, solid chest again, with the
feel of his arms strong and safe under her. 'I don't want to
break you.'

He laughed at that. 'I don't think you'll break me. Did you
find everything you needed? How's your room?'

She slipped her arm through his, conscious of the smell
of him again, refreshed now by his shower and overlaid with
soap and more of the citrusy cologne that had been haunting her nostrils all day. She wanted to press her nose to his
chest, to breathe him in, to absorb the warmth and scent and
maleness of him.

Not appropriate. She forced herself to concentrate.

'Lovely. The bath was utter bliss. I can't tell you how wonderful it was to get out of that awful dress. I hope Carlotta
hasn't burned it, I want to do it myself.'

He laughed again, a warm, rich sound that echoed round
the courtyard, and scanned her body with his eyes. 'It really

didn't do you justice,' he said softly, and in the gentle light she thought she caught a glimpse of whatever it was she'd seen in his eyes at the airport.

But then it was gone, and he was opening the door and ushering her through to a big, brightly lit kitchen. Carlotta was busy at the stove, and the children were seated at a large table in the middle of the room, Antonino kneeling up and leaning over to interfere with what Lavinia was doing.

She pushed him aside crossly, and Massimo intervened before a fight could break out, diffusing it swiftly by splitting them up. While he was busy, Carlotta came and helped her to the table. She smiled at her gratefully.

'I'm sorry to put you to so much trouble.'

'Is no trouble,' she said. 'Sit, sit. Is ready.'

She sniffed, and smiled. 'It smells wonderful.'

'*Buono.* You eat, then you feel better. Sit!'

She flapped her apron at Lydia, and she sat obediently at the last place laid at the long table. It was opposite Francesca, and Massimo was at the end of the table on her right, bracketed by the two younger ones who'd been split up to stop them squabbling.

They were fractious—overtired, she thought guiltily, and missing their father. But Francesca was watching her warily. She smiled at the girl apologetically.

'I'm sorry I kept your father away from you for so long. He's been so kind and helpful.'

'He is. He helps everybody. Are you better now?'

'I'm all right. I've just got a bit of a headache but I don't think it's much more than that. I was so stupid. I tripped over the hem of my dress and fell down the steps of the plane and hit my head.'

Behind her, there was a clatter, and Francesca went chalk white, her eyes huge with horror and distress.

'*Scusami,*' she mumbled, and pushing back her chair, she

ran from the room, her father following, his chair crashing over as he leapt to his feet.

'Francesca!' He reached the door before it closed, and she could hear his voice calling as he ran after her. Horrified, uncertain what she'd done, she turned to Carlotta and found her with her apron pressed to her face, her eyes above it creased with distress.

'What did I say?' she whispered, conscious of the little ones, but Carlotta just shook her head and picked up the pan and thrust it in the sink.

'Is nothing. Here, eat. Antonino!'

He sat down, and Lavinia put away the book he'd been trying to tug away from her, and Carlotta picked up Massimo's overturned chair and ladled food out onto all their plates.

There was fresh bread drizzled with olive oil, and a thick, rich stew of beans and sausage and gloriously red tomatoes. It smelt wonderful, tasted amazing, but Lydia could scarcely eat it. The children were eating. Whatever it was she'd said or done had gone right over their heads, but something had driven Francesca from the room, and her father after her.

The same something that had made Massimo go pale at the airport, as he'd knelt on the tarmac at her side? The same something that had made him stand, rigid with tension, staring grimly at a poster when he thought she was asleep in the room at the hospital?

She pushed back her chair and hopped over to the sink, where Carlotta was scrubbing furiously at a pot. 'I'm sorry, I can't eat. Carlotta, what did I say?' she asked under her breath, and those old, wise eyes that had seen so much met hers, and she shook her head, twisting her hands in the dishcloth and biting her lips.

She put the pot on the draining board, and Lydia automatically picked up a tea towel and dried it, her hip propped against the edge of the sink unit as she balanced on her good leg. Another pot followed, and another, and finally Carlotta stopped scouring the pots as if they were lined with demons and her hands came to rest.

She hobbled over to the children, cleared up their plates, gave them pudding and then gathered them up like a mother hen.

'Wait here. Eat. He will come back.'

They left her there in the kitchen, their footsteps echoing along a corridor and up stairs, and Lydia sank down at the table and stared blankly at the far wall, going over and over her words in her head and getting nowhere.

Carlotta appeared again and put Francesca's supper in a microwave.

'Is she coming down again? I want to apologise for upsetting her.'

'No. Is all right, *signorina*. Her *pàpa* look after her.' And lifting the plate out of the microwave, she carried it out of the room on a tray, leaving Lydia alone again.

She poked at her food, but it was cold now, the beans congealing in the sauce, and she ripped up a bit of bread and dabbed it absently in the stew. What had she said, that had caused such distress?

She had no idea, but she couldn't leave the kitchen without finding out, and there was still a pile of washing up to do. She didn't know where anything lived, but the table was big enough to put it all on, and there was a dishwasher sitting there empty.

Well, if she could do nothing else while she waited, she could do that, she told herself, and pushing up her sleeves, she hopped over to the dishwasher and set about clearing up the kitchen.

He had to go down to her—to explain, or apologise properly, at the very least.

His stomach growled, but he ignored it. He couldn't eat,

not while his daughter was just settling into sleep at last, her sobs fading quietly away into the night.

He closed his eyes. Talking to Lydia, dredging it all up again, was the last thing he wanted to do, the very last, but he had no choice. Leaning over Francesca, he pressed a kiss lightly against her cheek, and straightened. She was sleeping peacefully now; he could leave her.

Leave her, and go and find Lydia, if she hadn't had the sense to pack up her things and leave. It seemed unlikely, but he couldn't blame her.

He found her in the kitchen, sitting with Carlotta over a cup of coffee, the kitchen sparkling. He stared at them, then at the kitchen. Carlotta had been upstairs until a short while ago, settling the others, and the kitchen had been in chaos, so how?

'She's OK now,' he said in Italian. 'Why don't you go to bed, Carlotta? You look exhausted and Roberto's worried about you.'

She nodded and got slowly to her feet, then rested her hand on Lydia's shoulder and patted it before leaving her side. 'I *am* tired,' she said to him in Italian, 'but you need to speak to Lydia. I couldn't leave her. She's a good girl, Massimo. Look at my kitchen! A good, kind girl, and she's unhappy. Worried.'

He sighed. 'I know. Did you explain?'

'No. It's not my place, but be gentle with her—and yourself.' And with that pointed remark, she left them alone together.

Lydia looked up at him and searched his eyes. 'What did she say to you?'

He gave her a fleeting smile. 'She told me you were a good, kind girl. And she told me to be gentle with you.'

Her eyes filled, and she looked away. 'I don't know what I said, but I'm so, so sorry.'

His conscience pricked him. He should have warned her. He sighed and scrubbed a hand through his hair.

'No. I should be apologising, not you. Forgive us, we aren't normally this rude to visitors. Francesca was upset.'

'I know that. Obviously I made it happen. What I don't know is why,' she said, looking up at him again with grief-stricken eyes.

He reached for a mug, changed his mind and poured himself a glass of wine. 'Can I tempt you?'

'Is it one of yours?'

'No. It's a neighbour's, but it's good. We could take it outside. I don't know if it's wise, though, with your head injury.'

'I'll take the risk,' she said. 'And then will you tell me what I said?'

'You know what you said. What you don't know is what it meant,' he said enigmatically, and picking up both glasses of wine, he headed for the door, glancing back over his shoulder at her. 'Can you manage, or should I carry you?'

Carry her? With her face pressed up against that taunting aftershave, and the feel of his strong, muscled arms around her legs? 'I can manage,' she said hastily, and pushing back her chair, she got to her feet and limped after him out into the still, quiet night.

She could hear the soft chirr of insects, the sound of a motorbike somewhere in the valley below, and then she saw a single headlight slicing through the night, weaving and turning as it followed the snaking road along the valley bottom and disappeared.

He led her to a bench at the edge of the terrace. The ground fell away below them so it felt as if they were perched on the edge of the world, and when she was seated he handed her the glass and sat beside her, his elbows propped on his knees, his own glass dangling from his fingers as he stared out over the velvet blackness.

For a while neither of them said anything, but then the tension got to her and she broke the silence.

'Please tell me.'

He sucked in his breath, looking down, staring into his glass as he slowly swirled the wine before lifting it to his lips.

'Massimo?' she prompted, and he turned his head and met her eyes. Even in the moonlight, she could see the pain etched into his face, and her heart began to thud slowly.

'Angelina died of a brain haemorrhage following a fall,' he began, his voice expressionless. 'Nothing serious, nothing much at all, just a bit of a bump. She'd fallen down the stairs and hit her head on the wall. We all thought she was all right, but she had a bit of a headache later in the day, and we went to bed early. I woke in the night and she was missing, and I found her in the kitchen, slumped over the table, and one side of her face had collapsed.'

Lydia closed her eyes and swallowed hard as the nausea threatened to choke her. What had she *done*? Not just by saying what she had at the table—the same table? But by bringing this on all of them, on Claire, on him, on the children—most especially little Francesca, her eyes wide with pain and shock, fleeing from the table. The image would stay with her forever.

'It wasn't your fault,' he said gently. 'You weren't to know. I probably should have told you—warned you not to talk about it in that way, and why. I let you walk right into it.'

She turned back to him, searching his face in the shadows. She'd known something was wrong when he was bending over her on the tarmac, and again later, staring at the poster. And yet he'd said nothing.

'Why didn't you *tell* me? I knew something was wrong, something else, something more. Luca seemed much more worried than my condition warranted, even I knew that, and he kept looking at you anxiously. I thought he was worried about me, but then I realised it was you he was worried about. I just didn't know why. You should have told me.'

'How could I? You had a head injury. How could I say to you, "I'm sorry, I'm finding this a bit hard to deal with, my wife died of the same thing and I'm a bit worried I might lose you, too." How could I say that?'

He'd been worried he could lose her?

No. Of course he hadn't meant that, he didn't know her. He meant he was worried she might be about to die, too. Nothing more than that.

'You should have left us there instead of staying and getting distressed. I had no business tangling you all up in this mess—oh, Massimo, I'm so sorry.'

She broke off, clamping her teeth hard to stop her eyes from welling over, but his warm hand on her shoulder was the last straw, and she felt the hot, wet slide of a tear down her cheek.

'*Cara*, no. Don't cry for us. It was a long time ago.'

'But it still hurts you, and it'll hurt you forever,' she said unevenly.

'No, it just brought the memories back. We're all right, really. We're getting there. Francesca's the oldest, she remembers Angelina the most clearly, and she's the one who bears the brunt of the loss, because when I'm not there the little ones turn to her. She has to be mother to them, and she's been so strong, but she's just a little girl herself.'

He broke off, his jaw working, and she laid her hand gently against it and sighed.

'I'm so sorry. It must have been dreadful for you all.'

'It was. They took her to hospital, and she died later that day—she was on life support and they tested her brain but there was nothing. No activity at all. They turned off the machine, and I came home and told the children that their mother was gone. That was the hardest thing I've ever had to do in my life.'

His voice broke off again, turning away this time, and Lydia closed her eyes and swallowed the anguished response. There was nothing she could say that wouldn't be trite or meaningless, and so she stayed silent, and after a moment he let out a long, slow breath and sat back against the bench.

'So, now you know,' he said, his voice low and oddly flat.

Wordlessly, she reached out and touched his hand, and he turned it, his fingers threading through hers and holding on tight.

They stayed like that for an age, their hands lying linked between them as they sipped their wine, and then he turned to her in the dim light and searched her face. He'd taken comfort from her touch, felt the warmth of her generous spirit seeping into him, easing the ache which had been a part of him for so long.

How could she do that with just a touch?

No words. Words were too hard, would have been trite. Did she know that?

Yes. He could see that she did, that this woman who talked too much actually knew the value of silence.

He lifted her hand and pressed it to his lips, then smiled at her sadly. 'Did you eat anything?'

She shook her head. 'No. Not really.'

'Nor did I. Shall we see what we can find? It's a very, very long time since breakfast.'

It wasn't exactly *haute cuisine*, but the simple fare of olive bread and ham and cheese with sweetly scented baby plum tomatoes and a bowl of olive oil and balsamic vinegar just hit the spot.

He poured them another glass of wine, but it didn't seem like a good idea and so she gave him the second half and he found some sparkling water for her. She realised she'd thought nothing of handing him her glass of wine for him to finish, and he'd taken it without hesitation and drunk from it without turning a hair.

How odd, when they'd only met a scant twelve hours ago. Thirteen hours and a few minutes, to be more exact.

It seemed more like a lifetime since she'd watched him getting out of the taxi, wondered if he'd be The One to make it happen. The guy she'd been talking to was funny and seemed nice enough, but he wasn't about to give her a lift and she knew that. But Massimo had looked at her as he'd gone into the Jet Centre foyer, his eyes meeting hers and locking...

She glanced up, and found him watching her with a frown.

'Why are you frowning?' she asked, and his mouth kicked up a fraction in one corner, the frown ironed out with a deliberate effort.

'No reason. How's your head now?'

She shrugged. 'OK. It just feels as if I fell over my feet and spent the day hanging about in a hospital.' It was rather worse than that, but he didn't need to know about every ache and pain. The list was endless.

She reached out and covered his hand. 'Massimo, I'm all right,' she said softly, and the little frown came back.

'Sorry. It's just a reflex. I look after people—it's part of my job description. Everyone comes to me with their problems.'

She smiled at him, remembering her conversation with Francesca.

'I'm sorry I kept your father away from you for so long. He's been so kind and helpful.'

'He is. He helps everybody.'

'You're just a fixer, aren't you? You fix everything for everybody all the time, and you hate it when things can't be fixed.'

His frown deepened for a moment, and then he gave a wry laugh and pulled his hand away, swirling the wine in her glass before draining it. 'Is it so obvious?'

She felt her lips twitch. 'Only if you're on the receiving end. Don't get me wrong, I'm massively grateful and just so sorry I've dragged you into this awful mess and upset everyone. I'm more than happy you're a fixer, because goodness only knows I seemed to need one today. I think I need a guardian angel, actually. I just have such a gift for getting into a mess and dragging everybody with me.'

She broke off, and he tipped his head on one side and that little crease between his eyebrows returned fleetingly. 'A gift?'

She sighed. 'Jen's accident was sort of my fault.'

He sat back, his eyes searching hers. 'Tell me,' he said softly, so she did.

She told him about Russell, about their trip to her parents' farm for the weekend, because Jen and Andy were going to be there as well and she hadn't seen them for a while. And she'd shown him the farm, and he'd seen the quad bike, and suggested they went out on it so she could show him all the fields.

'I didn't want to go with him. He was a crazy driver, and I knew he'd want to go too fast, so I said no, but then Jen offered to show him round. She wanted to get him alone, to threaten him with death if he hurt me, but he hurt her instead. He went far too fast, and she told him to stop but he thought she was just being chicken and she wasn't, she knew about the fallen tree hidden in the long grass, and then they hit it and the quad bike cartwheeled through the air and landed on her.'

He winced and closed his eyes briefly. 'And she ended up in a wheelchair?'

'Not for a few weeks. She had a fractured spine, and she

was in a special bed for a while. It wasn't displaced, the spinal cord wasn't severed but it was badly bruised and it took a long time to recover and for the bones to heal. She's getting better now, she's starting to walk again, but she lost her job and so did Andy, so he could look after her. He took away everything from them, and if I'd gone with him, if it had been me, then I might have been able to stop him.'

'You really think so? He sounds like an idiot.'

'He is an idiot,' she said tiredly. 'He's an idiot, and he was my boss, so I lost my job, too.'

'He sacked you?'

She gave him a withering look. 'I walked…and then his business folded without me, and he threatened to sue me if I didn't go back. I told him to take a flying hike.'

'What business was he in?'

'He had a restaurant. I was his chef.'

Hence the tidy kitchen, he realised. She was used to working in a kitchen, used to bringing order to chaos, used to the utensils and the work space and the arrangement of them that always to him defied logic. And his restaurant had folded without her?

'You told me you were a cook,' he rebuked her mildly. 'I didn't realise you were a chef.'

She quirked an eyebrow at him mockingly. 'You told me you were a farmer and you live in a flipping fortress! I think that trumps it,' she said drily, and he laughed and lifted his glass to her.

'*Touché,*' he said softly, and her heart turned over at the wry warmth in his eyes. 'I'm sorry,' he went on. 'Sorry about this man who clearly didn't deserve you, sorry about your sister, sorry about your job. What a mess. And all because he was a fool.'

'Absolutely.'

'Tell me more about him.'

'Like what?'

'Like why your sister felt she needed to warn him not to hurt you. Had you been hurt before?'

'No, but she didn't really like him. He wasn't always a nice man, and he took advantage of me—made me work ridiculous hours, treated me like a servant at times and yet he could be a charmer, too. He was happy enough to talk me into his bed once he realised I was a good chef—sorry, you really didn't need to know that.'

He smiled slightly. 'Maybe you needed to say it,' he suggested, and her laugh was a little brittle.

'There are so many things I could tell you about him. I said I was a lousy judge of character. I think he had a lot in common with Nico, perhaps.'

He frowned. 'Nico?'

'The guy at the airport?'

'Yes, I know who you mean. In what way? Was he a drinker?'

'Yes. Definitely. But not just a drinker. He was a nasty drunk, especially towards the end of our relationship. He seemed to change. Got arrogant. He used to be quite charming at first, but it was just a front. He—well, let's just say he didn't respect women either.'

His mouth tightened. 'I'm sorry. You shouldn't have had to tolerate that.'

'No, I shouldn't. So—tell me about your house,' she said, changing the subject to give them both a bit of a break. She reached out and tore off another strip of bread, dunking it in the oil that she couldn't get enough of, and looked up to see a strange look on his face. Almost—tender?

Nonsense. She was being silly. 'Well, come on, then,' she mumbled round the bread, and he smiled, the strange look disappearing as if she'd imagined it.

'It's very old. We're not sure of the origins. It seems it

might have been a Medici villa, but the history is a little cloudy. It was built at the time of the Florentine invasion.'

'So how come your family ended up with it?'

His mouth twitched. 'One of our ancestors took possession of it at the end of the seventeenth century.'

That made her laugh. 'Took possession?'

The twitch again, and a wicked twinkle in his eye. 'We're not quite sure how he acquired it, but it's been in the family ever since. He's the one who renamed the villa *Palazzo Valtieri*.'

Palazzo? She nearly laughed at that. Not just a fortress, then, but a proper, full-on palace. Oh, boy.

'I'll show you round it tomorrow. It's beautiful. Some of the frescoes are amazing, and the formal rooms in the part my parents live in are fantastic.'

'Your parents live here?' she asked, puzzled, because there'd been no mention of them. Not that they'd really had time, but—

'*Si*. It's a family business. They're away at the moment, snatching a few days with my sister Carla and her new baby before the harvest starts, but they'll be back the day after tomorrow.'

'So how many rooms are there?'

He laughed. 'I have no idea. I've never counted them, I'm too busy trying not to let it fall down. It's crumbling as fast as we can patch it up, but so long as we can cheat time, that's fine. It's quite interesting.'

'I'm sure it is. And now it's your turn to run it?'

His mouth tugged down at the corners, but there was a smile in his eyes. '*Si*. For my sins. My father keeps trying to interfere, but he's supposed to be retired. He doesn't understand that, though.'

'No. It must be hard to hand it over. My father wouldn't be able to do it. And the harvest is just starting?'

He nodded. 'The grape harvest is first, followed by the chestnuts and the olives. It's relentless now until the end of November, so you can see why I was in a hurry to get back.'

'And I held you up.'

'*Cara*, accidents happen. Don't think about it any more.' He pushed back his chair. 'I think it's time you went to bed. It's after midnight.'

Was it? When had that happened? When they were outside, sitting in the quiet of the night and watching the twinkling lights in the villages? Or now, sitting here eating bread and cheese and olive oil, drinking wine and staring into each other's eyes like lovers?

She nodded and pushed back her chair, and he tucked her arm in his so she could feel the solid muscle of his forearm under her hand, and she hung on him and hopped and hobbled her way to her room.

'Ring me if you need anything. You have my mobile number on my card. I gave it to you on the plane. Do you still have it?'

'Yes—but I won't need you.'

Well, not for anything she'd dream of asking him for...

His brows tugged together. 'Just humour me, OK? If you feel unwell in the night, or want anything, ring me and I'll come down. I'm not far away. And please, don't lock your door.'

'Massimo, I'm feeling all right. My headache's gone, and I feel OK now. You don't need to worry.'

'You can't be too careful,' he said, and she could see a tiny frown between his brows, as if he was still waiting for something awful to happen to her.

They reached her room and he paused at the door, staring down into her eyes and hesitating for the longest moment. And then, just when she thought he was going to kiss her, he stepped back.

'Call me if you need me. If you need anything at all.'

'I will.'

'Good. *Buonanotte*, Lydia,' he murmured softly, and turned and walked away.

CHAPTER FOUR

WHAT was she *thinking* about?

Of course he hadn't been about to kiss her! That bump on the head had obviously been more serious than she'd realised. Maybe a blast of fresh air would help her think clearly?

She opened the French doors onto the terrace and stood there for a moment, letting the night air cool her heated cheeks. She'd been so carried along on the moment, so lured by his natural and easy charm that she'd let herself think all sorts of stupid things.

Of course he wasn't interested in her. Why would he be? She'd been nothing but a thorn in his side since the moment he'd set eyes on her. And even if he hadn't, she wasn't interested! Well, that was a lie, of course she was interested, or she wouldn't even be thinking about it, but there was no way it was going anywhere.

Not after the debacle with Russell. She was sworn off men now for life, or at least for a good five years. And so far, it hadn't been much more than five months!

Leaving the doors open, she limped back to the bed and pulled her pyjamas out of her flight bag, eyeing them dubiously. The skimpy top and little shorts she'd brought for their weightlessness had seemed fine when she was going to be sharing a hotel room with Claire, but here, in this ancient historic house—*palazzo*, even, for heaven's sake! She wondered what on earth he'd make of them.

Nothing. Nothing at all, because he wasn't going to see her in her nightclothes! Cross with herself, her head aching and her ankle throbbing and her bruises giving her a fair amount of grief as well, she changed into the almost-pyjamas, cleaned her teeth and crawled into bed.

Oh, bliss. The pillows were cloud-soft, the down quilt light and yet snuggly, and the breeze from the doors was drifting across her face, bringing with it the scents of sage and lavender and night-scented stocks.

Exhausted, weary beyond belief, she closed her eyes with a little sigh and drifted off to sleep...

Her doors were open.

He hesitated, standing outside on the terrace, questioning his motives.

Did he *really* think she needed checking in the night? Or was he simply indulging his—what? Curiosity? Fantasy? Or, perhaps...need?

He groaned softly. There was no doubt that he *needed* her, needed the warmth of her touch, the laughter in her eyes, the endless chatter and the brilliance of her smile.

The silence, when she'd simply held his hand and offered comfort.

Thinking about that moment brought a lump to his throat, and he swallowed hard. He hadn't allowed himself to need a woman for years, but Lydia had got under his skin, penetrated his defences with her simple kindness, and he wanted her in a way that troubled him greatly, because it was more than just physical.

And he really wasn't sure he was ready for that—would ever be ready for that again. But the need...

He'd just check on her, just to be on the safe side. He couldn't let her lie there alone all night.

Not like Angelina.

Guilt crashed over him again, driving out the need and leaving sorrow in its wake. Focused now, he went into her room, his bare feet silent on the tiled floor, and gave his eyes a moment to adjust to the light.

Had she sensed him? Maybe, because she sighed and shifted, the soft, contented sound drifting to him on the night air. When had he last heard a woman sigh softly in her sleep?

Too long ago to remember, too soon to forget.

It would be so easy to reach out his hand, to touch her. To take her in his arms, warm and sleepy, and make love to her.

Easy, and yet impossibly wrong. What was it about her that made him feel like this, that made him think things he hadn't thought in years? Not since he'd lost Angelina.

He stood over her, staring at her in the moonlight, the thought of his wife reminding him of why he was here. Not to watch Lydia sleep, like some kind of voyeur, but to keep her safe. He focused on her face. It was peaceful, both sides the same, just as it had been when he'd left her for the night, and she was breathing slowly and evenly. As he watched she moved her arms, pushing the covers lower. Both arms, both working.

He swallowed. She was fine, just as she'd told him, he realised in relief. He could go to bed now, relax.

But it was too late. He'd seen her sleeping, heard that soft, feminine sigh and the damage was done. His body, so long denied, had come screaming back to life, and he wouldn't sleep now.

Moving carefully so as not to disturb her, he made his way back to the French doors and out onto the terrace. Propping his hands on his hips, he dropped his head back and sucked in a lungful of cool night air, then let it out slowly before dragging his hand over his face.

He'd swim. Maybe that would take the heat out of his blood. And if it was foolish to swim alone, if he'd told the children a thousand times that no one should ever do it—well, tonight was different.

Everything about tonight seemed different.

He crossed the upper terrace, padded silently down the worn stone steps to the level below and rolled back the thermal cover on the pool. The water was warm, steaming billowing from the surface in the cool night air, and stripping off his clothes, he dived smoothly in.

Something had woken her.

She opened her eyes a fraction, peeping through the slit between her eyelids, but she could see nothing.

She could hear something, though. Not loud, just a little, rhythmic splash—like someone swimming?

She threw off the covers and sat up, wincing a little as her head pounded and the bruises twinged with the movement. She fingered the egg on her head, and sighed. *Idiot*. First thing in the morning she was going to track down that dress and burn the blasted thing.

She inched to the edge of the bed, and stood up slowly, her ankle protesting as she put weight through it. Not as badly as yesterday, though, she thought, and limped out onto the terrace to listen for the noise.

Yes. Definitely someone swimming. And it seemed to be coming from straight ahead. As she felt her way cautiously across the stone slabs and then the grass, she realised that this was the terrace they'd sat on last night, or at least a part of it. They'd been further over, to her left, and straight ahead of her were railings, the top edge gleaming in the moonlight.

She made her way slowly to them and looked down, and

there he was. Well, there someone was, slicing through the water with strong, bold strokes, up and down, up and down, length after length through the swirling steam that rose from the surface of the pool.

Exorcising demons?

Then finally he slowed, rolled to his back and floated spread-eagled on the surface. She could barely make him out because the steam clouded the air in the moonlight, but she knew instinctively it was him.

And as if he'd sensed her, he turned his head and as the veil of mist was drawn back for an instant, their eyes met in the night. Slowly, with no sense of urgency, he swam to the side, folded his arms and rested on them, looking up at her.

'You're awake.'

'Something woke me, then I heard the splashing. Is it sensible to swim on your own in the dark?'

He laughed softly. 'You could always come in. Then I wouldn't be alone.'

'I haven't got any swimming things.'

'Ah. Well, that's probably not very wise then because neither have I.'

She sucked in her breath softly, and closed her eyes, suddenly embarrassed. Amongst other things. 'I'm sorry. I didn't realise. I'll go away.'

'Don't worry, I'm finished. Just close your eyes for a second so I don't offend you while I get out.'

She heard the laughter in his voice, then the sound of him vaulting out of the pool. Her eyes flew open, and she saw him straighten up, water sluicing off his back as he walked calmly to a sun lounger and picked up an abandoned towel. He dried himself briskly as she watched, unable to look away, mesmerised by those broad shoulders that tapered down to lean hips and powerful legs.

In the magical silver light of the moon, the taut, firm globes of his buttocks, paler than the rest of him, could have been carved from marble, like one of the statues that seemed to litter the whole of Italy. Except they'd be warm, of course, alive...

Her mouth dry, she snapped her eyes shut again and made herself breath. In, out, in, out, nice and slowly, slowing down, calmer.

'Would you like a drink?'

She jumped and gave a tiny shriek. 'Don't creep up on people like that!' she whispered fiercely, and rested her hand against the pounding heart beneath her chest.

Yikes. Her all but bare chest, in the crazily insubstantial pyjamas...

'I'm not really dressed for entertaining,' she mumbled, which was ridiculous because the scanty towel twisted round his hips left very little to the imagination.

His fingers, cool and damp, appeared under her chin, tilting her head up so she could see his face instead of just that tantalising towel. His eyes were laughing.

'That makes two of us. I tell you what, I'll go and put the kettle on and pull on my clothes, and you go and find something a little less...'

'Revealing?'

His smile grew crooked. 'I was going to say alluring.'

Alluring. Right.

'I'll get dressed,' she said hastily, and limped rather faster than was sensible back towards her room, shutting the doors firmly behind her.

He watched her hobble away, his eyes tracking her progress across the terrace in the skimpiest of pyjamas, the long slender legs that had been hidden until now revealed by those tiny shorts in a way that did nothing for his peace of mind.

Or the state of his body. He swallowed hard and tightened his grip on the towel.

So much for the swimming cooling him down, he thought wryly, and went into the kitchen through the side door, rubbed himself briskly down with the towel again and pulled on his clothes, then switched on the kettle. Would she be able to find him? Would she even know which way to go?

Yes. She was there, in the doorway, looking deliciously rumpled and sleepy and a little uncertain. She'd pulled on her jeans and the T-shirt she'd been wearing last night, and her unfettered breasts had been confined to a bra. Pity, he thought, and then chided himself. She was a guest in his house, she was injured, and all he could do was lust after her. He should be ashamed of himself.

'Tea, coffee or something else? I expect there are some herbal teabags or something like that.'

'Camomile?' she asked hopefully.

Something to calm her down, because her host, standing there in bare feet, a damp T-shirt clinging to the moisture on his chest and a pair of jeans that should have had a health warning on them hanging on his lean hips was doing nothing for her equilibrium.

Not now she knew what was underneath those clothes.

He poured boiling water into a cup for her, then stuck another cup under the coffee maker and pressed a button. The sound of the grinding beans was loud in the silence, but not loud enough to drown out the sound of her heartbeat.

She should have stayed in her room, kept out of his way.

'Here, I don't know how long you want to keep the teabag in.'

He put the mug down on the table and turned back to the coffee maker, and as she stirred the teabag round absently she watched him. His hands were deft, his movements precise as he spooned sugar and stirred in a splash of milk.

'Won't that keep you awake?' she asked, but he just laughed softly.

'It's not a problem, I'm up now for the day. After I've drunk this I'll go and tackle some work in my office, and then I'll have breakfast with the children before I go out and check the grapes in each field to see if they're ripe.'

'Has the harvest started?'

'La vendemmia?' He shook his head. 'No. If the grapes are ripe, it starts tomorrow. We'll spend the rest of the day making sure we're ready, because once it starts, we don't stop till it's finished. But today—today should be pretty routine.'

So he might have time to show her round…

'Want to come with me and see what we do? If you're interested, of course. Don't feel you have to.'

If she was interested? She nearly laughed. *The farm*, she told herself firmly. He was talking about the *farm*.

'That would be great, if I won't be in your way?'

'No, of course not. It might be dull, though, and once I leave the house I won't be back for hours. I don't know if you're feeling up to it.'

Was he trying to get out of it? Retracting his invitation, thinking better of having her hanging around him all day like a stray kitten that wouldn't leave him alone?

'I can't walk far,' she said, giving him a get-out clause, but he shook his head.

'No, you don't have to. We'll take the car, and if you don't feel well I can always bring you back, it's not a problem.'

That didn't sound as if he was trying to get out of it, and she was genuinely interested.

'It sounds great. What time do you want to leave?'

'Breakfast is at seven. We'll go straight afterwards.'

It was fascinating.

He knew every inch of his land, every nook and cranny,

every slope, every vine, almost, and as he stood on the edge of a little escarpment pointing things out to her, his feet planted firmly in the soil, she thought she'd never seen anyone who belonged so utterly to their home.

He looked as if he'd grown from the very soil beneath his feet, his roots stretching down into it for three hundred years. It was a part of him, and he was a part of it, the latest guardian in its history, and it was clear that he took the privilege incredibly seriously.

As they drove round the huge, sprawling estate to check the ripeness of the grapes on all the slopes, he told her about each of the grape varieties which grew on the different soils and orientations, lifting handfuls of the soil so she could see the texture, sifting it through his fingers as he talked about moisture content and pH levels and how it varied from field to field, and all the time his fingers were caressing the soil like a lover.

He mesmerised her.

Then he dropped the soil, brushed off his hands and gave her a wry smile.

'I'm boring you to death. Come on, it's time for lunch.'

He helped her back to the car, frowning as she trod on some uneven ground and gave a little cry as her ankle twisted.

'I'm sorry, it's too rough for you. Here.' And without hesitating he scooped her off her feet and set her back on the passenger seat, shut the door and went round and slid in behind the wheel.

He must have been mad to bring her out here on the rough ground in the heat of the day, with a head injury and a sprained ankle. He hadn't been thinking clearly, what with the upset of yesterday and Francesca's scene at the table and then the utter distraction of her pyjamas—even if he'd been intending to go back to bed, there was no way he would have slept. In fact, he doubted if he'd ever sleep again!

He put her in the car, drove back to the villa and left her there with Carlotta. He'd been meaning to show her round the house, but frankly, even another moment in her company was too dangerous to contemplate at the moment.

He made a work-related excuse, and escaped.

He had a lot to do, he'd told her as he'd hurried off, because *la vendemmia* would start the following day.

So much for her tour of the house, she thought, but maybe it was as well to keep a bit of distance, because her feelings for him were beginning to confuse her.

Roberto brought the children home from school at the end of the afternoon, and she heard them splashing in the pool. She'd been contemplating the water herself, but without a suit it wasn't a goer, so she'd contented herself with sitting in the sun for a while and relaxing.

She went over to the railings and looked down, and saw all three of them in the water, with Carlotta and Roberto sitting in the shade watching them and keeping order. Carlotta glanced up at her and waved her down, and she limped down the steps and joined them.

It looked so inviting. Was her face a giveaway? Maybe, because Carlotta got to her feet and went to a door set in the wall of the terrace, under the steps. She emerged with a sleek black one-piece and offered it to her. 'Swim?' she said, encouragingly.

It was so, so tempting, and the children didn't seem to mind. Lavinia swam to the edge and grinned at her, and Antonino threw a ball at her and missed, and then giggled because she threw it back and bounced it lightly off his head. Only Francesca kept her distance, and she could understand why. It was the first time she'd seen her since supper last night, and maybe now she'd find a chance to apologise.

She changed in the cubicle Carlotta had taken the costume

from, and sat on the edge of the pool to take off her elastic
ankle support.

'Ow. It looks sore.'

She glanced up, and saw Francesca watching her warily,
her face troubled.

'I'm all right,' she assured her with a smile. 'I was really
stupid to fall like that. I'm so sorry I upset you last night.'

She shrugged, and returned the smile with a tentative one
of her own. 'Is OK. I was just tired, and *Pàpa* had been away
for days, and—I'm OK. Sometimes, I just remember…'

She nodded, trying to understand what it must be like to be
ten and motherless, and coming up with nothing even close,
she was sure.

'I'm sorry.' She slipped into the water next to Francesca,
and reached out and touched her shoulder gently. Then she
smiled at her. 'I wonder, would you teach me some words of
Italian?'

'Sure. What?'

'Just basic things. Sorry. Thank you. Hello, goodbye—just
things like that.'

'Of course. Swim first, then I teach you.'

And she smiled, a dazzling, pretty smile like the smile
of her mother in the photograph, and it nearly broke Lydia's
heart.

He came into the kitchen as she was sitting there with the
children, Francesca patiently coaching her.

'No! *Mee dees-pya-che*,' said Francesca, and Lydia repeated it, stretching the vowels.

'That's good. *Ciao, bambini*!'

'*Ciao, Pàpa!*' the children chorused, and he came over and
sat down with them.

'I'm teaching Lydia *Italiano*,' Francesca told him, grinning at him.

He smiled back, his eyes indulgent. *'Mia bella ragazza,'* he said softly, and her smile widened, a soft blush colouring her cheeks.

'So what do you know?' he asked Lydia, and she laughed ruefully.

'Mi dispiace—I thought sorry was a word I ought to master pretty early on, with my track record,' she said drily, and he chuckled.

'Anything else?'

'Grazie mille—I seem to need that a lot, too! And *per favore*, because it's rude not to say please. And *prego*, just in case I ever get the chance to do something that someone thanks me for. And that's it, so far, but I think it's the most critical ones.'

He laughed. 'It's a good start. Right, children, bedtime. Say goodnight.'

'Buonanotte, Lydia,' they chorused, and she smiled at them and said, *'Buonanotte,'* back.

And then she looked at Francesca, and added, *'Grazie mille*, Francesca,' her eyes soft, and Francesca smiled back.

'Prego. We do more tomorrow?'

'Si.'

She grinned, and then out of the blue she came over to Lydia and kissed her on both cheeks. 'Goodnight.'

'Goodnight, Francesca.'

He ushered them away, although Francesca didn't really need to go to bed this early, but she'd lost sleep the night before and she was always happy to lie in bed and read.

He chivvied them through the bathroom, checked their teeth, redid Antonino's and then tucked them up. As he bent to kiss Francesca goodnight, she slid her arms round his neck and hugged him. 'I like Lydia,' she said. 'She's nice.'

'She is nice,' he said. 'Thank you for helping her.'

'It's OK. How long is she staying?'

'I don't know. A few days, just until she's better. You go to sleep, now.'

He turned off her top light, leaving the bedside light on so she could read for a while, and went back down to the kitchen.

Lydia was sitting there studying an English-Italian dictionary that Francesca must have lent her, and he poured two glasses of wine and sat down opposite her.

'She's a lovely girl.'

'She is. She's very like her mother. Kind. Generous.'

Lydia nodded. 'I'm really sorry you lost her.'

He smiled, but said nothing. What was there to say? Nothing he hadn't said before.

'So, the harvest starts tomorrow,' Lydia said after a moment.

'*Si*. You should come down. Carlotta brings lunch for everyone at around twelve-thirty. Come with her, I'll show you what we do.'

Massimo left before dawn the following morning, and she found Carlotta up to her eyes in the kitchen.

'How many people are you feeding?' she asked.

Carlotta's face crunched up thoughtfully, and she said something in Italian which was meaningless, then held up her outspread hands and flashed them six times. Sixty. *Sixty?*

'Wow! That's a lot of work.'

'*Si*. Is lot of work.'

She looked tired at the very thought, and Lydia frowned slightly and began to help without waiting to be asked. They loaded the food into a truck at twelve, and Roberto, Carlotta's husband, drove them down to the centre of operations.

They followed the route she'd travelled with Massimo the day before, bumping along the gravelled road to a group of buildings. It was a hive of activity, small tractors and pickup trucks in convoy bringing in the grapes, a tractor and trailer with men and women crowded on the back laughing and joking, their spirits high.

Massimo met them there, and helped her down out of the truck with a smile. 'Come, I'll show you round,' he said, and led her to the production line.

Around the tractors laden with baskets of grapes, the air was alive with the hum of bees. Everyone was covered in sticky purple grape juice, the air heavy with sweat and the sweet scent of freshly pressed grapes, and over the sound of excited voices she could hear the noise of the motors powering the pumps and the pressing machines.

'It's fascinating,' she yelled, and he nodded.

'It is. You can stay, if you like, see what we do with the grapes.'

'Do you need me underfoot?' she asked, and his mouth quirked.

'I'm sure I'll manage. You ask intelligent questions. I can live with that.'

His words made her oddly happy, and she smiled. 'Thank you. They seem to be enjoying themselves,' she added, gesturing to the laughing workers, and he grinned.

'Why wouldn't they be? We all love the harvest. And anyway, it's lunchtime,' he said pragmatically as the machines fell silent, and she laughed.

'So it is. I'm starving.'

The lunch was just a cold spread of bread and cheese and ham and tomatoes, much like their impromptu supper in the middle of the first night, and the exhausted and hungry workers fell on it like locusts.

'Carlotta told me there are about sixty people to feed. Does she do this every day?'

'Yes—and an evening meal for everyone. It's too much for her, but she won't let anyone else take over, she insists on being in charge and she's so fussy about who she'll allow in her kitchen it's not easy to get help that she'll accept.'

She nodded. She could understand that. She'd learned the art of delegation, but you still had to have a handle on everything that was happening in the kitchen and that took energy and physical resources that Carlotta probably didn't have any more.

'How old is she?'

Massimo laughed. 'It's a state secret and more than my life's worth to reveal it. Roberto's eighty-two. She tells me it's none of my business, which makes it difficult as she's on the payroll, so I had to prise it out of Roberto. Let's just say there's not much between them.'

That made her chuckle, but it also made her think. Carlotta hadn't minded her helping out in the kitchen this morning, or the other night—in fact, she'd almost seemed grateful. Maybe she'd see if she could help that afternoon. 'I think I'll head back with them,' she told him. 'It's a bit hot out here for me now anyway, and I could do with putting my foot up for a while.'

It wasn't a lie, none of it, but she had no intention of putting her foot up if Carlotta would let her help. And it would be a way to repay them for all the trouble she'd caused.

It was an amazing amount of work.

It would have been a lot for a team. For Carlotta, whose age was unknown but somewhere in the ballpark of eighty-plus, it was ridiculous. She had just the one helper, Maria, who sighed with relief when Lydia offered her assistance.

So did Carlotta.

Oh, she made a fuss, protested a little, but more on the lines of 'Oh, you don't really want to,' rather than, 'No, thank you, I don't need your help.'

So she rolled up her sleeves and pitched in, peeling and

chopping a huge pile of vegetables. Carlotta was in charge of browning the diced chicken, seasoning the tomato-based sauce, tasting.

That was fine. This was her show. Lydia was just going along for the ride, and making up for the disaster of her first evening here, but by the time they were finished and ready to serve it on trestle tables under the cherry trees, her ankle was paying for it.

She stood on one leg like a stork, her sore foot hooked round her other calf, wishing she could sit down and yet knowing she was needed as they dished up to the hungry hordes.

They still looked happy, she thought. Happy and dirty and smelly and as if they'd had a good day, and there was a good deal of teasing and flirting going on, some of it in her direction.

She smiled back, dished up and wondered where Massimo was. She found herself scanning the crowd for him, and told herself not to be silly. He'd be with the children, not here, not eating with the workers.

She was wrong. A few minutes later, when the queue was thinning out and she was at the end of her tether, she felt a light touch on her waist.

'You should be resting. I'll take over.'

And his firm hands eased her aside, took the ladle from her hand and carried on.

'You don't need to do that. You've been working all day.'

'So have you, I gather, and you're hurt. Have you eaten?'

'No. I was waiting till we'd finished.'

He ladled sauce onto the last plate and turned to her. 'We're finished. Grab two plates, we'll go and eat. And you can put your foot up. You told me you were going to do that and I hear you've been standing all day.'

They sat at the end of a trestle, so she was squashed be-

tween a young girl from one of the villages and her host, and
the air was heady with the scent of sweat and grape juice and
the rich tomato and basil sauce.

He shaved cheese over her pasta, his arm brushing hers
as he held it over her plate, and the soft chafe of hair against
her skin made her nerve-endings dance.

'So, is it a good harvest?' she asked, and he grinned.

'Very good. Maybe the best I can remember. It'll be a vintage year for our Brunello.'

'Brunello? I thought that was only from Montalcino?'

'It is. Part of the estate is in the Montalcino territory. It's
very strictly regulated, but it's a very important part of our
revenue.'

'I'm sure.' She was. During the course of her training
and apprenticeships she'd learned a lot about wines, and she
knew that Brunellos were always expensive, some of them
extremely so. Expensive, and exclusive. Definitely niche market.

Her father would be interested. He'd like Massimo, she
realised. They had a lot in common, in so many ways, for all
the gulf between them.

Deep in thought, she ate the hearty meal, swiped the last
off the sauce from her plate with a chunk of bread and licked
her lips, glancing up to see him watching her with a smile on
his face.

'What?'

'You. You really appreciate food.'

'I do. Carlotta's a good cook. That was delicious.'

'Are you making notes?'

She laughed. 'Only mental ones.'

He glanced over her head, and a smile touched his face.
'My parents are back. They're looking forward to meeting
you.'

Really? Like this, covered in tomato sauce and reeking of

chopped onions? She probably had an orange tide-line round her mouth, and her hair was dragged back into an elastic band, and—

'Mamma, *Pàpa*, this is Lydia.'

She scrambled to her feet, wincing as her sore ankle took her weight, and looked up into the eyes of an elegant, beautiful, immaculately groomed woman with clear, searching eyes.

'Lydia. How nice to meet you. Welcome to our home. I'm Elisa Valtieri, and this is my husband, Vittorio.'

'Hello. It's lovely to meet you, too.' Even if she did look a fright.

She shook their hands, Elisa's warm and gentle, Vittorio's rougher, his fingers strong and hard, a hand that wasn't afraid of work. He was an older version of his son, and his eyes were kind. He reminded her of her father.

'My son tells me you've had an accident?' Elisa said, her eyes concerned.

'Yes, I was really stupid, and he's been unbelievably kind.'

'And so, I think, have you. Carlotta is singing your praises.'

'Oh.' She felt herself colour, and laughed a little awkwardly. 'I didn't have anything else to do.'

'Except rest,' Massimo said drily, but his smile was gentle and warmed her right down to her toes.

And then she glanced back and found his mother looking at her, curiosity and interest in those lively brown eyes, and she excused herself, mumbling some comment about them having a lot to catch up on, and hobbled quickly back to Carlotta to see if there was anything she could do to help.

Anything, other than stand there while his mother eyed her speculatively, her eyes asking questions Lydia had no intention of answering.

If she even knew the answers…

CHAPTER FIVE

'You ran away.'

She was sitting outside her room on a bench with her foot up, flicking through a magazine she'd found, and she looked up guiltily into his thoughtful eyes.

'I had to help Carlotta.'

'And it was easier than dealing with my mother,' he said softly, a fleeting smile in his eyes. 'I'm sorry, she can be a little…'

'A little…?'

He grinned slightly crookedly. 'She doesn't like me being on my own. Every time I speak to a woman under fifty, her radar picks it up. She's been interrogating me for the last three hours.'

Lydia laughed, and she put the magazine down, swung her foot to the ground and patted the bench. 'Want to hide here for a while?'

His mouth twitched. 'How did you guess? Give me a moment.'

He vanished, then reappeared with a bottle of wine and two glasses. 'Prosecco?'

'Lovely. Thanks.' She took a glass from him, sniffing the bubbles and wrinkling her nose as she sipped. 'Mmm, that's really nice. So, how was the baby?'

'Beautiful, perfect, amazing, the best baby in the world—

oh, apart from all their other grandchildren. This is the sixth, and Luca and Isabelle are about to make it seven. Their second is due any time now.'

'Wow. Lots of babies.'

'Yes, and she loves it. Nothing makes her happier. Luca and Isabelle and my brother Gio are coming over tomorrow for dinner with some neighbours, by the way. I'd like you to join us, if you can tolerate it.'

She stared at him. 'Really? I'm only here by default, and I feel such a fraud. I really ought to go home.'

'How's your head now?'

She pulled a face. 'Better. I'm still getting the odd headache, but nothing to worry about. It's my ankle and the other bruises and scrapes that are sorest. I think I hit every step.'

He frowned. 'I'm sorry. I didn't really think about the things I can't see.'

Well, that was a lie. He thought about them all the time, but there was no way he was confessing that to Lydia. 'So— will you join us?'

She bit her lip, worrying it for a moment with her teeth, which made him want to kiss her just to stop her hurting that soft, full mouth that had been taunting him for days. *Dio*, the whole damn woman had been taunting him for days—

'Can I think about it?'

A kiss? No. No! Not a kiss!

'Of course,' he said, finally managing to unravel his tongue long enough to speak. 'Of course you may. It won't be anything impressive, Carlotta's got enough to do as it is, but my mother wanted to see Isabelle and Luca before the baby comes, and Gio's coming, and so my mother's invited Anita and her parents, and so it gets bigger—you know how it is.'

She laughed softly. 'I can imagine. Who's Anita?'

'The daughter of our neighbours. She and Gio had a thing a

while back, and my mother keeps trying to get them together again. Can't see it working, really, but she likes to try.'

'And how do they feel?'

He laughed abruptly. 'I wouldn't dare ask Gio. He has a fairly bitter and twisted attitude to love. Comes from being a lawyer, I suppose. His first line of defence is always a pre-nuptial agreement.'

She raised an eyebrow. 'Trust issues, then. I can understand that. I have a few of my own after Russell.'

'I'm sure. People like that can take away something precious, a sort of innocence, a naivety, and once it's gone you can never get it back. Although I have no idea what happened to Gio. He won't talk about it.'

'What about Anita? What's she like?'

His low chuckle made her smile. 'Anita's a wedding planner. What do you think?'

'I think she might like to plan her own?'

'Indeed. But Gio can't see what's under his nose, even if Mamma keeps putting her there.' He tipped his head on one side. 'It could be an interesting evening. And if you're there, it might take the heat off Gio, so he'll probably be so busy being grateful he'll forget to quiz me about you, so it could be better all round!'

She started to laugh at that, and he joined in with another chuckle and topped up her glass.

'Here's to families and their politics and complications,' he said drily, and touched his glass to hers.

'Amen to that,' she said, remembering guiltily that she'd meant to phone Jen again. 'I heard from Claire, by the way—she's back home safely, and she said Jo's ecstatic about winning.'

'How's your sister about it?'

She pulled a face. 'I'm not sure. She was putting on a brave face, but I think she's gutted. I know none of us expected me to win but, you know, it would have been so nice.'

He nodded. 'I'm sorry.'

'Don't be. You've done more than enough.' She drained her glass and handed it to him. 'I'm going to turn in. I need to rest my leg properly, and tomorrow I need to think about arranging a flight back home.'

'For tomorrow?' He sounded startled, and she shook her head.

'No. I thought maybe the next day? I probably ought to phone the hospital and get the go-ahead to fly.'

'I can take you there if you want a check-up.'

'You've got so much to do.'

'Nothing that's more important,' he said, and although it wasn't true, she knew that for him there was nothing more important than making sure there wasn't another Angelina.

'I'll see what they say,' she compromised. There was always the bus, surely? She'd ask Carlotta in the morning.

She got to her feet, and he stood up and took her hand, tucking it in the crook of his arm and helping her to the French doors. Quite unnecessarily, since she'd been hobbling around without help since the second day, really, but it was still nice to feel the strength of his arm beneath her hand, the muscles warm and hard beneath the fine fabric of his shirt.

Silk and linen, she thought, sampling the texture with her fingertips, savouring it.

He hesitated at the door, and then just when she thought he was going to walk away, he lowered his head and touched his lips to hers, sending rivers of ice and fire dancing over her skin.

It was a slow kiss, lingering, thoughtful, their mouths the only point of contact, but then the velvet stroke of his tongue against her lips made her gasp softly and part them for him, and everything changed.

He gave a muffled groan and deepened the kiss, searching the secret recesses of her mouth, his tongue finding hers and dancing with it, retreating, tangling, coaxing until she thought her legs would collapse.

Then he eased away, breaking the contact so slowly so that for a tiny second their lips still clung.

'*Buonanotte*, Lydia,' he murmured unevenly, his breath warm against her mouth, and then straightening slowly, he took a step back and turned briskly away, gathering up the glasses and the bottle as he went without a backwards glance.

She watched him go, then closed the curtains and undressed, leaving the doors open. The night was warm still, the light breeze welcome, and she lay there in the darkness, her fingertips tracing her lips, and thought about his kiss…

He must have been mad to kiss her!

Crazy. Insane. If he hadn't walked away, he would have taken her right there, standing on the terrace in full view of anyone who walked past.

He headed for the stairs, but then hesitated. He wouldn't sleep—but what else could he do? His office was next to her room, and he didn't trust himself that close to her. The pool, his first choice of distraction for the sheer physical exertion it offered, was too close to her room, and she slept with her doors open. She'd hear him, come and investigate, and…

So not the pool, then.

Letting out a long, weary sigh, he headed slowly up the stairs to his room, and sat on the bed, staring at the photograph of Angelina on his bedside table.

He'd loved her—really, deeply and enduringly loved her. But she was gone, and now, as he looked at her face, another face seemed superimposed on it, a face with laughing eyes and a soft, full bottom lip that he could still taste.

He groaned and fell back against the pillows, staring up

at the ceiling. The day after tomorrow, she'd be gone, he told himself, and then had to deal with the strange and unsettling sense of loss he felt at the thought that he was about to lose her.

She didn't sleep well.

Her dreams had been vivid and unsettling, and as soon as she heard signs of life, she got up, showered and put on her rinsed-out underwear, and then sat down on the edge of the bed and sighed thoughtfully as she studied her clothes.

She couldn't join them for dinner—not if their neighbours were coming. She'd seen Elisa, seen the expensive and elegant clothes she'd worn for travelling back home from her daughter's house, and the only things she had with her were the jeans and top she'd been wearing now for two days, including all the cooking she'd done yesterday.

No way could she wear them to dinner, even if she'd earn Gio's undying gratitude and give Elisa something else to think about! She put the clothes on, simply because she had absolutely no choice apart from the wedding dress Carlotta had stuffed in a bag for her and which she yet had to burn, and went outside and round the corner to the kitchen.

Carlotta was there, already making headway on the lunch preparations, and the children were sitting at the table eating breakfast. For a slightly crazy moment, she wondered if they could tell what she'd been dreaming about, if the fact that she'd kissed their father was written all over her face.

She said good morning to them, in her best Italian learned yesterday from Francesca, asked them how they were and then went over to Carlotta. *'Buongiorno*, Carlotta,' she said softly, and Carlotta blushed and smiled at her and patted her cheek.

'Buongiorno, signorina,' she said. 'Did you have good sleep?'

'Very good,' she said, trying not to think of the dreams and blushing slightly anyway. 'What can I do to help you?'

'No, no, you sit. I can do it.'

'You know I can't do that,' she chided softly. She stuck a mug under the coffee machine, pressed the button and waited, then added milk and went back to Carlotta, sipping the hot, fragrant brew gratefully. 'Oh, that's lovely. Right. What shall I do first?'

Carlotta gave in. 'We need to cut the meat, and the bread, and—'

'Just like yesterday?'

'*Si.*'

'So I'll do that, and you can make preparations for tonight. I know you have dinner to cook for the family as well as for the workers.'

Her brow creased, looking troubled, and Lydia could tell she was worried. Exhausted, more like. 'Look, let me do this, and maybe I can give you a hand with that, too?' she offered, but that was a step too far. Carlotta straightened her gnarled old spine and plodded to the fridge.

'I do it,' she said firmly, and so Lydia gave in and concentrated on preparing lunch for sixty people in the shortest possible time, so she could move on to cooking the pasta sauce for the evening shift with Maria. At least that way Carlotta would be free to concentrate on dinner.

Massimo found her in the kitchen at six, in the throes of draining gnocci for the workers, and she nearly dropped the pan. Crazy. Ridiculous, but the sight of him made her heart pound and she felt like a gangly teenager, awkward and confused because of the kiss.

'Are you in here again?' he asked, taking the other side of the huge pan and helping her tip it into the enormous strainer.

'Looks like me,' she said with a forced grin, but he just

frowned and avoided her eyes, as if he, too, was feeling awkward and uncomfortable about the kiss.

'Did you speak to the hospital?' he asked, and she realised he would be glad to get rid of her. She'd been nothing but trouble for him, and she was unsettling the carefully constructed and safe status quo he'd created around them all.

'Yes. I'm fine to travel,' she said, although it wasn't quite true. They'd said they needed to examine her, and when she'd said she was too busy, they'd fussed a bit but what could they do? So she'd booked a flight. 'I've got a seat on a plane at three tomorrow afternoon from Pisa,' she told him, and he frowned again.

'Really? You didn't have to go so soon,' he said, confusing her even more.

'It's not soon. It'll be five days—that's what they said, and I've been under your feet long enough.'

And any longer, she realised, and things were going to happen between them. There was such a pull every time she was with him, and that kiss last night—

She thrust the big pot at him. 'Here, carry the *gnocci* outside for me. I'll bring the sauce.'

He followed her, set the food down for the workers and stood at her side, dishing up.

'So can I persuade you to join us for dinner?' he asked, but she shook her head.

'I've got nothing to wear,' she said, feeling safe because he couldn't argue with that, but she was wrong.

'You're about the same size as Serena. I'm sure she wouldn't mind if you borrowed something from her wardrobe. She always leaves something here. Carlotta will show you.'

'Carlotta's trying to prepare a meal for ten people this evening, Massimo. She doesn't have time to worry about clothes for me.'

'Then I'll take you,' he said, and the moment the serving was finishing, he hustled her back into the house before she could argue.

He was right. She and Serena were about the same size, something she already knew because she'd borrowed her costume to swim in, and she found a pair of black trousers that were the right length with her flat black pumps, and a pretty top that wasn't in the first flush of youth but was nice enough.

She didn't want to take anything too special, but she didn't think Serena would mind if she borrowed that one, and it was good enough, surely, for an interloper?

She went back to the kitchen, still in her jeans and T-shirt, and found Carlotta sitting at the table with her head on her arms, and Roberto beside her wringing his hands.

'Carlotta?'

'She is tired, *signorina*,' he explained worriedly. 'Signora Valtieri has many people for dinner, and my Carlotta…'

'I'll do it,' she said quickly, sitting down and taking Carlotta's hands in hers. 'Carlotta, tell me what you were going to cook them, and I'll do it.'

'But Massimo said…'

'Never mind what he said. I can cook and be there at the same time. Don't worry about me. We can make it easy. Just tell me what you're cooking, and Roberto can help me find things. We'll manage, and nobody need ever know.'

Her eyes filled with tears, and Lydia pulled a tissue out of a box and shoved it in her hand. 'Come on, stop that, it's all right. We've got cooking to do.'

Well, it wasn't her greatest meal ever, she thought as she sat with the others and Roberto waited on them, but it certainly didn't let Carlotta down, and from the compliments going back to the kitchen via Roberto, she knew Carlotta would be feeling much less worried.

As for her, in her borrowed top and trousers, she felt underdressed and overawed—not so much by the company as by the amazing dining room itself. Like her room and the kitchen, it opened to the terrace, but in the centre, with two pairs of double doors flung wide so they could hear the tweeting and twittering of the swallows swooping past the windows.

But it was the walls which stunned her. Murals again, like the ones in the cloistered walkway around the courtyard, but this time all over the ornate vaulted ceiling as well.

'Beautiful, isn't it?' Gio said quietly. 'I never get tired of looking at this ceiling. And it's a good way to avoid my mother's attention.'

She nearly laughed at that. He was funny—very funny, very quick, very witty, very dry. A typical lawyer, she thought, used to brandishing his tongue in court like a rapier, slashing through the opposition. He would be formidable, she realised, and she didn't envy the woman who was so clearly still in love with him.

Anita was lovely, though. Strikingly beautiful, but warm and funny and kind, and Lydia wondered if she realised just how often Gio glanced at her when she'd looked away.

Elisa did, she was sure of it.

And then she met Massimo's eyes, and realised he was studying her thoughtfully.

'Excuse me, I have to go and do something in the kitchen,' she murmured. 'Carlotta very kindly let me experiment with the dessert, and I need to put the finishing touches to it.'

She bolted, running along the corridor and arriving in the kitchen just as Carlotta had put out the bowls.

'Roberto say you tell them I cook everything!' she said, wringing her hands and hugging her.

Lydia hugged her back. 'You did, really. I just helped you. You told me exactly what to do.'

'You *know* what to do. You such good *cuoca*—good cook. Look at this! So easy—so beautiful. *Bellisima!*'

She spread her hands wide, and Lydia looked. Five to a tray, there were ten individual gleaming white bowls, each containing glorious red and black frozen berries fogged with icy dew, and in the pan on the stove Roberto was gently heating the white chocolate sauce. Sickly sweet, immensely sticky and a perfect complement to the sharp berries, it was her favourite no-frills emergency pud, and she took the pan from Roberto, poured a swirl around the edge of each plate and then they grabbed a tray each and went back to the dining room.

'I hope you like it,' she said brightly. 'If not, please don't blame Carlotta, I made her let me try it!'

Elisa frowned slightly, but Massimo just gave her a level look, and as she set the plate down in front of him, he murmured, 'Liar,' softly, so only she could hear.

She flashed him a smile and went back to her place, between Gio and Anita's father, and opposite Isabelle. 'So, tell me, what's it like living in Tuscany full-time?' she asked Isabelle, although she could see that she was blissfully contented and the answer was going to be biased.

'Wonderful,' Isabelle said, leaning her head against Luca's shoulder and smiling up at him. 'The family couldn't have been kinder.'

'That's not true. I tried to warn you off,' Gio said, and Luca laughed.

'You try and warn everybody off,' he said frankly, 'but luckily for me she didn't listen to you. Lydia, this dessert is amazing. Try it, *cara.*'

He held a spoonful up to Isabelle's lips, and Lydia felt a lump rise in her throat. Their love was so open and uncomplicated and genuine, so unlike the relationship she'd had with Russell. Isabelle and Luca were like Jen and Andy, unashamedly devoted to each other, and she wondered with a little ache what it must feel like to be the centre of someone's world, to be so clearly and deeply loved. *That* would be amazing.

She glanced across the table, and found Massimo watching her, his eyes thoughtful. He lifted his spoon to her in salute.

'Amazing, indeed.'

She blinked. He was talking about the dessert, not about love. Nothing to do with love, or with her, or him, or the two of them, or that kiss last night.

'Thank you,' she said, a little breathlessly, and turned her attention to the sickly, sticky white chocolate sauce. If she glued her tongue up enough with that, maybe it would keep it out of trouble.

'So how much of that was you, and how much was Carlotta?'

It was midnight, and everyone else had left or gone to bed. They were alone in the kitchen, putting away the last of the serving dishes that she'd just washed by hand, and Massimo was making her a cup of camomile tea.

'Honestly? I gave her a hand.'

'And the dessert?'

'Massimo, she was tired. She had all the ingredients for my quick fix, so I just improvised.'

'Hmm,' he said, but he left it at that, to her relief. She sensed he didn't believe her, but he had no proof, and Carlotta had been so distraught.

'Right, we're done here,' he said briskly. 'Let's go outside and sit and drink this.'

They went on her bench, outside her room, and sat in companionable silence drinking their tea. At least, it started out companionable, and then last night's kiss intruded, and she felt the tension creep in, making the air seem to fizz with the sparks that passed between them.

'You don't have to go tomorrow, you know,' he said, breaking the silence after it had stretched out into the hereafter.

'I do. I've bought a ticket.'

'I'll buy you another one. Wait a few more days.'

'Why? So I can finish falling for you? That's not a good idea, Massimo.'

He laughed softly, and she thought it was the saddest sound she'd ever heard. 'No. Probably not. I have nothing to offer you, Lydia. I wish I did.'

'I don't want anything.'

'That's not quite true. We both want something. It's just not wise.'

'Is it ever?'

'I don't know. Not for us, I don't think. We've both been hurt enough by the things that have happened, and I don't know about you but I'm not ready to try again. I have so many demands on me, so many calls on my time, so much *duty*.'

She put her cup down very carefully and turned to face him. 'We could just take tonight as it comes,' she said quietly, her heart in her mouth. 'No strings, just one night. No duty, no demands. Just a little time out from reality, for both of us.'

The silence was broken only by the beating of her heart, the roaring in her ears so loud that she could scarcely hear herself think. For an age he sat motionless, then he lifted a hand and touched her cheek.

'Why, *cara*? Why tonight?'

'Because it's our last chance?'

'Why me?'

'I don't know. It just seems right.'

Again he hesitated, then he took her hand and pressed it to his lips. 'Give me ten minutes. I need to check the children.'

She nodded, her mouth dry, and he brushed her lips with his and left her there, her fingers resting on the damp, tingling skin as if to hold the kiss in place.

Ten minutes, she thought. Ten minutes, and my life will change forever.

He didn't come back.

She gave up after half an hour, and went to bed alone, humiliated and disappointed. How stupid, to proposition a man so far out of her league. He was probably still laughing at her in his room.

He wasn't. There was a soft knock on the door, and he walked in off the terrace. 'Lydia? I'm sorry I was so long. Are you still awake?'

She propped herself up on one elbow, trying to read his face, but his back was to the moonlight. 'Yes. What happened? I'd given up on you.'

'Antonino woke. He had a nightmare. He's all right now, but I didn't want to leave him till he was settled.'

He sat on the edge of the bed, his eyes shadowed in the darkness, and she reached for the bedside light. He caught her hand. 'No. Leave it off. Let's just have the moonlight.'

He opened the curtains wide, but closed the doors—for privacy? She didn't know, but she was grateful that he had because she felt suddenly vulnerable as he stripped off his clothes and turned back the covers, lying down beside her and taking her into his arms.

The shock of that first contact took their breath away, and he rested his head against hers and gave a shuddering sigh. 'Oh, Lydia, *cara*, you feel so good,' he murmured, and then after that she couldn't understand anything he said, because his voice deepened, the words slurred and incoherent. He was speaking Italian, she realised at last, his breath trembling over her body with every groaning sigh as his hands cupped and moulded her.

She arched against him, her body aching for him, a need like no need she'd ever felt swamping her common sense and turning her to jelly. She ran her hands over him, learning his contours, the feel of his skin like hot silk over the taut, corded muscles beneath, and then she tasted him, her tongue testing the salt of his skin, breathing in the warm musk and the lingering trace of cologne.

He seemed to be everywhere, his hands and mouth caressing every part of her, their legs tangling as his mouth returned to hers and he kissed her as if he'd die without her.

'Please,' she whispered, her voice shaking with need, and he paused, fumbling for something on the bedside table.

Taking care of her, she realised, something she'd utterly forgotten, but not him. He'd remembered, and made sure that she was safe with him.

No strings. No repercussions.

Then he reached for her, taking her into his arms, and as he moved over her she stopped thinking altogether and just *felt*.

He woke to the touch of her hand on his chest, lying lightly over his heart.

She was asleep, her head lying on his shoulder, her body silvered by the moonlight. He shifted carefully, and she sighed and let him go, so he could lever himself up and look down at her.

There was a dark stain over one hipbone. He hadn't noticed it last night, but now he did. A bruise, from her fall. And there was another, on her shoulder, and one on her thigh, high up on the side. He kissed them all, tracing the outline with his lips, kissing them better like the bruises of a child.

It worked, his brother Luca told him, because the caress

released endorphins, feel-good hormones, and so you really could kiss someone better, but only surely if they were awake—

'Massimo?'

He turned his head and met her eyes. 'You're hurt all over.'

'I'm all right now.'

She smiled, reaching up and cradling his jaw in her hand, and he turned his face into her hand and kissed her palm, his tongue stroking softly over the sensitive skin.

'What time is it?'

He glanced at his watch and sighed. 'Two. Just after.'

Two. Her flight was in thirteen hours.

She swallowed hard and drew his face down to hers. 'Make love to me again,' she whispered.

How could he refuse? How could he walk away from her, even though it was madness?

Time out, she'd said, from reality. He needed that so badly, and he wasn't strong enough to resist.

Thirteen hours, he thought, and as he took her in his arms again, his heart squeezed in his chest.

Saying goodbye to the children and Carlotta and Roberto was hard. Saying goodbye to Massimo was agony.

He'd parked at the airport, in the short stay carpark, and they'd had lunch in the café, sitting outside under the trailing pergola. She positioned herself in the sun, but it didn't seem to be able to warm her, because she was cold inside, her heart aching.

'Thank you for everything you've done for me,' she said, trying hard not to cry, but it was difficult and she felt a tear escape and slither down her cheek.

'Oh, *bella*.' He sighed, and reaching out his hand, he brushed it gently away. 'No tears. Please, no tears.'

'Happy tears,' she lied. 'I've had a wonderful time.'

He nodded, but his eyes didn't look happy, and she was sure hers didn't. She tried to smile.

'Give my love to the children, and thank Francesca again for my Italian lessons.'

He smiled, his mouth turning down at the corners ruefully. 'They'll miss you. They had fun with you.'

'They'll forget me,' she reassured him. 'Children move on very quickly.'

But maybe not if they'd been hurt in the past, he thought, and wondered if this had been so safe after all, so without consequences, without repercussions.

Maybe not.

He left her at the departures gate, standing there with his arms round her while she hugged him tight. She let him go, looked up, her eyes sparkling with tears.

'Take care,' she said, and he nodded.

'You, too. Safe journey.'

And without waiting to see her go through the gate, he walked away, emotions raging through him.

Madness. He'd thought he could handle it, but—

He'd got her address from her, so he could send her a crate of wine and oil.

That was all, he told himself. Nothing more. He certainly wasn't going to contact her, or see her again—

He sucked in a breath, surprised by the sharp stab of loss. Ships in the night, he told himself more firmly. They'd had a good time but now it was over, she was gone and he could get on with his life.

How hard could it be?

CHAPTER SIX

'WHY don't you just go and see her?'

Massimo looked up from the baby in his arms and forced himself to meet his brother's eyes.

'I don't know what you mean.'

'Of course you do. You've been like a grizzly bear for the last two weeks, and even your own children are avoiding you.'

He frowned. Were they? He hadn't noticed, he realised in horror, and winced at the wave of guilt. But...

'It's not a crime to want her, you know,' Luca said softly.

'It's not that simple.'

'Of course not. Love never is.'

His head jerked up again. 'Who's talking about love?' he snapped, and Luca just raised an eyebrow silently.

'I'm *not* in love with her.'

'If you say so.'

He opened his mouth to say, 'I do say so,' and shut it smartly. 'I've just been busy,' he said instead, making excuses. 'Carlotta's been ill, and I've been trying to juggle looking after the children in the evenings and getting them ready for school without neglecting all the work of the grape harvest.'

'But that's over now—at least the critical bit. And you're wrong, you know, Carlotta isn't ill, she's old and tired and she needs to stop working before she becomes ill.'

Massimo laughed out loud at that, startling his new nephew

and making him cry. He shushed him automatically, soothing the fractious baby, and then looked up at Luca again. 'I'll let you tell her that.'

'I have done. She won't listen because she thinks she's indispensable and she doesn't want to let anybody down. And she's going to kill herself unless someone does something to stop her.'

And then it dawned on him. Just the germ of an idea, but if it worked...

He got to his feet, wanting to get started, now that the thought had germinated. He didn't know why he hadn't thought of it before, except he'd been deliberately putting it—her—out of his mind.

'I think I'll take a few days off,' he said casually. 'I could do with a break. I'll take the car and leave the children here. Mamma can look after them. It'll keep her off Gio's back for a while and they can play with little Annamaria while Isabelle rests.'

Luca took the baby from him and smiled knowingly.

'Give her my love.'

He frowned. 'Who? I don't know what you're talking about. This is a business trip. I have some trade samples to deliver.'

His brother laughed and shut the door behind him.

'Do you know anyone with a posh left-hand-drive Mercedes with a foreign number plate?'

Lydia's head jerked up. She did—but he wouldn't be here. There was no way he'd be here, and certainly not without warning—

'Tall, dark-haired, uber-sexy. Wow, in fact. Very, *very* wow!'

Her mouth dried, her heart thundering. No. Surely not—not when she was just getting over him—

'Let me see.'

She leant over Jen's shoulder and peeped through the door-way, and her heart, already racing, somersaulted in her chest. Over him? Not a chance. She'd been fooling herself for over two weeks, convincing herself she didn't care about him, it had just been a holiday romance, and one sight of him and all of it had come slamming back. She backed away, one hand on her heart, trying to stop it vaulting out through her ribs, the other over her mouth holding back the chaotic emotions that were threatening to erupt.

'It's him, isn't it? Your farmer guy. You never said he was that hot!'

No, she hadn't. She'd said very little about him because she'd been desperately trying to forget him and avoid the inevitable interrogation if she so much as hinted at a rela-tionship. But—farmer? Try millionaire. More than that. Try serious landowner, old-money, from one of Italy's most well-known and respected families. Not a huge brand name, but big enough, she'd discovered when she'd checked on the in-ternet in a moment of weakness and aching, pathetic need.

And try lover—just for one night, but the most magical, memorable and relived night of her life.

She looked down at herself and gave a tiny, desperate scream. She was cleaning tack—old, tatty tack from an even older, tattier pony who'd finally met his maker, and they were going to sell it. Not for much, but the saddle was good enough to raise a couple of hundred pounds towards Jen's wedding.

'He's looking around.'

So was she—for a way to escape from the tack room and back to the house without being seen, so she could clean up and at least look slightly less disreputable, but there was no other way out, and...

'He's seen me. He's coming over. Hi, there. Can I help?'

'I hope so. I'm looking for Lydia Fletcher.'

His voice made her heart thud even harder, and she backed into the shadows, clutching the filthy, soapy rag in a desperate fist.

'She's here,' Jen said, dumping her in it and flashing him her most charming smile. 'I'm her sister, Jen—and she's rather grubby, so she probably doesn't want you to see her like that, so why don't I take you over to the house and make you a cup of tea—'

'I don't mind if she's grubby. She's seen me looking worse, I'm sure.'

And before Jen could usher him away, he stepped past her into the tack room, sucking all the air out of it in that simple movement.

'Ciao, bella,' he said softly, a smile lurking in his eyes, and she felt all her resolve melt away to nothing.

'Ciao,' she echoed, and then toughened up. 'I didn't expect to see you again.'

She peered past him at Jen, hovering in the doorway. 'Why don't you go and put the kettle on?' she said firmly.

With a tiny, knowing smile, Jen took a step away, then mouthed, 'Be nice!'

Nice? She had no intention of being anything *but* nice, but she also had absolutely no intention of being anything more accommodating. He'd been so clear about not wanting a relationship, and she'd thought she could handle their night together, thought she could walk away. Well, she wasn't letting him in again, because she'd never get over it a second time.

'You could have warned me you were coming,' she said when Jen had gone, her crutches scrunching in the gravel. 'And don't tell me you lost my phone number, because it was on the same piece of paper as my address, which you clearly have or you wouldn't be here.'

'I haven't lost it. I didn't want to give you the chance to avoid me.'

'You thought I would?'

'I thought you might want to, and I didn't want you to run away without hearing me out.' He looked around, studying the dusty room with the saddle racks screwed to the old beams, the saddle horse in the middle of the room with Bruno's saddle on it, half-cleaned, the hook dangling from the ceiling with his bridle and stirrup leathers hanging from it, still covered in mould and dust and old grease.

Just like her, really, smeared in soapy filth and not in any way dressed to impress.

'Evocative smell.' He fingered the saddle flap, rubbing his fingertips together and sniffing them. 'It takes me back. I had a friend with horses when I was at boarding school over here, and I stayed with him sometimes. We used to have to clean the tack after we rode.'

He smiled, as if it was a good memory, and then he lifted his hand and touched a finger to her cheek. 'You've got dirt on your face.'

'I'm sure. And don't you dare spit on a tissue and rub it off.'

He chuckled, and shifting an old riding hat, he sat down on a rickety chair and crossed one foot over the other knee, his hands resting casually on his ankle as if he really didn't care how dirty the chair was.

'Well, don't let me stop you. You need to finish what you're doing—at least the saddle.'

She did. It was half-done, and she couldn't leave it like that or it would mark. She scrunched the rag in her fingers and nodded. 'If you don't mind.'

'Of course not. I didn't know you had a horse,' he added, after a slight pause.

'We don't—not any more.'

His eyes narrowed, and he leant forwards. 'Lydia?' he said

softly, and she sniffed and turned away, reaching for the saddle soap.

'He died,' she said flatly. 'We don't need the tack, so I'm going to sell it. It's a crime to let it rot out here when someone could be using it.'

'I'm sorry.'

'Don't be. He was ancient.'

'But you loved him.'

'Of course. That's what life's all about, isn't it? Loving things and losing them?' She put the rag down and turned back to him, her heart aching so badly that she was ready to howl her eyes out. 'Massimo, why are you here?'

'I promised you some olive oil and wine and balsamic vinegar.'

She blinked, and stared at him, dumbfounded. 'You drove all this way to deliver me *olive oil*? That's ridiculous. Why are you really here, in the middle of harvest? And what was that about not wanting me to run away before hearing you out?'

He smiled slowly—reluctantly. 'OK. I have a proposition for you. Finish the saddle, and I'll tell you.'

'Tell me now.'

'I'll tell you while you finish,' he compromised, so she picked up the rag again and reapplied it to the saddle, putting on rather more saddle soap than was necessary. He watched her, watched the fierce way she rubbed the leather, the pucker in her brow as she waited for him to speak.

'So?' she prompted, her patience running out.

'So—I think Carlotta is unwell. Luca says not, and he's the doctor. He says she's just old, and tired, and needs to stop before she kills herself.'

'I agree. She's been too old for years, probably, but I don't suppose she'll listen if you tell her that.'

'No. She won't. And the trouble is she won't allow anyone else in her kitchen.' He paused for a heartbeat. 'Anyone except *you*.'

She dropped the rag and spun round. 'Me!' she squeaked, and then swallowed hard. 'I—I don't understand! What have I got to do with anything?'

'We need someone to feed everybody for the harvest. After that, we'll need someone as a housekeeper. Carlotta won't give that up until she's dead, but we can get her local help, and draft in caterers for events like big dinner parties and so on. But for the harvest, we need someone she trusts who can cater for sixty people twice a day without getting in a flap—someone who knows what they're doing, who understands what's required and who's available.'

'I'm not available,' she said instantly, and he felt a sharp stab of disappointment.

'You have another job?'

She shook her head. 'No, not really, but I'm helping with the farm, and doing the odd bit of outside catering, a bit of relief work in the pub. Nothing much, but I'm trying to get my career back on track and I can't do that if I'm gallivanting about all over Tuscany, however much I want to help you out. I have to earn a living—'

'You haven't heard my proposition yet.'

She stared at him, trying to work out what he was getting at. What he was offering. She wasn't sure she wanted to know, because she had a feeling it would involve a lot of heartache, but—

'What proposition? I thought that was your proposition?'

'You come back with me, work for the harvest and I'll give your sister her wedding.'

She stared at him, confused. She couldn't have heard him right. 'I don't understand,' she said, finding her voice at last.

'It's not hard. The hotel was offering the ceremony, a reception for—what, fifty people?—a room for their wedding night, accommodation for the night before for the bridal party, a food and drink package—anything I've missed?'

She shook her head. 'Flowers, maybe?'

'OK. Well, we can offer all that. There's a chapel where they can marry, if they're Catholic, or they could have a blessing there and marry in the Town Hall, or whatever they wanted, and we'll give them a marquee with tables and chairs and a dance floor, and food and wine for the guests. And flowers. And if they don't want to stay in the guest wing of the villa, there's a lodge in the woods they can have the use of for their honeymoon.'

Her jaw dropped, and her eyes suddenly filled with tears. 'That's ridiculously generous! Why would you do this for them?'

'Because if I hadn't distracted you on the steps, you wouldn't have fallen, and your sister would have had her wedding.'

'No! Massimo, it wasn't your fault! I don't need your guilt as well as my own! This is not your problem.'

'Nevertheless, you would have won if you hadn't fallen, and yet when I took you back to my home that night you just waded in and helped Carlotta, even though you were hurt and disappointed. You didn't need to do that, but you saw she was struggling, and you put your own worries and injuries out of your mind and just quietly got on with it, even though you were much more sore than you let on.'

'What makes you say that?'

He smiled tenderly. 'I saw the bruises, cara. All over your body.'

She blushed furiously, stooping to pick the rag up off the floor, but it was covered in dust and she put it down again. The saddle was already soaped to death.

'And that dinner party—I know quite well that all of those dishes were yours. Carlotta doesn't cook like that, and yet you left an old woman her pride, and for that alone, I would give you this wedding for your sister.'

The tears spilled down her cheeks, and she scrubbed them away with the backs of her hands. Not a good idea, she realised instantly, when they were covered in soapy filth, but he was there in front of her, a tissue in his hand, wiping the tears away and the smears of dirt with them.

'Silly girl, there's no need to cry,' he tutted softly, and she pushed his hand away.

'Well, of course I'm crying, you idiot!' she sniffed, swallowing the tears. 'You're being ridiculously generous. But I can't possibly accept.'

'Why not? We need you—and that is real and genuine. I knew you'd refuse the wedding if I just offered it, but we really need help with the harvest, and it's the only way Carlotta will allow us to help her. If we do nothing, she'll work herself to death, but she'll be devastated if we bring in a total stranger to help out.'

'I was a total stranger,' she reminded him.

He gave that tender smile again, the one that had unravelled her before. 'Yes—but now you're a friend, and I'm asking you, as a friend, to help her.'

She swallowed. 'And in return you'll give Jen this amazing wedding?'

'*Si.*'

'And what about us?'

Something troubled flickered in his eyes for a second until the shutters came down. 'What about us?'

'We agreed it was just for one night.'

'Yes, we did. No strings. A little time out from reality.'

'And it stays that way?'

He inclined his head. '*Si.* It stays that way. It has to.'

Did it? She felt—what? Regret? Relief? A curious mixture of both, probably, although if she was honest she might have been hoping...

'Can I think about it?'

'Not for long. I have to return first thing tomorrow morning. I would like to take you with me.'

She nodded. 'Right. Um. I need to finish this—what are you *doing*?'

He'd taken off his jacket, slung it over the back of the chair and was rolling up his sleeves. 'Helping,' he said, and taking a clean rag from the pile, he buffed the saddle to a lovely, soft sheen. 'There. What else?'

It took them half an hour to clean the rest of Bruno's tack, and then she led him back to the house and showed him where he could wash his hands in the scullery sink.

'Don't mention any of this to Jen, not until I've made up my mind,' she warned softly, and he nodded.

Her sister was in the kitchen, and she pointed her in the direction of the kettle and ran upstairs to shower. Ten minutes later, she was back down in the kitchen with her hair in soggy rats' tails and her face pink and shiny from the steam, but at least she was clean.

He glanced up at her and got to his feet with a smile. 'Better now?'

'Cleaner,' she said wryly. 'Is Jen looking after you?'

Jen was, she could see that. The teapot was on the table, and the packet of biscuits they'd been saving for visitors was largely demolished.

'She's been telling me all about you,' he said, making her panic, but Jen just grinned and helped herself to another biscuit.

'I've invited him to stay the night,' she said airily, dunking it in her tea while Lydia tried not to panic yet again.

'I haven't said yes,' he told her, his eyes laughing as he

registered her reaction. 'There's a pub in the village with a sign saying they do rooms. I thought I might stay there.'

'You can't stay there. The pub's awful!' she said without thinking, and then could have kicked herself, because realistically there was nowhere else for miles.

She heard the door open, and the dogs came running in, tails wagging, straight up to him to check him out, and her mother was hard on their heels.

'Darling? Oh!'

She stopped in the doorway, searched his face as he straightened up from patting the dogs, and started to smile. 'Hello. I'm Maggie Fletcher, Lydia's mother, and I'm guessing from the number plate on your car you must be her Italian knight in shining armour.'

He laughed and held out his hand. 'Massimo Valtieri—but I'm not sure I'm any kind of a knight.'

'Well, you rescued my daughter, so I'm very grateful to you.'

'She hurt herself leaving my plane,' he pointed out, 'so really you should be throwing me out, not thanking me!'

'Well, I'll thank you anyway, for trying to get her there in time to win the competition. I always said it was a crazy idea.'

'Me, too.' He smiled, and Lydia ground her teeth. The last thing she needed was him cosying up to her mother, but it got worse.

'I promised her some produce from the estate, and I thought, as I had a few days when I could get away, I'd deliver it in person. I'll bring it in, if I may?'

'Of course! How very kind of you.'

It wasn't kind. It was an excuse to bribe her into going back there to feed the troops by dangling a carrot in front of her that he knew perfectly well she'd be unable to resist. Two carrots, really, because as well as Jen's wedding, which was giving her the world's biggest guilt trip, there was the problem of the aging and devoted Carlotta, who'd become her friend.

'I'll help you,' she said hastily, following him out to the car so she could get him alone for a moment.

He was one step ahead of her, though, she realised, because as he popped the boot open, he turned to her, his face serious. 'Before you say anything, I'm not going to mention it to your family. This is entirely your decision, and if you decline, I won't say any more about it.'

Well, damn. He wasn't even going to *try* to talk her into it! Which, she thought with a surge of disappointment, could only mean that he really wasn't interested in picking up their relationship, and was going to leave it as it stood, as he'd said, with just that one night between them.

Not that she wanted him to do anything else. She really didn't want to get involved with another man, not after the hatchet job Russell had done on her self-esteem, and not when she was trying to resurrect her devastated career, but...

'Here. This is a case of our olive oils. There are three types, different varietals, and they're quite distinctive. Then this is a case of our wines—including a couple of bottles of vintage Brunello. You really need to save them for an important occasion, they're quite special. There's a nice *vinsanto* dessert wine in there, as well. And this is the *aceto balsamico* I promised you, from my cousin in Modena.'

While she was still standing there open-mouthed, he reached into a cool box and pulled out a leg of lamb and a whole Pecorino cheese.

'Something for your mother's larder,' he said with a smile, and without any warning she burst into tears.

'Hey,' he said softly, and wrapping his arms around her, he drew her up against his chest. He could feel the shudders running through her, and he cradled her against his heart and rocked her, shushing her gently. 'Lydia, please, *cara*, don't cry.'

'I'm not,' she lied, bunching her fists in his shirt and burrowing into his chest, and he chuckled and hugged her.

'I don't think that's quite true,' he murmured. 'Come on, it's just a few things.'

'It's nothing to do with the things,' she choked out. Her fist hit him squarely in the chest. 'I didn't think I'd ever see you again, and I was trying to move on, and then you just come back into my life and drop this bombshell on me about the wedding, and of all the times to choose, when I'm already…'

Realisation dawned, and he stroked her hair, gentling her. 'Oh, *cara*, I'm sorry. When did he die, the pony?'

She sniffed hard and tried to pull away, but he wouldn't let her, he just held her tight, and after a moment she went still, unyielding but resigned. 'Last week,' she said, her voice clogged with tears. 'We found him dead in the field.'

'And you haven't cried,' he said.

She gave up fighting and let her head rest against his chest. 'No. But he was old.'

'We lost our dog last year. She was very, very old, and she'd been getting steadily worse. After she died, I didn't cry for weeks, and then one day it suddenly hit me and I disintegrated. Luca said he thought it was to do with Angelina. Sometimes grief is like that. We can't acknowledge it for the things that really hurt, and then something else comes along, and it's safe then to let go, to let out the hurt that you can't face.'

She lifted her head and looked up at him through her tears.

'But I don't hurt.'

'Don't you? Even after Russell treated you the way he did? For God's sake, Lydia, he was supposed to be your lover, and yet when he'd crippled your sister, his only reaction was anger that you'd left him and his business was suffering! What kind of a man is that? Of course you're hurting.'

She stared at him, hearing her feelings put into words somehow making sense of them all at last. She eased away from him, needing a little space, her emotions settling now.

'You know I can't say no, don't you? To your proposition?'

His mouth quirked slightly and he nodded slowly and let her go. 'Yes. I do know, and I realise it's unfair to ask this of you, but—I need help for Carlotta, and you need the wedding. This way, we both win.'

Or lose, depending on whether or not he could keep his heart intact, seeing her every day, working alongside her, knowing she'd be just there in the room beside his office, taunting him even in her sleep.

She met his eyes, her own troubled. 'I don't want an affair. I can't do it. One night was dangerous enough. I'm not ready, and I don't want to hurt your children.'

He nodded. 'I know. And I agree. If I wanted an affair, it would be with a woman my children would never meet, someone they wouldn't lose their hearts to. But I would like to be your friend, Lydia. I don't know if that could work but I would like to try.'

No. It couldn't work. It was impossible, because she was already more than half in love with him, but—Jen needed her wedding, and she'd already had it snatched away from her once. This was another chance, equally as crazy, equally as dangerous, if not more so.

It was a chance she had to take.

'OK, I'll do it,' she said, without giving herself any further time to think, and his shoulders dropped slightly and he smiled.

'*Grazie, cara. Grazie mille.* And I know you aren't doing it for me, but for your sister and also for Carlotta, and for that, I thank you even more.'

He hugged her—just a gentle, affectionate hug between friends, or so he told himself as she slid her arms round him and hugged him back, but the feel of her in his arms, the soft pressure of her breasts, the smell of her shampoo and the warmth of her body against his all told him he was lying.

He was in this right up to his neck, and if he couldn't hold it together for the next two months—but he had to. There was no choice. Neither of them was ready for this.

He let her go, stepped back and dumped the lamb and the cheese in her arms. 'Let's go back in.'

'Talk to me about your dream wedding,' he said to Jen, after they'd taken all the things in from the car.

Her smile tugged his heartstrings. 'I don't dream about my wedding. The last time I did that, it turned into a nightmare for Lydia, so I'm keeping my feet firmly on the ground from now on, and we're going to do something very simple and quiet from here, and it'll be fine.'

'What if I was to offer you the *palazzo* as a venue?' he suggested, and Jen's jaw dropped.

'What?' she said, and then shook her head. 'I'm sorry, I don't understand.'

'The same deal as the hotel.'

She stared, looking from Lydia to Massimo and back again, and shook her head once more. 'I don't…'

'They need me,' Lydia explained. 'Carlotta's not well, and if I cook for the harvest season, you can have your wedding. I don't have another job yet, and it's good experience and an interesting place to work, so I thought it might be a good idea.'

'I've brought a DVD of my brother's wedding so you can see the setting. It might help you to decide.'

He handed it to her, and she handed it straight back.

'There's a catch,' she said, her voice strained. 'Lydia?'

'No catch. I work, you get the wedding.'

'But—that's so generous!'

'Nonsense. We'd have to pay a caterer to do the job, and it would cost easily as much.'

'But—Lydia, what about you? You were looking for another job, and you were talking about setting up an outside catering business. How can you do that if you're out of the country? No, I can't let you do it!'

'Tough, kid,' she said firmly, squashing her tears again. Heavens, she never cried, and this man was turning her into a fountain! 'I'm not doing it just for you, anyway. This is a job—a real job, believe me. And you know what I'm like. I'd love to know more about Italian food—real, proper country food—and this is my chance, so don't go getting all soppy on me, all right? My catering business will keep. Just say thank you and shut up.'

'Thank you and shut up,' she said meekly, and then burst into tears.

Lydia cooked the leg of lamb for supper and served it with rosemary roast potatoes and a redcurrant *jus*, and carrots and runner beans from the garden, and they all sat round at the battered old kitchen table with the dogs at their feet and opened one of the bottles of Brunello.

'It seems wrong, drinking it in here,' she said apologetically, 'but Andy's doing the accounts on the dining table at the moment and it's swamped.'

'It's not about the room, it's about the flavour. Just try it,' he said, watching her closely.

So she swirled it, sniffed it, rolled it round on her tongue and gave a glorious sigh. 'That is *the* most gorgeous wine I have ever tasted,' she told him, and he inclined his head and smiled.

'Thank you. We're very proud of it, and it's a perfect complement to the lamb. It's beautifully cooked. Well done.'

'Thank you. Thank you for trusting me with it.' She smiled back, suddenly ridiculously happy, and then the men started to talk about farming, and Jen quizzed her about the *palazzo*, because she'd hardly said anything about it since she'd come home.

'It sounds amazing,' Jen said, wide-eyed. 'We'll have to look at that video.'

'You will. It's great. The frescoes are incredible, and the view is to die for, especially at night, when all you can see is the twinkling lights in the distance. It's just gorgeous, and really peaceful. I know it'll sound ridiculous, but it reminded me of home, in a way.'

'I don't think that's ridiculous,' Massimo said, cutting in with a smile. 'It's a home, that's all, just in a beautiful setting, and that's what you have here—a warm and loving family home in a peaceful setting. I'm flattered that you felt like that about mine.'

The conversation drifted on, with him telling them more about the farm, about the harvest and the soil and the weather patterns, and she could have sat there for hours just listening to his voice, but she had so much to do before they left in the morning, not least gathering together her clothes, so she left them all talking and went up to her room.

Bearing in mind she'd be flying back after the harvest was over, she tried to be sensible about the amount she took, but she'd need winter clothes as well as lighter garments, and walking boots so she could explore the countryside, and something respectable in case he sprang another dinner on her—

'You look lost.'

She looked up from her suitcase and sighed. 'I don't know what to take.'

'Your passport?'

'Got that,' she said, waggling it at him with a smile. 'It's clothes. I want enough, but not too much. I don't know what the weather will be like.'

'It can get cold. Bring warm things for later, but don't worry. You can buy anything you don't have.'

'I'm trying to stick to a sensible baggage allowance for when I come back.'

'Don't bother. I'll pay the excess. Just bring what you need.'

'What time are we leaving?'

'Seven.'

'Seven?' she squeaked, and he laughed.

'That's a concession. I would have left at five, or maybe six.'

'I'll be ready whenever you tell me. Have you been shown to your room?'

'*Si*. And the bathroom is opposite?'

'Yes. I'm sorry it doesn't have an *en suite* bathroom—'

'Lydia, stop apologising for your home,' he said gently. 'I'm perfectly capable of crossing a corridor. I'll see you at six for breakfast, OK?'

'OK,' she said, and for a heartbeat she wondered if he'd kiss her goodnight.

He didn't, and she spent a good half-hour trying to convince herself she was glad.

They set off in the morning shortly before seven, leaving Jen and Andy still slightly stunned and busy planning their wedding, and she settled back in the soft leather seat and wondered if she'd completely lost her mind.

'Which way are we going?' she asked as they headed down to Kent.

'The quickest route—northern France, across the Alps in Switzerland, past Lake Como and onto the A1 to Siena. We'll stay somewhere on the way. I don't want to drive through the Alps when I'm tired, the mountain roads can be a little tricky.'

Her heart thudded. They were staying somewhere overnight?

Well, of course they were, he couldn't possibly drive whatever distance it was from Suffolk to Tuscany in one day, but somehow she hadn't factored an overnight stop into her calculations, and the journey, which until now had seemed simple and straightforward, suddenly seemed fraught with the danger of derailing their best intentions.

CHAPTER SEVEN

'LYDIA?'

She stirred, opened her eyes and blinked.

He'd pulled up in what looked like a motorway service area, and it was dark beyond the floodlit car park. She yawned hugely and wrapped her hand around the back of her neck, rolling her head to straighten out the kinks.

'Oh, ow. What time is it? I feel as if I've been asleep for hours!'

He gave her a wry, weary smile. 'You have. It's after nine, and I need to stop for the night before I join you and we have an accident.'

'Where are we?'

'A few miles into Switzerland? We're getting into the mountains and this place has rooms. It's a bit like factory farming, but it's clean and the beds are decent. I'd like to stop here if they have any vacancies.'

'And if they don't?'

He shrugged. 'We go on.'

But he must be exhausted. They'd only stopped twice, the last time at two for a late lunch. What if they only have one room? she thought, and her heart started to pound. How strong was her resolve? How strong was his?

She never found out. They had plenty of space, so he booked two rooms and carried her suitcase for her and put it down at the door. 'We should eat fairly soon, but I thought you might want to freshen up. Ten minutes?'

'Ten minutes is fine,' she said, and let herself into her lonely, barren motel room. It was clean and functional as he'd promised, just another generic hotel room like all the rest, and she wished that for once in her life she had the courage to go after the thing she really wanted.

Assuming the thing—the person—really wanted her, of course, and he'd made it clear he didn't.

She stared at herself in the bathroom mirror. What was she *thinking* about? She didn't want him! She wasn't ready for another relationship. Not really, not if she was being sensible. She wanted to get her career back on track, to refocus her life and remember where she was going and what she was doing. She certainly didn't need to get her heart broken by a sad and lonely workaholic ten years her senior, with three motherless children and a massively demanding business empire devouring all his time.

Even if he was the most fascinating and attractive man she'd ever met in her life, and one of the kindest and most thoughtful. He was hurting, too, still grieving for his wife, and in no way ready to commit to another relationship, no matter how deeply she might fall in love with him. He wouldn't hurt her intentionally, but letting herself get close to him— that was a recipe for disaster if nothing else was.

'Lydia?'

There was a knock at the bedroom door, and she turned off the bathroom light and opened it. Massimo was standing there in the corridor, in a fresh shirt and trousers, his hair still damp from the shower. He looked incredible.

'Are you ready for dinner?'

She conjured up a smile. 'Give me ten seconds.'

She picked up her bag, gave her lips a quick swipe of translucent colour as a concession to vanity and dragged a comb through her hair. And then, just out of defiance, she added a spritz of scent.

She might be travel weary, and she might not be about to get involved with him, but she still had her pride.

The dinner was adequate. Nothing more, nothing less.

He was tired, she was tired—and yet still they lingered, talking for an hour over their coffee. She asked about Isabelle and Luca's baby, and how the children were, and he asked her about Jen's progress and if she'd be off the crutches by the time of the wedding, whenever it would be.

They talked about his time at boarding school, and she told him about her own schooling, in a village just four miles from where she lived.

And then finally they both fell silent, and he looked at his watch in disbelief.

'It's late and tomorrow will be a hard drive,' he said. 'We should go to bed.'

The word *bed* reverberated in the air between them, and then she placed her napkin on the table and stood up a little abruptly. 'You're right. I'm sorry, you should have told me to shut up.'

He should. He should have cut it short and gone to bed, instead of sitting up with her and hanging on her every word. He paid the bill and escorted her back to her room, leaving a clear gap between them as he paused at her door.

Not because he wanted to, but because he didn't, and if he got any closer, he didn't trust himself to end it there.

'Buonanotte, bella,' he said softly. 'I'll wake you at five thirty.'

She nodded, and without looking back at him, she opened the door of her room, went in and closed it behind her. He stared at it for a second, gave a quiet, resigned laugh and let himself into his own room.

This was what he'd wanted, wasn't it? For her to keep her distance, to enable him to do the same?

So why did he suddenly feel so lonely?

It was like coming home.

This time, when she saw the fortress-like building standing proudly on the hilltop, she felt excitement and not trepidation, and when the children came tumbling down the steps to greet them, there was no look of horror, but shrieks of delight and hugs all round.

Antonino just wanted his father, but Francesca hugged her, and Lavinia hung on her arm and grinned wildly. 'Lydia!' she said, again and again, and then Carlotta appeared at the top of the steps and welcomed her—literally—with open arms.

'*Signorina*! You come back! Oh!'

She found herself engulfed in a warm and emotional hug, and when Carlotta let her go, her eyes were brimming. She blotted them, laughing at herself, and then taking Lydia by the hand, she led her through the courtyard to her old room.

This time there were flowers on the chest of drawers, and Roberto brought in her luggage and put it down and hugged her, too.

'*Grazie mille, signorina,*' he said, his voice choked. 'Thank you for coming back to help us.'

'Oh, Roberto, it's my pleasure. There's so much Carlotta can teach me, and I'm really looking forward to learning.'

'I teach,' she said, patting her hand. 'I teach you everything!'

She doubted it. Carlotta's knowledge of traditional dishes was a rich broth of inheritance, and it would take more than a few experiments to capture it, but it would still be fascinating.

They left her to settle in, and a moment later there was a tap at the French doors.

'The children and I are going for a swim. Want to join us?'

She was so tempted. It was still warm here, much warmer than in England, although she knew the temperature would drop once it was dark. The water in the pool would be warm and inviting, though, and it would be fun playing with the children, but she felt a shiver of danger, and not just from him.

'I don't think so. I'm a bit tired. I might rest for a little while.'

He nodded, smiled briefly and walked away, and she closed the door and shut the curtains, just to make the point.

The children were delightful, but they weren't why she was here, and neither was he. And the more often she reminded herself of that, the better, because she was in serious danger of forgetting.

She didn't have time to think about it.

The harvest season was in full swing, and from first thing the following morning, she was busy. Carlotta still tried to do too much, but she just smiled and told her she was allowed to give orders and that was all, and after the first two days she seemed happy to do that.

She even started taking a siesta in the middle of the day, which gave Lydia time to make a lot of the preparations for the evening without prodding Carlotta's conscience.

And every evening, she dished up the food to the workers and joined them for their meal.

They seemed pleased to see her, and there was a bit of flirting and whistling and nudging, but she could deal with that. And then Massimo appeared at her side, and she heard a ripple of laughter and someone said something she'd heard a few times before when he was about. She'd also heard him say it to Francesca on occasions.

'What does *bella ragazza* mean?' she asked in a quiet moment as they were finishing their food, and he gave a slightly embarrassed laugh.

'Beautiful girl.'

She studied his face closely, unconvinced. 'Are you sure? Because they only say it when you're near me.'

He pulled a face. 'OK. It's usually used for a girlfriend.'

'They think I'm your *girlfriend*?' she squeaked, and he cleared his throat and pushed the food around his plate.

'Ignore them. They're just teasing us.'

Were they? Or could they see the pull between them? Because ignore it as hard as she liked, it wasn't going away, and it was getting stronger with every day that passed.

A few days later, while she was taking a breather out on the terrace before lunch, Isabelle appeared. She was pushing a pram, and she had a little girl in tow.

'Lydia, hi. I was hoping to find you. Mind if we join you?'

She stood up, pleased to see her again, and hugged her. 'Of course I don't mind. Congratulations! May I see?'

'Sure.'

She peered into the pram, and sighed. 'Oh, he's gorgeous. So, so gorgeous! All that dark hair!'

'Oh, yes, he's his daddy's boy. Sometimes I wonder where my genes went in all of this.' She laughed, and Lydia smiled and reached out to touch the sleeping baby's outstretched hand.

It clenched reflexively, closing on her fingertip, and she gave a soft sigh and swallowed hard.

He looked just like the picture of Antonino with his mother in the photo frame in the kitchen. Strong genes, indeed, she thought, and felt a sudden, shocking pang low down in her abdomen, a need so strong it was almost visceral.

She eased her finger away and straightened up. 'Can I get you a drink? And what about your little girl?'

'Annamaria, do you want a drink, darling?'

'Juice!'

'Please.'

'P'ees.'

'Good girl. I'd love a coffee, if you've got time? And anything juice-related with a big slosh of water would be great. We've got a feeder cup.'

They went into the kitchen, and she found some biscuits and took them out into the sun again with the drinks, and sat on the terrace under the pergola, shaded by the jasmine.

'Are you completely better now, after your fall?' Isabelle asked her, and she laughed and brushed it aside.

'I'm fine. My ankle was the worst thing, really, but it's much better now. It still twinges if I'm careless, but it's OK. How about you? Heavens, you've had a baby, that's much worse!'

Isabelle laughed and shook her head. 'No. It was harder than when Annamaria was born, but really very straightforward, and you know Luca's an obstetrician?'

'Yes, I think so. I believe Massimo mentioned it. I know he's a doctor, he met us at the hospital when I had the fall and translated everything for me. So did he deliver him? What's he called, by the way?'

'Maximus—Max for short, after his uncle. Maximus and Massimo both mean the greatest, and my little Max was huge, so he really earned it. And yes, Luca did help deliver him, but at home with a midwife. Not like last time. He nearly missed Annamaria's birth, and I was at home on my own, so this time he kept a very close eye on me!'

'I'll bet. Wow. You're very brave having them at home.'

'No, I just have confidence in the process. I'm a midwife.'

'Is that how you met?'

She laughed. 'No. We met in Florence, in a café. We ended

up together by a fluke, really.' She tipped her head on one side. 'So what's the story with you and Massimo?'

She felt herself colour and pretended to rearrange the biscuits. 'Oh, nothing, really. There is no story. He gave me a lift, I had an accident, he rescued me, and now I'm doing Carlotta's job so she doesn't kill herself.'

Isabelle didn't look convinced, but there was no way Lydia was going into details about her ridiculous crush or their one-night stand! But Luca's wife wasn't so easily put off. She let the subject drop for a moment, but only long enough to lift the now-crying baby from the pram and cradle him in her arms as she fed him.

Spellbound, Lydia watched the baby's tiny rosebud mouth fasten on his mother's nipple, saw the look of utter contentment on Isabelle's face, and felt a well of longing fill her chest.

'He's a good man, you know. A really decent guy. He'd be worth the emotional investment, but only if you're serious. I'd hate to see him hurt.'

'He won't get hurt. We're not getting involved,' she said firmly. 'Yes, there's something there, but neither of us want it.'

Isabelle's eyes were searching, and Lydia felt as if she could see straight through her lies.

Lies? Were they?

Oh, yes. Because she did want it, even though it was crazy, even though she'd get horribly badly hurt. And she'd thought Russell had hurt her? He didn't even come close to what Massimo could do if she let him into her heart.

'He's not interested in an emotional investment,' she said, just in case there was any misunderstanding, but Isabelle just raised a brow slightly and smiled.

'No. He doesn't *think* he is, but actually he's ready to love again. He just hasn't realised it.'

'No, he isn't. We've talked about it—'

'Men don't talk. Not really. It's like pulling teeth. He's telling you what he thinks he ought to feel, not what he feels.'

She glanced up, at the same time as Lydia heard crunching on the gravel.

'Talk of the devil, here they are,' Isabelle said, smiling at her husband and his brother, and not wanting to get involved any deeper in this conversation, Lydia excused herself and went back to the kitchen.

Seconds later Massimo was in there behind her. 'I've come to tell you we've almost finished. The last of the vines are being stripped now and everyone's having the afternoon off.'

'So no lunch?'

He raised an eyebrow. 'I don't think you'll get away with that, but no evening meal, certainly. Not today. And tomorrow we're moving on to the chestnut woods. So tonight I'm taking you out for dinner, to thank you.'

'You don't need to do that. You're paying for my sister's wedding. That's thanks enough.'

He brushed it aside with a flick of his hand, and smiled. 'Humour me. I want to take you out to dinner. There's a place we eat from time to time—fantastic food, Toscana on a fork. The chef is Carlotta's great-nephew. I think you'll find it interesting. Our table's booked for eight.'

'What if I want an early night?'

'Do you?'

She gave in and smiled. 'No, not really. It sounds amazing. What's the dress code?'

'Clean. Nothing more. It's where the locals eat.'

'Your mother's a local,' she said drily, and he chuckled.

'My mother always dresses for the occasion. I'll wear jeans and a jacket, no tie. Does that help?'

She smiled. 'It does. Thank you. Help yourselves to coffee, I need to get on with lunch.'

* * *

Jeans and a jacket, no tie.

So what did that mean for her? Jeans? Best jeans with beaded embroidery on the back pockets and a pretty top?

Black trousers and a slinky top with a cardi over it?

A dress? How about a long skirt?

Clean. That was his first stipulation, so she decided to go with what was comfortable. And by eight, it would be cool, and they'd be coming back at about eleven, so definitely cooler.

Or maybe...

She'd just put the finishing touches to her makeup, not too much, just enough to make her feel she'd made the effort, when there was a tap on her door.

'Lydia? I'm ready to go when you are.'

She opened the door and scanned him. Jeans—good jeans, expensive jeans, with expensive Italian leather loafers and a handmade shirt, the leather jacket flung casually over his shoulder hanging from one finger.

He looked good enough to eat, and way up the scale of clean, so she was glad she'd changed her mind at the last minute and gone for her one decent dress. It wasn't expensive, but it hung like a dream to the asymmetric hem and made her feel amazing, and from the way he was scanning her, he wasn't disappointed.

'Will I do?' she asked, twirling slowly, and he said nothing for a second and then gave a soft huff of laughter.

'Oh, yes. I think so.'

His eyes were still trailing over her, lingering on the soft swell of her breasts, the curve of her hip, the hint of a thigh—

He pulled himself together and jerked his eyes back up to meet hers. 'You look lovely,' he said, trying not to embarrass himself or her. 'Are you ready to go?'

'I just need a wrap for later.' She picked up a pretty pashmina the same colour as her eyes, and her bag, and shut the door behind her. 'Right, then. Let's go get Toscana on a fork!'

It was a simple little building on one side of a square in the nearby town.

From the outside it looked utterly unpretentious, and it was no different inside. Scrubbed tables, plain wooden chairs, simple décor. But the smell was amazing, and the place was packed.

'Massimo, *ciao!*'

He shook hands with a couple on the way in, introduced her as a friend from England, and ushered her past them to the table he'd reserved by the window.

'Is it always this busy?'

His lips twitched in a smile. 'No. Sometimes it's full.'

She looked around and laughed. 'And these are all locals?'

'Mostly. Some will be tourists, people who've bothered to ask where they should eat.'

She looked around again. 'Is there a menu?'

'No. He writes it on a board—it's up there. Tonight it's a casserole of wild boar with plums in a red wine reduction.'

'And that's it?'

'No. He cooks a few things every night—you can choose from the board, but the first thing up is always his dish of the day, and it's always worth having.'

She nodded. 'Sounds great.'

He ordered a half-carafe of house wine to go with it— again, the wine was always chosen to go with the meal and so was the one to go for, he explained—and then they settled back to wait.

'So—are you pleased with the harvest?' she asked to fill the silence, and he nodded.

'*Si.* The grapes have been exceptional this year, it should be an excellent vintage. We need that. Last year was not so good, but the olives were better, so we made up for it.'

'And how are the olives this year?'

'Good so far. It depends on the weather. We need a long, mild autumn to let them swell and ripen before the first frosts. We need to harvest early enough to get the sharp tang from the olives, but not so early that it's bitter, or so late that it's sweet and just like any other olive oil.'

She smiled. 'That's farming for you. Juggling the weather all the time.'

'*Si.* It can be a disaster or a triumph, and you never know. We're big enough to weather it, so we're fortunate.'

'We're not. We had a dreadful year about three years ago, and I thought we'd go under, but then the next year we had bumper crops. It's living on a knife edge that's so hard.'

'Always. Always the knife edge.'

Her eyes met his, and the smile that was hovering there was driven out by an intensity that stole her breath away. 'You look beautiful tonight, *cara*,' he said softly, reaching out to touch her hand where it lay on the table top beside her glass.

She withdrew it, met his eyes again warily. 'I thought we weren't going to do this?'

'We're not doing anything. It was a simple compliment. I would say the same to my sister.'

'No, you wouldn't. Not like that.' She picked up her glass of water and drained the last inch, her mouth suddenly dry. 'At least, I hope not.'

His mouth flicked up briefly at the corners. 'Perhaps not quite like that.'

He leant back as the waiter appeared, setting down bread and olive oil and balsamic vinegar, and she tore off a piece of bread and dunked it, then frowned thoughtfully as the taste exploded on her tongue. 'Is this yours?'

He smiled. 'Yes. And the *balsamico* is from my cousin.'

'And the wild boar?'

'I have no idea. If it's from our estate, I don't know about it. The hunting season doesn't start until November.'

She smiled, and the tension eased a little, but it was still there, simmering under the surface, the compliment hovering at the fringes of her consciousness the whole evening. It didn't spoil the meal. Rather, it heightened the sensations of taste and smell and texture, as if somehow his words had brought her alive again and set her free.

'This casserole is amazing,' she said after the first mouthful. 'I want the recipe.'

He laughed at that. 'He won't give it to you. Women offer to sleep with him, but he never reveals his secrets.'

'Does he sleep with them anyway?'

He chuckled again. 'I doubt it. His wife would skin him alive.'

'Good for her. She needs to keep him. He's a treasure. And I've never been that desperate for a recipe.'

'I'm glad to hear it.' He was. He didn't even want to think about her sleeping with anybody else, even if she wasn't sleeping with him. And she wasn't.

She really, really wasn't. He wasn't going to do that again, it was emotional suicide. It had taken him over a week before he could sleep without waking aroused and frustrated in a tangle of sheets, aching for her.

He returned his attention to the casserole, mopping up the last of the sauce with a piece of bread until finally the plate was clean and he had no choice but to sit back and look up and meet her eyes.

'That was amazing,' she said. 'Thank you so much.'

'Dessert?'

She laughed a little weakly. 'I couldn't fit it in. Coffee, though—I could manage coffee.'

He ordered coffee, and they lingered over it, almost as if

they daren't leave the safety of the little *trattoria* for fear of what they might do. But then they ran out of words, out of stalling tactics, and their eyes met and held.

'Shall we go?'

She nodded, getting to her feet even though she knew what was going to happen, knew how dangerous it was to her to leave with him and go back to her room—because they would end up there, she was sure of it, just as they had before, and all their good intentions would fall at the first hurdle...

CHAPTER EIGHT

THEY didn't speak on the way back to the *palazzo*.

She sat beside him, her heart in her mouth, the air between them so thick with tension she could scarcely breathe. They didn't touch. All the way to her bedroom door, there was a space between them, as if they realised that the slightest contact would be all it took to send them up in flames.

Even when he shut the door behind them, they still hesitated, their eyes locked. And then he closed his eyes and murmured something in Italian. It could have been a prayer, or a curse, or just a 'what the hell am I doing?'

She could understand that. She was doing it herself, but she was beyond altering the course of events. She'd been beyond it, she realised, the moment he'd walked into the tack room at home and smiled at her.

He opened his eyes again, and there was resignation in them, and a longing that made her want to weep. He lifted his hand and touched her cheek, just lightly, but it was enough.

She turned her face into his hand, pressing her lips to his palm, and with a ragged groan he reeled her in, his mouth finding hers in a kiss that should have felt savage but was oddly tender for all its desperation.

His jacket hit the floor, then his shirt, stripped off over his head, and he spun her round, searching for the zip on her dress and following its progress with his lips, scorching a trail of fire down her spine. It fell away, and he unclipped her bra and turned her back to face him, easing it away and sighing softly as he lowered his head to her breasts.

She felt the rasp of his stubble against the sensitised skin, the heat of his mouth closing over one nipple, then the cold as he blew lightly against the dampened flesh.

She clung to his shoulders, her legs buckling, and he scooped her up and dropped her in the middle of the bed, stripping off the rest of his clothes before coming down beside her, skin to skin, heart to heart.

There was no foreplay. She would have died if he'd made her wait another second for him. Incoherent with need, she reached for him, and he was there, his eyes locking with hers as he claimed her with one long, slow thrust.

His head fell against hers, his eyes fluttering closed, a deep groan echoing in her ear. Her hands were on him, sliding down his back, feeling the powerful muscles bunching with restraint, the taut buttocks, the solid thighs bracing him as he thrust into her, his restraint gone now, the desperation overwhelming them, driving them both over the edge into frenzy.

She heard a muffled groan, felt his lips against her throat, his skin like hot, wet silk under her hands as his hard body shuddered against hers. For a long time he didn't move, but then, his chest heaving, he lifted his head to stare down into her eyes.

'Oh, *cara*,' he murmured roughly, and then gathering her against his heart he rolled to his side and collapsed against the pillows, and they lay there, limbs entangled, her head on his chest, and waited for the shockwaves to die away.

'I thought we weren't going to do that.'

He glanced down at her, and his eyes were filled with regret and despair. 'It looks like we were both wrong.'

His eyes closed, as if he couldn't bear to look at her, and easing away from her embrace he rolled away and sat up on the edge of the bed, elbows braced on his knees, dropping his head into his hands for a moment. Then he raked his fingers through his hair and stood up, pulling on his clothes.

'I have to check the children,' he said gruffly.

'We need to talk.'

'Yes, but not now. Please, *cara*. Not now.'

He couldn't talk to her now. He had to get out of there, before he did something stupid like make love to her again.

Make love? Who was he kidding? He'd slaked himself on her, with no finesse, no delicacy, no patience. And he'd promised her—promised himself, but promised *her*—that this wouldn't happen again.

Shaking his head in disgust, he pushed his feet into his shoes, slung his jacket over his shoulder and then steeled himself to look at her.

She was still lying there, curled on her side on top of the tangled bedding, her eyes wide with hurt and confusion.

'Massimo?'

'Later. Tomorrow, perhaps. I have to go. If Antonino wakes—'

She nodded, her eyes closing softly as she bit her lip. Holding back the tears?

He was despicable. All he ever did was make this woman cry.

He let himself out without another word, and went through to his part of the house, up the stairs to the children to check that they were all in bed and sleeping peacefully.

They were. Antonino had kicked off the covers, and he eased them back over his son and dropped a kiss lightly on his forehead. He mumbled in his sleep and rolled over, and he went out, leaving the door open, and checked the girls.

They were both asleep, Francesca's door closed, Lavinia's open and her nightlight on.

He closed the landing door that led to his parents' quarters, as he always did when he was in the house, and then he made his way back down to the kitchen and poured himself a glass of wine.

Why? Why on earth had he been so stupid? After all his lectures to himself, how could he have been so foolish, so weak, so self-centred?

He'd have to talk to her, he realised, but he had no idea what he would say. He'd promised her—promised! And yet again he'd failed.

He propped his elbows on the table and rested his face in his hands. Of all the idiotic things—

'Massimo?'

Her voice stroked him like a lover's touch, and he lifted his head and met her eyes.

'What are you doing here?' he asked, his voice rough.

'I came to get a drink,' she said uncertainly.

He shrugged. 'Go ahead, get it.'

She stayed there, her eyes searching his face. 'Oh, Massimo, don't beat yourself up. We were deluded if we thought this wouldn't happen. It was so obvious it was going to and I can't believe we didn't realise. What we need to work out is what happens now.'

He gave a short, despairing laugh and pushed back his chair. 'Nothing, but I have no idea how to achieve that. All I know that whenever I'm with you, I want you, and I can't just have what I want. I'm not a tiny child, I understand the word no, I just can't seem to use it to myself. Wine?'

She shook her head. 'Tea. I'll make it.'

He watched her as she took out a mug from the cupboard, put a teabag in it, poured on boiling water, her movements automatic. She was wearing a silky, figure-hugging dressing gown belted round her waist, and he'd bet his life she had those tiny little pyjamas on underneath.

'Just tell me this,' she said at last, turning to face him. 'Is there any reason why we can't have an affair? Just—discreetly?'

'Here? In this house? Are you crazy? I have children here and they have enough to contend with without waking in the night from a bad dream and finding I'm not here because I'm doing something stupid and irresponsible for my own gratification.'

She sat down opposite him, cradling the tea in her hands and ignoring his stream of self-hatred. 'So what do you normally do?'

Normally? *Normally?* he thought.

'Normally, I don't have affairs,' he said flatly. 'I suppose, if I did, it would be elsewhere.' He shrugged. 'Arranged meetings—afternoon liaisons when the children are at school, lunchtimes, coffee.'

'And does it work?'

He laughed a little desperately. 'I have no idea. I've never tried.'

She stared at him in astonishment. 'What? In five years, you've never had an affair?'

'Not what you could call an affair, no. I've had the odd liaison, but nothing you could in any way call a relationship.' He sighed shortly, swirled his wine, put it down again.

'You have to see it from my point of view. I have obligations, responsibilities. I would have to be very, very circumspect in any relationship with a woman.'

'Because of the children.'

'Mostly, but because of all sorts of things. Because of my duties and responsibilities, the position I hold within the family, the business—any woman I was to become involved with would have to meet a very stringent set of criteria.'

'Not money-grabbing, not lying, not cheating, not looking for a meal ticket or an easy family or status in the community.'

'Exactly. And it's more trouble than it's worth. I don't need it. I can live without the hassle. But it's more than that. If I make a mistake, many people could suffer. And besides, I don't have the time to invest in a relationship, not to do it justice. And nor do you, not if you're going to reinvent yourself and relaunch your career.'

He'd be worth the emotional investment, but only if you're serious.

Oh, Isabelle, you're so right, she thought. But was she serious? Serious enough? Could she afford to dedicate the emotional energy needed, to a man who was so clearly focused on his family life and business that women weren't considered necessary?

If she felt she stood the slightest chance, then yes, she realised, she could be very, very serious indeed about this man. But he wasn't ever going to be serious about her. Not serious enough to let her into all parts of his life, and there was no way she'd pass his stringent criteria test.

No job, for a start. No independent wealth—no wealth of any sort. And besides, he was right, she needed to get her career back on track. It had been going so well...

'So what happens now? We can't have an affair here, because of the children, and yet we can't seem to stick to that. So what do we do? Because doing nothing doesn't seem to work for us, Massimo. We need a plan.'

He gave a wry laugh and met her eyes again, his deadly serious. 'I have no idea, *cara*. I just know I can't be around you.'

'So we avoid each other?'

'We're both busy. It shouldn't be so hard.'

They were busy, he was right, but she felt a pang of loss even though she knew it made sense.

'OK. I'll keep out of your way if you keep out of mine.'

He inclined his head, then looked up as she got to her feet.

'You haven't finished your tea.'

'I'll take it with me,' she said, and left him sitting there wondering why he felt as if he'd just lost the most precious thing in the world, and yet didn't quite know what it was.

Nice theory, she thought later, when her emotions had returned to a more even keel. It just didn't have a hope of working in practice.

How could they possibly avoid each other in such an intimate setting?

Answer—they couldn't. He was in and out of the kitchen all the time with the children, and she was in and out of his workspace twice a day at least with food for the team of workers.

They were gathering chestnuts this week, in the *castagneti*, the chestnut woods on the higher slopes at the southern end of the estate. Carlotta told her all about it, showed her the book of chestnut recipes she'd gathered, many handed down from her mother or her grandmother, and she wanted to experiment.

So she asked Massimo one lunchtime if she could have some for cooking.

'Sure,' he said briskly. 'Help yourself. Someone will give you a basket.'

She shouldn't have been hurt. It was silly. She knew why he was doing it, why he hadn't met her eyes for more than a fleeting second, because in that fleeting second she'd seen something in his eyes that she recognised.

A curious mixture of pain and longing, held firmly in check.

She knew all about that.

She gathered her own chestnuts, joining the workforce and taking good-natured and teasing advice, most of which she didn't understand, because her Italian lessons with Francesca hadn't got that far yet—and in any case, she was very conscious of not getting too close to his children, for fear of them forming an attachment to her that would only hurt them when she went home again, so she hadn't encouraged it.

But she understood the gist. Sign language was pretty universal, and she learned how to split open the cases without hurting her fingers and remove the chestnuts—huge chestnuts, *marrone*, apparently—and that night after she'd given them all their evening meal, she went into the kitchen to experiment.

And he was there, sitting at the kitchen table with a laptop and a glass of wine.

'Oh,' she said, and stood there stupidly for a moment.

'Problem?'

'I was going to try cooking some of the chestnuts.'

His eyes met hers, and he shut the laptop and stood up. 'It's fine. I'll get out of your way.'

She looked guarded, he thought, her sunny smile and open friendliness wiped away by his lack of control and this overwhelming need that stalked him hour by hour. It saddened him. Greatly.

'You don't have to go.'

'I do,' he said wearily. 'I can't be around you, *cara*. It's too difficult. I thought I could do this, but I can't. The only way is to keep my distance.'

'But you can't. We're falling over each other all the time.'

'There's no choice.'

There was, she thought. They could just go with the flow, make sure they were discreet, keep it under control, but he didn't seem to think they could do that successfully, and he'd left the kitchen anyway.

She sat down at the table, in the same chair, feeling the warmth from his body lingering in the wood, and opened Carlotta's recipe book. Pointless. It was in Italian, and she didn't understand a word.

Frustration getting the better of her, she dropped her head into her hands and growled softly.

'Lydia, don't.'

'Don't what? I thought you'd gone,' she said, lifting her head.

'I had.' He sat down opposite her and took her hand in his, the contact curiously disturbing and yet soothing all at once.

'This is driving me crazy,' he admitted softly.

'Me, too. There must be another way. We can't avoid each other successfully, so why don't we just work alongside each other and take what comes? We know it's not long-term, we know you're not looking for commitment and I'm not ready to risk it again, and I have to go back and try and relaunch my career in some direction.'

He let go of her hand and sat back. 'Any ideas for that?' he said, not running away again as she'd expected, but staying to have a sensible conversation, and she let herself relax and began to talk, outlining her plans, such as they were.

'I've been thinking more and more about outside catering, using produce from my parents' farm. There are plenty of people with money living in the nearby villages, lots of second homes with people coming up for the weekend and bringing friends. I'm sure there would be openings, I just have to be there to find them.'

'It could be a bit seasonal.'

'Probably. Easter, summer and winter—well, Christmas and New Year, mostly. There's always lots of demand around

Christmas, and I need to be back by then. Will the olive harvest be over?'

'Almost certainly. If it's not, we can manage if you need to return.' He stood up and put the kettle on. 'I was thinking we should invite your sister and her fiancé over to meet Anita so she can start the ball rolling.'

'Anita?'

'*Si*. They'll need a wedding planner.'

'They can't afford a wedding planner!'

'It's part of the package. I'm not planning it, I simply don't have the time or the expertise, and Jen can't plan a wedding in a strange place from a distance of two thousand kilometres, so we need Anita.'

'I could do it. I'm here.'

'But do you have the necessary local contacts? No. And besides, you're already busy.'

'Can I do the catering?'

He smiled tolerantly. 'Really? Wouldn't you rather enjoy your sister's wedding?'

'No. I'd rather cut down the cost of it to you. I feel guilty enough—'

'Don't feel guilty.'

'But I do. I know quite well what cooks get paid, and it doesn't stack up to the cost of a wedding in just three months!'

He smiled again. 'We pay our staff well.'

She snorted rudely, and found a mug of tea put down in front of her.

'Don't argue with me, *cara*,' he said quietly. 'Just ask your sister when she could come over, and arrange the flights and check that Anita is free to see them.'

'Only if you'll let me do the catering.'

He rolled his eyes and laughed softly. 'OK, you can do the catering, but Anita will give you menu options.'

'No. I want to do the menus.'

'Why are you so stubborn?'

'Because it's my job!'

'To be stubborn?'

'To plan menus. And don't be obtuse.'

His mouth twitched and he sat down opposite her again, swirling his wine in the glass. 'I thought you were going to cook chestnuts?'

'I can't read the recipe book. My Italian is extremely limited so it's a non-starter.'

He took it from her, opened it and frowned. 'Ah. Well, some of it is in a local dialect anyway.'

'Can you translate?'

'Of course. But you'd need to know more than just classic Italian to understand it. Which recipe did you want to try?'

She raised an eyebrow. 'Well, how do I know? I don't know what they are.'

'I'll read them to you.'

'You know what? I'll do it in the morning, with Carlotta. She'll be able to tell me which are her favourites.'

'I can tell you that. She feeds them to us regularly. She does an amazing mousse for dessert, and stuffing for roast boar which is incredible. You should get her to teach you those if nothing else. Anyway, tomorrow won't work. There's a fair in the town.'

'Carlotta said there was a day off, but nobody told me why.'

'To celebrate the end of *La Vendemmia*. They hold one every year. Then in a few weeks there's the chestnut fair, and then after *La Raccolta*, the olive harvest, there's another one. It's a sort of harvest festival gone mad. You ought to go tomorrow, it's a good day out.'

'Will you be there?'

He nodded. 'All of us will be there.'

'I thought we were avoiding each other?'

He didn't smile, as she'd expected. Instead he frowned,

his eyes troubled. 'We are. I'll be with my children. Roberto and Carlotta will be going. I'm sure they'll give you a lift.'

And then, as if she'd reminded him of their unsatisfactory arrangement, he stood up. 'I'm going to do some work. I'll see you tomorrow.'

She did see him, but only because she kept falling over him.

Why was it, she thought, that if you lost someone in a crowd of that size you'd never be able to find them again, and yet every time she turned round, he was there?

Sometimes he didn't see her. Equally, probably, there were times when she didn't see him. But there were times when their eyes met, and held. And then he'd turn away.

Well, this time she turned away first, and made her way through the crowd in the opposite direction.

And bumped into Anita.

'Lydia! I was hoping I'd see you. Come, let's find a quiet corner for a coffee and a chat. We have a wedding to plan!'

She looked around at the jostling crowd and laughed. 'A quiet corner?'

'There must be one. Come, I know a café bar on a side street. We'll go there.'

They had to sit outside, but the sunshine was lovely and it was relatively quiet away from the hubbub and festival atmosphere of the colourful event.

'So—this wedding. Massimo tells me your sister's coming over soon to talk about it. Do you know what she wants?'

Lydia shrugged, still uncomfortable about him spending money on Anita's services. 'The hotel was offering a fairly basic package,' she began, and Anita gave a soft laugh.

'I know the hotel. It would have been basic, and they would have talked it up to add in all sorts of things you don't really need.'

'Well, they wouldn't, because she hasn't got any money, which is why I'm working here now.'

Anita raised an eyebrow slightly. 'Is that the only reason?' she asked softly. 'Because I know these Valtieri men. They're notoriously addictive.'

Poor Anita. Lydia could see the ache in her eyes, knew that she could understand. Maybe, for that reason, she let down her guard.

'No. It's not the only reason,' she admitted quietly. 'Maybe, subconsciously, it gave me an excuse to spend time with him, but trust me, it's not going to come to anything.'

'Don't be too sure. He's lonely, and he's a good man. He can be a bit of a recluse—he shuts himself away and works rather than deal with his emotions, but he's not alone in that. It's a family habit, I'm afraid.'

She shook her head. 'I *am* sure nothing will come of it. We've talked about it,' she said, echoing her conversation with Isabelle and wondering if both women could be wrong or if it was just that they were fond of him and wanted him to be happy.

'He needs someone like you,' Anita said, 'someone honest and straightforward who isn't afraid of hard work and understands the pressures and demands of an agricultural lifestyle. He said your family are lovely, and he felt at home there with them. He said they were refreshingly unpretentious.'

She laughed at that. 'We've got nothing to be pretentious about,' she pointed out, but Anita just smiled.

'You have to understand where he's coming from. He has women after him all the time. He's a very, very good catch, and Gio is worried that some money-seeking little tart will get her claws into him.'

'Not a chance. He's much too wary for that, believe me. He has strict criteria. Anyway, I thought we were talking about the wedding?'

Anita smiled wryly and let it go, but Lydia had a feeling that the subject was by no means closed...

'What are you doing?'

A pair of feet appeared in her line of sight, slender feet clad in beautiful, soft leather pumps. She straightened up on her knees and looked up at his mother, standing above her on the beautiful frescoed staircase.

'I'm helping Carlotta.'

'It's not your job to clean. She has a maid for that.'

'But the maid's sick, so I thought I'd help her.'

Elisa frowned. 'I didn't know that. Why didn't Carlotta tell me?'

'Because she doesn't?' she suggested gently. 'She just gets on with it.'

'And so do you,' his mother said softly, coming down to her level. 'Dear girl, you shouldn't be doing this. It's not part of your job.'

'I don't have a job, Signora Valtieri. I have a bargain with your son. I help out, my sister gets her wedding, which is incredibly generous, so if there's some way I can help, I just do it.'

'You do, don't you, without any fuss? You are a quite remarkable girl. It's a shame you have to leave.'

'I don't think he thinks so.'

'My son doesn't know what's good for him.'

'And you do?'

'Yes, I do, and I believe you could be.'

She stared at Elisa, stunned. 'But—I'm just a chef. A nobody.'

'No, you are not a nobody, Lydia, and we're just farmers like your people.'

'No.' She laughed at that and swept an arm around her to underline her point. 'No, you're not just farmers, *signora*. My family are just farmers. You own half of Tuscany and a *pala-zzo*, with incredibly valuable frescoes on the walls painted by Old Masters. There is a monumental difference.'

'I think not—and please stop calling me *signora*. My name, as you well know, is Elisa. Come. Let's go and get some coffee and have a chat.'

She shook her head. 'I can't. I have work to do—lunch to prepare for everyone in a minute. I was just giving the stairs a quick sweep.'

'So stop now, and come, just for a minute. Please? I want to ask you something.'

It was a request, but from his mother it was something on the lines of an invitation to Buckingham Palace. You didn't argue. You just went.

So she went, leaving the ornate and exquisitely painted staircase hall and following her into the smaller kitchen which served their wing of the house.

'How do you take your coffee? Would you like a cappuccino?'

'That would be lovely. Thank you.'

Bone china cups, she thought, and a plate with little Amaretti biscuits. Whatever this was about, it was not going to be a quick anything, she realised.

'So,' Elisa said, setting the tray down at a low table between two beautiful sofas in the formal *salon* overlooking the terrace. 'I have a favour to ask you. My son tells me you're contemplating starting a catering business. I would like to commission you.'

Lydia felt her jaw drop. 'Commission?' she echoed faintly. 'For what?'

'I'm having a meeting of my book group. We get together every month over dinner and discuss a book we've read, and this time it's my turn. I would like you to provide the meal for us. There will be twenty people, and we will need five courses.'

She felt her jaw sag again. 'When?'

'Wednesday next week. The chestnuts should be largely harvested by then, and the olive harvest won't have started yet. So—will you do it?'

'Is there a budget?'

Elisa shrugged. 'Whatever it takes to do the job.'

Was it a test? To see if she was good enough? Or a way to make her feel valued and important enough to be a contender for her son? Or was it simply that she needed a meal provided and Carlotta was too unwell?

It didn't matter. Whatever the reason, she couldn't refuse. She looked into Elisa's eyes.

'Yes. Yes, I'll do it,' she said. 'Just so long as you'll give me a reference.'

Elisa put her cup down with a satisfied smile. 'Of course.'

CHAPTER NINE

THE book club dinner seemed to be going well.

She was using her usual kitchen—the room which histori-cally had always been the main kitchen in the house, although it was now used by Massimo and his children, and for pre-paring the harvest meals.

She needed the space. Twenty people were quite hard to cater for if the menu was extravagant, and she'd drafted in help in the form of Maria, the girl who'd been helping her with the meals all along.

The *antipasti* to start had been a selection of tiny canapés, all bite-sized but labour intensive. Massimo had dropped in and tasted them, and she'd had to send him away before he'd eaten them all.

Then she'd served penne pasta with crayfish in a sauce of cream with a touch of fresh chilli, followed by a delicate lemon sorbet to cleanse the palette.

For the main, she'd sourced some wild boar with Carlotta's help, and she'd casseroled it with fruit and lots of wine and garlic, reducing it to a rich, dark consistency. Massimo, yet again, had insisted on tasting it, dipping his finger in the sauce and sucking it, and said it was at least as good as Carlotta's great-nephew's. Carlotta agreed, and asked her for the recipe, which amazed her.

She'd served it on a chestnut, apple and sweet potato mash,

with fresh green beans and fanned Chantenay carrots. And now it was time for the dessert, individual portions of perfectly set and delicate pannacotta under a spun sugar cage, with fresh autumn raspberries dusted with vanilla sugar and drizzled with dark chocolate. If that didn't impress them, nothing would, she thought with satisfaction.

She carried them through with Maria's help, set them down in front of all the guests and then left them to it. She put the coffee on to brew in Elisa's smaller kitchen, with homemade *petit fours* sitting ready on the side, and then headed back to her kitchen to start the massive clean-up operation.

But Massimo was in there, up to his wrists in suds, scrubbing pans. The dishwasher was sloshing quietly in the background, and there was no sign of Maria.

'I sent her home,' he said in answer to her question. 'It's getting late, and she's got a child.'

'I was going to pay her.'

'I've done it. Roberto's taken her home. Why don't you make us both a coffee while I finish this?'

She wasn't going to argue. Her head was aching, her feet were coming out in sympathy and she hadn't sat down for six hours. More, probably.

'Are they happy?'

She shrugged. 'They didn't say not and they seemed to eat it all, mostly.'

'Well, that's a miracle. There are some fussy women amongst them. I don't know why my mother bothers with them.'

He dried his hands and sat down opposite her, picking up his coffee. 'Well done,' he said, and the approval in his voice warmed her.

'I'll reserve judgement until I get your mother's verdict,' she said, because after all he hadn't been her client.

'Don't bother. It was the best food this house has seen in decades. You did an amazing job.'

'I loved it,' she confessed with a smile. 'It was great to do something a bit more challenging, playing with flavours and presentation and just having a bit of fun. I love it. I've always loved it.'

He nodded slowly. 'Yes, I can see that. And you're very good at it. I don't suppose there's any left?'

She laughed and went to the fridge. 'There's some of the boar casserole, and a spare pannacotta. Haven't you eaten?'

He pulled a face. 'Kid's food,' he admitted. 'My father and I took them out for pizza. There didn't seem to be a lot of room in here.'

She plated him up some of the casserole with the vegetables, put it in the microwave and reheated it, then set it down in front of him and watched him eat. It was the best part of her job, to watch people enjoying the things she'd created, and he was savouring every mouthful.

She felt a wave of sadness and regret that there was no future for them, that she wouldn't spend the rest of her life creating wonderful, warming food and watching him eat it with relish.

She'd had the girls in with her earlier in the day, and she'd let them help her make the *petit fours* from homemade marzipan. That, too, had given her pangs of regret and a curious sense of loss. Silly, really. She'd never had them, so how could she feel that she'd lost them?

And after he'd eaten so much marzipan she was afraid he'd be sick, Antonino had stood up at the sink on an upturned box and washed up the plastic mixing bowls, soaking himself and the entire area in the process and having a great time with the bubbles. Such a sweet child, and the spitting image of his father. He was going to be a good-looking man one day, but she wouldn't be there to see it.

Or watch his father grow old.

She took away his plate, and replaced it with the pannacotta. He pressed the sugar cage with his fingertip, and frowned as it shattered gently onto the plate. 'How did you make it?' he asked, fascinated. 'I've never understood.'

'Boil sugar and water until it's caramelised, then trail it over an oiled mould. It's easy.'

He laughed. 'For you. I can't even boil an egg. Without Carlotta my kids would starve.'

'No. They'd eat pizza,' she said drily, and he gave a wry grin.

'Probably.' He dug the spoon into the pannacotta and scooped up a raspberry with it, then sighed as it melted on his tongue. 'Amazing,' he mumbled, and scraped the plate clean.

Then he put the spoon down and pushed the plate away, leaning back and staring at her. 'You really are an exceptional chef. If there's any justice, you'll do well in your catering business. That was superb.'

'Thank you.' She felt his praise warm her, and somehow that was more important than anyone else's approval. She washed his plate and their coffee cups, then turned back to him, her mind moving on to the real reason she was here.

'Massimo, I need to talk to you about Jen and the wedding. They'll be here in two days, and I need to pick them up from the airport somehow.'

'I'll do it,' he offered instantly. 'My mother's preparing the guest wing for them, but she wanted to know if they needed one room or two.'

'Oh, one. Definitely. She needs help in the night sometimes. Is there a shower?'

'A wet room. That was one of the reasons for the choice. And it's got French doors out to the terrace around the other

side. Come. I'll show you. You can tell me which room would
be the best for them.'

She went, and was blown away by their guest suite. Two
bedrooms, both large, twin beds in one and a huge double in
the other, with a wet room between and French doors out onto
the terrace. And there was a small sitting room, as well, a private retreat, with a basic kitchen for making drinks and snacks.

'This will be just perfect. Give them the double room. She
wakes in the night quite often, having flashbacks. They're
worse if Andy's not beside her.'

'Poor girl.'

She nodded, still racked with guilt. She always would be,
she imagined. It would never go away, just like his guilt over
Angelina slumped over the kitchen table, unable to summon
help.

She felt his finger under her chin, tilting her face up to his
so he could look into her eyes.

'It was not your fault,' he said as if he could read her mind.

Her eyes were steady, but sad. 'Any more than Angelina's
death was your fault. Bad things happen. Guilt is just a natural human reaction. Knowing it and believing it are two different things.'

He felt his mouth tilt into a smile, but what kind of a smile
it was he couldn't imagine. It faded, as he stared into her eyes,
seeing the ache in them, the longing, the emptiness.

He needed her. Wanted her like he had never wanted anyone, but there was too much at stake to risk upsetting the status quo, for any of them.

He dropped his hand. 'What time do they arrive?' he asked,
and the tension holding them eased.

For now.

They collected Jen and Andy from Pisa airport at midday on
Friday, and they were blown away by their first view of the

palazzo. By the time they'd pulled up at the bottom of the steps, Jen's eyes were like saucers, but all Lydia could think about was how her sister would get up the steps.

She hadn't even thought about it, stupidly, and now—

'Come here, gorgeous,' Andy said, unfazed by the sight of them, and scooping Jen up, he grinned and carried her up the steps to where Roberto was waiting with the doors open.

Massimo and Lydia followed, carrying their luggage and the crutches, and as they reached the top their eyes met and held.

The memory was in her eyes, and it transfixed him. The last woman to be carried up those steps had been her in that awful wedding dress—the dress that was still hanging on the back of his office door, waiting for her to ask for it and burn it.

He should let her. Should burn it himself, instead of staring at it for hour after hour and thinking of her.

He dragged his eyes away and forced himself to concentrate on showing them to their rooms.

'I'll leave you with Lydia. If you need anything, I'll be in the office.'

And he walked away, crossing the courtyard with a firm, deliberate stride. She dragged her eyes off him and closed the door, her heart still pounding from that look they'd exchanged at the top of the steps.

Such a short time since he'd carried her up them, and yet so much had happened. Nothing obvious, nothing apparently momentous, and yet nothing would ever be quite the same as it had been before.

Starting with her sister's wedding.

'Wow—this is incredible!' Jen breathed, leaning back on Andy and staring out of the French doors at the glorious view. 'So beautiful! And the house—my God, Lydia, it's fantastic! Andy, did you see those paintings on the wall?'

Lydia gave a soft laugh. 'Those are the rough ones. There are some utterly stunning frescoes in the main part of the house, up the stairwell, for instance, and in the dining room. Absolutely beautiful. The whole place is just steeped in history.'

'And we're going to get married from here. I can't believe it.'

'Believe it.' She glanced at her watch. 'Are you hungry? There's some soup and cheese for lunch, and we'll eat properly tonight. Anita's coming over before dinner to talk to you and show you where the marquee will go and how it all works—they've had Carla's wedding and Luca's here, so they've done it all before.'

'Not Massimo's?'

She had no idea. It hadn't been mentioned. 'I don't know. Maybe not. So—lunch. Do you want a lie down for a while, or shall I bring you something over?'

'Oh, I don't want to make work for you,' Jen said, but Lydia could see she was flagging, and she shook her head.

'I don't mind. I'll bring you both something and you can take it easy for a few hours. Travelling's always exhausting.'

Anita arrived at five, and by six Gio had put in an appearance, rather as she'd expected.

He found Lydia in the kitchen, and helped himself to a glass of Prosecco from the fridge and a handful of canapés.

'Hey,' she said, slapping his wrist lightly when he went back for more. 'I didn't know you were involved in the wedding planning.'

'I'm not,' he said with a cocky grin. 'I'm just here for the food.'

And Anita, she thought, but she didn't say that. She knew he'd turn from the smiling playboy to the razor-tongued lawyer the instant she mentioned the woman's name. Instead she did a little digging on another subject.

'So, how many weddings have there been here recently?' she asked.

'Two—Carla and Luca.'

'Not Massimo?'

'No. He got married in the *duomo* and they went back to her parents' house. Why?'

She shrugged. 'I just didn't want to say anything that hit a nerve.'

'I think you hit a nerve,' he said, 'even without speaking. You unsettle him.'

Was it so obvious? Maybe only to someone who was looking for trouble.

'Relax, Gio,' she said drily. 'You don't need to panic and get out your pre-nup template. This is going nowhere.'

'Shame,' he said, pulling a face, 'you might actually be good for him,' and while she was distracted he grabbed another handful of canapés.

She took the plate away and put it on the side. 'Shame?' she asked, and he shrugged.

'He's lonely. Luca likes you, so does Isabelle. And so does our mother, which can't be bad. She's a hard one to please.'

'Not as hard as her son,' she retorted. 'And talking of Massimo, why don't you go and find him and leave me in peace to cook? You're distracting me.'

'Wouldn't want to do that. You might ruin the food, and I've come all the way from Florence for it.'

And he sauntered off, stealing another mouthful from the plate in passing.

The dinner went well, and Anita came back the following day to go through the plans in detail, after talking to Jen and Andy the night before.

'She's amazing,' Jen said later. 'She just seems to know what I want, and she's got the answers to all of my questions.'

'Good,' she said, glad they'd got on well, because hearing the questions she'd realised there was no way someone without in-depth local knowledge could have answered them.

They were getting married the first weekend in May, in the town hall, and coming back to the *palazzo* for the marquee reception. They talked food, and she asked Anita for the catering budget and drew a blank. 'Whatever you need,' she was told, and she shook her head.

'I need to know.'

'I allow between thirty and eighty euros a head for food. Do whatever you want, he won't mind. Just don't make it cheap. That would insult him.'

'What about wine?'

'Prosecco for reception drinks, estate red and white for the meal, estate vinsanto for the dessert, champagne for toasts— unless you'd rather have prosecco again?'

'Prosecco would be fine. I prefer it,' Jen said, looking slightly stunned. 'Lydia, this seems really lavish.'

'Don't worry, Jen, she's earned it,' Anita said. 'He's been working her to the bone over the harvest season, and it's not finished yet.'

It wasn't, and there was a change in the weather. Saturday night was cold and clear, and there was a hint of frost on the railings. Winter was coming, and first thing on Monday morning Roberto, not Massimo, took Jen and Andy to the airport because *la Raccolta*, the olive harvest, was about to begin.

Jen hugged her goodbye, her eyes welling. 'It's going to be amazing. I don't know how to thank you.'

'You don't need to thank me. Just go home and concentrate on getting better, and don't buy your wedding dress until I'm there. I don't want to miss that.'

'What, with your taste in wedding dresses?' Massimo said, coming up behind them with a teasing smile that threatened to double her blood pressure.

'It was five pounds!'

'You were cheated,' he said, laughing, and kissed Jen good-bye, slapping Andy on the back and wishing them a safe journey. 'I have to go—I'm needed at the plant. We have a problem with the olive press. I'll see you in May.'

She waved them off, feeling a pang of homesickness as they went, but she retreated to the kitchen where Carlotta was carving bread.

'Here we go again, then,' she said with a smile, and Carlotta smiled back and handed her the knife.

'I cut the *prosciutto*,' she said, and turned on the slicer.

He was late back that night—more problems with the *frantoio*, so Roberto told her, and Carlotta was exhausted.

Elisa and Vittorio were out for dinner, and so apart from Roberto and Carlotta, she was alone in the house with the children. And he was clearly worried for his wife.

'Go on, you go and look after her. Make her have an early night. I'll put the children to bed and look after them.'

'Are you sure?'

'Of course. They don't bite.'

He smiled gratefully and went, and she found the children in the sitting room. Antonino and Lavinia were squabbling again, and Francesca was on the point of tears.

'Who wants a story?' she asked, and they stopped fighting and looked up at her.

'Where's *Pàpa*?' Lavinia asked, looking doubtful.

'Working,' she said, because explaining what he was doing when she didn't really understand was beyond her. But they seemed to accept it, and apart from tugging his sister's hair again, even Antonino co-operated.

More or less. There was some argument about whether or not they needed a bath, but she was pretty sure no child had died from missing a single bath night, so she chivvied them into their pyjamas, supervised the teeth cleaning and ushered them into Antonino's bedroom.

It was a squeeze, but they all fitted on the bed somehow, and he handed her his favourite story book.

It was simple enough, just about, that she could fudge her way through it, but her pronunciation made them all laugh, and Francesca coached her. Then she read it again, much better this time, and gradually Antonino's eyelids began to wilt.

She sent the girls out, tucked him up and, on impulse, she kissed him goodnight.

He was already asleep by the time she reached the door, and Lavinia was in bed. Francesca, though, looked unhappy still, so after she'd settled her sister, she went into the older girl's room and gave her a hug.

She wasn't surprised when she burst into tears. She'd been on the brink of it before, and Lydia took her back downstairs and made her a hot drink and they curled up on the sofa in the sitting room next to the kitchen and talked.

'He's always working,' she said, her eyes welling again. 'He's never here, and Nino and Vinia always fight, and then Carlotta gets cross and upset because she's tired, and it's always me to stop them fighting, and—'

She broke off, her thin shoulders racked with sobs, and Lydia pulled her into her arms and rocked her, shushing her gently as she wept.

'—she's the one who bears the brunt of the loss, because when I'm not there the little ones turn to her. She has to be mother to them, and she's been so strong, but she's just a little girl herself—'

Poor, poor little thing. She was so stoic, trying to ease the burden on her beloved *pàpa*, and he was torn in half by his responsibilities. It was a no-win situation, and there was nothing she could do to change it, but maybe, just this one night, she'd made it a little easier.

She cradled Francesca in her arms until the storm of weeping had passed, and then they put on a DVD and snuggled up together to watch it.

Lydia couldn't understand it, but it didn't matter, and after a short while Francesca dropped off to sleep on Lydia's shoulder. She shifted her gently so she was lying with her head on her lap, and she stroked her hair as she settled again.

Dear, sweet child. Lydia was falling for her, she realised. Falling for them all. For the first time in her life she felt truly at home, truly needed, as if what she did really made a difference.

She sifted the soft, dark curls through her fingers and wondered what the future held for her and for her brother and sister.

She'd never know. Her time here was limited, they all knew that, and yet she'd grown to love them all so much that to leave them, never to know what became of them, how their lives panned out—it seemed unthinkable. She felt so much a part of their family, and it would be so easy to imagine living here with them, maybe adding to the family in time.

She squeezed her eyes shut and bit her lips.

No. It was never going to happen. She was going, and she had to remember that.

But not yet, she thought, a fine tendril of hair curled around her finger. Not now. For now, she'd just sit there with Francesca, and they'd wait for Massimo to return.

It was so late.

His mother would have put the children to bed, he thought, but yet again he'd missed their bedtime story, yet again he'd let them down.

The lights were on in the sitting room, and he could hear the television. Odd. He paused at the door, thinking the children must have left everything on, and he saw Lydia asleep on the sofa, Francesca sprawled across her lap.

Why Lydia? And why wasn't Francesca in bed?

He walked quietly over and looked down at them. They were both sound asleep, and Lydia was going to have a dreadful crick in her neck, but he was filthy, and if he was to carry Francesca up to bed, he needed a shower.

He backed out silently, went upstairs and showered, then threw on clean clothes and ran lightly downstairs.

'Lydia?' he murmured softly, touching her on the shoulder, and she stirred slightly and winced.

'Oh—you're home,' she whispered.

'*Sì.* I'll take her.'

He eased her up into his arms, and Francesca snuggled close.

'She missed you,' Lydia said. 'The little ones were tired and naughty.'

'I'm sorry.'

'Don't be. It's not your fault.'

'Why are you here? My mother should be putting them to bed. I sent her a text.'

'They're out for dinner.'

He dropped his head back with a sigh. 'Of course. Oh, Lydia, I'm so sorry.'

'It's fine. Put her to bed.'

He did, settling her quickly, earning a sleepy smile as he kissed her goodnight. But by the time he got downstairs again, the television was off and the sitting room was in darkness.

It was over.

La Raccolta was finished, the olive oil safely in the huge lidded terracotta urns where it would mature for a while before being bottled.

The fresh olive oil, straight from the press, was the most amazing thing she'd ever tasted, and she'd used it liberally in the cooking and on *bruschetta* as an appetiser for the family's meals.

Of all the harvests, she'd found the olive harvest the most fascinating. The noise and smell in the pressing room was amazing, the huge stone wheels revolving on edge in the great stainless steel bowl of the *frantoio*, the olive press, crushing the olives to a purple paste. It was spread on circular felt discs and then stacked and pressed so that the oily juice dribbled out and ran into a vat, where it separated naturally, the bright green oil floating to the top.

Such a simple process, really, unchanged for centuries, and yet so very effective.

Everything in there had been covered in oil, the floor especially, and she knew that every time she smelt olive oil now, she'd see that room, hear the sound of the *frantoio* grinding the olives, see Massimo tossing olives in the palm of his hand, or checking the press, or laughing with one of the workers.

It would haunt her for the rest of her life, and the time had come so quickly.

She couldn't believe she was going, but she was. She'd grown to love it, not just because of him, but because of all his family, especially the children.

They were sad she was leaving, and on her last night she cooked them a special meal of their own, with a seafood risotto for their starter, and a pasta dish with chicken and pesto, followed by the dessert of frozen berries with hot white chocolate sauce that was always everyone's favourite.

'I don't want you to go,' Francesca said sadly as they finished clearing up.

Massimo, coming into the room as she said it, frowned. 'She has to go, *cara*. She has a business to run.'

'No, she doesn't. She has a job here, with us.'

Her heart squeezed. 'But I don't, sweetheart,' she said gently. 'I was only here to help Carlotta with the harvest. It's finished now. I can't just hang around and wait for next year. I have to go and cook for other people.'

'You could cook for us,' she reasoned, but Lydia shook her head.

'No. Carlotta would feel hurt. That's her job, to look after you. And your *pàpa* is right, I have to go back to my business.'

'Not go,' Lavinia said, her eyes welling. '*Pàpa, no!*' She ran to him, begging him in Italian, words she couldn't understand.

'What's she saying?' she asked, and Lavinia turned to look at her, tugging at her father and pleading, and he met her eyes reluctantly.

'She wants you to stay. She said—'

He broke off, but Francesca wouldn't let him stop.

'Tell her what Lavinia said, *Pàpa*,' she prompted, and he closed his eyes briefly and then went on.

'*Pàpa* is unhappy when aren't you're here,' he said grudgingly, translating directly as Lavinia spoke. 'Please don't go. We missed you when you went home before.' He hesitated, and she nudged him. 'It's lovely when you're here,' he went on, his bleak eyes locked with hers, 'because you make *Pàpa* laugh. He never laughs when you're not here.'

A tear slipped over and slid down her cheek, but she didn't seem to notice. Their eyes were locked, and he could see the anguish in them. He swallowed hard, his arm around Lavinia's skinny little shoulders holding her tight at his side.

Was it true? Was he unhappy when she wasn't there, unhappy enough that even the children could see it? Did he really not laugh when she wasn't there?

Maybe.

Lydia pressed her fingers to her lips, and shook her head. 'Oh, Lavinia. I'm sorry. I don't want to make your *pàpa* unhappy, or any of you, but I have to go home to my family.'

She felt little arms around her hips, and looked down to find Antonino hugging her, his face buried in her side. She laid a hand gently on his hair and stroked it, aching unbearably inside. She'd done this, spent so much time with them that she was hurting them now by leaving, and she never meant to hurt them. 'I'm sorry,' she said to him, *'mi dispiace.'* And his little arms tightened.

'Will you read us a story?' Francesca asked.

She'd be leaving for the airport before three in the morning, long before the children were up, so this was her last chance to read to them. Her last chance ever? 'Of course I will,' she said, feeling choked. She'd done it a few times since the night of the *frantoio* breakdown, and she loved it. Too much.

They were already in their pyjamas, and she ushered them up to bed, supervised the teeth cleaning as she'd done before, and then they settled down on Antonino's bed, all crowded round while she read haltingly to them in her awful, amateurish Italian.

She could get the expressions right, make it exciting—that was the easy bit. The pronunciation was harder, but it was a book they knew, so it didn't really matter.

What mattered was lying propped up against the wall, with Antonino under one arm and Lavinia under the other, and Francesca curled up by her knees leaning against the wall and watching her with wounded eyes.

She was the only one of them to remember her mother, and for a few short weeks, Lydia realised, she'd slipped into the role without thinking, unconsciously taking over some of the many little things a mother did. Things like making cupcakes, and birthday cards for Roberto. She'd stopped the two little ones fighting, and hugged them when they'd hurt themselves, and all the time she'd been playing happy families and ignoring the fact that she'd be going away soon, going back to her real life at home.

And now she had to go.

She closed the book, and the children snuggled closer, stretching out the moment.

Then Massimo's frame filled the doorway, his eyes shadowed in the dim light.

'Come on. Bedtime now. Lydia needs to pack.'

It was a tearful goodnight, for all of them, and as soon as she could she fled to her room, stifling the tears.

She didn't have to pack. She'd done it ages ago, been round all the places she might have left anything, and there was nothing to do now, nothing to distract her.

Only Lavinia's words echoing in her head.

He never laughs when you're not here.

The knock was so quiet she almost didn't hear it.

'Lydia?'

She opened the door, unable to speak, and met his tortured eyes.

And then his arms closed around her, and he held her hard against his chest while she felt the shudders run through him.

They stayed like that for an age, and then he eased back and looked down at her.

His eyes were raw with need, and she led him into the room and closed the door.

Just one last time…

CHAPTER TEN

'Is it true?'

He turned his head and met her eyes in the soft glow of the bedside light, and his face was shuttered and remote.

'Is what true?'

'That you don't laugh when I'm not here?'

He looked away again. 'You don't want to listen to what the children say.'

'Why not, if it's true? Is it?'

He didn't answer, so she took it as a yes. It made her heart ache. If only he'd believe in them, if only he'd let her into his heart, his life, but all he would say was no.

'Talk to me,' she pleaded.

He turned his head back, his eyes unreadable.

'What is there to say?'

'You could tell me how you really feel. That would be a good start.'

He laughed, a harsh, abrupt grunt full of pain. 'I can't,' he said, his accent stronger than she'd ever heard it. 'I can't find the words, I don't have the language to do this in English.'

'Then tell me in Italian. I won't understand, but you can say it then out loud. You can tell me whatever you like, and I can't hold you to it.'

He frowned, but then he reached out and stroked her face, his fingers trembling. His mouth flickered in a sad smile, and

then he started to speak, as if she'd released something inside
him that had been held back for a long, long time.

She didn't understand it, but she understood the tone—the
gentleness, the anguish, the pain of separation.

And then, his eyes locked with hers, he said softly, *'Ciao,
mia bella ragazza. Te amo...'*

She reached out and cradled his jaw, her heart breaking.
Ciao meant hello, but it also meant goodbye.

'It doesn't have to be goodbye,' she said softly. 'I love you,
too—so much.'

He shook his head. 'No. No, *cara*, please. I can't let you
love me. I can't let you stay. You'll be hurt.'

'No!'

'Yes. I won't let you.'

'Would you stop that?' she demanded, angry now. 'The
first time I met you, you said I couldn't go in the plane with
Nico because it wasn't safe. Now you're telling me I can't
love you because I'll get hurt! Maybe I want to take the risk,
Massimo? Maybe I *need* to take the risk.'

'No. You have a life waiting for you, and one day there
will be some lucky man...'

'I don't want another man, I want you.'

'No! I have nothing to give you. I'm already pulled in so
many ways. How can I be fair to you, or the children, or my
work, my family? How can I do another relationship justice?'

'Maybe I could help you. Maybe I could make it easier.
Maybe we could work together?'

'No. You love your family, you have your career. If I let
you give it all up for me, what then? What happens when
we've all let you into our hearts and then you leave?'

'I won't leave!'

'You don't know that. You've been here less than three
months. What happens in three years, when we have another
child and you decide you're unhappy and want to go? I don't

have time for you, I can't give you what you need. I don't even have enough time now to sleep! Please, *cara*. Don't make it harder. You'll forget me soon.'

'No. I'll never forget you. I'll never stop loving you.'

'You will. You'll move on. You'll meet someone and marry him and have children of your own in England, close to your family, and you'll look back and wonder what you saw in this sad and lonely old man.'

'Don't be ridiculous, you're not old, and you're only sad and lonely because you won't let anybody in!'

His eyes closed, as if he couldn't bear to look at her any longer. 'I can't. The last time I let anyone into my life, she lost her own, and it was because I was too busy, too tired, too overstretched to be there for her.'

'It wasn't your fault!'

'Yes, it was! I was *here*! I was supposed to be looking after her, but I was lying in my bed asleep while she was dying.'

'She should have woken you! She should have told you she was sick. It was not your fault!'

'No? Then why do I wake every night hearing her calling me?'

He threw off the covers and sat up, his legs over the edge of the bed, his head in his hands, his whole body vibrating with tension. 'I can't do this, Lydia! Please, don't ask me to. I can't do it.'

Why do I wake every night hearing her calling me?

His words echoing in her head, her heart pounding, she knelt up behind him, her arms around him, her body pressed to his in comfort.

'It wasn't your fault,' she said gently. 'You weren't responsible, but you're holding yourself responsible, and you have to forgive yourself. It wasn't my fault Jen had her accident, but I've blamed myself, and it has taken months to accept that it wasn't my fault and to forgive myself for not stopping him.

You have to do the same. You have to accept that you weren't at fault—'

'But I was! I should have checked on her.'

'You were asleep! What time of year was it?'

'Harvest,' he admitted, his voice raw. 'The end of *La Raccolta.*'

Right at the end of the season. Now, in fact. Any time now. Her heart contracted, and she sank back down onto her feet, her hands against his back.

'You were exhausted, weren't you? Just as you're exhausted now. And she didn't want to disturb you, so she went down to the kitchen for painkillers.'

He sucked in a breath, and she knew she was right.

'She probably wasn't thinking clearly. Did she suffer from headaches?'

'Yes. All the time. They said she had a weakness in the vessels.'

'So it could have happened at any time?'

'*Si.* But it happened when I was there, and it happened slowly, and if I'd realised, if I hadn't thought she was with the baby, if I'd known…'

'If you'd been God, in fact? If you'd been able to see inside her head?'

'They could have seen inside her head. She'd talked of going to the doctor about her headaches, but we were too busy, and she'd just had the baby, and it was the harvest, and…'

'And there was just no time. Oh, Massimo. I'm so sorry, but you know it wasn't your fault. You can't blame yourself.'

'Yes, I can. I can, and I have to, because my guilt and my grief is all I have left to give her! I can't even love her any more because you've taken that from me!' he said harshly, his voice cracking.

The pain ran through her like a shockwave.

How could he tell her that he loved her, and yet cling to his guilt and grief so that he could hold onto Angelina?

He couldn't. Not if he really loved her. Unless…

'Why are you doing this to me?' she asked quietly. 'To yourself? To your children? You wear your grief and your guilt like a hair shirt to torture yourself with, but it's not just you you're torturing, you're torturing me, as well, and your children. And they don't deserve to be tortured just because you're too much of a coward to let yourself love again!'

'I am not a coward!'

'Then prove it!' she begged. 'Let yourself love again!'

He didn't answer, his shoulders rigid, unmoving, and after what felt like forever, she gave up. She'd tried, and she could do no more.

Shaking, she eased away from him and glanced at her watch.

'We have to leave in half an hour. I'm going to shower,' she said, as steadily as she could.

And she walked into the bathroom, closed the door and let the tears fall…

He didn't come into the airport building this time.

He gave her a handful of notes to pay for her excess baggage, put her luggage on the pavement at the drop-off point and then hesitated.

'I'll see you in May,' he said, his voice clipped and harsh.

His eyes were raw with pain, and she wanted to weep for him, and for herself, and for the children, but now wasn't the time.

'Yes. I'll be in touch.'

'Anita will email you. She's in charge. I'll be too busy.'

Of course he would.

'Take care of yourself,' she said softly. And going up on tiptoe, she pressed her lips to his cheek.

His arms came round her, and for the briefest moment he rested his head against hers. *'Ciao, bella,'* he said softly, so softly that she scarcely heard him, and then he was straightening up, moving back, getting into the car.

He started the engine and drove away, and she watched his tail lights until they disappeared. Then she gathered up her luggage and headed for the doors.

It was the worst winter of her life.

The weather was glorious, bright winter sunshine that seemed to bounce right off her, leaving her cold inside. She found work in the pub down the road, and she created a website and tried to promote her catering business.

It did well, better than she'd expected, but without him her life was meaningless.

Jen found her one day in mid-January, staring into space.

'Hey,' she said softly, and came and perched beside her on the back of the sofa, staring out across the valley.

'Hey yourself. How are you doing?'

'OK. We've had another email from Anita. She wants to know about food.'

She could hardly bring herself to think about food. For a while she'd thought she was pregnant she'd felt so sick, but she wasn't. The test said no, her body said no and her heart grieved for a child that never was and never would be. And still she felt sick.

'What does she want to know? I've given her menu plans.'

'Something about the carpaccio of beef?'

She sighed. 'OK. I'll contact her.'

It was nothing to do with the beef. It was about Massimo.

'He's looking awful,' Anita said. 'He hasn't smiled since you left.'

Nor have I, she thought, *but there's nothing I can do, either for him or me.*

She didn't reply to the email. Two hours later her phone rang.

'I can't help you, Anita,' she said desperately. 'He won't listen to me.'

'He won't listen to anyone—Luca, Carlotta, his mother—even Gio's on your side, amazingly, but he just says he doesn't want to talk about it. And we're all worried. We're really worried.'

'I'm sorry, I can't do any more,' she said again, choked, and hung up.

Jen found her in her room, face down on the bed sobbing her heart out, and she lay down beside her and held her, and gradually it stopped hurting and she was numb again.

Better, in a strange kind of way.

January turned into February, and then March, and finally Jen was able to walk without the crutches.

'That's amazing,' Lydia said, hugging her, her eyes filling with tears. 'I'm so glad.'

'So am I.' Jen touched her cheek gently. 'I'm all right now, Lydia. I'm going to be OK. Please stop hurting yourself about it.'

'I'm not,' she said, and realised it was true, to an extent. Oh, it would always hurt to know that she'd been part of the sequence of events that had led to Jen's accident, but she'd stopped taking the blame for it, and now she could share in the joy of Jen's recovery. If only Massimo...

'You need to buy your wedding dress, we're leaving it awfully late,' she said, changing the subject before her mind dragged her off down that route.

'I know. There's a shop in town that does them to take away, so they don't need to be ordered. Will you come with me?'

She ignored the stab of pain, and hugged her sister. 'Of course I will.'

* * *

It was bittersweet.

They all went together—Lydia, Jen and their mother and she found a dress that laced up the back, with an inner elasticated corset that was perfect for giving her some extra back support.

'Oh, that's so comfy!' she said, and then looked in the mirror and her eyes filled.

'Oh...'

Lydia grabbed her mother's hand and hung on. It was definitely The Dress, and everybody's eyes were filling now.

'Oh, darling,' her mother said, and hugged her, laughing and crying at the same time, because it might never have come to this. They could have lost her, and yet here she was, standing on her own two feet, unaided, and in her wedding dress. Their tears were well and truly earned.

After she'd done another twirl and taken the dress off, the manageress of the little wedding shop poured them another glass of Prosecco to toast Jen's choice.

As the bubbles burst in her mouth, Lydia closed her eyes and thought of him.

Sitting on the terrace outside her bedroom, sipping Prosecco and talking into the night. They'd done it more than once, before the weather had turned. Pre-dinner drinks when Jen and Andy had come to visit. Sitting in the *trattoria* waiting for their food to come, the second time they'd made love.

'Lydia?'

She opened her eyes and dredged up a smile. 'You looked stunning in it, Jen. Absolutely beautiful. Andy'll be bowled over.'

'What about you?'

'I don't need a wedding dress!' she said abruptly, and then remembered she was supposed to be Jen's bridesmaid, and suddenly it was all too much.

'Can we do this another day?' she asked desperately, and Jen, seeing something in her eyes, nodded.

'Of course we can.'

She went back on her own a few days later, and flicked through the rails while she was waiting. And there, on a mannequin in the corner, was the most beautiful dress she'd ever seen.

The softest, heaviest silk crepe de Chine, cut on the cross and hanging beautifully, it was exquisite. So soft, she thought, fingering it with longing, such a far cry from the awful thing she'd worn for the competition, and she wondered, stupidly, if she'd worn it instead, would she have fallen? And if not, would she have known what it was to love him? Maybe, if he'd seen her wearing a dress like that...

'It's a beautiful dress, isn't it? Why don't you try it on?'

'I don't need a wedding dress,' she said bluntly, dropping her hand to her side. 'I'm here for a bridesmaid's dress.'

'You could still try it on. We're quiet today, and I'd love to see it on you. You've got just the figure for it.'

How on earth had she let herself be talked into it? Because, of course, it fitted like a dream on her hourglass figure, smoothing her hips, showing off her waist, emphasising her bust.

For a moment—just a moment—she let herself imagine his face as he saw her in it. She'd seen that look before, when he'd been making love to her—

'This is silly,' she said, desperate to take it off now. 'I'm not getting married.'

Not ever...

The awful wedding dress was still hanging on the back of his door.

He stared at it numbly. It still had her blood on it, a dark brown stain on the bodice where she'd wiped her fingers after she'd touched the graze on her head.

He missed her. The ache never left him, overlying the other ache, the ache that had been there since Angelina died.

Their wedding photo was still on his desk, and he picked it up and studied it. Was Lydia right? Was her wearing a metaphorical hair shirt, punishing himself for what was really not his fault?

Rationally, he knew that, but he couldn't let it go.

Because he hadn't forgiven himself? Or because he was a coward?

It's not just you you're torturing, you're torturing me, as well, and your children. And they don't deserve to be tortured just because you're too much of a coward to let yourself love again!

Getting up from the desk, he went and found Carlotta and told her he was going out. And then he did what he should have done a long time ago.

He went to the place where she was buried, and he said goodbye, and then he went home and took off his wedding ring. There was an inscription inside. It read *'Amor vincit omnia'*.

Love conquers everything.

Could it? Not unless you gave it a chance, he thought, and pressing the ring to his lips, he nestled it in Angelina's jewellery box, with the lock of her hair, the first letter she'd ever sent him, a rose from her bouquet.

And then he put the box away, and went outside into the garden and stood at the railings, looking out over the valley below. She'll be here soon, he thought, and then I'll know.

Jen and Andy saw her off at the airport.

She put on a bright face, but in truth she was dreading this part of the wedding.

She was going over early to finalise the menu and meet the people who were going to be helping her. Carlotta's nephew, the owner of the *trattoria*, had loaned her one of his chefs and sourced the ingredients, and the waiting staff were all from local families and had worked for Anita before, but the final responsibility for the menu and the food was hers.

None of that bothered her. She was confident about the menu, confident in the ability of the chef and the waiting staff, and the food she was sure would be fine.

It was seeing Massimo that filled her with dread.

Dread, and longing.

She was thinner.

Thinner, and her face was drawn. She looked as if she'd been working too hard, and he wondered how her business was going. Maybe she'd been too successful?

He hoped not—no! That was wrong. If it was going well, if it was what she wanted, then he must let her go.

Pain stabbed through him and he sucked in a breath. For the past few weeks he'd put thoughts of failure out of his mind, but now—now, seeing her there, they all came rushing to the fore.

He walked towards her, and as if she sensed him there she turned her head and met his eyes. All the breath seemed to be sucked out of his body, and he had to tell his feet how to move.

'*Ciao, bella,*' he said softly, and her face seemed to crumple slightly.

'*Ciao,*' she said, her voice uneven, and then he hugged her, because she looked as if she'd fall down if he didn't.

'Is this everything?'

She nodded, and he took the case from her and wheeled it out of the airport to his car.

He was looking well, she thought. A little thinner, perhaps, but not as bad as she'd thought from what Anita had said. Because he was over her?

She felt a sharp stab of pain, and sucked in her breath. Maybe he'd been right. Maybe he couldn't handle it, and he'd just needed to get back onto an even keel again.

And then he came round and opened the car door for her, and she noticed his wedding ring was missing, and her heart began to thump.

Was it significant?

She didn't know, and he said nothing, just smiled at her as he got into the car and talked about what the children had been up to and how the wedding preparations were going, all the way back to the *palazzo*.

It was like coming home, she thought.

The children were thrilled to see her, especially Francesca who wrapped her arms around her and hugged her so hard she thought her ribs might break.

'Goodness, you've all grown so tall!' she said, her eyes filling. Lavinia's arms were round her waist, and Antonino was hanging on her arm and jumping up and down. It made getting up the steps a bit of a challenge, but they managed it, and Massimo just chuckled softly and carried her luggage in.

'I've put you in the same room,' he said, and she felt a shiver of dread. The last time she'd been in here, he'd broken her heart. She wasn't sure she wanted to be there again, but it felt like her room now, and it would be odd to be anywhere else.

'So, what's the plan?' she asked as he put her case down.

He smiled wryly. 'Anita's coming over. I've told her to give you time to unwind, but she said there was too much to do. Do you want a cup of tea?'

'I'd love a cup of tea,' she said fervently. 'But don't worry. I'll make it.'

He nodded. 'In that case, I'll go and get on. You know my mobile number—ring me if you need me.'

She didn't have time to need him, which was perhaps just as well. The next few days were a whirlwind, and by the time the family arrived, she was exhausted.

Anita was brilliant. She organised everything, made sure everyone knew what they were to do and kept them all calm and focused, and the day of the wedding went without a hitch.

Lydia's involvement in the food was over. She'd prepared the starters and the deserts, the cold buffet was in the refrigerated van beside the marquee, and all she had to do was dress her sister and hold her bouquet.

And catch it, apparently, when it was all over.

Jen wasn't subtle. She stood just a few feet from her, with everyone standing round cheering, and threw it straight at Lydia.

It hit her in the chest and she nearly dropped it, but then she looked up and caught Massimo's eye, and her heart began to pound slowly.

He was smiling.

Smiling? Why? Because he was glad it was all over? Or because the significance of her catching it wasn't lost on him?

She didn't know. She was too tired to care, and after Andy scooped his glowing, blushing bride up in his arms and carried her off at the end of the reception in a shower of confetti and good wishes, she took the chance and slipped quietly away.

There was so much to do—a mountain of clearing up in the kitchen in the *palazzo*, never mind all the catering equipment which had been hired in and had to be cleaned and returned.

Plates, cutlery, glasses, table linen.

'I thought I might find you in here.'

She looked up.

'There's a lot to do.'

'I know.'

He wasn't smiling. Not now. He was thoughtful. Maybe a little tense?

He took off his suit jacket and rolled up his sleeves and pitched in alongside her, and for a while they worked in silence. He changed the washing up water three times, she used a handful of tea towels, but finally the table was groaning with clean utensils.

'Better. The guests are leaving. Do you want to say goodbye?'

She smiled slightly and shook her head. 'They're not my guests. Let my parents do it. I've got enough to do.'

'I'll go and clear up outside,' he said, and she nodded. There was still a lot to do in there, and she worked until she was ready to drop.

Her feet hurt, her shoes were long gone and she wanted to lie down. The rest, she decided, would keep, and turning off the light, she headed back to her room.

She passed her parents in the colonnaded walkway around the courtyard, on their way in with Massimo's parents.

They stopped to praise the food yet again, and Elisa hugged her. 'It was wonderful. I knew it would be. You have an amazing talent.'

'I know,' her mother said. 'We're very proud of her.'

She was hugged and kissed again, and then she excused herself and finally got to her room, pausing in surprise in the doorway.

The door was open, the bedside light was on, and the bed was sprinkled with rose petals.

Rose petals?

She picked one up, lifting it to her nose and smelling the delicately heady fragrance.

Who—?

'May I come in?'

She spun round, the rose petal falling from her fingers, and he was standing there with a bottle of sparkling water and two glasses. 'I thought you might be thirsty,' he said.

'I don't know what I am,' she said. 'Too tired to know.'

He laughed softly, and she wondered—just briefly, with the small part of her brain that was still functioning—how often he'd done that since she went away.

'Lie down before you fall.'

She didn't need telling twice. She didn't bother to take the dress off. It was probably ruined anyway, and realistically when would she wear it again? She didn't go to dressy events very often. She flopped onto the bed, and he went round the other side, kicked off his shoes and settled himself beside her, propped up against the headboard.

'Here, drink this,' he said, handing her a glass, and she drained the water and handed the glass back.

'More.'

He laughed—again?—and refilled it, then leant back and sighed.

'Good wedding.'

'It was. Thank you. Without you, it wouldn't have happened.'

'It might have been at the hotel.'

'No. Nobody was giving me a lift—well, only Nico, and we both know how that might have ended.'

'Don't.' He took the empty glass from her again, put them both down and slid down the bed so he was lying flat beside her. His hand reached out, and their fingers linked and held.

'How are you, really?' he asked softly.

He wasn't talking about tonight, she realised, and decided she might as well be honest. It was the only thing she had left.

'All right, I suppose. I've missed you.'

'I've missed you, too. I didn't know I could hurt as much as that, not any more. Apparently I can.'

She rolled to her side to face him, and he did the same, his smile gone now, his eyes serious.

'Massimo,' she said, cutting to the chase, 'where's your wedding ring?'

'Ah, *cara*. So observant. I took it off. I didn't need it any more. You were right, it was time to let the past go and move on with my life.'

'Without guilt?'

His smile was sad. 'Without guilt. With regret, perhaps. The knowledge that things probably wouldn't have been very different whatever I'd done. I'd lost sight of that. And you?' he added. 'Are you moving on with your life?'

She tried to laugh, but she was too tired and too hurt to make it believable. 'No. My business is going well, but I don't care. It's all meaningless without you.'

'Oh, *bella*,' he said softly, and reached for her. 'My life is the same. The only thing that's kept me going the last few weeks has been the knowledge that I'd see you again soon. Without that I would have gone insane. I nearly did go insane.'

'I know. Anita rang me. They were all worried about you.'

He eased her up against his chest, so that her face lay against the fine silk shirt, warm from his skin, the beat of his heart echoing in her ear, slow and steady.

'Stay with me,' he said. 'I have no right to ask you, after I sent you away like that, but I can't live without you. No. That's not true. I can. I just don't want to, because without you, I don't laugh. Lavinia was right. I don't laugh because there's nothing to laugh at when you're not here. Nothing seems funny, everything is cold and colourless and futile. The days are busy but monotonous, and the nights—the nights are so lonely.'

She swallowed a sob, and lifted her hand and cradled his stubbled jaw. 'I know. I've lain awake night after night and missed you. I can fill the days, but the nights...'

'The nights are endless. Cold and lonely and endless. I've tried working, but there comes a time when I have to sleep, and then every time I close my eyes, I see you.'

'Not Angelina?'

'No. Not Angelina. I said goodbye to her. I hadn't done it. I hadn't grieved for her properly, I'd buried myself in work and I thought I was all right, but then I met you and I couldn't love you as you deserved because I wasn't free. And instead of freeing myself, I sent you away.'

'I'm sorry. It must have been hard.'

His eyes softened, and he smiled and shook his head. 'No. It was surprisingly easy. I was ready to do it—more than ready. And I'm ready to move on. I just need to know that you're ready to come with me.'

She smiled and bit her lip. 'Where are we going?'

'Wherever life takes us. It will be here, because this is who I am and where I have to be, but what we do with that life is down to us.'

He took her hand from his cheek and held it, staring intently into her eyes. 'Marry me, Lydia. You've set me free, but that freedom is no use to me without you. I love you, *bella. Te amo*. If you still love me, if you haven't come to your senses in all this time, then marry me. Please.'

'Of course I'll marry you,' she breathed, her heart overflowing. 'Oh, you foolish, silly, wonderful man, of course I'll marry you! Just try and stop me. And I'll never, never stop loving you.'

'I've still got the dress,' he told her some time later, his eyes sparkling with mischief. 'It's hanging on my office door. I thought I'd keep it, just in case you said yes.'

Did the woman in the wedding dress shop have second sight? 'I think I might treat myself to a new one,' she said, and smiled at him.

They were married in June, in the town hall where Jen and Andy had been married.

It had been a rush—she'd had to pack up all her things in England and ship them over, and they'd moved, on his parents' insistence, into the main part of the *palazzo*.

A new start, a clean slate.

It would take some getting used to, but as Massimo said, it was a family home and it should have children in it. It was where he and his brothers and sisters had been brought up, and it was family tradition for the eldest son to take over the formal rooms of the *palazzo*. And hopefully, there would be other children to fill it.

She held onto that thought. She'd liked the simplicity of the other wing, but there was much more elbow room in the central part, essential if they were to have more children, and the views were, if anything, even more stunning. And maybe one day she'd grow into the grandeur.

But until their wedding night, she was still using the room she'd always had, and it was in there that Jen and her mother helped her put on the beautiful silk dress. It seemed woefully extravagant for such a small and simple occasion, but she was wearing it for him, only for him, and when she walked out to meet him, her heart was in her mouth.

He was waiting for her in the frescoed courtyard, and his eyes stroked slowly over her. He said nothing, and for an endless moment she thought he hated it. But then he lifted his eyes to hers, and the heat in them threatened to set her on fire.

She looked stunning.

He'd thought she was beautiful in the other wedding dress, much as he'd hated it. In this, she was spectacular. It hugged her curves like a lover, and just to look at her made him ache.

She wasn't wearing a veil, and the natural curls of her fine blonde hair fell softly to her shoulders. It was the way he liked it. Everything about her was the way he liked it, and at last he found a smile.

'*Mia bella ragazza,*' he said softly, and held out his hand to her.

It was a beautiful, simple ceremony.

Their vows, said by both of them in both English and Italian, were from the heart, and they were witnessed by their closest family and friends. Both sets of parents, his three sisters, Jen and Andy, Luca and Isabelle, Gio, Anita, Carlotta and Roberto, and of course the children.

Francesca and Lavinia were bridesmaids, and Antonino was the ring bearer. There was a tense moment when he wobbled and the rings started to slide, but it was all right, and with a smile of encouragement for his son, Massimo took her ring from the little cushion and slid it onto her finger, his eyes locked with hers.

He loved her. When he'd lost Angelina, he'd thought he could never love again, but Lydia had shown him the way. There was always room for love, he realised, always room for another person in your heart, and his heart had made room for her. How had he ever thought it could do otherwise?

She slid the other ring onto his finger, her fingers firm and confident, and he cupped her shoulders in his hands and bent his head and kissed her.

'*Te amo,*' he murmured, and then his words were drowned out by the clapping and cheering of their family.

* * *

Afterwards they went for lunch to the little *trattoria* owned by Carlotta's nephew. He did them proud. They drank Prosecco and ate simple, hearty food exquisitely cooked, and when it was over, they drove back to the *palazzo*. The others were going back to Luca and Isabelle's for the rest of the day, to give them a little privacy, and Massimo intended to take full advantage of it.

He drove up to the front door, scooped her up in his arms and carried her up the steps. The last time he'd done this she'd been bloodstained and battered. This time—this time she was his wife, and he felt like the luckiest man alive.

Pausing at the top he turned, staring out over the valley spread out below them. Home, he thought, his heart filled with joy, and Lydia rested her head on his shoulder and sighed.

'It's so beautiful.'

'Not as beautiful as you. And that dress…' He nuzzled her neck, making her arch against him. 'I've been wanting to take it off you all day.'

'Don't you like it? I wasn't sure myself. I thought maybe I should have stuck to the other one,' she teased, and he laughed, the sound carrying softly on the night air.

It was a sound she'd never tire of, she thought contentedly as he turned, still smiling, and carried his bride over the threshold.

* * * * *

LORENZO'S REWARD

CATHERINE GEORGE

Catherine George was born in Wales, and early on developed a passion for reading which eventually fuelled her compulsion to write. Marriage to an engineer led to nine years in Brazil, but on his later travels the education of her son and daughter kept her in the UK. And, instead of constant reading to pass her lonely evenings, she began to write the first of her romantic novels. When not writing and reading she loves to cook, listen to opera, and browse in antiques shops.

CHAPTER ONE

THE crowded pub was hot, smoke-filled, and full of men in suits talking business over lunch. Jess eyed her watch impatiently, willing Simon to hurry, then looked up to find a complete stranger watching her intently from the far end of the bar. Jess felt an odd plummeting sensation in the pit of her stomach when dark, heavy-lidded eyes lit with incredulous recognition as they met hers. She glanced over her shoulder, sure he must be looking at some other woman, but there was no other female in sight.

Jess looked back again, which was a mistake. This time she couldn't look away. Heat rose in her face. Irritably she ordered herself to stop sitting there like a hypnotised rabbit, her pulse suddenly erratic as the man put down his drink and with purpose began to push his way through the crowd towards her. But before he could reach her two other men joined him, barring his way. The stranger shrugged expressively, signalling regret, and Jess finally broke eye contact. Then it dawned on her that one of his companions was Mr Jeremy Lonsdale, unrecognisable for a moment minus his barristers wig and gown. But when the third member of the trio turned his head she gasped in utter consternation. He was all too familiar, with eyes which blazed in incredulous affront when Jess panicked at the sight of him, spun around and fled from the pub, with Simon Hollister, her astonished lunch companion, in hot pursuit.

Jess dodged through honking traffic, and ran like a deer

5

up the road to the courthouse, to subject herself to the usual security process inside. She was still gasping for breath when Simon caught up with her in the jury restaurant.

"What the hell was all that about?" he panted.

"Prosecuting—Counsel—was there. With chums." Jess heaved in a lungful of air. "One of them was Roberto Forli, my sister's ex-boyfriend," she finished in a rush.

Simon whistled. "And we jurors are forbidden connection to anyone at all on the case."

"Exactly!"

"How well do you know the man?"

"I've only met him once."

"Did Lonsdale see you?"

"I don't think so. He had his back to me."

Simon smiled reassuringly. "Then it's probably all right. Anyway, we'll soon know if your friend grassed on you. Let's grab something to eat before we're called. I left our lunch on the bar when you took off."

But after her mad dash in the midday heat Jess couldn't face the thought of food. Her mind was too full of the unexpected meeting with Roberto Forli. And with the stranger in his company. The memory of those dark, intent eyes sent shivers down her spine. The man had obviously recognised her from somewhere. But where? And when? Jess forced herself back to the present with an effort, and gulped down the rest of her mineral water as the jury was called back into the court.

As she took her seat in the jury box Jess buttoned her jacket against the cold of the courtroom, which was arctic compared with the summer day outside. According to bus driver Phil, the comedian in their group, the courtroom was kept cool to keep the jury awake during the longer discourses, and at the same time prevent heatstroke for the judge and barristers in their archaic horsehair wigs and black gowns.

While they waited for the judge Jess firmly blanked the lunchtime incident from her mind by thinking back over her two weeks of jury service. She was glad, now, of the experience, but the first day had been daunting. After waiting in line to pass through an airport-style metal detector she had been directed to the jury restaurant, an airport-style cafeteria packed with people queuing for coffee, reading newspapers, or just sitting staring into space if they'd managed to find a chair. Later, in an empty courtroom with the other newcomers, she had watched a video which set out the rules, but a wait of two days had elapsed before she was called into service.

The clerk of the court had shuffled cards and read out names as usual, but this time Jessamy Dysart was among the chosen. She had been led off to a courtroom, and with eleven of her peers sworn in as a member of the jury. At first glance the dark wood and leather of the courtroom, though impressive enough, had seemed a lot smaller than on television. Jess had been rather disconcerted to find herself at such close quarters not only with the prisoner in the dock, but with the barristers and solicitors facing the judge in the well of the court.

Now there was only another day of a different trial to go, with a different batch of jurors. This time Jess was seated in the front of the jury box next to Simon Hollister. He had made a beeline for her from the first day, and frankly admitted that his original intention had been to avoid jury duty by pleading pressure of work in his marketing job in the City. But once actually there in the courthouse an unexpected sense of civic duty had made him stay.

"Added to the prospect of a fortnight coming into close contact with you, Jess," he'd added, with a grin.

Jess had taken this with a pinch of salt. Simon was a charmer, and she liked him, but she also liked Edward, the ex-headmaster, and June, the office cleaner, and most of her fellow jurors. However, she longed for this particular trial to be over. The young woman in the dock, Prosecuting Counsel alleged, had knowingly smuggled drugs into the country in her luggage. Like Jess she was in her mid-twenties, but with eyes dark-ringed in a pale, strained face, and from the evidence there seemed little doubt that she was guilty.

Previously Jess had preferred to eat a sandwich lunch in the jury restaurant with the others. But today she had given in to Simon's coaxing, glad to escape from the memory of the defendant's hopeless eyes. Now Jess wished she'd stayed put as usual. The fascinating stranger's interest had intrigued her, and in other circumstances she would have liked to meet him. But not when he came as one of a package with Roberto Forli and Prosecuting Counsel.

Jess waited in trepidation as the afternoon session began, fully expecting the judge to stop the proceedings. But to her vast relief everything went on as usual, and instead of pointing a dramatic finger at her Mr Jeremy Lonsdale merely got to his feet to make his closing speech for the prosecution. When the barrister sat down at last Simon gave a discreet thumbs-up sign. Afterwards Defence Counsel's speech proved to be mainly a criticism of Prosecution's case, with interminable reminders to the jury about burden of proof and miscarriages of justice. Long before he finished Jess bitterly regretted the reckless volume of water downed before coming into court. Hot with embarrassment, she was forced to raise a hand at last when the barrister paused for breath. With the judge's permission the usher escorted all members of the jury from the box to lock them in the jury room where eleven of them waited while Jess, crimson-faced, retired to their private cloakroom. Afterwards they all filed back into the court again to hear Defence Counsel come to a conclusion. When he achieved this at long last the judge ruled that it was time to finish for the day. He would leave his summing up for the morning.

"Not to worry, love," whispered June afterwards. "Don't be embarrassed. Nature calls everyone—even the judge."

The June sunshine was warm as Jess drove home through rush hour. Moving from one set of traffic lights to the next in slow progression, she was so preoccupied with the thoughts of the fascinating stranger she almost shot a red light at one point, and glued her attention to the traffic afterwards instead. The hot, crowded city streets filled Jess with sudden longing for Friars Wood, the cool house perched on the cliffs overlooking the Wye Valley, and the meal her mother would be concocting for the family at that very moment. Just one more day to go, she consoled herself, then she could go home for a break.

Jess managed to park near her flat in Bayswater, then trudged along the terrace of tall white houses, glad to get back to a home far more peaceful these days, since Fiona Todd had moved out to live with her man. Jess and her remaining flatmate, Emily Shaw, were now the only tenants, an arrangement which worked very amicably.

When Jess got in Emily was lying on the sofa, watching television. "Hi," she said, turning the set off. "My word, you look done in. What's up?"

Jess groaned. "Have I had a fraught day!"

"Is it desperately hush-hush, or are you allowed to tell me?"

"This bit I can! I ran into Roberto Forli in a pub at lunchtime."

Emily's big eyes widened. "*Really?* Your sister's ex from Florence? What's he doing here in London?"

"No idea. Whatever it was I wish he'd been doing it somewhere else," said Jess irritably.

"Why?" said Emily, astonished.

"It's a long story."

"But jolly interesting, by the sound of it."

Jess took a deep breath. "Simon Hollister, the marketing bloke on the jury with me, asked me out for a swift lunch. By sheer bad luck we hit on the same pub as Prosecuting Counsel."

"No!"

Jess described the incident with Roberto Forli to her riveted friend. But, for reasons she wasn't quite sure of, made no mention of the stranger. "We're forbidden contact with anyone connected to the court, of course, so when I saw Roberto all chummy with Prosecuting Counsel I shot out of the pub like greased lightning and did a runner back to the courthouse."

"Did Roberto see you?"

"You bet he did." Jess collapsed into a chair, grateful for the fruit juice her friend handed over. "Wonderful. I needed this. Thank goodness you were home early today."

Emily Shaw worked for an executive in a credit card company, and it was rare that she was home at this hour. "Mr Boss Man's away, and I've been slaving like mad to get everything shipshape before I take off on my hols. I developed a nasty little headache after lunch, so I knocked off early for once."

"I should think so." Jess eyed her closely. "You look horribly peaky. Have you taken any painkillers?"

"Yes, Nurse. And I'm going to bed early." Emily grinned. "You should do the same for once."

"I probably will." Jess smiled ruefully. "Pity I had to offend Roberto like that. You should have seen his face when I bolted!"

"Well, don't keep me in suspense—what happened when you went back into the jury box? Did the judge excommunicate you, or whatever?"

"No, thank goodness. But while Defence Counsel was droning on I realised I shouldn't have drunk so much water." Jess giggled as she described the trooping out of the entire jury on her account. "There's only one loo in the jury room, and it's not exactly soundproof. I think I'm still blushing."

"Oh, bad luck!" Emily laughed, then eyed Jess speculatively. "I wonder why Leonie's ex is in London?"

"No idea." Jess sighed. "Pity he was with Prosecuting Counsel. In any other circumstances I'd have enjoyed a chat with him very much." And, more to the point, achieved an introduction to the interesting stranger at the same time.

"Never mind," consoled Emily. "Perhaps Leo will know when you go home for the wedding."

Jess brightened. "Which now seems plain sailing, thank goodness. I was getting a bit tense about the way things were dragging on, in case I had to dash straight back after the wedding to go to court on Monday, but with a bit of luck the case will finish tomorrow. Lucky for me, anyway," she added, sobering.

"Cheer up—the weekend forecast looks good." Emily grinned. "The sun is sure to shine for Leonie on Sunday, anyway. The minute I set foot in a plane to fly away from it Britain always swelters in a heatwave.''

''Since you're off to sunny Italy it doesn't matter.'' Jess sighed. ''I wish I was going with you. After seven years apart Jonah and Leo were all for dashing off to a register office right away, of course, but when they were persuaded to wait for a conventional June wedding I hadn't the heart to say the date clashed with my holiday.''

''You know nothing would have kept you from Leonie's wedding! Not to worry; we'll do a holiday together some other time. And *my* sister was in raptures when I suggested she stepped into the breach.''

''Who's looking after the children?''

''My mother's taking turns with the other grandma. And Jack gets home to supervise bathtime and bed, anyway. I told Celia to relax—they'll all cope.''

''Of course they will. And I'll use the time off to laze about at home.'' Jess yawned widely. ''I'm off for a bath.''

Jess was towelling thick layers of flaxen hair when Emily banged on the bathroom door.

''Phone call for you,'' she called. ''Guess who?''

''Surprise me.''

''A sexy-sounding gent by the name of Forli!''

''*What*? Tell me you're pulling my leg, Em!'' said Jess, throwing open the door in dismay.

''Of course I'm not,'' said Emily indignantly. ''He's hanging on as we speak, dearie, so get yourself to the phone.''

Jess shook her head violently. ''I still can't talk to him.''

''What on earth shall I say?''

"Tell him I'm in the bath. Asleep. Anything. Why didn't you say I was out?"

"I didn't realise a phone call was taboo as well." Emily shook her head. "Honestly, Jess, any woman in her right mind would *kill* to listen to that voice purring down the line. Who would know?" She flung up her hands. "All right, all right. I'll lie through my teeth and swear you're prostrate with a migraine."

"Perfect. If I'm not I should be!"

When Jess joined Emily minutes later her friend grinned as she ladled cream and smoked salmon over bowls of steaming pasta.

"I'm afraid the gentleman didn't believe a word of it. But he was much too civilised to blame the messenger."

"Damn, damn, damn!" said Jess bitterly. "Any other time I'd have been delighted to talk to him."

"I believe you. Is he tall, dark and handsome to match the voice?"

"Not quite." That particular description belonged to the third man in the equation. "Roberto's tall enough, but fairish in that olive-skinned, Latin sort of way. A bit of a star on the ski-slopes, according to Leo."

"Smouldering blue eyes, of course," said Emily, smacking her lips.

"What *have* you been reading lately? Actually his eyes are dark like mine."

"Smouldering *black* eyes, then. Even better."

Jess's heart gave a sudden lurch at the memory of dark eyes which had smouldered so effectively she couldn't get them out of her mind. She ground her teeth in frustration. If only she'd been able to talk to Roberto he could have introduced her. Why did this kind of thing never go right for her? She eyed Emily hopefully. "I don't suppose Roberto gave you his number? I could happily ring him tomorrow, *after* the trial.''

"Sorry. A second rebuff must have been too much for the poor guy.''

"I'll bet. Especially as it's not long since my sister jilted him. We Dysart girls really know how to treat a man, don't we?'' Jess ate her favourite supper with less relish than it deserved. "Maybe Leo knows his number. If so I'll ring to apologise.'' And casually ask who the friend might be.

"Don't just apologise—grovel!'' advised Emily.

"You haven't even met the man.''

"I don't have to! Just listening to that voice was enough.''

Next day the proceedings in court were over sooner than expected. The judge reminded the jury of the exact meaning of the indictment, of what the Prosecution was obliged to prove to win its case and what the Defence must have done to persuade the jury to acquit, and concluded by telling the jury it was entirely up to them to decide. The ushers took an oath to keep the jury in a private and convenient place, and Jess and her fellow jurors were led off to the jury room and locked in to make their deliberations.

This time the facts were so conclusive that the jury members were reluctantly unanimous, and back in court later Edward, their foreman, delivered the verdict of guilty. Up to that point Jess had been very sorry for the young woman in the dock, but to her surprise Prosecuting Counsel justified the jury's verdict by disclosing a prior conviction of a similar nature before the judge passed sentence.

Afterwards the twelve jury members went off to the

pub Jess had raced from the day before. But this time there was no sign of Roberto Forli and Jeremy Lonsdale, nor, most disappointing of all, of the third member of the trio.

"Let's keep in touch, Jess," said Simon Hollister, as they emerged with the others into hot afternoon sunlight. "If I give you a ring soon, will you have dinner with me?"

"I'd love to," agreed Jess. "Not yet awhile, though. I'm off home to Gloucestershire for my sister's wedding tomorrow, and I'm staying on for a few days."

"Lucky old you," he said enviously. "I'm back to the City grind on Monday. I'll ring you in a week or so, then."

Jess nodded, then beckoned to June. "Time I went. I'm giving our friend a lift. See you, Simon."

The moment she got back to the flat Jess rang home. "Hi, Mother, it's me. The trial finished today after all, so I can stay on after the wedding with a light heart."

"Thank heavens for that," said Frances Dysart with relief. "How are you, darling? Tired?"

"Exhausted. How are things there? Mad panic on all sides?"

"Not a bit of it. The bride is floating about on a pink cloud and Fenny, needless to say, is bursting with excitement. But Kate's a bit tense. She's only halfway through her exams."

"I can't believe she's worried about failing! Kate's the brains of the family." Jess chuckled ruefully. "Leo got the looks and Adam the charm, whereas poor old me—"

"Whereas poor old you," echoed her mother dryly, "are the sexiest, according to your brother."

Jess was astounded. "*Really?* When did Adam say that?"

"This morning. He arrived with a carload of laundry—in time for lunch, of course."

Jess laughed. "How did his Finals go?"

"He refuses to commit himself. He's going back to Edinburgh to paint it red after the wedding, but for now I think he's just relieved the exams are over."

"I bet he is. And how about you and Dad? Are you worn out with all the excitement?"

"Not in the least. Everything's under control. What time are you arriving tomorrow?"

"I'll ring when I start off. Jury work's more tiring than I expected—I really need a lie-in tomorrow before I have my hair cut. I should be with you some time in the afternoon. And mind you take it easy, Mother, don't work too hard. See you tomorrow. Can you float the bride towards the phone now?"

Leonie Dysart greeted her sister with such exuberance Jess felt wistful, wondering how it felt to be so much in love. And to know with such certainty that her feelings were returned.

"Sorry, Leo, what did you say?" she said quickly.

"I asked how you were feeling after your stint in court."

"A bit tired, as we speak, but don't worry. I'll be firing on all cylinders on the day." Jess paused. "Leo, this is a bit of a long shot, but I don't suppose you'd know how to contact Roberto Forli? Here in this country, I mean? You'll never believe this, but I bumped into him yesterday—"

"Don't I know it! What on earth was all that about? He rang here afterwards and told me you took one look at him in a pub somewhere and ran for your life. He sounded so stroppy I was surprised when he asked for your telephone number. Did he get in touch last night?"

"Yes, he did. But I couldn't speak to him then, either."

"Why not?" demanded her sister in astonishment. "I thought you liked him."

"I *do*." Jess heaved a sigh, then explained the problem in detail.

"Oh, Jess, what bad luck! I knew Roberto had a barrister friend he sometimes stays with in London."

"Unfortunately the friend was Prosecuting Counsel on the case I was sitting in on. So I thought if I could ring him to explain—"

"You don't have to," said Leonie, sounding rather odd. "You'll see him on Sunday. I've invited him to the wedding."

"What? And he's actually *coming*?" said Jess, astonished. "How does Jonah feel about that? Doesn't he mind having his wedding cluttered up with your former lovers?"

"Just one," said Leonie tartly. "Not that Roberto was ever my lover, as you well know. Anyway, I invited the Ravellos, who own the school in Florence. And since it's through them that I met Roberto when I was teaching there it seemed only polite to send him an invitation, too. Mind you, I never dreamed he'd accept."

"Jonah's not put out?"

"He's all for it."

Jess chuckled. "You mean he's very happy for Roberto to look on, grinding his teeth, while you take Jonah Savage for your lawful wedded husband."

"Exactly." Leonie gave a wry little laugh. "Anyway, Jess, do try to smooth things over with Roberto. He's a good friend of mine, remember, and I'm fond of him. Poor man. Women invariably chase after Roberto Forli, not run away from him."

CHAPTER TWO

THE DRIVE home was long and hot, the motorway crowded with holiday traffic, and Jess felt her spirits lift when she saw the twin towers of the older Severn bridge soaring white against the blue sky. She hummed happily in tune with the car radio as she drove across the bridge, then down through Chepstow and on for the remaining miles towards home. She swept in through the gates of Friars Wood at last, gunned the car up the bends of the drive past the Stables where Adam lived, and roared past the main house to park in a crunch of gravel in her usual spot under the trees near the summerhouse at the end of the terrace.

Jess sounded her horn, indignant when no one came rushing out of the house to greet her. Then she jumped out of the car, laughing, as six-year-old Fenella came hurtling up the garden, with a large golden retriever in panting pursuit. Leonie came following behind in more leisurely fashion, attired in shrunken vest top, khaki shorts and battered old sneakers, her bronze hair bundled up in an untidy knot.

"You're a very messy bride, Leo!" called Jess, hugging Fenny as she fended off Marzi, who was frisking around them in a frenzy of excitement. "Where is everyone?"

"Adam's driven Kate to her friend's house to get some books," panted Fenny, gazing, round-eyed, at Jess's hair.

"And Dad's taken Mother to the hairdresser," said Leonie. "Fenny got impatient, waiting for you, so we

18

went off to throw a ball for the dog before he's banished to the farm for the weekend.'' She gave Jess a kiss, then stood back, grinning. ''I love the hair.''

''Do you? Really?'' Jess smiled, relieved. ''I suppose I should have asked your approval first. It's your wedding. But I was tired of my girly bob. I fancied something wilder for a change.''

''Dad will hate it,'' said Leonie, laughing. ''But I love the way it falls over one eye like that. Dead sexy. Come and have tea; you must be hot after the drive. Fen, shall I take Marzi's lead?''

''No, I can do it,'' insisted the little girl.

''You're obviously not bothering with a hairdresser, Leo,'' commented Jess, as they went into the cool house together.

''Nope. I'll wash the flowing locks myself, as usual. I just want to look my normal self.''

''Which is exactly what Jonah requires, of course. Always has,'' added Jess.

Leonie nodded, her dark eyes luminous. ''I know. I'm so lucky.''

''So is Jonah,'' said Jess gruffly. ''Now, where's that tea?''

''Mother said you'd probably skip lunch,'' said Leonie. ''So I made you some salad, and hid some of Mother's little mushroom tarts from Adam.''

''And the coconut cake,'' said Fenny, eyes gleaming as they fastened on the snowy confection under a glass dome. ''Can I have some, Leo? Please?''

''So what's happening tonight?'' said Jess, helping herself to salad.

''Jonah's having dinner with his family in Pennington tonight, at the company flat, and we'll just have a family supper here.'' Leonie cut a slice of cake for Fenny.

"Roberto's staying in Pennington too, with the Ravellos," she said casually. "So you could ring the Chesterton tonight and have a chat with him. If you like."

Jess choked on a crumb of pastry, her dark eyes bright with dismay as they met her sister's. "Must I?"

"I thought you might like to. So that everything's nice and friendly for tomorrow."

Jess's groan was cut off by the arrival of Tom and Frances Dysart, who came hurrying in with Adam and Kate close behind them. Jess sprang up to embrace them all, and there was general laughter when her father blenched theatrically as he noticed her hair. The kitchen filled with exuberant noise as all the Dysarts began talking at once and the dog began barking in excitement in counterpoint. Jess breathed in a deep, happy sigh. She was home.

After supper, which they ate early so that Fenny could share it with them, Adam went for a run down to the farm to hand over the dog, Kate took herself off to revise for her next exam, and Frances and Tom Dysart retired to the study for some peace and quiet while Jess admired wedding presents in Leonie's room.

"I hope Jonah won't be disappointed because I'm not wearing a meringue-type wedding dress and veil and so on," said Leonie, as she repacked a Baccarat crystal vase.

"Of course he won't!" said Jess with scorn. "The dress is perfect. What did you decide on for your hair in the end?"

"I wasn't going to wear anything at first. But when Dad mentioned a jewellery auction he was holding at Dysart's, Jonah bid for the most amazing pair of antique earrings for a wedding present—showers of baroque pearls on tiny gold chains, with a matching brooch. I've

sewn the brooch to a silk barrette to fasten in my hair.''
Leonie took it from its nest of tissue paper and secured
a tress of bronze hair back with it. "What do you think?"

Jess eyed the result with approval. "Perfect! Now put
the earrings on so I can see the full effect."

Leonie rummaged in a drawer, then spun round, her
eyes meeting her sister's in sudden panic. "Jess, they're
not here—Jonah took them into a jeweller in Pennington
to rethread some of the pearls. And it's Saturday night!
What if he's forgotten to collect them?" Sudden tears
poured down her face, astonishing her sister. "I wanted
everything to be so *perfect*—"

"Hey, hey," said Jess, dismayed.
"Don't get upset. Ring him now and ask him."

"I'm not supposed to," sobbed Leonie. "It's unlucky
the night before the wedding!"

"Then I will." Jess passed her sister a bunch of tissues. "Calm down, Leo. This isn't like you!"

"Sorry." Leonie blew her nose, then gave Jess a wa-
tery, radiant smile. "It must be hormones. Can you keep
a secret? I haven't told Mother, in case she's worried
about me tomorrow, in fact I haven't told a soul yet—
not even Jonah—but I found out today for sure that I'm
pregnant."

Jess enveloped her sister in a crushing hug. "And
you're thrilled to bits, obviously. Wonderful! When are
you going to give Jonah the glad news?"

Leonie gave a wicked grin. "I thought tomorrow night,
maybe? *Late* tomorrow night, in the honeymoon suite in
our hotel in Paris. A sort of extra wedding present."

Jess chuckled, then reached for her sister's cellphone.
"Right, then. Let's ring the bridegroom. You want ear-
rings, little mother, you shall have earrings—even if
Jonah has to bribe the jeweller to open up again tonight."

But when Jonah was questioned it seemed he'd collected them the day before and merely forgotten to hand them over. Jess gave him a laughing telling-off, and, when he was all for driving over right away, informed him that Leonie forbade him to set foot in the vicinity of Friars Wood that night.

"You stay put. I'll come and collect them." She made a face at Leonie. "But the Chesterton's a lot nearer for me than your flat, Jonah, so be a love and save me a trip right across town on a Saturday night. Meet me in the bar there to hand them over? Right. Yes, I'll tell her. She's blowing a kiss as we speak. See you in half an hour or so."

"You're going to kill two birds with one stone?" said Leonie, eyes sparkling.

Jess sighed, resigned. "I suppose so. Anything to make your day perfect. So I'll fetch the earrings and make my peace with your ex-lover at the same time, and if ever I get married I'll think of something *really* difficult you can do for me in exchange."

"Anything," said Leonie fervently.

"I'll hold you to that. Jonah sent his love, of course." Jess glanced down at her halter top and ivory linen trousers. "If I just wear the jacket belonging to these will I do?"

"Slap some more make-up on and take those stilt-heeled strappy things to change into when you get there." Leonie grinned and kissed her fingertips. "Before he met me Roberto was very partial to sexy blondes. He'll melt at the sight of you."

And in doing so impart some information about his companion at the pub, maybe. Unknown to Leonie, Jess had secretly jumped at the chance to go out. She felt oddly restless. Wedding fever, she decided, as she neared

the outskirts of the town. Until recently a committed relationship of any kind had held little attraction for her,
except as something far off in the future. But since
Leonie and Jonah's reunion a gradual feeling of discon-
tent had crept up on her, a hankering after something
different from the no-strings, light-hearted arrangements
she'd preferred up to now. But the fleeting encounter with
the dark stranger had jolted her into a sudden longing for
the kind of relationship Leo had with Jonah Savage. Not
that she was likely to achieve that in the foreseeable future, Jess thought irritably as she picked her way across
the gravel of the Chesterton car park.

Relieved to find that Roberto Forli was nowhere in
sight for the moment, Jess made for the bar, and spotted
the tall figure of Jonah Savage talking to the barman.

"Jess," exclaimed Jonah, smiling, his green eyes
alight with welcome as he came forward to give her a
hug. "Sexy haircut!"

"Hi, Jonah. Glad you approve."

"You look positively edible. Shame I'm promised to
Another," he teased. "What can I get you?"

"Just some fruit juice, then I must go straight back."

Jonah gave the order, then leaned close to Jess with a
probing look. "So tell me. How is she?"

"Leo's fine. A bit emotional when she remembered
the earrings, but otherwise in perfectly good nick, I promise you." Jess nursed her sister's secret with hidden glee
as she sipped her orange juice. "How's the groom?"

"Nervous as hell. God knows why," he added, "marrying Leo is all I've ever wanted since the day I met
her."

"I know." Jess drained the glass, feeling edgy, for
once wanting Jonah to make himself scarce so she could

find Roberto and get her apologies over and done with. "Thanks, Jonah. Must dash."

He looked surprised. "Why the rush? My parents hoped you'd come to the flat for a drink. My aunt's with them."

"Sorry, I must get back to Leo. The earrings were a vital necessity before the bride could go happy to bed. Give the three of them my love."

"Jess," said Jonah, frowning. "Are you being straight with me? You'd tell me if something was wrong?"

She laughed indulgently, and reached up to pat his cheek. "Scout's honour, the blushing bride can't wait to sprint down the aisle to you. But we all want an early night tonight. Ditto for you, too—you can stay up late tomorrow."

Jonah grinned. "I seriously doubt that."

"Spare my blushes, please!" she retorted, fluttering her eyelashes.

"Jess, I really appreciate your coming all this way for Leo's sake," said Jonah as they left the bar. "Drive carefully."

"I will." She returned his affectionate hug and kiss with warmth, took the box he gave her, and stowed it carefully in her bag. "Must make a pitstop before I go back. Don't wait. See you tomorrow, brother-in-law."

Jess waved Jonah off, then hurried off to the cloakroom, needing to make a few repairs as self-defence before she went in search of Roberto Forli. But no search was necessary. When she returned to the foyer, lips retouched and hair in place, he was waiting for her. And he had company. Jess's heart gave a great lurch, missed a couple of beats, then resumed with a force which made her feel giddy. She felt hollow, hardly able to breathe,

the blood pounding through her veins at a dizzying rate as she recognised Roberto's companion.

Like Roberto, he wore a pale linen suit, but his hair was thick and dark, and the unforgettable black eyes held hers with the look Jess had persuaded herself she'd imagined. A faint smile played at the corners of his mouth while she gazed at him mutely, for the first time in her life struck completely dumb.

"Will you not introduce us, Roberto?" said the stranger at last, his voice deep-toned and husky, with a hint of accent which accelerated Jess's pulse to an alarming degree.

"I will do so at once, before she runs away again." Roberto, who had been looking from one to the other with narrowed eyes, bowed formally. "Miss Jessamy Dysart, allow me to present my brother, Lorenzo Forli."

Jess murmured an incoherent greeting, and Lorenzi Forli took her hand and raised it to his lips. Jess disengaged her hand swiftly, and forced her attention back to Roberto. She had met him only once before, when she'd played an unwanted third at dinner in this very hotel the night Leonie had informed Roberto Forli she was marrying another man. Then, they had spent a pleasant hour together after Jonah had arrived to take Leonie home, and Roberto, despite the circumstances, had been charm itself to Jess. Tonight, however, his manner was hostile. Nor did Jess blame him for it.

"I'm glad to see you again, Roberto." She held out her hand to him. "How are you?"

He took the hand and bowed, unsmiling. "I am well. And you?"

His chill courtesy made it difficult to embark on the apology she was very conscious that he deserved. "I'm fine. I came on an errand for Leo. My sister,'' she explained, turning to Lorenzo.

"I am acquainted with the beautiful Leonie," he informed her. And Leo had never thought fit to *mention* him?

"How is the bride?" asked Roberto. "Radiant and beautiful as always?"

"Even more so at the moment," Jess informed him.

Roberto's eyes flickered for an instant. "Ah, yes. You know I am invited to the wedding?"

"Leo told me. But I was surprised you'd want to come," she said frankly.

Roberto shrugged his shoulders in the way Jess remembered well from their first meeting. "I was coming to your country at this time for other reasons."

"Is it a business trip?" asked Jess. "I've forgotten what you actually do, I'm afraid."

"We are involved in hotels," said Lorenzo, moving closer. "Miss Dysart, please drink a glass of wine with us."

"I'm sorry, I can't," said Jess with deep regret. "I'm driving, I must get back."

"We saw you with Leonie's *fidanzato*." Roberto informed her, his eyes bright with unexpected malice. "But he left before we could congratulate him."

"I came to collect some earrings from Jonah," said Jess. "Leo's wearing them tomorrow, and he'd forgotten to hand them over."

"Neither your brother nor your father could do this?"

Jess stiffened at his tone. "They wanted to," she said shortly. "But I had my reasons for coming myself."

"Of course you did," said Roberto with open sarcasm.

"Enough, Roberto," commanded Lorenzo. "Rejoin the Ravellos. I will escort Miss Dysart to her car."

Roberto, obviously about to protest, received a quelling look from his brother, and reluctantly acquiesced. He nodded coldly to Jess. "Please give my—my regards to Leonie. *Arrivederci!*" And before she could embark on her apology he strode off.

"There's something I must explain to Roberto," began Jess in a rush, and would have gone after him, but Lorenzo Forli took her arm.

"Leave him.".

"But he's obviously put out with me—I need to apologise for running away that day in London," she said, ignoring the fact that Lorenzo Forli's touch seemed to be scorching through her sleeve.

"Roberto is 'put out' as you say, not only because you ran away at the sight of him, but because he believes that you are in love with Leonie's *fidanzato*," he informed her, as he escorted her outside to the car park.

"*What?*" Jess stared up at him in disbelief.

Lorenzo shrugged. "He is sure that you came here tonight for a few stolen moments before your sister's lover lost you tomorrow."

Jess stopped dead, and wrenched her arm away, her eyes blazing as she glared up into the dark, imperious face. "That's nonsense," she snapped.

"Is it?" he demanded.

"Of course it is!" Jess looked him in the eye. "Look, Signor Forli, I came here tonight purely to please my sister, and to explain to Roberto why it was impossible to speak to him on Thursday—"

"All of which may be true. But I think Roberto can be forgiven for his mistake." Lorenzo Forli's eyes locked with hers. "I also saw you embrace your sister's lover," he informed her.

"So did several other people," she retorted, incensed.

"There was nothing furtive about it. I find Roberto's insinuations deeply offensive. Yours, too, Goodnight, Signor Forli." Jess stormed off blindly towards the car, in such a tearing hurry she caught one tall, slender heel in a patch of loose gravel and fell heavily on her hands and knees.

Lorenzo raced to pull her to her feet. "*Dio*—are you hurt?"

"Only my dignity," she snapped, scarlet to the roots of her hair as she pulled away.

"Take care," he said sternly, and bent to retrieve the impractical sandal. "You could have broken your ankle. Put your hand on my shoulder and give me your foot, *Cenerentola*."

Jess complied unwillingly to let him slide on the offending shoe, then bit her lip when Lorenzo took her by the wrists.

He said something brief in his own tongue as he examined the grazed, bleeding palms. "I will take you inside to cleanse your wounds."

"No, *please*," she protested, in an agony of embarrassment. "I'm fine."

Lorenzo shook his head firmly. "You cannot drive with hands which bleed. How far is it to your home?"

"Twenty miles or so—"

"Then I shall drive you. Leave your car here."

"Certainly not," she snapped, then spread her hands wide suddenly as blood threatened to drip on her jacket.

Lorenzi handed her an immaculate handkerchief. "You cannot control a car in this condition. And if you have an accident it will spoil the day for your sister tomorrow."

Unexpectedly hurt by his thought for Leonie rather

than herself, Jess mopped blood and dirt from her grazed palms without looking at him.

"Come," he said imperiously. "I will ask the receptionist for dressings."

Twenty minutes later Lorenzo Forli was driving his mutinous passenger towards Stavely in the car he'd hired for his stay in Britain. "Your hands are still hurting?"

"A little," she muttered, still hot with embarrassment over the fuss made by the assistant manager, who'd been in the foyer when they went back into the hotel. In short order she'd been presented with plasters and antiseptic, offered brandy, and Roberto had been sent for to explain his brother's proposed absence. Roberto's prompt offer to drive Jess to Stavely himself had been summarily dismissed by his brother, and Jess hustled off with only a brief goodnight.

"Perhaps you should have rung Leonie to explain the delay," said Roberto, as he followed her directions to Stavely.

"No need." She said stiffly. "Leo won't be expecting me just yet."

Jess fixed her eyes on the road, cursing the fate which had actually allowed her a meeting with the charismatic stranger, only to find he believed her capable of lusting after her sister's bridegroom. Jess seethed in silence while Lorenzo Forli drove smoothly along the winding road which hugged the river. The scene was very peaceful in the fading light. Later the traffic would increase as Saturday night revellers made for home, but at this hour the journey would have been restful in almost any other circumstances. With Lorenzo Forli at the wheel, however, expert driver though he was, Jess felt anything but restful, consumed with a volcanic mixture of resentment and excitement which made it hard for her to sit still in her seat.

"Why did you run away from me that day?" Lorenzo asked abruptly, startling her. "I think you knew very well I wished to meet you. Was the prospect so intolerable?"

She raised her chin disdainfully.

"It was nothing to do with you, Signor Forli. It was Roberto I was running away from. Because of Jeremy Lonsdale."

"Roberto's friend, the *avvocato*?" He frowned, baffled. "I do not understand."

With resignation Jess once again explained her dilemma as a juror. Lorenzo heard her out, then gave a long smouldering look before returning his attention to the road.

"This does not explain why you refused to speak to *me* when I rang that night."

Jess shot him another startled look. "That was you?"

"Did your friend not tell you?" His expressive mouth tightened. "She said you had the migraine. Was that true?"

"No," said Jess faintly, shaken by the discovery that Lorenzo had rung her on the strength of one fleeting, chance encounter. She cleared her throat. "Emily said it was Signor Forli, so naturally I assumed it was Roberto." She eyed his aloof profile in appeal. "There was another day to go in court so I still couldn't speak to him."

"And if you had known it was I who wished to speak to you? What then?" he demanded, throwing a challenging glance at her.

Jess thought about it for a while. "I'm not sure," she said at last.

Lorenzo's jaw set. "I see."

"I don't think you do. I mean," added Jess in desperation, "that if I had known who you were I would have—

have liked to speak to you, but I'm still not sure whether I would have been breaking any rules if I had.''

He turned to her with a smile of such blatant triumph it took her breath away. ''Ah! That is better. Much better.''

Jess turned away sharply, so floored by her body's response to the smile she spent the next mile or two in pulling herself together, uncertain whether she was sorry or glad when they reached the turning which led past the church and on up to Friars Wood. In command of herself at last, she gave concise instructions as Lorenzo negotiated the steep bends of the drive, telling him to park in front of the Stables, well away from the main house.

''This is my brother's private retreat,'' Jess told him, wincing as she tried to undo the seat belt.

''*Permesso,*'' said Lorenzo, and leaned across her to release the catch, giving her a close-up of thick black lashes and the type of profile seen on Renaissance sculptures. He turned away to get out of the car, and came round to help her out, taking her elbow very carefully. ''I must not hurt your hands. Are they giving you pain?''

''I'm fine,'' she assured him, which was a lie. In actual fact, she felt so weirdly different from usual she was relieved when her brother emerged from the stable block to inject a note of normality.

''Hi, Jess,'' said Adam, eyeing the stranger with curiosity. ''Where's your car?''

''I left it at the Chesterton,'' she explained, and introduced Lorenzo.

''Nice to meet you,'' said Adam as he shook hands.

''*Piacere,*'' said Lorenzo Forli, smiling. ''Your sister fell and hurt her hands, so I drove her home.''

''How the devil did you manage that, Jess?'' demanded Adam. "Don't tell me," he added, resigned, noticing her feet. "Life-threatening heels, as usual."

"I tripped on some gravel," said Jess tersely. "So you'll have to drive me back to Pennington after the wedding, to collect my car."

"No problem," said Adam cheerfully. "Right then, Jess, bring Lorenzo in to meet the family. I was just going to ask Mother to make me a snack."

"You are most kind," said Lorenzo, after a questioning look at Jess's face. "But I will not intrude on this special night."

When it became clear that Lorenzo had no immediate intention of getting back in the car, Adam threw his sister a bright, knowing look, said goodnight, and loped off in search of food.

"Thank you for driving me home," said Jess at last, desperate to break the silence once Adam had gone.

"It was my pleasure." Lorenzo reached out a hand to touch hers. "Jessamy, I can tell that you are angry."

"How perceptive," she snapped, backing away.

"Why?" he asked, advancing on her.

Her head went up. "I would have thought it was obvious. I object to wild accusations about my morals, especially from strangers," she added coldly.

"Ah!" His eyes held hers relentlessly. "We return to the subject of your sister's *fidanzato*. You insist you do not love him?"

"On the contrary, I do," she assured him airily, gratified when his dark eyes blazed with anger.

"You admit this?" he said incredulously.

"Only to you," she said sweetly. "They say it's easier to confide in strangers. So I can share my little secret, Signor Forli."

"Then Roberto was right," said Lorenzo grimly. "He

suspected this when he first met you. No matter. You will be made to change your mind.'' His smile was so arrogant it raised every hackle Jess possessed. ''I swore this the first moment I saw you.''

''But you didn't know who I was.''

He moved closer. ''Ah, but I did.''

Jess stared at him wildly. ''I don't understand.''

''You lie, Jessamy.'' He held her wrists loosely, one finger on her tell-tale pulse.

''I'm not lying,'' she retorted, and pulled her hands away. ''So explain. Had you seen me somewhere before?''

''Only in my dreams,'' he said, routing her completely. He smiled into her eyes. ''But now I've met you in the alluring flesh, Jessamy Dysart, you will forget all other men in your life from this day on, including your sister's husband. I forbid you to gaze at him with longing tomorrow.''

''*What?* You can't *forbid* me to do anything,'' she said, incensed, desperate to hide the tumult of delight beneath her outrage. ''We're complete strangers. I don't know what you think gives you the right to talk to me like this—''

''Why did you cut off your beautiful hair?'' he interrupted, changing the subject with an abruptness which knocked her off balance again.

Jess blinked. ''Not—not quite all of it.''

''Far too much. Almost you look like a boy, now.''

''Do I really!''

''I said almost!'' Lorenzo gave her a slow smile, his eyes lingering on the place where her jacket hung open. ''You are all contradiction, *tesoro*. You wear trousers and cut off your hair, yet choose feminine shoes and a *camicetta* which clings to your breasts. Why can you not glory in the fact that you are a desirable woman? A woman,'' he added relentlessly, his eyes clashing with hers, ''who must no longer yearn for a man forbidden to her.''

Jess gave an exclamation of pure frustration, afraid that at any moment the entire Dysart clan would come pouring from the house to press the stranger at their gates to whatever hospitality he would accept. ''I don't know why I'm saying this to a man who I'd never met until an hour ago, but I do *not* yearn for Jonah. Nevertheless I've known him for a long time, and it's true that I love him. But like a brother. Or a brother-in-law.'' She looked him in the eye. ''So let's forget all this nonsense, shall we? I'd give you my hand to shake on it, but both of them hurt rather a lot at the moment.''

He nodded, his face relaxing visibly. ''Very well, we shall talk no more of this.'' He smiled down at her. ''And since we cannot shake hands, English style, we shall say goodnight Italian style—like this.'' He took her by the shoulders and planted a kiss on both her flushed cheeks. He raised his head to look down at her, no longer smiling, then with an oddly helpless shrug he bent to kiss her mouth, his hands tightening on her shoulders when the kiss went on for a considerable time. He raised his head at last, his eyes slitted. ''*Mi scusi!* That was unfair,'' he said unevenly.

''Unfair?'' managed Jess.

''To take advantage when you are injured. But I could not resist.'' Lorenzo smiled into her dazed eyes, dropped his hands and stood back. ''Now, since I cannot see you tomorrow, tell me when you return to London.''

''Not for a while.''

He moved nearer. ''Where are you going?''

''I'm not going anywhere. I'm staying here.''

"Then I shall also."

Jess stared at him disbelief.

"You would not like it if I did?" he demanded.

"That's not the point. I don't know you. I just can't believe that you took one look at me that day and decided—"

"That I wanted you," he finished for her.

Jess felt her face flame. "Are you always this direct with women?" she demanded. "Or is this approach commonplace in Florence?"

He shrugged negligently. "I am not concerned with how the other men behave, either in Florence or London. So, Jessamy. When will you be free? Or am I not asking correctly? Should I entreat? Implore? Forgive my lack of English vocabulary. Tell me what to say." He took her by the shoulders again. "Or are *you* saying you have no wish to see me again?"

Jess looked down. "No," she said gruffly. "I'm not saying that."

He put a finger under her chin and smiled down at her in triumph. "Tomorrow, then, after the wedding. You will dine with me."

She shook her head reluctantly. "I can't. I must stay with my family."

"Then Monday."

"Are you staying on that long?"

He bent nearer. "Do you doubt it?" he whispered, and kissed her gently. He raised his head to look into her eyes, muttered something inaudible in his own language and pulled her close, crushing her to him as he kissed her again, no longer gentle, his lips parting hers, his tongue invading, and she responded, shaking, her body curving into his as she answered the demand of the skilful, passionate mouth. For a while Jess was lost to everything other than the engulfing pleasure of Lorenzo Forli's kiss. Then she came back to earth abruptly at the sound of footsteps on the terrace, and pulled away, her face burning.

Breathing a little rapidly Lorenzo looked up to smile in greeting when Leonie came hurrying towards them. "*Buona sera*, Leonie. Please forgive my intrusion."

"Lorenzo, how nice to see you! I couldn't believe it when Adam said you'd driven Jess home. Roberto didn't tell me you were here in England with him." Leonie held up her face and Lorenzo kissed her on both cheeks, sending shamed little pang of jealousy through Jess.

"I joined him only a short time ago. Roberto is here to visit his friend, but he will return to Florence after your wedding. I shall stay awhile, and explore your beautiful countryside." Lorenzo glanced at Jess, sending the colour rushing to her face again. "I was most fortunate, Leonie, to meet your sister tonight."

"Come and meet the rest of my family as well, Lorenzo," she said promptly, but he shook his head.

"I must not keep the bride from her beauty sleep." He smiled at her. "Not, of course, that you need this, Leonie."

"Thank you, kind sir." She exchanged a look with Jess, then gave him a cajoling smile. "Lorenzo, feel free to say no, of course, but since Roberto and Ravellos are coming to my wedding why don't you come too? It's a very informal affair. Just a garden party after the church ceremony tomorrow afternoon. My family would be delighted to welcome you. Wouldn't they, Jess?"

Jess nodded mutely.

Lorenzo's eyes searched her face for a moment, then, apparently satisfied she approved the idea, he smiled at Leonie. "You are very kind. I am most happy to accept.

Until tomorrow. *Buona notte!*'' He gave them both a graceful little bow, got back in the car and drove off down the winding drive.

Leonie put an arm round her sister's shoulders and drew her slowly along the terrace to the house. "Well, well, what have you been up to, sister dear?" she teased gently. "I was sent out to invite Lorenzo in, but I beat a hasty retreat when I saw him kiss you. I waited for a bit, but then he started kissing you again, and it seemed unlikely that he was about to stop for the foreseeable future, so I decided to interrupt. Sorry!"

"I tripped and fell in the Chesterton car park and hurt my hands, so he volunteered to drive me home," said Jess, flushing.

"With the greatest of pleasure, by the look of it. I don't know Lorenzo as well as Roberto, of course—"

"Obviously," retorted Jess. "You never mentioned him."

"I haven't met him often. He doesn't socialise much. In fact, Roberto told me that Lorenzo's marriage changed his brother into something of a recluse."

CHAPTER THREE

"He's married?" Jess stopped dead in her tracks, her world disintegrating about her.

"Renata died about three years ago," said Leonie hastily, bringing Jess back to life. "It was a great shock to Lorenzo. He was married very young, I think. I'm not sure of the details. Actually, I think Roberto's a bit in awe of his older brother, though they see a lot more of each other these days." She gave Jess a sparkling look. "Not that Lorenzo looked much like the grieving widower just now."

"He took me by surprise," muttered Jess as they went in.

Leonie chuckled. "I can see that. You're still in shock!"

Jess shivered a little, and Leonie urged her inside the house.

"Come on I'll make you a hot drink while mother inspects those hands. By the way," she added, "in all the excitement I hope you didn't forget the earrings!"

To the disappointment of Tom Dysart, who rather fancied himself in his father's morning coat and top hat, his daughter had insisted on a very informal wedding. Lounge suits would be worn instead of morning dress for the men. The female guests could splash out on hats. But otherwise she wanted very much the same kind of garden party Jonah's parents had put on in their Hampstead house seven years before, to celebrate their first, ill-fated engagement.

"Only this time," Leonie had declared, "we'll be celebrating a wedding at Friars Wood and nothing will go wrong. The sun will shine, and we'll live happily ever after."

She was right about the weather. The June Sunday was glorious from the start, with just enough breeze to mitigate the heat without endangering the umbrellas shading the tables on the lawn. When the kitchen in the main house was given over to the caterers, quite soon after breakfast, the family moved out into Adam's quarters until it was time to get ready for the main event.

"Rounded up any more guests this morning, Leo?" quizzed Adam, over an early lunch.

"Cheek!" The bride smiled at her mother. "But when I found Lorenzo Forli was here with Roberto it seemed a shame not to ask him. You don't mind, do you, Mother?"

"Not in the least," said Frances placidly. "Numbers don't matter at this kind of thing. And it was very good of him to drive Jess home last night. How on earth did you come to fall like that, darling?"

"Death-defying heels, no doubt," said Tom Dysart. "I hope you're trotting down the aisle in something safer, Jess."

"She has to," said Kate, who measured only an inch or so over five feet. "Today *I'm* in the high heels and Jess is down to something safer to even us out."

"Just make sure *you* don't fall over, then, half-pint," advised her brother.

"As if!" she retorted, giving him a push.

"My shoes don't have any heels at all," said Fenny

with regret, then brightened. "But they've got little yellow rosebuds on the toes."

"Time enough for high heels where you're concerned," said Tom lovingly, then looked at the bride's
plate with disapproval. "For pity's sake eat something
else, Leo. I can't have you fainting as we march up the
aisle."

"No chance," Leonie assured him. "But my dress fits
so perfectly I'm leaving the pigging out bit until the wedding feast."

"You're very quiet, Jess," observed her mother. "Are
your hands still hurting?"

"Not so much." Jess yawned a little. "I'm just a bit
tired after my jury stint, I suppose. Don't worry," she
added, "no one will be looking at me today."

"I wouldn't count on that. How about Lorenzo the
Magnificent?" said Adam, carving off a sliver of ham
with a deft hand. "The man couldn't take his eyes off
you last night."

"Rubbish!" Jess made a face at him. "I'd never even
met Lorenzo Forli until—until last night."

"So you hadn't," said Leonie, smiling slyly. "Just
think how much better you can get to know him today!"

"Talking of today," said Frances, holding out a hand
to Fenny, "we'd better get ready. Mrs Briggs will clear
away before she sets off for the church, so get a move
on everyone. You don't want to be late, Leo."

"Perish the thought," teased Jess, pulling her sister up.
"Jonah admitted to nerves last night, so don't keep the
poor man waiting on tenterhooks at the altar."

"Don't worry—I'll be punctual to the second."

Leonie was true to her word. Long before it was time
to leave the house she was ready, in a slim, unadorned
column of ivory slipper satin. Jess secured the pearl

brooch into her sister's gleaming hair, handed over the earrings, then stood back to admire the effect.

"How do I look?" she asked.

"Absolutely beautiful," said her mother fondly. "And your bridesmaids do you proud, darling."

Jess and Kate were in bias-cut chiffon the creamy yellow shade of Fenny's layers of organdie, the child in such a state of excitement by this time that Kate had to hold her still for Jess to secure a band of rosebuds on her hair.

The photographer arrived a few minutes later. Frances collected a dramatic straw hat decorated with black ostrich feathers, then herded the entire family off to the drawing room for the indoor pictures. The bride requested the first pose alone with Adam, his lanky frame elegant in a new suit with an Italian label, his mop of black curls severely brushed for once for the photograph, before he rushed off to drive down the lane to the church to do his duty as usher.

Tom Dysart, tall as his son, but with greying hair that had once been flaxen fair as Jess's shining locks, wore a magnificent dark suit with grey brocade waistcoat, and looked as proud as a peacock as he posed, first with the radiant bride, then with his wife, and finally with all his women folk around him.

"Like a sultan in his harem," said Jess, laughing.

"And a damn good-looking bunch you are," said her father fondly.

Later, as Jess waited for the bride with Kate and Fenny in the church porch, she found that her posy was shaking a little in her still tender hand.

"Nervous?" whispered Kate.

"Only of this thing falling out of my hair," lied Jess, controlling an urge to peer into the church to see if Lorenzo had arrived. But it was true that her new haircut, unlike Kate's flowing dark curls, had made it difficult to fix the trio of rosebuds attached to a tiny comb. Kate put her posy down on the porch seat, removed the flowers, then anchored them again very firmly into one of the longer gilt strands.

"How's that?"

"Fine, love, thanks. Here we go. The bride's arrived."

Leonie smiled radiantly at her sisters as she glided up the path, then, to the strains of Mendelssohn, began the walk up the aisle on her father's arm towards the bridegroom and best man at the altar.

Jonah's tense face relaxed into a smile of such tenderness at the sight of his bride Jess felt her throat thicken, and dropped her eyes to the flowers she held, as she walked down the aisle. When they came to a halt she turned to make sure Fenny was happy behind her and caught a glimpse of Lorenzo, standing with his brother towards the rear of the church. She met his eyes for a long, charged instant, then turned to take charge of Leonie's flowers as the service began.

When Tom Dysart rejoined his wife after giving his daughter away, Jonah took Leonie's hand and held it in his. After the moving ceremony was over the wedding party moved to the vestry to sign the register, and during the kissing and congratulations Jess slipped out into the church to stand beside Helen Savage's wheelchair for a chat while the organist went through a spectacular repertoire before launching into Wagner for the triumphal exit.

Jess hurried back to the vestry and took the best man's proffered arm, laughing up at Angus Buchanan as he joked about his terror over his speech. As they drew level with the Forli brothers Jess surprised such a dark, smouldering look from Lorenzo she realised he was jealous, and glowed with secret gratification as the wedding party emerged into the sunlight for the inevitable photo session.

Back at Friars Wood, the bride and groom's happiness pervaded the entire scene on the sunlit lawn as they greeted their guests. Everyone milled about with glasses of champagne, laughing and talking, and introducing themselves. First Roberto Forli, then his brother, shook Jonah's hand, and asked smiling permission to kiss the bride. When he reached Jess, to her surprise Roberto saluted her on both cheeks in the same way.

"Lorenzo has told me about your legal problem," he whispered. "I am glad it was not the sight of *my* face which made you run!"

She gave him a wry little smile. "Absolutely not. Jeremy Lonsdale's face did that. Sorry I had to be so rude, Roberto."

"I am sorry also. I should not have said such bad things to you last night." He pulled a face. "Lorenzo was very angry with me when he returned."

"Let's forget it, shall we?" Jess smiled at him warmly, then introduced him to Kate. When Jess turned at last to Lorenzo, he took her hand to draw her closer so that he could kiss both her cheeks.

"You look very beautiful—all woman today," he whispered, and raised a black, quizzical eyebrow. "The best man thought this also, no?"

"Angus is very charming," she said demurely, and gave Lorenzo a smile so radiant his eyes lit up in response. She turned away hastily to welcome Angela and Luigi Ravello. Jess chatted with them for a while, introduced them to other people, then did the rounds of the other guests, all the time finding it a dangerously exciting experience to know that Lorenzo Forli rarely took his eyes from her. This all-out intensity of his was something new in her experience. And gloriously addictive.

Eventually Leonie and Jonah took their places with their respective parents at a table in the centre of the lawn, and Adam and the best man directed guests to the tables grouped casually around the central focus of the bride and groom. Adam wheeled Helen Savage's chair to the nearest table, with Jess and Fenny, and invited the guests from Florence to join them.

Jess made the necessary introductions, and Adam, giving her a surreptitious wink, seated Lorenzo next to her, put Kate between the two brothers, and took his place beside Fenny, who was next to Helen Savage's chair, as she usually was lately, her eyes sparkling as they inspected the tempting canapés and patisserie Leonie had chosen for the meal.

"You obeyed me, Jessamy," said Lorenzo, under cover of the general conversation and laughter.

She eyed him narrowly. "I *obeyed* you?"

"You did not gaze with longing at the bridegroom."

"I should think not," she retorted, looking across at Leonie. "I *told* you how wrong you were about all that. Don't you think the bride looks breathtaking today?" she added.

Lorenzo's eyes followed hers. "Leonie dazzles because she is so happy." He smiled wryly. "Unlike my brother, who was very sad during the ceremony."

Jess glanced at Roberto, who, if he was nursing a broken heart, showed little sign of it as he laughed with Kate. "I'm sure a man like Roberto won't pine unconsoled for long."

"True. Robert leads a very active social life. I," he added very deliberately, "do not." Lorenzo gave her a long, unsmiling look, then noticed Fenny, who was watching them with interest as she munched on a meringue. "Jessamy, will you introduce me to this very elegant little lady?"

"Of course." Jess smiled affectionately at the youngest bridesmaid. "May I present Miss Fenella Dysart? Fen, this gentleman's name is Lorenzo Forli."

"How do you do?" said Fenny politely, as she'd been taught.

"*Piacere,*" said Lorenzo, and got up to kiss her hand.

"Ooh!" Fenny went scarlet with delight. "Did Mummy see, Jess?"

"Run across and ask her, if you like."

Lorenzo laughed as he watched the little girl race across the grass. "She will break hearts, that one." Then his eyes narrowed as he watched Fenny chattering to Jonah. He frowned. "Strange. Now that I see them together the child greatly resembles the bridegroom. How can that be?" Colour ran up suddenly beneath his olive skin. "*Dio*—she is Leonie's child?" he whispered.

"Certainly not!"

Lorenzo turned to look at Jess, his eyes narrowed in sudden, dark suspicion.

"It's not what you think," she whispered hastily, relieved when Angus Buchanan stood up and put an end to conversation by tapping his glass for silence. The circumstances of Fenny's birth were complicated, and not something to discuss with a man who, difficult though it was for her to remember, was nevertheless still very much a stranger.

But Jess could sense Lorenzo's preoccupation as the speeches began. Stranger or not, she found it all too easy to tell he was brooding beneath the surface. Roberto was no happier either, she suspected. His smiling mask slipped a little when Jonah got up to make his speech, and though Roberto applauded afterwards Jess knew, beyond any doubt, that Roberto Forli would have given much to change places with the bridegroom.

But none of that mattered, Jess reminded herself. Leonie and Jonah were deliriously happy, and deserved to be, after the long years of estrangement they'd suffered before coming together again.

"It was all over so quickly," sighed Leonie afterwards, as she changed for the trip to Paris. "I hope everyone had a good time. I certainly did."

"It's been a beautiful day," Jess assured her.

"Everything was perfect, Leo. So get your skates on—it's time to start the happy-ever-after bit."

"Are you ready, darling?" asked Frances Dysart, coming in. "Jonah's getting a bit impatient down there."

Leonie smiled luminously, then collected her bag and her bridal posy. "Right, then. How do I look?"

"Lovely," said her mother, blinking away a sudden tear as she hugged her daughter carefully. "Mustn't crease that heavenly suit before you start."

Jess kissed her sister's glowing cheek. "Have a wonderful time, Mrs Savage."

"I certainly will!"

The guests had all come up from the lawn to the terrace to see the pair off in the car that Kate, Adam and Angus had festooned with balloons and streamers. With Jonah's arm round her, Leonie tossed her posy into the cheering crowd, where it was caught, much to her astonishment, by Kate.

"No good to me," she said, laughing, "I've got exams to do."

There was a round of kisses and embraces, then cheers as the guests waved the newly-weds off down the drive, and soon afterwards people began to drift away.

"Jessamy," said Lorenzo Forli urgently, when Roberto accompanied the Ravellos to take their leave of Tom and Frances Dysart. "I must talk with you. Is there no way that you can dine with me later?"

"I told you last night that just isn't possible," she whispered. "Jonah's family are staying for a meal with us tonight."

His eyes held hers. "But if I return later tonight, would your family spare you for a little while afterwards? I shall ask them myself, if you permit."

Jess nodded. "If you want to."

"You know very well that I do. Let us join your parents." Lorenzo walked with Jess to thank the Dysarts, and stood talking to them for a while, complimenting them on the perfection of the day. When Tom Dysart was called away, Lorenzo turned to Frances. "It was most kind of you to welcome a stranger to your celebration, Signora Dysart."

"It's always a pleasure to welcome my family's friends," she assured him. "I gather you're returning to London tonight?"

He shook his head. "Roberto is travelling there with our good friends the Ravellos, but I shall stay for a while, and explore this beautiful part of your country."

"Then you must come and visit us again," she said promptly.

"You are most kind. I should be delighted." Lorenzo cast a look at Jess before turning again to her mother. "*Signora*, I was just asking your daughter if you would spare her to me for a while later tonight after you have dined."

"I explained that it was difficult, because of the family supper," said Jess hastily.

Frances Dysart, rarely slow on the uptake, smiled on

them both. "That won't take long, darling. Jonah's family will probably leave early, after all the excitement. Kate and Adam are having some friends over at the Stables to party for a while later, as you know, but you won't fancy that, Jess. If Lorenzo's on his own, by all means keep him company for a while."

After Frances left them to see departing guests on their way Lorenzo looked at Jess urgently. "How soon may I come for you? Is there some quiet place nearby where we can drink a glass of wine together and talk for a while?"

Jess nodded. "But I can't leave before eight-thirty at the earliest. Is that too late?"

"Yes," he said promptly. "Much too late. So when I come you will not keep me waiting, *per favore*."

She gave him a wry, considering look. "I'll try. Now I really must help my parents with the remaining wedding guests. And by his body language I think Roberto wants to leave."

"I have no doubt that he does, now Leonie has departed for her honeymoon. Also he must catch the train for London." Lorenzo raised her hand to his lips. "While I must wait with what patience I can until I see you tonight, Jessamy Dysart. I shall count the minutes. *Arrivederci*."

CHAPTER FOUR

ALL evening while Jess helped her mother and Kate serve their guests, she found it difficult to concentrate on the buzz of animated post wedding conversation going on around her. She managed to contribute the odd remark now and then, but otherwise she functioned on auto-pilot, hoping her excitement wasn't too obvious as the time drew nearer to Lorenzo's arrival.

"Everything went like a dream today, Frances," said Flora Savage with satisfaction. "You did a fantastic job. Even the weather was perfect."

"Thank God," said Tom Dysart with feeling. "Otherwise everyone would have been crammed into the house."

"Leo was determined to have the reception at home, rain or shine," said Frances serenely. "Which was just as well. The good hotels in these parts need a year's notice for a June wedding."

James Savage chuckled. "Jonah found it hard enough to wait until *this* June once he got Leo back. I don't blame him, either. Your turn next, Jess?"

"Not me," she assured him.

"Leo's Italian friend was very attentive," said Helen casually. "Have you known him long, Jess?"

"She only met him last night," said Adam, grinning.

"Really, dear?" Flora Savage stared in surprise. "I thought you were old friends."

"They soon will be at this rate," said Kate mischievously. "He's taking her out again tonight."

"You mean you're not gracing the Stables with your presence?" demanded Adam.

"And spoil your fun, children? Not a chance." Jess grinned at him, then noticed that Fenny's eyelids were beginning to droop. "Come on, bridesmaid," she coaxed. "Time for bath and bed. I'll take you up tonight."

"But I was going to read Aunt Helen a story," objected Fenny.

"And so you shall," promised Frances. "When you're in your dressing gown you can read to her in the study for a little while."

Once Jess had delivered a clean and shining Fenny into the care of Helen Savage, she raced back upstairs and rushed through a shower, then rummaged frantically through her wardrobe, rattling hangers and discarding one thing after another in a frenzy. Nothing too clingy or sexy, no trousers tonight, something feminine... Suddenly she laughed at herself. Practically anything she'd packed would do for a trip to a country pub, even with Lorenzo Forli.

Eventually, in sleeveless indigo lawn, the skirt of the dress drifting just above her ankles, Jess went downstairs to find that Fenny had fallen fast asleep on the sofa.

"She's had a very exciting day," whispered Helen. "I didn't like to leave her to call someone."

Jess smiled warmly. "I expect you enjoyed a little lull with her on your own."

"I did, indeed." Helen brushed a gentle hand over the dark, shining hair. "She's such a darling."

Also a little enigma that had very plainly disturbed Lorenzo Forli, Jess reminded herself, and went off to get Adam and Kate. "Will you two take Fenny off to bed, while I wheel Helen back to the others?"

"Of course," said Kate, eyeing her sister. "Wow! You look terrific, Jess."

"*Flat* shoes?" said Adam with awe, eyeing his sister's linen sling-backs.

"Only because they match the dress," she assured him.

"You be careful tonight," he said sternly, only half joking.

"I'm careful every night!"

Jess wheeled Helen back to the others, to face a chorus of approval on her appearance, and much kindly teasing from Jonah's parents. Eventually she was rescued by the doorbell, and hurried back along the hall, her heart thumping at the sight of Lorenzo's tall silhouette through the stained glass panels of the inner door. She threw it open, smiling, feeling a rush of reaction at the sight of him. He was less formal tonight, in a lightweight jacket and a shirt open at the throat. And so much everything she'd ever dreamed of in a man she had to swallow before she could speak.

"Hello," she said at last. "You're very punctual."

Lorenzo said nothing for a moment, surveying her with such undisguised pleasure Jess found it hard to stand still.

"*Bellissima,*" he said at last. "But why do you look so small tonight?"

She held up a foot. "Different shoes. Now you see why I like high heels. Would you care to come in for a while?"

"I would like that very much," he said, rather to her surprise. Jess had assumed he would decline politely and whisk her off the first moment he could, as eager to be alone with her as she was with him.

"Would you like a drink?" she asked as she led him to the drawing room.

"Alas, no." He smiled down at her. "I shall wait until later."

The visitor was given a warm welcome. He sat very much at his ease, adding his own comments about the wedding, stressing how privileged he felt to have been a guest. Then, just when Jess thought they could decently take their leave, Kate and Adam joined them, and it was more than half an hour later before Lorenzo got up to go.

"I trust you did not mind that I spent time with your family?" he asked, as he opened the car door for Jess.

"Not in the least." But she did. Just a little.

"I am in your hands, Jessamy," he told her, sliding behind the wheel. "Where shall we go?"

She gave him directions to a country pub a few miles away. "They have a pretty garden there, so perhaps we can sit outside. It's a beautiful evening."

"Very beautiful," he agreed, giving her a swift, all-encompassing glance.

Lorenzo professed himself delighted with the picturesque inn. He led Jess to a rustic bench in the surprisingly deserted garden, then went off to discover the extent of the wine list. The garden was secluded behind high laurel hedges, the scent of roses heavy in the warm summer night, and Lorenzo looked around in surprise as he rejoined her.

"Inside it is very crowded and very hot. Yet this delightful garden is deserted. Not," he added, sitting beside her, "that I complain! And to my surprise they keep a good prosecco here. I hope this pleases you?"

"Perfect," said Jess, who at this particular moment in time would have accepted tap water with equal pleasure. "I'm surprised they keep such a cosmopolitan cellar. I haven't been here for ages."

After a waitress arrived with bottle and glasses, and

departed, smiling, the richer for a generous tip, Lorenzo filled the glasses, then sat back with a sigh of contentment and took Jess's hand in his.

"Ah, Jessamy, this is so perfect."

She smiled up at him. "First of all, Lorenzo, no one uses my proper name. I'm always known as Jess."

He shook his head. "Not to me, *cara*. I shall always call you Jessamy."

Jess saw no point in contradicting him and looked down at their clasped hands, wondering if his reaction to the contact was anything like her own. Which brought her to something she was desperately curious to know. "Lorenzo, can I ask you something?"

"Anything you wish."

"When you first saw me in the pub in London, you seemed to recognise me. How? And no more moonshine about dreams, please."

He laughed. "*Va bene*, I confess. I had seen you in a photograph. When she lived in Firenze Leonie suffered much from *la nostalgia*, I think, and one day she showed me some pictures of your home. You were sitting on the lawn with a large dog, the sun shining on your hair, and those big dark eyes smiling into mine."

"So the first time you saw me," said Jess, feeling a little deflated, "you already knew I was Leo's sister." Not love at first sight after all. Just recognition from a photograph.

Lorenzo smoothed a slim finger over the back of her hand. "It would not have mattered who you were. After only one glimpse of your face in the photograph I could not rest until I met you. When Roberto was invited to Leonie's wedding fate played into my hands. I decided to join him and contrive to meet her sister." He shook his head in wonder. "I could not believe my good fortune when I saw you walk into that London bar. But you ran away before Roberto could introduce us.''

''I've told you why.'' She raised her head and met a look in his eyes which made her pulse race.

''Jessamy,'' he whispered, bending closer. ''You are so charming, so appealing, it amazes me that you have no man in your life.''

''Would you have gone away without meeting me if I had?''

''No.'' He shrugged negligently. ''I knew you had no husband. A lesser relationship would not have deterred me.''

She shook her head, smiling. ''In other words you always get your own way!''

''No.'' His face darkened. ''Not always.''

Jess shivered, cursing herself for her habit of speaking without thinking first.

''You are cold?'' he said swiftly. ''You wish to go inside?''

''No, please.'' Jess looked at him squarely. ''Look, Lorenzo, before you say anything else, I know you were married. Leo told me.''

He nodded, resigned. ''Of course. It is no secret.''

''It must be terrible to lose someone you love,'' she said with sympathy, and shivered again.

''You *are* cold,'' he accused.

''Only a little. But I want to stay here.'' Where they were alone.

''Then there is no alternative.'' Lorenzo put an arm round her and drew her close, and Jess leaned against him as naturally as though they'd sat together like this a hundred times before.

''Will you tell me about your wife?'' she said gently.

He was silent for a time. ''Since she died,'' he said at

last, choosing his words with care, "I have never talked of Renata. But perhaps now it is time that I do. So that there is truth between us, Jessamy."

She tensed, wondering what he meant, and he put a finger under her chin and turned her face up to him.

"You fear what I have to say?"

"No." Jess held his eyes steadily. "I'm a fan of the truth myself."

He nodded in approval, and drew her closer. "First you must know that though I was very fond of Renata, ours was not a love match. Our families were close, and we were brought up almost as brother and sister. I always knew that I was expected to marry her. It was our parents' dearest wish."

"You mean it was an arranged marriage?"

"I was not forced into it. And I believed Renata loved me. I had no choice." He shrugged. "You do not approve of arranged marriages?"

"Absolutely not. If ever I do have a husband I expect to choose him myself!"

His arm tightened. "It is a miracle you are not married already."

"No miracle." She smiled a little. "It's Jonah's fault, really."

Lorenzo stiffened, his eyes suddenly blazing into hers. "What are you saying?"

"Not what you think," she said hastily. "I meant that Jonah met Leo when I was still in school. After seeing them together, so much in love, the way they could hardly bear to be apart for a second, I was determined never to settle for anything less."

He let out an explosive breath. "You take delight in tormenting me."

She leaned closer. "I didn't mean to."

"No?" He raised a quizzical eyebrow, then grew thoughtful. "Jessamy," he said slowly, "are you saying you have never been in love?"

"Yes." She gave him a wry little smile. "I thought I'd come close to it once or twice. But I was mistaken. Both times the gentleman in question went off in a huff, never to return."

"A huff? What is that?"

"Rage, I suppose."

"This I can understand! To believe he is loved and then find he is not—" Lorenzo made a chopping motion with his hand. "This would enrage any man."

"Exactly. So after that I made a conscious decision to wait until I find a death-do-us part kind of thing…" She breathed in sharply in dismay. "Lorenzo—I'm so sorry!"

He shook his head. "Do not apologise, *cara*. I would not have you guard your tongue over every word."

"I thought of you during the ceremony today, wondering if it made you sad."

He raised her hand to his lips, pressing a kiss on it. "It was Roberto who was sad, not I, Jessamy. It is a long time since my own wedding. Sometimes I can almost believe it happened to some other man, not I."

"How old were you?"

"I was twenty-one, Renata was a year younger."

"As young as that!" She hesitated. "Would it be painful to describe her to me?"

Lorenzo was quiet for a while, as though picturing his dead wife in his mind. "Renata had long black hair," he began at last, "and pale blue eyes inherited from some northern ancestor. She was much too thin, with an intensity which seemed to hint at a passionate nature. We were married with all the usual ceremony in a church full of lilies. And later that night," he added with sudden bitterness, "my bride became hysterical with fear when I tried to consummate our marriage."

Jess stared at him in horror. "But you said she loved you."

"She did. In her way. But this was not as a wife loves a husband." Lorenzo stared unseeingly into the scented twilight. "Renata had no wish to be wife to any man. That night, once she was sure I would not force her, she confessed she had always longed to enter a convent. Her parents forbade this." He shrugged. "They were elderly, Renata was their only child, and a loving, obedient daughter, so she surrendered to their wishes. Which was disaster for both of us."

"That's so sad," said Jess huskily. She hesitated. "Did—did things ever improve?"

"If you talk of a normal married relationship, no." Lorenzo shrugged. "Do not mistake me, Jessamy. I was fond of Renata. I would have done my best to make her happy and give her children. But all hope of that died on our wedding night, killed by her frenzied rejection. We were both trapped by our marriage vows. So. We agreed to act out our pathetic little *commedia*, and keep the true state of our marriage secret. When my unsuspecting parents died, years later, their only regret was the lack of grandchildren."

There was a sudden eruption of people from the hotel, accompanied by a burst of laughter as they made for the car park. Jess stirred instinctively, but Lorenzo held her fast.

"Did Roberto know the truth?" she asked, settling back against him.

Lorenzo shrugged. "He knew that my marriage was not—not perfect. But for many reasons I have never told him the truth."

Jess stared down at their clasped hands. "It must have been so hard for a man like you," she said with difficulty.

"A man like me?"

"Lorenzo, you know very well what I mean. You're a healthy, virile male. A marriage like yours must have been hell for you."

"In that way it was." He rubbed his cheek over her hair. "During my marriage my pride prevented me from seeking consolation elsewhere, you understand. But afterwards," he added carefully, "when certain privileges were offered I have not refused."

"You mean that if a woman gives out certain signals you don't fight her off!" teased Jess, in an effort to lighten the atmosphere.

He laughed a little. "I am expressing myself in a foreign language, remember."

"And very well you do it," she assured him.

"Good. Because there must be no misunderstandings between us, Jessamy. Now or in the future."

Jess peered up at him uncertainly in the gathering dusk, her heart racing at his mention of the future.

"What is it, *carissima*?" he asked softly.

She tried to laugh, make light of it. "Now and then I get this little attack of unreality."

"Make no mistake," he said fiercely. "This *is* reality, Jessamy. Since my marriage I have never felt truly alive until now."

Jess trembled, and he put his other arm round her.

"I should not keep you out here like this."

"I'm not cold," she blurted. "It's just the effect you have on me."

Lorenzo was utterly still for an instant, then he crushed her close and kissed her with a tender ferocity which sent shock waves through her entire body. "Do you know what it means to me to hear you say such things, *amore*?'' he demanded raggedly, raising his head at last. ''Forgive me, Jessamy, this is a public place—''

''I don't care,'' she said recklessly, and kissed him back.

Lorenzo responded without reserve, his body shaking with the intensity of the feelings she'd aroused, and Jess exulted, proud of her power. Then he gave a groan like a man in pain and dropped his arms. ''We must go,'' he panted. ''Now!''

Jess took the hand he held out to her and stood up, then saw the untouched glasses of wine on the table, the half-full bottle beside them. ''Lorenzo! What a terrible waste. I forgot all about the wine.''

''And why did you forget?'' he demanded, his fingers tightening on hers.

''I was too wrapped up in you,'' she said gruffly.

Lorenzo said something unintelligible in his own tongue and pulled her into his arms to kiss her at such length they were both speechless when he let her go. Without another word he took her by the hand and led her to the car, neither of them saying another word during the journey to Stavely. Inside the car the tension between them mounted to such heights Jess could hardly breathe by the time Lorenzo turned up the lane which led to Friars Wood. Suddenly he stood on the brakes, and she saw a cat streak across the lane, a blur of pale fur in the headlights.

''*Scusa*,'' said Lorenzo through his teeth. He drove on at a snail's pace, then stopped the car under a tree which shaded a spot wide enough to park. He wrenched his seat belt free, then reached over to release Jess and pulled her into his arms like a man at the end of his tether. He kissed her with a barely suppressed frenzy she responded to equally fiercely, and it was a long time before he raised his head to gaze down into her dazed, heavy eyes.

"Forgive me, *amore*," he said, in a tone which melted her very bones.

"For what?"

"For making love to you in a car, like some callow Romeo." His wide, sensuous mouth curved in self-mockery. "You give me back my youth, Jessamy. I have no defence against my desire for you."

"How old *are* you?" she demanded.

"Thirty-four."

"I thought you were older than that."

He drew back, eyeing her ruefully. "I look so ancient?"

"Not ancient—mature!" She pulled his head down to hers and kissed him hard, then rubbed her cheek against his.

He shrugged wryly. "I learned maturity very early."

Jess ached with sympathy. "Which is why you seem so assured, I suppose, so much in control."

"In control!" He gave a breathless laugh. "With you I am twenty again, with no control at all." He trailed his lips over her eyelids and down her cheeks, pressing light, tantalising kisses which left Jess wanting more. She wound her arms round his neck, kissing him with a passion she'd never known she was capable of, and reaped a reward which transcended anything she'd ever imagined.

It was a long time before Lorenzo let her go. "Tomorrow," he panted at last. "How soon can we meet?"

"How early do you want me—?" She bit her lip as he laughed deep in his throat.

"I want you now, Jessamy. So much I ache with longing. You know this." He kissed her nose and settled her back in her seat, reaching over to do up the seat belt. When it was fastened he stayed arched over her, looking down into her eyes. "If I come early in the morning, would your family find this strange?"

Jess gave him a demure little smile. "How early?"

"Ten?"

"Done. What do you want to do?"

"I have come to explore your beautiful countryside, so you shall be my guide. We shall spend the day together." He stretched out a hand to the ignition key, but Jess put a hand on his arm.

"Don't start the car yet. Before we get back there's something I forgot to tell you."

"What is it?" he demanded, his voice harsh with sudden tension.

"I meant to bring the subject up earlier," said Jess ruefully, "but it—it went out of my head."

"What is this subject?" he asked very quietly.

"This afternoon, at the reception, you were a bit remote after you saw Fenny with Jonah."

Lorenzo let out a deep breath, and settled back in his seat.

Jess could tell he was relieved. What had he expected her to say?

"I was a jealous fool," he said with remorse. "I soon realised that the child could not be yours. Forgive me, Jessamy, I had no right to intrude on something so personal to your family."

"I knew you were coming to all the wrong conclusions, so after you left this afternoon I asked permission to tell you Fen's history." Jess sighed. "Poor unsuspecting mite—she's caused enough trouble already."

"Trouble?" queried Lorenzo, frowning. "In what way?"

"Leo broke her engagement to Jonah all those years ago because she thought he was the unborn Fenny's father."

"Dio!" he said, startled.

"My father's sister Rachel was in her early forties, working as personal assistant to Jonah's father, when she met the love of her life at last. Leo overheard Rachel telling Jonah she was pregnant, begging him never to reveal the truth to her. She assumed he was the father, of course, flew back to Italy, and broke up with Jonah, refusing to give any explanation. And because Rachel was Dad's much-loved sister Leo couldn't tell my parents why, either."

Lorenzo shook his head in amazement. "I confess I am curious." He eyed her questioningly. "Who *is* the little one's father?"

"Richard Savage, Jonah's uncle. You met Richard's wife, Helen, today. She was the one Rachel was desperate not to hurt, not Leo." Jess sighed. "Richard looked a lot like Jonah, especially the hazel eyes he handed down to Fenny."

Lorenzo smoothed a caressing hand down her cheek. "Will you forgive me for my wild imaginings, Jessamy?"

She smiled wryly. "Wild imaginings are right. Jonah never had eyes for anyone other than Leo from the first moment they met."

"This I can believe!"

"She's beautiful, isn't she?"

"True." He lifted her hand to her mouth. "But you mistake me. I also know how one look is enough to recognise one's fate."

Jess looked away, her heart thumping, and went on with her story. "Helen's brain tumour resulted in paralysis, which ended the physical side of her marriage, but Richard never looked at another woman until he fell madly in love with Rachel. He was killed in a car accident before she could tell him she was pregnant. Rachel was so heartbroken she died giving birth to Fenny.''

Lorenzo flinched. *''Che tragedia!''* he said harshly. ''Does the little one know this?''

''No. Not yet. My parents intend telling her as soon as she's old enough to understand.''

''And for one crazy moment I suspected you, Jessamy!'' Lorenzo threw out his hands in appeal. ''Forgive me, *tesoro.* I have not experienced jealousy before. It seems it deprives a man of his wits.''

Jess smiled at him, beginning to think she could forgive this man anything. ''It's late. Time I was home.''

''You are right. I have no wish to anger your charming parents. It is most necessary that they approve of me.''

''Why?''

Lorenzo smiled into her eyes. ''I think you know the answer very well, Jessamy Dysart.''

When they arrived at Friars Wood, to the sound of music thumping from the Stables, Jess exclaimed in surprise when Adam came hurtling from the party to intercept them.

''Sorry to interrupt,'' he panted.

''What's wrong?'' demanded Jess in alarm. ''Not Leo—?''

''No, it's your pal Emily. She rang from Florence about an hour ago. In a right old state, apparently. Mother's hoping you can help out, Lorenzo.''

CHAPTER FIVE

TOM DYSART opened the door to them in obvious relief. "Come in, come in, Lorenzo. Are we glad to see you. If we'd known where you were, Jess, we'd have contacted you before."

"What on earth's happened, Dad?" said Jess anxiously. "Is it something to do with Emily's sister?"

"No, darling," said Frances. "Celia never made it after all. The children went down with chicken pox."

Jess eyed her in consternation. "Emily's on her *own*? Don't say she's had an accident!"

"No, no, nothing like that. She's feeling very unwell, poor dear."

"In what way can I help, *signora*?" asked Lorenzo swiftly.

Frances smiled at him gratefully and handed him a card with a number. "Would you ring the hotel and find out what help we can arrange for Emily?"

"I'd have had a shot at it myself if it had been France," said Tom apologetically. "I could have managed in French—just. But not Italian."

"First, I think, Jessamy must speak with her friend and discover the problem." Lorenzo keyed in the number, waited for a while, then conducted a quick-fire exchange in Italian and handed the receiver to Jess. "They are putting you through to your friend's room."

Jess waited a moment, then heard her friend's hoarse, fearful response.

"Hi, Em," she said quickly. "It's me, Jess. What's the matter, love?"

"*Jess*! Oh, Jess, thank heavens. I'm so glad to hear your voice." Emily broke off to cough. "Sorry to make a fuss like this," she gasped, "but I feel ghastly. I'm so hot, and I've got this terrible pain."

Jess blenched. "Have you rung the desk to ask for a doctor?" she demanded.

"It's the middle of the night. I didn't like to—" Emily broke off into painful coughing again, and dissolved into tears.

"All right, love, all right," soothed Jess. "Don't cry, Em. Hang in there. Listen, I'll get the first flight I can, I promise, so you won't be on your own for long. I'll be in Florence before you know it. In the meantime Lorenzo will organise things from this end, and get a doctor to see you right away."

"Who's Lorenzo?" croaked her friend.

"I'll explain later. Must ring off now, to let him get on with it."

When Jess explained Emily's symptoms Lorenzo took the phone from her swiftly. "I shall arrange for a doctor at once."

Jess shuddered at the thought of her friend alone and ill in a strange country. But as she listened to Lorenzo's flow of musical, expressive Italian she had to fight down a guilty pang of disappointment. There would be no idyll with Lorenzo after all.

Lorenzo finally gave the Dysart telephone number, reiterated his thanks, then rang off and turned to the others. "I was fortunate to get through to my own doctor, Bruno Tosti. He is a personal friend, and will go immediately to the hotel." He smiled reassuringly at Jess. "Do not worry. Bruno speaks English. Your friend is in good hands. The hotel will report here to me on his diagnosis.''

''Wonderful! Thank you so much, Lorenzo,'' said Frances in relief. ''Will they really ring back from the hotel at this time of night?''

''But of course, *signora*.'' He smiled a little. ''The hotel is part of the group run by my family.''

''Ah! Splendid,'' said Tom Dysart, relieved. ''That's a load off my mind.''

''While you're waiting I'll make some coffee and a few sandwiches,'' said Frances, looking happier. ''You hardly ate a thing at dinner tonight, Jess. Come and help me, Tom.''

Jess took Lorenzo into the comfortably shabby study, smiling at him with heartfelt gratitude. ''I don't know how to thank you, Lorenzo—''

''I know a very good way,'' he said promptly, and took her in his arms to kiss her. ''This is all I need,'' he muttered against her mouth. He raised his head, his dark eyes gleaming as they gazed down into hers. ''I would do anything in the world for you, Jessamy. Never doubt this.''

In her dealings with the opposite sex shyness had never been a problem for Jess. But Lorenzo's words deprived her of speech.

''You said you like the truth,'' he reminded her.

''I know.'' She smiled shakily. ''It's my unreality problem again.''

Lorenzo smiled indulgently. ''I know ways to cure this, but not here, not now.'' He frowned. ''Your mother said you did not eat tonight. Why?''

''I was too excited,'' she admitted, flushing.

''Jessamy!'' He made an instinctive move towards her,

then halted, smiling ruefully, as he heard her parents returning.

"If you don't mind," said Tom Dysart, setting a tray down, "we'll turn in now. It's been quite a day, one way and another. Kate's in bed, by the way, Jess, and the party should break up soon. But we insist you stay the night, Lorenzo."

"Absolutely," said Frances firmly. "We can't have you driving back to Pennington in the small hours. Adam's old room is always ready for visitors."

Lorenzo smiled with gratitude. "This is most kind. I thank you both."

"The least we can do," Tom assured him. "Right, then, we'll leave you to it. Jess will show you where to sleep. And thanks again, Lorenzo. You've been a great help."

"*Prego*. I am only too glad."

When the goodnights had been said, and they were alone again Lorenzo took Jess by the hand and sat down with her on the sofa, smiling a little. "I am very sorry that your friend is ill, *carissima*, but secretly I cannot help feeling grateful to her. Otherwise we should not be sitting here alone together at this time of night."

"True." Jess sighed guiltily. "Poor Emily. I just hope it's nothing serious."

"Bruno will do everything necessary, I promise," Lorenzo assured her. "Now. You must eat."

"But—"

"I insist." He wagged a reproving finger at her. "Or I shall feed you, mouthful by mouthful—" Sudden heat flared in his eyes, and he blinked and turned away. "*Dio*, it seems I cannot be trusted. I must sit somewhere else."

"No. Please." Jess caught his hand. "Let's have some

coffee. Or would you prefer wine, since we never got round to the prosecco?''

''*Grazie*, no,'' he said firmly, ''Just to be close to you like this intoxicates me enough!''

''Then we'll both be sensible and drink coffee.'' Jess eyed him cajolingly. ''Please eat a sandwich, Lorenzo, or Mother will be offended.''

''I repeat, Jessamy,'' he said huskily. ''For you I would do anything.''

A statement which made it very hard for Jess to apply herself to a sandwich she didn't want. Nothing, short of measles and the odd bout of flu, had ever deprived her of her appetite in her entire life. This was new. She finished her coffee in sudden dejection.

''What is it, Jessamy?'' he said quickly.

''We won't have our day together after all. I must get to Florence as soon as I possibly can.'' She got up to put cups and plates on the tray.

''There will be other days.'' Lorenzo drew her down beside him. He put an arm round her and drew her close, his cheek on her hair. For a moment or two they sat quietly, savouring each other's nearness, but at last Lorenzo gave a deep sigh and turned her face up to his. ''It is no use, amore, I cannot hold you without wanting to kiss and caress—''

The phone cut off the rest of his words, and with a muffled oath Lorenzo seized it from the table beside him and barked his name. He listened intently for some time, asked some questions, then spoke afterwards at length, and put the phone down.

''What did they say?'' demanded Jess.

''Your friend is suffering from *la pleurite*, I think you call this pleurisy.''

Jess eyed him in consternation, then made for the

bookshelves along the wall and took down a medical dictionary to leaf quickly through the pages. "Inflammation of the pleura," she reported. "The thin membrane round the lungs. Pain caused by deep breaths or coughing. What a thing to happen on holiday alone! Emily can't speak a word of Italian. Did they mention treatment?"

"She has been given antibiotics and something to make her sleep. Bruno is arranging for a nurse to come immediately, and suggests you ring your friend in the morning." Lorenzo smiled caressingly. "There, Jessamy. Do you feel better now?"

"Much better!" She leaned over the arm of the sofa to kiss him, and he pulled her down beside him, returning the kiss with a hunger she responded to without reserve. After the anxiety of the past hour her relief swiftly changed to desire as she felt Lorenzo's heart thudding through the thin material of her dress. The rhythm accelerated when her lips closed in welcome over his seeking tongue, but at last he held her away a little, his eyes dilating as they dropped to her turbulent breasts. With a smothered groan he caressed the pointing nipples through their filmy covering, and kissed her parted mouth with a passion she responded to in total abandon.

At last Lorenzo drew away, his hands cupping her flushed face. "You set me ablaze, Jessamy," he said unevenly. "But you must believe that it was not for this that I travelled to England to see you."

"What did you expect, then?"

"To meet you, and to get to know you at least a little. But even in my dreams I never aspired to such delight as this—nor such torment!"

"Neither did I," she said with feeling. "It's all so new it's frightening."

His eyes narrowed in incredulous question.

She smiled a little. "Whatever this is that happens between us has never happened for me before."

"*Carissima*!" Lorenzo seized her in his arms and kissed her again, but this time with such protective tenderness Jess relaxed against him like a tired child, suddenly exhausted. "Come," he said, and stood up, holding out his hand. "You must sleep." He smiled at her. "Is your brother's room close to yours?"

"Next door," she said, turning out lights.

Lorenzo sighed heavily. "Then I will probably not sleep at all."

Jess was up early the following morning, but Lorenzo was before her. She went into the kitchen to find him eating breakfast with her family, looking very much at home.

"*Buon giorno*!" he said, jumping up to pull out a chair. "How are you this morning, Jessamy?"

"Tired." She flushed as she met interested looks on all sides.

"Lorenzo told us about Emily's pleurisy, Jess," said Kate. "How awful for her! Mother says you're going out to join her as soon as you can."

"You'd better get on the phone straight after breakfast," said her father. "Could be tricky getting a flight this time of year."

"Have no fear, Signor Dysart, I shall arrange all that," said Lorenzo at once, and passed a jug of orange juice to Jess. "Drink a little of this, *cara*. It will revive you."

Jess sipped obediently, feeling her colour deepen under Kate's fascinated gaze.

"Lorenzo lives in Italy, Jess," announced Fenny, impressed. "Just like Leo did."

"I know, poppet."

"Is that a long way?"

"Two hours only in an aeroplane," Lorenzo informed her, smiling.

"Is your house big?"

"Big enough, *piccola*. You must come and visit me there one day."

"Yes, please!" Fenny nodded with enthusiasm. "Kate and Adam, too?"

"Of course," he assured her gravely.

"Honestly, Fen," said Kate, embarrassed. "Come *on*, we'll be late. Are you ready, Dad?"

Tom Dysart downed the last of his coffee and stood up. Lorenzo followed suit to shake hands. Thanks were exchanged and there was a round of hugs and kisses—Fenny not at all pleased when she heard Jess might not be there when she got back from school.

"Fenny thinks we should all live here all the time, with no going away to college and jobs and so on," explained Frances, after her husband had taken his daughters off.

"And who can blame her?" said Lorenzo. "This is a beautiful part of the world."

"So is yours," said Jess.

"You have eaten nothing, *cara*," he accused.

"Come on, Jess, this isn't like you," said her mother. "Have some toast, at least."

"And while you eat your breakfast, *signora*, with your permission I shall make use of the telephone," said Lorenzo.

"Of course. Use the one in the study." When he'd gone Frances looked at her daughter in wry amusement as she passed the toast. "You're very quiet."

"Just tired," said Jess, with a yawn.

"Were you late getting to bed?"

"Very. It took ages for Lorenzo to get things sorted out."

"He told us. Poor Emily. What a thing to happen alone on holiday!"

"Do you think I should ring her mother?" asked Jess, frowning.

Frances thought for a moment. "I should wait until you see Emily. Let her decide. If Mrs Shaw is involved with the chicken pox she has more than enough to cope with already, poor dear."

Breakfast had been cleared away, and Frances had gone over to the Stables to rouse Adam by the time Lorenzo returned to the kitchen to report.

"It took some time to get through this morning, Jessamy. But eventually I spoke to the nurse, who said your friend is improving."

"Thank heavens for that," said Jess in relief. "I'll ring through in a minute and speak to Emily myself."

"She is now sleeping, therefore I told the nurse you would be with your friend later today," he informed her.

"Have you arranged a flight, then?" she said, surprised.

Lorenzo smiled. "But of course. Your plane leaves Heathrow this afternoon. Do you need much time to pack, *cara*?"

"No, I did that last night." Jess smiled a little. "One way and another I just couldn't get to sleep. I should imagine you did better after all that telephoning."

Lorenzo shook his head, and touched a finger to the curve of her bottom lip. "How could I sleep? When you were so close, but not close enough!" He frowned suddenly. "But I regret that I have added much to your father's phone bill."

"Don't offer to pay! Not if you want to come here again—" She halted, flushing, and he smiled indulgently.

"You know very well that I do."

"I'm sure they'll be delighted to see you any time during your stay," said Jess forlornly.

He stared at her in amazement. "But I am not staying, Jessamy. What possible reason could I have for remaining here if you are in Firenze? I travel with you."

Travel with Lorenzo Forli was very different from anything Jess had experienced before. After Lorenzo's farewells she had submitted to Adam's bear hug, reminded him to fetch her car, then kissed her mother goodbye and rushed out to the car with Lorenzo to drive to Pennington for his luggage before going on to Heathrow to catch the plane.

In a remarkably short time, it seemed to Jess, they were in the sky, bound for Italy. Air travel was normally an evil she endured as the quickest way to get from one point to another. But travelling first class with Lorenzo had a magic carpet quality about it. Sitting close to him, her hand in his, Jess found herself enjoying the entire process for the first time, so absorbed in his company she had no attention to spare for the food they were served.

"It is my ambition to see you eat something one day," he observed, resigned, after the trays were removed.

"Normally I eat like a horse," she assured him. "The last few days have been a bit hectic, that's all, with the wedding straight on top of my jury duty, and now this with poor Emily."

"Try not to worry—you will soon be with her. Instead tell me more about your jury service. Did you enjoy this?" he asked, reaching for her hand again.

"Not enjoy, exactly. But I'm glad, now, that I did it."

Lorenzo frowned. "It occurs to me, regrettably late, Jessamy, that I have told you many things I have confided to no one. Yet I have asked nothing about the work you do. Forgive me, *cara*. Are you a teacher, like Leonie?"

Jess pulled a face. "No, not my scene at all. I'm a booker in a model agency."

"A booker?" he said, puzzled. "What is this?"

"I book the models for a London agency. I work with the chief scout, help with new faces, deal with their anxious parents and so on. But actually I prefer my work with the older models, who tend to be more relaxed than the young ones."

Lorenzo looked surprised. "But I thought models must always be very young, also very thin."

"They are, mostly. But modelling isn't just catwalks and glossy magazines. It involves a lot of advertising and catalogue work, which is where the more mature ladies come into their own."

"Have you done modelling yourself, Jessamy?"

She laughed. "No way. Not my sort of thing. Besides, I've never had the right shape for the catwalk, and I'm not old enough yet to promote anti-wrinkle cream."

"Your skin is flawless, and I think your shape is perfect," he whispered, and leaned closer. "I would like very much to kiss you right now, *carissima*, but I think you would not like that."

"Oh, yes, I would," she said in his ear. "But I'd rather be kissed in private."

"I will remind you of that later!"

She suppressed a shiver at the mere thought of it, and changed the subject. "You haven't told me how you managed to get a flight so easily."

"I told Roberto to transfer his reservation to you. He

will stay on with his friend the *avvocato* until he can reserve another."

"Goodness," said Jess, impressed. "Does Roberto always jump when you tell him to?"

"Always," Lorenzo assured her.

"But what about *your* ticket?"

He smiled smugly. "I already had one."

"Oh. I see." She smiled, enlightened. "You were all prepared to fly home with Roberto if I'd been a disappointment!"

"You are wrong, *tesoro*. I knew in my heart that you would be all I had ever hoped for." He shrugged. "However, it was possible that you might not have liked *me*."

"I find that hard to imagine," she said involuntarily, and caught her breath as she saw his eyes dilate.

"If you do not wish me to kiss you here and now," he said through his teeth, "it is best you do not say such things."

"It's the truth, Lorenzo."

He raised her hand to his lips and pressed a kiss into the palm. "I begin to suffer from this unreality of yours. When I think of my past loneliness—" He breathed in deeply, and smiled with such tenderness Jess felt her throat thicken. "You know that when I first saw your face in the photograph I vowed I would do everything in my power to meet you. But I did not recognise you then."

She eyed him questioningly. "You knew who I was."

"True. " He frowned in concentration. "How I wish you spoke my language, Jessamy, so that I could make my meaning clear. What I try to say is now I have met you at last, I know *what* you are."

"What I am?" repeated Jess, eyes narrowed.

He nodded triumphantly. "You are my reward!"

CHAPTER SIX

WHEN Jess arrived in the hotel room her heart contracted at the first glimpse of her friend. The brown glossy hair Emily took such care of hung lank around her face, and streaks of hectic colour along her cheekbones contrasted alarmingly with her pallor.

"*Jess!* Oh, Jess—you came!" Emily's sunken grey eyes lit up with pure relief, then brimmed over with tears when her friend gave her a careful hug.

"My word, Em," Jess teased, sitting on the edge of the bed. "If you're improving I dread to think what you looked like before!"

Emily accepted the wad of tissues a motherly little nurse handed her, and mopped herself up. "Think Bride of Frankenstein," she said hoarsely, and sniffed hard, doing her best to smile. "I should have rung my mother, not you, Jess, I know, but I hated the thought of scaring her silly until I knew what was wrong with me. Sorry to be such a nuisance."

"Rubbish," said Jess fiercely, needing to sniff a little herself. "Due to Lorenzo I was the best one to contact, anyway." She stood up and held out her hand to the hovering nurse. "Hello. I'm Jess Dysart. Thank you so much for looking after my friend."

"*Piacere,*" said the woman, smiling cheerfully. "I am glad to be of service."

"Sorry!" said Emily in remorse. "I'm forgetting my manners. Jess, this is Anna, my angel of mercy. She's been so kind."

''I can see you're in good hands.'' Jess smiled warmly at the nurse. ''Signor Forli would like a word with you, Nurse. He's waiting in the lobby.''

''And while you're away please take a break, Anna,'' said Emily quickly. ''Have some coffee and a rest. You deserve it.''

Anna nodded, smiling. ''*Va bene*. Now your friend is here I shall leave you together for half an hour.''

''Lorenzo obviously wants to ask her if you need anything,'' said Jess, when they were alone.

''Who on earth *is* this Lorenzo?'' said Emily, struggling to sit up.

''Hang on, I'll prop your pillows up.''

''Never mind my pillows! This morning *that* arrived.'' Emily waved a hand at the vast basket of fruit on the dressing table. ''And after you rang last night masses of mineral water and fruit juice arrived for me. Then Dr Tosti came, with Anna. He's very nice, and speaks English, thank heavens. He gave me an examination, assured me I wasn't dying, and prescribed some antibiotics. Then he left Anna behind to take care of me. So tell. Who is this Lorenzo?''

''Oddly enough,'' said Jess casually, ''you've already spoken to him.''

''I have?''

''That night at the flat. He's the one with the sexy voice you fancied so much.''

Emily stared in astonishment. ''But I thought that was Roberto!''

''No.'' Jess stretched luxuriously. ''It was Lorenzo Forli, Roberto's older brother, chairman of the group that owns this hotel.'' She paused, then gave her friend a wry, crooked little smile. ''But much more important than that, he's the man I'm truly, madly, deeply in love with.''

Emily flopped back against the pillows, pole-axed. "You're serious!" she accused, heaved in a deep breath and began to cough painfully.

Alarmed, Jess handed her a glass of water. "Hey—steady on, love."

Emily swallowed the water, then waved a peremptory arm at the other bed. "Right then, Jess Dysart," she ordered. "You can't stop there. Curl up on that and tell me everything. Right from the beginning."

Jess was only too happy to oblige, from the fall at the Chesterton, which had resulted in the drive home to Friars Wood with Lorenzo, to the flight he'd arranged to bring her rushing to Emily's aid. "And as the icing on the cake," she added with satisfaction, "the moment you're well enough for a car ride, Em, he's taking us to stay at his home in the country. I'll keep you company there while you get yourself better."

"How *kind* of him!" Emily shook her head in wonder. "He must be some man, this Lorenzo."

"He is." Jess swung her legs over the edge of the bed and leaned forward, suddenly serious. "Now then, Em. Have you rung your mother?"

"I spoke to her as soon as I arrived, but didn't let on I was feeling rough—told her the flight had made my voice dry." She eyed Jess guiltily. "The thing is, love, when Celia had to cancel I knew perfectly well I should have done the same. I'd been feeling a bit off for a day or two before I left."

"Which is why you were home early that day!" Jess bit her lip in remorse. "And I was too wrapped up in my own concerns to notice."

"I didn't feel so bad then, Jess. I just thought I had a cold coming on. But I was utterly determined to get to Florence. Serves me right, I suppose, because I just wanted to crawl into bed and die by the time I finally got to the hotel.''

When the nurse returned she had a message from Lorenzo. ''Signor Forli wishes to speak to you, Miss Dysart. He awaits you downstairs.''

''On your mark, get set, then, Jess,'' said Emily, grinning. ''Don't keep the man waiting.''

Jess flushed, her eyes like stars as she flew to the bathroom to tidy up. ''Shan't be long,'' she said breathlessly, as she hurried from the room.

When the lift doors opened into the lobby Lorenzo was waiting for her. Aware of rapt attention from everyone behind the reception desk, Jess returned his greeting sedately, then accompanied him to a large lounge, where they sat on a brocade sofa screened by a vast palm, with coffee on a silver tray on the table in front of them.

''*Allora*, how is your friend?'' asked Lorenzo.

''She's not very well at all,'' Jess handed him his cup. ''In fact she looks terrible. But Emily assures me she's much better than she was.''

''I have been speaking to Bruno Tosti, and he confirms this, but he thinks it best your friend remains here for tonight. Tomorrow I will drive you both to the Villa Fortuna.'' Lorenzo smiled at her. ''I have sent word for everything to be made ready.''

''Where exactly is the house?'' asked Jess.

''A short journey from Firenze—it should not be too exhausting for your friend.''

''Do you commute into the city every day, then?''

''No. I have an apartment here. I use the villa only at weekends.'' He lowered his voice. ''But while you are there, *tesoro*, I shall remain there also. Roberto will return tomorrow, or the next day. He can take my place for a while.'' He moved closer, and touched her hand fleetingly. "What is it, Jessamy? Something troubles you."

She shook her head. "Not troubles, exactly. It's just that I'm totally overwhelmed by your kindness, Lorenzo—Emily, too."

He shrugged negligently. "It is no great thing. Later this evening, when I collect you for dinner, you shall present me to your friend."

Jess raised a mocking eyebrow. "So I'm having dinner with you, am I?"

Lorenzo smiled indulgently. "But of course. When you return to your friend, Anna can take time to herself for an hour or two. She will return at eight. You look doubtful," he added, eyes narrowed. "You do not wish this?"

"You know I do," she assured him. "But I'd rather not go too far, Lorenzo, just in case Emily wants me."

"Of course. We shall dine here in the hotel, *cara*. You could be with your friend in minutes, should this be necessary, I shall come for you at eight." Lorenzo escorted her to the lift, bowing very formally as the doors closed on her.

When Jess got back to the room Emily was sitting in a chair, looking tired, but a lot more like herself in a fresh nightgown, with her hair brushed into something more like its normal shine.

"Anna's given me a sponge bath and changed the bed," she said cheerfully. "Then she's going off for an hour or so."

The nurse helped Emily back into bed, and straightened the bedclothes with precision. "I have ordered a light meal, *cara*, and your friend must make sure you eat it,'' she said firmly, and gathered up the discarded linen. ''I shall return at eight. *A presto!*''

Jess saw the nurse out, then returned to sit on the other bed. ''Lorenzo wants me to have dinner with him, Em.''

''I know. Anna told me.''

''Do you mind terribly?'' Jess pulled a face. ''I feel a bit guilty flying to your side and all that, then leaving you alone for the evening.''

''Of course I don't mind,'' said Emily, chuckling. ''Besides, I won't be alone. I'll have Anna. She can snooze on your bed while I read.''

''Which reminds me.'' Jess dived for her luggage, and produced two paperback novels. ''I bought these at the airport. One thriller, one sexy romance.''

Emily beamed. ''Wonderful! So what are you wearing for your romantic dinner for two, then?''

''We're on the move tomorrow, so there's no point in unpacking.'' Jess took out a dress and held it up, eyeing it critically. ''This knitted silky stuff travels well. I packed in such a terrible hurry nothing else is fit to be seen. I'll hang it on the bathroom door to get the creases out. But first I'm going out on that balcony to look at the view!''

Outside the full moon was just rising over the Arno. All the traffic noise and bustle and scents of Florence came rising up on the balmy evening air, and Jess breathed in deeply, savouring it as she craned her neck to get a glimpse of the Ponte Vecchio in the distance.

''Fantastic,'' she said, going inside. ''Shall I leave the doors open?''

''Yes, please.'' Emily smiled ruefully. ''At last I can listen to Florence, even though I can't explore the city just yet. Hurry up, Jess. I want a blow-by-blow description of the wedding.''

Jess showered quickly, dried her hair and brushed it into shape, then curled up on the other bed and settled down to take Emily through the wedding day from start to finish. "I know brides are supposed to look beautiful, but you needed sunglasses just to look at Leo. Jonah couldn't take his eyes off her. Neither," she added ruefully, "could Roberto Forli."

"I'm amazed he was there!"

"So was I—but I'm very glad he was, because in the end it meant Lorenzo came to the wedding, too." Jess was silent for a moment. "Do you realise, Em," she said at last, "that this time last week I'd never even heard of Lorenzo Forli, let alone set eyes on him? And now—"

"And now?"

"I feel as though I've known him for ever." Jess leapt off the bed. "Right. Enough of me. Let's think about you. What are you having for supper?"

When a tempting herb omelette arrived Emily managed to eat some of it, under her friend's watchful eye, but asked for mercy eventually, and Jess removed the tray and plumped up the pillows.

"I'll help you tidy up, shall I?"

"If you like. Do I look so awful, then?"

"No. But Lorenzo's coming to meet you before he takes me to dinner."

This piece of news threw the invalid into a panic. She demanded help to the bathroom, managed to wash her own face afterwards, then brushed her own hair while Jess remade the bed.

"Right then, Em. In you go."

When Emily was sitting up against the pillows with her new book she flapped a hand at Jess. "Shoo! Go and gild the lily. It's you Lorenzo wants, not me."

A little before eight Jess was ready, in a sleeveless,

V-necked jersey dress, the lustrous bitter chocolate shade a perfect match for eyes which gleamed with anticipation beneath the gleaming fall of hair across her forehead.

"Yummy," said Emily as Jess gave a pirouette. "Like a gorgeous hand-made chocolate. Lorenzo will take one look and want to gobble you up." She grinned as a knock on the door silenced Jess's protests. "Go on. Let him in."

When Jess opened the door Lorenzo gave her an all-encompassing scrutiny, then kissed his fingers to her in reverent silence. She mimed a kiss in return, then ushered him into the room and introduced him to Emily.

"Piacere." Lorenzo smiled gently and took the hand the invalid held out, retaining it in his for a moment. "How are you feeling, Miss Shaw?"

"Emily, please!" She returned the smile shyly. "I can hardly help but feel better after all you've done for me, Mr—"

"Lorenzo, *per favore,*" he corrected quickly. "I am here not only for the pleasure of meeting you, but to make sure there is nothing you need."

"You've thought of everything," she assured him. "I can't tell you how grateful I am. I wish there was some way I could repay you."

"That is easy. You have only to make a full recovery," he assured her. "Jessamy has told you I am driving you to my home tomorrow?"

Emily went very pink. "Yes, indeed. It's amazingly kind of you."

"Lorenzo, how do you think she looks?" said Jess later, as they walked towards the lift.

"Very fragile, *cara.* But do not worry. I have asked Anna to accompany us for a few days to look after her."

"This is all a huge expense for you," said Jess, frowning.

"I am being selfish. I do not wish you to tire yourself with constant nursing." Lorenzo shrugged. "I promise you I can afford professional medical care for a few days. Otherwise where is the problem? You will be living in my house, with my cook preparing your meals. But none of that matters," he added, as they entered the lift. "As I have said before, *carissima*, for you I would do anything."

Jess reached up to touch a caressing hand to his cheek, her eyes narrowing suddenly as it dawned on her that the lift was going up, instead of down. "Do you have two restaurants in the hotel, then?"

"No. One only." When the lift stopped at the top floor Jess gave him a questioning look as she stepped out into a corridor with arched windows which gave it the look of a colonnade. Lorenzo led her towards a pair of double doors at the end, unlocked them and gave her a little bow as he led her through a small foyer, and opened one of the doors to usher her into what was very obviously the salon of a private apartment.

Jess stood very still just inside a large, beautiful room which opened out onto a balcony. The furniture was elegant: chairs and sofas upholstered in velvet and brocade, paintings and mirrors in carved, gilded frames on the walls. And in eye-catching prominence in the centre of the room a small table was laid for two, complete with a silver vase of flowers. She eyed it all with dismay, only now realising how much she'd wanted to dine in the hotel restaurant, with Lorenzo attentive at her side, displaying pride in his companion to the world. His world.

"The apartment you spoke of," said Jess tonelessly at

last. "I assumed it was somewhere else in the city. But I was wrong, wasn't I? You live here, in the hotel."

Lorenzo frowned. "Yes. Of course. What is wrong, Jessamy? I thought you would prefer to dine alone with me here. Downstairs in the restaurant all my staff would naturally take much interest in my—my companion."

"Instead," she said lightly, "they'll think you've brought me here for a lot more than just dinner. This, I assume, is where you bring the ladies who allow those privileges you talked about."

The animation drained from Lorenzo's face, leaving it blank as a Venetian carnival mask. "I bring no one here except family," he said, after a long, painful interval. "This is my private place." He strode past her towards a telephone on the carved credenza. "Like a fool I thought you would be happier here than in the public restaurant. That you would want to be alone with me." He shrugged negligently. "No matter. I shall ring to reserve a table."

"Not much point in that," said Jess, disappointment sharpening her voice. "The damage is done."

"The only damage is to my pride," he retorted with arrogance. "No one knows the identity of my guest, Jessamy. However, since you so obviously do not wish to dine with me after all, I shall ask for a table for one in the restaurant. You may eat there alone."

Jess stared at him in utter dismay. "I can't do that."

"Then I shall escort you back to your friend, and you shall ring for room service." His eyes glittered coldly, and Jess shivered, appalled at the sudden chasm yawning between them. One unconsidered step, she realised in sudden panic, could plunge her into it, with no way out. And belatedly she remembered how much she was indebted to him.

"I'm sorry," she said in a constricted voice quite unlike her own. "I didn't mean to offend you. Especially after you've been so kind—"

"Do not insult me by talking of expense again," he flung at her.

"Lorenzo, please," she said in desperation. "If I've jumped to the wrong conclusion I apologise."

He stared at her malevolently. "You thought I brought you here to rush you straight into my bed, it seems. Perhaps even before I allowed you to eat dinner."

"Like Lord Byron—" Jess bit her lip, cursing, not for the first time, her tendency to say the first thing that came into her head when she was nervous.

Lorenzo looked blank. "*Mi scusi?* What is your poet to do with this?" The cold glitter faded from his eyes as they followed the tide of colour which rose from the neckline of her dress to the roots of her hair.

"I read a book about him once. A biography," she said gruffly, unable to look at him. "On his wedding day he—he disposed of his wife's virginity on the sofa before dinner."

Lorenzo breathed in so deeply she could tell, even without looking at him, that he was fighting to master his temper. "And when you saw this room you expected me to do the same?"

"No. Not exactly." Jess raised her head and looked him in the eye. "That wouldn't have been possible."

Without taking his eyes from hers he gestured towards a deep-cushioned couch upholstered in honey-coloured velvet. "I have a sofa," he said very quietly.

Jess nodded. "But I'm not a virgin."

CHAPTER SEVEN

THE WORDS echoed in the room, and, suddenly desperate for air, Jess turned on her heel and went out onto the balcony. By this time the moon was high enough to paint a glittering path across the Arno. She leaned her hands on the balcony rail to gaze down at it blindly, cursing herself for a fool. She was twenty-four years old, without a shred of false modesty about her appeal to men. No one in the world she came from would expect her to be inexperienced. Yet she been mad enough to fling the fact in Lorenzo's face like a gauntlet because she wanted him to know before... Before she became his lover, of course. And if that was her intention, *and* her desire, as she now so clearly saw it was, it seemed a touch irrational to make a fuss about dining alone with him in his apartment.

Slim brown hands appeared beside hers to grasp the balcony rail.

Jess stood very still, conscious in every nerve of the male presence beside her. She glanced up at last at the dauntingly stern profile. "Lorenzo, I'm sorry. I've behaved like an idiot. But it was something Emily said just before you came for me."

He looked down at her, frowning. "Emily? What did she say?"

"When I was ready she said I looked—"

"Incantevole?"

"What does that mean?"

"Ravishing," he informed her, something in his voice

87

telling her that hostilities, if not over, were at least suspended.

"She actually said you'd want to gobble me up," Jess muttered.

"What is this 'gobble'?" he demanded.

"Devour, I suppose."

"Ah!" Lorenzo nodded. "I see. And when I brought you here you assumed she was right."

Jess slanted a troubled look at him. "I wouldn't blame you. From the night we met I've given you every reason to believe that the moment the opportunity arose I would share your bed. I won't lie. I want this, too. Some time soon."

"But not as soon as this."

"Exactly. Which is why I was upset and nervous and started babbling about Byron."

"Unlike the poet, I would have given you dinner first, I swear," he assured her, and took her hand. When she curled her fingers round his in relief he gave her a very direct look. "You are a woman of much allure, Jessamy. I did not imagine for one moment that you were a virgin. Why did you feel you had to tell me that?"

She stared down at their clasped hands. "I suppose because you said there should be truth between us. And after that nonsense about Byron it just came out. I thought that maybe here, in Italy, even someone my age might be expected—"

"To be a virgin," he finished for her.

"Right. And after your experience with Renata I wanted you to know this first. Not—" She halted, her face hot again.

"Not during the rapture of our first night together," he said, a deepened note in his voice which sent a great shiver down her spine. "You are cold," he said instantly, but she shook her head.

"No. Not in the least." She looked at him in appeal. "As I've told you before, it's the effect you have on me. Would you put your arms around me, Lorenzo? Please?"

His eyes dilated, his fingers suddenly cruelly tight on hers. "Come inside, then. Out here I feel as if the eyes of the world are on us."

Once inside the beautiful, formal room he dropped her hand, removed his jacket, then stood very still, just looking at her, and after a moment or two Jess realised it was up to her to make the first move. She went to him, arms outstretched, and with a smile which made her bones feel hollow Lorenzo drew her close against him, bending his dark head to hers. She could felt his heart thudding against hers, and clutching him closer so that he could kiss her and make everything better. The kiss made everything so much better that in a very short time both of them were ravenous for more than mere food. Then Jess's stomach gave a great, unromantic grumble and Lorenzo put her away from him, laughing uproariously.

"You are hungry!"

She nodded, giggling like a schoolgirl. "Yes. I am. Now."

He raised a quizzical eyebrow. "Now?"

"I couldn't have eaten a thing a while ago, when you were angry with me."

He grasped her by the shoulders and shook her gently. "You were angry with me, also, Jessamy."

She bit her lip. "I've said I'm sorry."

"I need more than words to heal my hurt!"

Jess reached up to wind her arms round his neck and kissed him with such passionate contrition Lorenzo put her away at last, breathing hard.

"We must eat," he said unsteadily. "Before you tempt
me into behaving like your mad, bad Byron. But first,"
he added with sudden emphasis, "my only reason for
bringing you here tonight was something you said during
the flight."

She eyed him in surprise. "What did I say?"

"You said you would prefer me to kiss you in private,
Jessamy. So. Instead of showing you off in triumph in
the restaurant I chose to bring you here." His eyes held
hers. "But only to kiss, and to touch, perhaps. Nothing
more. You believe this?"

"Yes," said Jess in deep remorse. "Of course I do."

Lorenzo seated her with much ceremony at the table.
"Our dinner is in the refrigerator in my seldom-used
kitchen. For this, our first meal together, I chose dishes
which would wait as long as we wished. So tonight I
must play waiter." He went from the room, then returned
with a tray he placed on the credenza. He set two plates
on the table, then opened the bottle of wine, his eyes
dancing. "And tonight we shall actually drink some prosecco, no?"

"Yes!" Jess smiled radiantly as he filled her glass.

He sat down, gazing into her eyes. "What shall we
drink to?"

She thought for a moment, then raised her glass. "To
truth—always!"

"Sempre la verità," he echoed.

The meal would have been tempting if Jess had possessed no appetite at all. As it was, with their first quarrel
behind them, her relief was intense at surviving it without
alienating Lorenzo for ever. Suddenly hungry, she was
quick to start on the salad of San Daniele ham and figs,
and savoured the flavours of mint and basil with enthusiasm Lorenzo viewed with open approval.

"At last, I see you eat," he said with satisfaction.

"I do it all the time—too much, sometimes," she assured him indistinctly. "Which is why I'm never going to be like Leo or Kate."

"Why should you wish to be?" he said, frowning.

"They can eat anything they like and stay slim." She smiled at him philosophically. "I tend to get a bit too rounded if I indulge too often."

"Rounded," he repeated, lingering on the word with pleasure. "I like this very much. I prefer a woman who curves in and out in certain delectable places. Like you, *amore*."

So she was *amore* again. Euphoric with relief, Jess began with enthusiasm on the main course of filleted salmon served with anchovy and caper mayonnaise, and sat back at last with a blissful sigh. "That was perfect," she informed him, and got up to take their plates, waving Lorenzo back when he would have done it for her. "No, let me. I need to make up to you for being so horrible." She shook her head. "When I think of all you've done—"

"Please! I do not wish to hear this." He paused, eyeing her intently. "Jessamy, when I spoke of my reward on the plane, did you really think I meant to claim this tonight? In payment for an air fare and a few medical bills for your friend?"

"*No!* That never occurred to me. But when you brought me here and I saw the scene set like this—" She shrugged ruefully. "I was afraid that history was repeating itself."

Lorenzo's eyes narrowed. "What is this history, Jessamy?"

"Are you sure you want to hear? The story of my love-life is short enough, goodness knows, but *very* boring."

"Not to me," he assured her. "Nothing about you could bore me. Tell me. Start at the very beginning of this love-life of yours. The very first man in your life."

Jess sat down and put out a hand and Lorenzo grasped it, smiling in encouragement. "Very well, then," she began, resigned. "I experienced my first run-in with sex— it certainly wasn't love—with the boy who took me home from the farewell dance at my school. I was seventeen."

Lorenzo's grasp tightened. "He was also young?"

Jess nodded. "But older than me. In more ways than one. He was captain of games at his own school, and good-looking in a hunky kind of way."

"Hunky?"

"More muscles and hormones than brains."

"Ah." Lorenzo nodded, enlightened.

"I'd had such a good time. Mother bought me a great dress, Leo did my hair, and all my friends envied me my partner because he was the best-looking boy there. He drove me home in the moonlight in his father's car, and on the way back he parked in a lane, took a rug from the back seat and suggested a stroll down to the river. I thought he just wanted a few kisses. Which he did, to start with. But he'd come prepared for a lot more than that. In every way." She pulled a face. "He was a big, muscular lad and very fit. I didn't stand a chance."

Lorenzo frowned darkly. "He hurt you?"

"He certainly did. I fought like a wildcat, which was not only useless and gave me bruises, but excited him so much that when he got his way at last it was over almost as soon as it had begun. He was furious and humiliated, I was hysterical with rage, and he drove me home at such speed it's a wonder we both got there in one piece. I never heard from him again. Nor," she added, eyes flashing, "did I want to."

Lorenzo said something short and expressive in his own tongue, then raised her hand to his lips, eyeing her questioningly. "And this came back to haunt you tonight?"

"Heavens, no!" Jess drank some of her wine. "I just mentioned it to explain my reluctance to repeat the experience. It would be different, I told myself, when I actually fell in love. I just had to wait until that happy day arrived." She shook her head sadly. "One day I really thought it had. But when we got as far as bed at last the whole thing left me cold. So the man vanished into the night in a huff."

"Were you heartbroken?" asked Lorenzo tenderly.

"Not in the slightest." Jess pulled a face. "In fact, I was beginning to wonder if I really *had* a heart. Emily falls in and out of love with amazing regularity, but I prefer men who just want to be friends."

"Do you know many men like that?" he asked, astonished.

"Not many, no. But eventually, quite a long time after fiasco number two, I met a man who'd just survived a divorce, and he agreed that platonic relationships were less trouble than the other kind."

"Ah!" A smile played at the corners of Lorenzo's mouth. "But he failed to keep to this, of course?"

"Right. He got in the habit of inviting me to his new flat to watch a video, order in Chinese, that kind of thing. But one night I arrived to find a table set for two, with champagne, candles, even red roses. You can guess the rest. The champagne didn't work. Nothing worked. At least not for me." Her eyes darkened. "He became quite objectionable, so this time *I* went off in a huff."

Lorenzo nodded slowly. "Now I understand your feelings when I brought you here tonight."

Jess smiled. Lorenzo's apartment was a far cry from the London flat she'd stormed out of in such a rage. "My disappointment tonight," she said with precision, "was for a quite different reason."

"Tell me this reason," he commanded.

"It's hard to put into words."

"Try!"

"I was really looking forward to eating in the hotel dining room with you," she admitted, flushing. "I liked the idea of everyone looking at us and knowing that you, that I—" She halted, her eyes locked with his.

"That you were mine?" he said softly.

Jess went pale, her dark, startled eyes wide as they stared into his. "Is that how you think of me?"

"Yes," he said simply. "Since the moment I first saw you I feel this. There is no way to explain it—"

"Wise men never try," she said huskily.

There was a sudden, charged silence between them.

"This is dangerous," said Lorenzo abruptly. "You were right. We should have dined in the restaurant."

"I'm glad now that we didn't," she assured him.

"Why?" he demanded.

"Because we couldn't have talked like this. Nor," she added, looking him in the eye, "could you have kissed me, touched me, just as you said you wanted."

Lorenzo tensed, like a panther about to spring, and for a moment Jess was sure he would pull her out of her chair and kiss her senseless. Instead, to her intense disappointment, he fetched a plate from the credenza and set it in front of her. "This is a *torta*, made of almonds and lemon and ricotta," he said, the uneven huskiness of his voice at odds with the prosaic words. "Is this to your taste?"

Jess stared at the confection blankly. "Normally, yes.

But not right now. Perhaps I could take it down to Emily later. She loves this kind of thing. Do have some yourself, of course.''

"No," he said explosively. "You know very well that it is not cake that I want." His eyes lit with a heat which dried her mouth. "I cannot forget that tonight, Jessamy, may be the only time we can be together like this. At the Villa Fortuna it will be difficult for me."

Jess stiffened. Was there some sinister reason why he wouldn't want to make love to her at the villa? Suddenly the reason hit her like a punch in the stomach.

"What is it?" he demanded, and at last pulled her up out of her chair. "Tell me! Why do you look like that?"

"I never thought to ask," she said in a rush. "Is the Villa Fortuna the home you shared with Renata?"

"Ah, no, *carssima*, it is not!" he assured her, and held her close for a moment, then led her across the room to a deep, comfortable sofa and drew her down beside him.

"I should have made this clear before, Jessamy. When Renata died I sold the house we lived in. The Villa Fortuna is my family home, where I grew up with Roberto and my sister."

"I didn't know you had a sister." Jess let out a deep sigh and relaxed against him, limp with relief. The prospect of staying in a house haunted by the ghost of Lorenzo's wife was the stuff of nightmares. "What's your sister's name? Where does she live? Is she married?"

He laughed and kissed the top of her head. "Isabella is younger than Roberto. She is married to a lawyer called Andrea Moretti. They have two small sons and live in Lucca." He turned her face to his. "*Allora*, you feel better?"

"Yes. Much better. Where *did* you live, Lorenzo?"

"Renata's parents wanted us to make our home with them, but to hide the truth of our marriage it was necessary for us to live alone. I bought a house far away from them, in Oltrano, over there." He gestured towards the balcony, his eyes sombre. "It became a prison for both of us."

"Is that why you wanted to come inside just now? Because you can't bear to look over there?"

"No!" His arm tightened. "It was solely a burning desire for privacy with you, *amore.*"

Deeply gratified, Jess leaned up to kiss his cheek. "Poor Renata. Though in some ways I think she was very fortunate."

"*Fortunate?*"

"To be married to you, Lorenzo. Other men, in the same circumstances, might not have been so forbearing."

He shook his head. "Do not endow me with virtues I lack, Jessamy."

"What do you mean?"

"I was forbearing, as you say, because I had no desire to be otherwise. Something died inside me the night Renata rejected me. My youth, perhaps," he added, with a twist to his mouth. "After that night, unless we were in public and it was unavoidable, I never touched her again." Lorenzo put a finger under her chin and raised her face to his. When I met you, *amore*, feelings I thought were dead for ever came to life, as though a dam had burst and all the suppressed longings of those empty years came rushing through." He smiled wryly into her startled eyes. "I am being very Italian and emotional, am I not? Does it embarrass you, *piccola*?"

"Not in the least," she assured him. To be called 'little one' in that husky, caressing voice ignited several emotions inside Jess, but not one of them was embarrassment.

"If you want the truth, I just love it when you get all Latin and passionate. It thrills me to bits—''

Lorenzo smothered the rest of her words with his mouth, and she responded with such ardour it was a long time before there was any more conversation. And when Lorenzo began to speak at last they were words Jess understood only by their intonation as he made love to her in his own tongue, the liquid flow of musical endearments as seductive as the slim, sure hands that moved over her in light, delicate caresses which, even through the clinging silk of her dress, sent fiery streaks of longing to a secret place which throbbed in unaccustomed response.

After only minutes of the delicate torture Jess longed for Lorenzo to undress her, and carry her to his bed and show her, at last, just how wonderful the act of love could be. But she knew he wasn't going to do that. At least, not tonight. Assailed by emotions and physical longings unfamiliar to her, she began to cry, and Lorenzo crushed her close in remorse.

"Do not weep, *amore*. Forgive me—I have frightened you.''

"No, you haven't,'' she said thickly. "I'm not frightened, I'm *frustrated*. I—I long for you, Lorenzo. You're driving me crazy. I've never felt like this before.''

He groaned. "Do not say such things to me, *carissima*.'' He held her face in his hands, his eyes questioning as they met the look in hers. "What is it?''

"You said that it would be difficult to be alone together at the Villa Fortuna. Is this because of Emily, and the nurse?''

Lorenzo nodded, resigned. "Also there is Carla, who cooks for me, and Mario, her husband, who takes care of the property, and the moment Isabella learns I have guests, she will come rushing to meet you.''

Jess bit her lip. "Won't your sister find it odd? That you've invited me to stay at your house?"

Lorenzo sat in silence for some time, his eyes fixed on their entwined hands. "She will be very surprised," he said at last, his voice deeper and more uneven than it had been. "Because I have never invited a woman there before." He looked up again, his eyes alight with an urgency which took her breath away. "I did not mean to say this. At least, not tonight. I told myself I must wait, be patient. But, *Dio*, I have wasted enough of my life already." His grasp tightened. "I knew from the first moment I saw you that I wanted you for my own. Not for a *relazione*—a love affair—but for ever. I want you for my wife, Jessamy."

CHAPTER EIGHT

JESS sat very still, gazing at him in silence broken only by the night-time sounds of Florence coming through the open balcony doors. A voice in her head suggested, without much hope, that this was too sudden, too soon, but her turbulent heart brushed it aside, clamouring that this was what she'd been waiting for all her adult life.

"It is too soon," said Lorenzo bitterly, and thrust a hand through his thick black hair. "I am a fool. I should have waited—"

"No," said Jess swiftly. She gave him a smile so incandescent his eyes blazed in response. "I'm glad you couldn't wait."

He seized her hands in a grasp which threatened to crack her bones. "You mean this?"

"Yes."

"You are saying you will marry me, Jessamy?"

"Yes."

"Then tell me that you love me!"

"Of course I love you," she said unevenly. "Otherwise we wouldn't be having this conversation."

Lorenzo leapt to his feet, pulling her with him, his face stern as he gazed down into hers. "You realise that the world will say you have known me too short a time to be sure of your feelings."

"Do you care?" she demanded.

He cupped her face in his hands. "I care only for you. And for what your parents will think. We must talk to them—"

"Not yet," Jess said hastily. "I don't want to tell anyone yet."

"Not even your friend?"

"Emily knows already," Jess assured him, then laughed at his look of astonished delight. "That I love you, I mean. I've never been madly in love before—I had to tell someone!"

"Meraviglioso!" His eyes lit with a triumphant gleam. "If your friend knows this life will be easier at the Villa Fortuna than I thought. She will expect us to want time alone together, no?"

"She will, yes," agreed Jess, and smiled at him expectantly. "I don't know how you do things in Italy, darling, but in my part of the world it's the custom to exchange a kiss once a proposal is accepted."

Lorenzo's eyes kindled. "Say 'darling' again!"

"Kiss me first."

Lorenzo picked her up instead, and for a wild moment Jess wondered if he meant to carry her straight to bed now their relationship had altered. Instead he sank down with her on the sofa, settling her in his lap as he kissed the mouth she held up in invitation.

"Now, *amore*," he breathed against her parted lips, "it is I who cannot believe this is real."

"If it's a dream, we're sharing it," she whispered, and responded with uninhibited delight to the mouth which showed her that mere kissing itself was an art form in which Lorenzo Forli possessed so much skill that Jess pulled away a little at last, smiling in challenge.

"Who taught you to kiss like that?" she demanded breathlessly.

He laughed, and ruffled the bright hair falling over her forehead. "Francesca."

"Who was *she*?" demanded Jess, sitting up.

Lorenzo pulled her back down against his shoulder. "Just a girl I knew when I was young, long before my marriage. She was older than me, and taught me that kisses and caresses are as important as the act of love itself. Not," he added with regret, "that Francesca ever allowed me more than the kisses, you understand."

"But you wanted more!"

His sudden grin stripped years from him. "Men always want more, *tesoro*." He breathed in deeply. "Now I must be practical. I am asking a great deal of you—I know this. Are you really willing to give up your career to share my life here with me, Jessamy?"

She hesitated, then nodded. "Yes, I am."

"You have doubts?" he asked quietly.

"No. None. In fact—" Jess smiled a little, then shrugged. "This is something I've never admitted to another soul. My so-called career has never really been important to me at all. I just pretended it was."

Lorenzo frowned. "But why should you need to pretend, *carissima*?"

"I had to have something special in my life. I'm not brainless, nor am I lazy, but I'm not in the least academic, like the rest of my family. Leo got a good degree, and I'm sure Adam has done well in Edinburgh, too, while Kate will do brilliantly, probably better than either of them." She smiled wryly. "I'm the odd one out, even to the straight hair—"

"Your hair is beautiful," he contradicted, and smoothed it back from her forehead. "And it will be even more beautiful when it grows longer, Jessamy," he added slyly, then kissed the mouth she opened to protest. "Go on," he said unevenly. "I am listening, *carassima*."

Jess took a deep breath. "After school I did a course which made me computer-literate, and I got a job in advertising, making it clear to all concerned that I was intent on a career. Eventually I worked for one of the men I told you about.'' She sighed. ''This meant that when the relationship went wrong I was forced to resign. So much for my advertising career. My present job is interesting, and I enjoy it.'' Jess looked at him squarely. ''But to be honest I hate the thought of doing it for the rest of my working life.''

Lorenzo pulled her closer, his eyes gleaming with relief. ''I am delighted to hear this. Also very happy that your career in London will not come between us.''

''Maybe I could do something here in Florence, or—'' She halted.

''Or?'' he prompted.

''Or perhaps we'll have a baby right away.'' Jess kept her eyes on the brown muscular throat visible through the open collar of Lorenzo's shirt, and saw it grow taut in response to her words.

''You mean this, *amore*?'' he demanded incredulously. ''You would like a baby?''

''Not *a* baby,'' she corrected breathlessly. ''*Your* baby.''

He crushed her close, his English deserting him as he unleashed a flood of passionate Italian which flowed over Jess in a torrent of feeling which left her in no doubt as to his reaction.

''I had given up all hope of children of my own,'' he said at last in English, his voice rough with emotion.

''But surely you must have met women who would have been only too delighted to give you babies?'' said Jess.

Lorenzo gave a very Latin shrug. ''Perhaps. But I swore never to marry again without love. Once,'' he added grimly, ''was enough.''

Jess pulled his head down to hers, experiencing a great urge to comfort him any way she could. She kissed him passionately, her arms locked round his neck, telling him without words how much she cared, feeling his heart thudding against hers as he whispered a great many things she knew would be gratifying if she could only understand them.

"I will teach you Italian," he said in between kisses. "I cannot make love in English."

"You're doing brilliantly," she gasped.

"I can do much better—"

There was sudden silence between them. They gazed at each other, both pairs of eyes dilated with shared desire.

Lorenzo jumped to his feet, pulling her with him. "I must take you back to your friend."

"It's early," objected Jess.

"No matter." He stared down at her wildly. "I want you so much, *amore*, you know this. I feel such fire, such longing to possess, I have no—no confidence in my power to—*Dio*!" he added in frustration. "I cannot find the words." He drew in a deep, steadying breath. "Jessamy, I swear that my intention was not the same as those other men. The meal, the wine, they were merely food and drink, not a means to lure you to my bed."

"I know that now," she said disconsolately, and laid her head against his shoulder. "Lorenzo."

"*Si?*"

"Are you saying you're not going to make love to me until we're married?"

"If that is your wish, most certainly."

She put her arms round his lean waist and tipped her face back, shaking her head. "It's not. I want you to

make love to me before then. Even—even if it's not perfect between us at first.''

''You confuse me with your other lovers!'' he said
arrogantly, and smiled. ''We were meant for each other,
Jessamy. How could it not be perfect?''

''It might not be. But that isn't important. I meant that
by our wedding night I wanted it to *be* perfect,'' she said
urgently, and saw comprehension blaze in his eyes.

''To erase bad memories? Ah, Jessamy. *Amore*. I am
so right to think of you as my reward.'' Lorenzo kissed
her with fierce tenderness, then drew away a little to
smile into her eyes. ''Now you have consented to be
mine,'' he whispered, ''very soon I shall show you just
what love can be. But in the meantime—''

''You're going to take me back to Emily,'' she said,
resigned.

He shook his head and drew her down to the deep
velvet couch again. ''Not yet. Anna can look after your
friend for at least another hour. This is a very special
moment in our lives, *innamorata*. I need to hold you in
my arms for a while.''

Lorenzo began to kiss her, gently at first, with subtle
kisses which moved over her eyelids and cheeks and
along her jaw before coming to rest on her waiting
mouth. Her lips parted eagerly, her tongue meeting his
with an ardour which hurried Lorenzo's breathing. He
laid her back against the velvet cushions and hung over
her, looking down into her face as though watchful for
any look of dissent as his hands sought her breasts,
smoothing and stroking through the thin, clinging fabric.
Jess gazed back, mesmerised, stirring restlessly beneath
caresses she could only just bear. Then the long, skilful
fingers slid beneath the neckline of her dress, and his

touch on her erect, sensitive nipples took her breath away.

Lorenzo kissed her deeply, drawing her down to lie full length against him, and Jess felt heat flood through her as she came into contact with his arousal. Feeling him hard and throbbing with explicit promise ignited something wild and new inside her, and she pulled away to reach behind her back, tugging down the zip of her dress to let it slide from her shoulders. Lorenzo breathed in sharply, pushed scraps of flesh-coloured silk aside and bent his head to her breasts, his mouth hot against her skin as he captured a diamond-hard nipple between his lips. Jess shook from head to foot as his lips, teeth and subtle, expert fingers swiftly roused her to a fever-pitch of need. She thrust her hands into his thick black hair to clutch him closer still, but after a moment or two Lorenzo sat up to strip off his shirt and crush her against his bare chest, kissing her mouth with a frenzied hunger she met with equal fire.

At long last Lorenzo lifted his dark, dishevelled head to look in her eyes. *"Innamorata,"* he said hoarsely.

"I want you so much, Lorenzo," she gasped.

"I want you more!" He closed his eyes in anguish for a moment, then leapt up, reaching for his shirt.

Jess got to her feet, and turned her back on him to reach for her zip, silent tears sliding down her cheeks as she struggled to do up her dress.

"Let me!" Lorenzo put her hands aside gently, then stiffened and spun her round in his arms. "You are cry-ing," he accused.

"No, I'm not," she croaked, and sniffed inelegantly.

"It is no sin to cry," he assured her, and bent to kiss the tears away. The fleeting contact was too much for either of them. In an instant their arms were straining each other close as their lips met in an engulfing kiss which vanquished any last shred of control either of them possessed. Lorenzo picked her up, his eyes wild and questioning on hers, and Jess gave him a look of such smouldering invitation he carried her from the room and set her on her feet at last beside a wide bed bathed in moonlight.

"You are sure?" he demanded hoarsely.

"Utterly sure," she whispered, and shrugged the dress from her shoulders, stepping out of it as it slithered to the floor.

Lorenzo sank to his knees before her, burying his face against the satiny skin of her waist. "I love you so much—I burn for you. I am not sure I can be gentle."

"I don't *want* you to be gentle," she said fiercely. "I just need to know."

He raised his head. "To know?"

"That I'm not frigid, or abnormal, or any of those things I've been accused of in the past—" She gasped as in one lithe movement Lorenzo leapt to his feet, swept her up in his arms and laid her on the bed.

He hung over her, his eyes blazing darkly in a face rendered pale as marble by the bleaching moonlight. "They were fools! You are perfect."

Tears slid from the corners of her eyes again. "Darling, I wish—"

"What is it you wish, *amore*?"

"That there had never been anyone else."

"Forget the past!" Lorenzo licked the tears away. "You and I," he promised huskily, "will find rapture together."

And when the final barriers of clothes were gone and they lay naked in each other's arms all memory of things past was blotted out for both of them as Lorenzo kissed and caressed her into hunger as great as his own. Jess shivered and gasped as his lips and hands wrought magic so overwhelming that she could bear it no longer. She uttered a hoarse, desperate little plea and Lorenzo thrust home to make their union complete. For a moment he lay tense and still, controlling his urgency, but Jess moved in urgent invitation, and Lorenzo responded with delight, increasing the rhythm by subtle degrees, kissing and caressing her and telling her how exquisite, how beautiful she felt in his arms, before his English deserted him and he resorted to liquid Italian endearments as he took her along the path to their mutual goal. Her eyes dilated and her breathing grew ragged, and her head began to toss back and forth on the pillow. At last Jess dug desperate, demanding fingers into his shoulders, and they surged together in hot, throbbing turbulence which mounted to a final paroxysm of pulsating sensation she experienced seconds before Lorenzo let out a great gasp and surrendered to the release he'd denied himself until he felt her convulse in the ultimate pleasure beneath him.

They lay in each other's arms for a long time before Lorenzo, with deep reluctance, stirred at last. He raised his head to smile into her heavy eyes.

"So, *mi amore*, tell me how you feel."

Jess considered it gravely. "Triumphant," she decided at last.

He let out a deep, relishing sigh, and rubbed his cheek against hers. "So you will not go away in this huff of yours?"

"No, indeed. I'm not sure I can even move."

"I do not wish you to move! But it is time I returned you to your friend."

"I wish I could stay."

He kissed her swiftly. "When we are married I shall hold you in my arms all night."

Jess stretched happily at the thought, then winced.

"What is it?" he said in alarm.

"A good thing you can't see me properly," she said gruffly. "I'm blushing."

He laughed and held her close. "Why?"

"Certain muscles unused to such activity are protesting," she said ruefully, then raised a hand to touch his cheek. "Thank you, Lorenzo. For making such magic for me."

"*You* are thanking *me*?" he said incredulously. "It was so beautiful, Jessamy, to feel your body so responsive to mine. When I brought you here tonight I did not expect such rapture."

"Before I met you I never expected it at all. Ever." Jess smiled at him radiantly, and he held her close, rubbing his cheek against hers until she asked for mercy.

"*Scusi!*" he said penitently. "When we are married I promise I shall shave every night before we go to bed."

The intimacy of this struck Jess with such force she breathed in sharply. "I still can't believe this is happening, darling."

Lorenzo nodded vigorously. "I know, *piccola*. I feel this also." He raised himself on an elbow to look down at her. "Believe that I love you, Jessamy Dysart," he said very quietly.

"I do." Jess returned the look very steadily. "I love you too, Lorenzo Forli."

And as though they'd exchanged a vow, Lorenzo picked up her hand and kissed the finger which would wear his ring. "Come, *carissima*. It is time to go."

Jess heaved a sigh. "If we must. But first I need to tidy up."

After an interval spent in Lorenzo's bathroom Jess presented herself for inspection in the soft lamplight of the beautiful outer room.

"Do I look all right?" she asked anxiously.

He smiled appreciatively. "Good enough to gobble up, as your friend would say."

"Lorenzo," said Jess suddenly. "There's something you should know."

His smile faded. "Tell me, then."

Her eyes fell. "I don't count the fiasco with the schoolboy, but I'd known the other two a long time before—"

"Before you became lovers?"

She nodded, flushing as she slid her feet into the famous sandals. "I wouldn't describe the arrangement like that, but that's what I meant, yes."

Lorenzo took her hands in his, looking down at her very soberly. "You are telling me that it is not your habit to make love with a man you've known such a short time. But for you and for me it is different. I love you, Jessamy."

"I love you, too," she said, oddly shy now.

"I asked you to marry me. And you consented. A church ceremony will make no difference to the way I feel," he assured her. "To me you are already my wife."

Jess felt tears well up in her eyes, and smiled at him damply. "Sorry. I'm not usually the weepy kind."

"Do not apologise, *carissima*, I love to kiss your tears away—"

"Remember what happened last time," she reminded him, sniffing hard.

He heaved in a deep sigh. "I do. Most vividly. So come. Let us go before I scandalise Anna by returning you after midnight."

"Hold me for a moment," she said gruffly.

"For the rest of my life!" he assured her, and held her up against him so that she stood on tiptoe and had to wreath her arms round his waist to keep her balance.

"I need your arms around me to convince myself this is all happening," she whispered.

Lorenzo looked deep into her eyes. "This is no fairytale, *Cenerentola*, this is real life. Our life." His arms tightened. "Now you have given yourself to me you are mine. I shall never let you go."

CHAPTER NINE

EMILY was too sleepy to do more than ask if Jess had enjoyed herself, and once Anna had gone to the room Lorenzo had reserved for her, Jess showered swiftly and slid into bed, reliving the evening over and over again before she slept at last. She woke only when the nurse arrived early next morning to see to Emily, which ruled out any private conversation with her friend, and Jess was grateful for it. The magic with Lorenzo was a glorious, private secret. And in the bright light of morning, despite Lorenzo's parting words, it was still hard to believe that the whole episode wasn't some figment of her imagination.

When her last relationship had soured Jess had been philosophical when Leonie questioned her about it. "Some day my prince will come," she'd said flippantly, but had never really expected a fairy tale scenario for herself. Ever. Yet now, with Lorenzo, it seemed that the dreams she'd once dreamed had finally come true.

While she shared an early breakfast with a slightly improved Emily, Jess described the delicious dinner she'd eaten, but because Anna was bustling about, preparing for the journey to the Villa Fortuna, she made no mention of dining alone with Lorenzo in his private apartment.

"I'm entitled to loss of appetite, but you're not," Emily accused, when Jess contented herself with orange juice and coffee.

"You know I never eat breakfast!"

Emily cast a knowing eye on her friend's dreaming face and raised an expressive eyebrow, Anna's presence preventing any teasing.

Due to Anna's efficiency Emily was bathed and dressed and ready well before time, but looked even less robust once she was on her feet.

"Take it easy, Em," said Jess, sitting her down in a chair near the open balcony doors. "Apparently it's not far to the villa, and when we get there you can go straight to bed, if you want."

"It is most necessary that she does so after the journey," said Anna firmly. "Dottore Tosti orders this. Tomorrow, Emily, you shall get up for a longer time."

"Yes, Nurse," said the invalid, so meekly it was plain that the thought of bed was more welcome than Emily cared to let on.

A few minutes later a porter arrived to take their luggage, then Jess and the nurse supported a very shaky Emily on the short distance to the lift.

"I feel like a new-born lamb," gasped Emily, wincing as the familiar pain gripped her ribs. She leaned gratefully against Jess as the lift descended.

"You'll soon be stronger," said Jess firmly, catching Anna's eye anxiously for confirmation.

The nurse nodded benignly. "A few days of fresh air and rest will see much improvement."

Lorenzo was waiting for them in the foyer, dressed more casually than usual, and to Jess's eyes so irresistible she wanted to throw herself into his arms there and then, regardless of the staff gathered to expedite their departure.

"*Buon giorno!*" he said, smiling at all three of them, but the quickly veiled look he gave Jess told her he was controlling a similar impulse to her own. "How are you feeling this morning, Miss Emily?"

"Fine," she said manfully, but even with Jess holding her tightly by the arm it was obvious to everyone that this was a polite lie.

"Actually, Lorenzo," said Jess in an undertone, "she's not too good. Is it far to the car?"

"No. It waits outside." He turned to Anna and gave her some swift instructions, then, with a smile at Emily, said *"Permesso,"* and picked her up, telling Jess to follow them as he carried the invalid outside and down the red-carpeted steps to the car. He settled Emily gently in the back seat alongside Anna, held the front passenger door for Jess, then excused himself to go back into the hotel to talk to the manager.

"Are you all right, love?" Jess turned anxiously to peer at her friend.

"Of course I am." Emily smiled valiantly. "How could I be anything else with all this star treatment?"

Lorenzo Forli drove out of Florence with due care for the welfare of the invalid, and after a short journey on the autostrada turned off on to a quiet minor road, slowing down to allow his passengers time to admire the views. The narrow, winding route was lined in places with groups of flame-shaped cypresses used as windbreaks for the olive groves and vines grown on the slopes of rolling amber hills. Here and there a patch of brighter gold indicated a crop of sunflowers, and in some places Lorenzo pointed out fields of the barley and maize used to feed cattle and poultry.

Jess was entranced by it all, smiling radiantly in response to the occasional questioning glance Lorenzo sent in her direction. It amazed her that in such a short distance from the sophistication of Florence they were deep in a timeless landscape which seemed little changed from those in the Renaissance paintings she'd seen in the Uffizi.

A few kilometres later Lorenzo turned off on a much narrower road which he informed them was one of the *strade vicinali*, the neighbourhood roads which wander over the Italian countryside. This one was little more than a track which wound up to the summit of one of the rounded hills, where the car nosed through a gap in a ring of cypresses to bring them to a house very different from the formal, classical villa Jess had expected. Lorenzo's country home was a long, two-storey house with cinnamon roof tiles and white-shuttered windows, the natural stone of the walls gilded by the morning sun. There were outbuildings in the background, and big earthenware pots of geraniums stood in a paved courtyard where a table and several chairs sheltered under a group of trees from the heat of the Tuscan sun.

"How lovely!" exclaimed Emily.

"Villa Fortuna," announced Lorenzo. He looked at Jess, a question in his eyes. "You approve?"

"How could I not?" she said with fervour. "It's heavenly!"

Then there was a commotion as a small, plump woman came hurrying from the house, followed by a thin, dark man, both of them talking at once to welcome the lord of the manor and his guests.

Lorenzo jumped out of the car, smiling broadly in return, and suddenly Jess saw a different side of him. This was the man who'd been born here, and these the exuberant, affectionate couple who had known him from his birth. He greeted them with warm affection, then presented Jess to them with a proprietary air no one watching could fail to interpret.

"This is Carla, who cooks like an angel from heaven," he told her, "and Mario who takes care of everything else." He translated rapidly, bring much bridling laughter from the woman and a pleased smile from her husband.

Jess held out her hand. *"Piacere,"* she said, with as good an accent as she could muster.

Her essay into Italian brought forth an incomprehensible stream of it in return, though the gist of it was easy enough to understand. The fact that Signor Lorenzo had brought guests to stay was the cause of much happiness for Carla and Mario Monti, and much sympathy for a white-faced Emily when, despite her protests that she could walk, Lorenzo carried her from the car to one of the shaded chairs.

"La poverina!" said Carla with sympathy, then hurried off to fetch refreshments, taking Anna with her while her husband saw to the luggage.

"We shall sit here for a few minutes," said Lorenzo, pulling up a chair for Jess. "It is not too hot for you, Emily?"

"Not in the least," she assured him. "Besides, there's a lovely cool breeze here."

"We Tuscans build our houses on top of hills for just this purpose," he assured her, and turned to Jess. "And you, Jessamy? How do you feel?"

Knowing that Lorenzo meant a great deal more than whether she'd survived the journey without ill effect, Jess smiled at him luminously, and leaned back in her chair with a sigh of pleasure. "I feel wonderful," she assured him, and waved at the view. "I'd be happy just to sit here all day, gazing at this fabulous landscape. When I stayed with Leo I never went outside the city."

"I am pleased you like my home." He looked up with a smile for Carla, who was returning with a tray of coffee and almond biscuits recently taken from the oven. *"Grazie,"* he said as she put it down in front of Jess, then listened, nodding in approval, as Carla spoke at length before bestowing a smile on the guests and hurrying back into the house.

"Anna is putting your clothes away, Emily," he reported. "And the nurse says that once you have finished your coffee you must rest on your bed, so that you will feel strong enough to join us for lunch."

Jess grinned at the mutinous expression on her friend's face. "Anna's quite a tyrant, isn't she? But she's right, Em. Take it easy for a while."

"I will." Emily smiled ruefully. "In fact I'll be quite glad to lie down again. Feeble, isn't it?"

"You cannot expect to recover from *la pleurite* overnight," said Lorenzo gently. "Soon, once the medication has had more time to take effect, I shall take you exploring with Jessamy." He stood up. "But for the moment forgive me if I leave you for a while to speak with Mario."

When he'd gone Jess poured coffee with a steady hand, aware that Emily was watching her speculatively. "What?" she asked, adding cream and sugar.

"When you said all that about truly, madly, deeply and so on," began Emily in an undertone.

"Yes."

"Lorenzo feels the same about you, doesn't he?"

Jess smiled happily as she sat back with her coffee. "He says he does."

Emily pulled a face. "Which makes the situation a tad awkward for me, old love."

Jess shot a surprised glance at her. "Why?"

"Would *you* like playing gooseberry if the situation were reversed?"

Jess was quiet for a moment, trying to find words of reassurance. She took her sunglasses off and leaned forward to emphasise her words. "Actually, Em, it doesn't matter whether we're alone or not. To be in love with someone doesn't mean one has to *make* love."

"Not for you, Snow Queen, I know. But for most people it does."

Jess smiled crookedly. "Actually it does for me, too. This time."

Emily chuckled. "I thought as much. We've lived together for quite a while, Jess Dysart, but I've never seen you like this before."

"I know. But don't worry. I'm happy just as long as Lorenzo's somewhere near at hand. I promise there'll be no embarrassing displays of affection," Jess assured her. "Besides," she added, "there's not only you, but Anna, Carla and Mario, to name but a few. And Lorenzo said his sister, Isabella, will come rushing to inspect us when she discovers he's got guests."

"Is that a habit of hers?"

"Apparently he's never brought anyone to stay before. A woman, I mean."

Emily whistled softly, and held out her cup for more coffee. "Which means, I hazard a guess, that Signor Forli's intentions are strictly honourable where you're concerned."

Jess wasn't listening. She was smiling in a way which plainly dazzled the man who came to join them. "Is everything all right, Lorenzo?"

"Yes," he said simply, taking the chair beside her. "Everything." His eyes detached themselves from hers with an effort, which plainly delighted the third member of the trio. "How are you feeling, Emily?"

"She's feeling awkward," said Jess bluntly.

Emily went scarlet and Lorenzo frowned.

"Awkward?" he queried.

"She feels she's playing gooseberry," Jess informed him.

Lorenzo thought for a moment, mentally translating the unfamiliar term, then his face cleared, and he smiled at Emily with such warmth her colour receded a little. "Ah! I see." He nodded. "Jessamy has told you that she—she cares for me, no?"

"Yes," said Emily. "But she put it a lot more strongly than that."

Lorenzo exchanged a gleaming look with Jess, then turned back to her friend. "I shall be frank. I fell in love with Jessamy the moment I first saw her. And I consider myself the most fortunate of men, because last night she told me—"

"That it was the same for me," interrupted Jess. "And for the very first time, as you know better than anyone, Em."

"I do indeed. I'm very happy for you." Emily beamed on them both, then turned away a little to cough painfully. "Sorry. I think maybe it's time I found that bed. And not," she added breathlessly, "because I feel in the way. I just feel a bit weary."

Jess looked at her watch. "And in a few minutes it's time for the next dose of pills. Lorenzo, could you show us where we're to sleep?"

"Of course." He went over to Emily. "Come. I shall carry you upstairs."

"No, really!" she protested, looking horrified. "I can walk."

"Let us see how you are once you are inside," he compromised, and took her arm while Jess held on to the other.

Inside the house it was cool, and both Lorenzo's guests exclaimed with pleasure at the sight of gleaming tiled floors and stone walls, with arched doorways leading off the large hall into the various ground-floor rooms. A mixture of comfortable modern furniture lived in harmony with antique pieces, giving a very different effect from the formality of Lorenzo's apartment in the hotel.

"You shall explore the rooms later," he said, looking down into Emily's suddenly wan face as she eyed the flight of stone stairs which led to the upper floor. *"Permesso,"* he said again, and picked her up, leaving Jess to follow behind as he carried her friend to a room situated at the back of the house, with a view of the rolling countryside from its windows.

Anna was already there, setting out bottles of water and fruit juice on a table beside the wrought-iron bed, where crisp white covers were turned down in invitation. The nurse clucked in alarm at the sight of Emily's face, scolding gently as Lorenzo lowered the invalid into a wicker chair under the open window.

"Run away and play, children," said Emily, managing a grin. "I'm in good hands."

"Let me help you undress," said Jess, but Anna should her head.

"No, *signorina*, I shall take care of Emily. She needs to rest, then perhaps she can join you for lunch. We shall see."

On the gallery which ran the length of the upper floor, Lorenzo led Jess to a room at the far end of the house. It was similar in size and furnishing to Emily's, complete with a small bathroom, but with a slightly different view. And, to Jess's dismay, she found that her belongings had been unpacked and neatly put away.

"This is lovely, but Anna shouldn't have bothered with my things as well," said Jess, embarrassed.

"It was Carla who unpacked for you, not Anna," he informed her, and smiled as he took her in his arms. The door of the bedroom was open, so that anyone who passed could see in, and the kiss Lorenzo gave her was fleeting, but so possessive Jess was left in no doubt that their relationship had taken a new turn. "Do you mind that she suspects how things are with us, *amore*?"

"You told her?"

"Officially, no." He shrugged, smiling. "But I have brought no woman here since my marriage, so she takes my relationship with you for granted. Does this trouble you?"

"Not in the least," Jess assured him. "Soon, when we're more used to the idea ourselves, the whole world can know."

Lorenzo took her on a quick tour of the upper rooms, one of which was Roberto's when he cared to use it instead of his apartment in the city. Downstairs there was a big, formal room Lorenzo called a *salone*, beyond it a dining room and a *salotto*, an informal sitting room with comfortable, well-worn furniture. Finally Lorenzo showed Jess a room he used as a study, complete with the latest technology to keep him in touch with the family business when he was at the villa. Carla and Mario, he informed her, lived in the cottage outside at the back of the house, but during the day Carla reigned over their last port of call, the all-important kitchen. It was very large, filled with fragrant smells of the meal Carla was preparing with the help of a young girl Lorenzo introduced as Gina, Carla's niece.

Lorenzo conducted a rapid, teasing conversation with

Carla, then Jess said her goodbyes after miming her rapture at the enticing smells in the air.

"She loves you very much, Lorenzo," said Jess as they went outside into the courtyard.

"When I was young she was my nursemaid," he explained, "so for Carla I have always been her special charge."

"Did she go with you to Oltrarno when you married Renata?" asked Jess.

Lorenzo shook his head, looking bleak. "She wished to. But by this time Carla had been cook and housekeeper here for years, and my mother could not spare her, thank God. Otherwise I would have been forced to break Carla's heart by refusing to let her work for us. I could not have hidden the misery of my marriage from her."

Jess frowned. "But if she knows you that well she must have seen that your marriage was unhappy, darling."

The endearment won Jess a kiss before Lorenzo drew her down on a wicker sofa beside him.

"You are right, of course. Carla knew very well that my marriage was a failure. But not why. No one knows this, *carissima*. Only you."

To give Emily time to recover from the journey, lunch was served late in the cool dining room, by which time Jess was as ready as Lorenzo for the plates of steaming pasta put before them, rich with tomato and basil and scattered with pine nuts and crisp-fried morsels of pancetta.

Emily, who looked a lot better for her rest, ate more than Jess had expected, exclaiming over the heavenly flavour.

Lorenzo looked on with indulgent approval as Jess

wiped a hunk of crusty bread round her plate to enjoy the last scrap of sauce. "Do you know, Emily, that our dinner last night was the first meal I had seen Jessamy eat?" he remarked.

Emily stared at him in astonishment. "Really? But normally she—"

"Eats like a horse," said Jess, resigned, and grinned at Lorenzo. "I told you that, but you didn't believe me. And until last night we hadn't actually shared a proper meal, remember."

"You ate nothing of the meal served to us on the plane," he reminded her.

"She never does. She hates flying," Emily informed him.

Lorenzo eyed Jess in surprise. "You said nothing, *carissima*. You should have told me."

"I wasn't nervous this time."

"With Lorenzo for company you probably forgot you were even in a plane," said Emily, chuckling.

Jess made a face at her. "Something like that."

"I am flattered," said Lorenzo, looking unashamedly smug.

When Carla came in with dessert she smiled in satisfaction when Lorenzo translated his guests' appreciation.

"She says that's the way to get well, Emily," said Lorenzo, then exchanged a look with Jess when Carla placed a familiar cake in front of her before going back to the kitchen.

"That looks yummy," said Emily, then looked at the other two with narrowed eyes. "What's wrong?"

"Nothing," said Jess hastily. "Just a coincidence. We were given this for pudding last night."

"Is it nice?" asked Emily, as Jess served her with a modest slice.

"She did not eat it," said Lorenzo, poker-faced.

To avoid explanations Jess cut a piece for herself, but Lorenzo refused.

"It is not cake that I want," he informed her, smiling into her eyes. "Just a little of this cheese to eat with Carla's bread," he added innocently.

Emily, plainly aware of undercurrents, tactfully ignored her friend's hot cheeks and applied herself to the cake. "It's gorgeous," she pronounced. "What's in it?"

"Almonds, lemon and ricotta," said Jess promptly, tasting her own. "And you're right. It's delicious."

After dinner that first evening Emily asked permission to ring her mother. "In case she rings the hotel and finds I've vanished! But I didn't want to ring until I at least sounded better."

"Invite your mother to come and stay here with you until you are well," suggested Lorenzo. "After helping with the little ones she must also be in need of rest."

Emily, though deeply grateful for Lorenzo Forli's kindness, flatly refused to take advantage of it to such an extent. "In fact," she added, "I should be fit enough to return with Jess on Saturday."

"Are you sure you're up to that on your own?" said Jess.

"*This* Saturday?" said Lorenzo swiftly, eyes narrowed. "You did not tell me, Jessamy."

Jess looked at him in distress. "I just have to get back next week because other people at the agency are on holiday. Could you arrange a flight for me?"

After Emily had gone off to ring her mother Lorenzo seized Jess by the shoulders. "Stay with me. Tell this agency of yours that you are not returning."

"I must go back, darling. Please—don't look at me

like that; I can't bear it.'' To her dismay Jess began to sob, and Lorenzo swept her into his arms.

"I cannot endure your tears," he said huskily. "So. I shall let you go back. But not for long. If you love me—"

"I do, I do," she assured him passionately.

"Then resign at once. And I shall come to England and ask your father's permission to marry his daughter," Lorenzo said with decision, and kissed her hard by way of emphasis.

By the time Emily rejoined them they were drinking coffee in the small sitting room, Jess composed and harmony restored.

"The little girls are better," Emily reported, and sat down rather wearily.

"How did your mother take the news about the pleurisy?" asked Jess, passing her a cup of coffee.

"Not terribly well. On top of the chicken pox it was a bit much, poor dear."

"She is naturally anxious," said Lorenzo. "It is Anna's opinion that you will not be well enough to travel on Saturday, Emily. Ask your mother to join you here in a day or two. Next week, after Jessamy has gone, I shall return to the apartment in Firenze. You may have the house to yourselves, except for Carla and Mario, of course."

But Emily wouldn't hear of it. "It's very kind of you, Lorenzo, but I must go back with Jess," she said firmly. "I already feel much better—"

"Well, you don't look it," said Jess flatly, but just then Anna appeared and put an end to the discussion by stating that it was time her patient was in bed.

Later Jess went out into the courtyard with Lorenzo, to look at the stars in the cool of the evening. "I wish I could stay," she said wistfully.

"Soon you shall stay with me for ever!"

"Will we live here all the time?" asked Jess.

"Some of the time only." Lorenzo put his arm round her and drew her close. "We shall spend our weekends here, the rest of the time at the *appartamento*." He rubbed his cheek against her hair. "There are occasions when I curse living so close to my work, but last night I gave thanks for such an arrangement," he whispered, his breath warm against her skin.

"So did I," she whispered back, and turned her face up for his kiss.

To her surprise Jess soon found she was as tired as Emily. "I don't know why," she said apologetically, after a second yawn. "Heaven knows I haven't done much today."

"It is the air," said Lorenzo, pulling her to her feet.

"And I had a very strenuous day yesterday—" Jess halted, biting her lip, and Lorenzo laughed softly and held her close.

"We should have such strenuous days more often, *tesoro*."

Jess was pensive as they went in the house. "The thing is, Lorenzo," she said, as he began turning out lights, "Emily won't ask her mother to come because Mrs Shaw is a widow on a pension. She just wouldn't have the spare cash for the flight."

"Ah, I see!" Lorenzo frowned. "It would be simple to buy a ticket. But how can we arrange it so that the lady is not offended?"

"Tomorrow I'll ring Celia, Emily's sister, and see what can be done."

When Emily was resting after lunch next day Jess made her phone call and found that Celia thought a trip to Tuscany was an excellent idea for her mother. After a

rapid consultation with her husband Celia reported that
Daddy was taking a fortnight off to help with the con-
valescence, and would be very happy to provide an air-
line ticket to Pisa for Mrs Shaw as a gift for all her hard
work.

"Or maybe Jack wants his mother-in-law out of the
way now he's home," said Emily privately to Jess, after
her mother rang in great excitement to say that she would
soon be on her way to Italy.

"Don't they get on?" asked Jess.

"Reasonably well. But Jack works long hours, so he
doesn't see much of his family during the week. He'll be
glad of time alone with them. Nothing more sinister than
that. I hope." Emily sipped her iced fruit juice, frowning.
"It seems so hard on you, though, Jess. You're back to
the grind, while I'm staying on here where you should
be. How are you going to tear yourself away from
Lorenzo?"

"With the utmost difficulty," said Jess despondently.

"Tell me to mind my own business, but has he popped
the question yet?"

"Yes. But that's not for publication yet, Em. To anyone."

Emily's grey eyes opened wide. "You said yes, of
course—" She breathed in sharply, and began to cough,
and Anna came hurrying to suggest her patient went in-
doors where it was cooler.

"You stay here, Jess," said Emily when she could
speak. "I think I'll go and have a bath, then read for a
while on my bed."

"Not suffering from gooseberry complex by any
chance?" demanded Jess suspiciously.

Emily grinned and went off with Anna, leaving Jess
alone to gaze at the view. It would be agony to part with

Lorenzo, she knew very well, there was no possible way out of it. And she would need to warn her family about his proposal before he contacted them himself. Jess tried to imagine the general Dysart reaction to the news, and decided to ask Lorenzo to leave it for a while before breaking it to them, so that the whole idea didn't smack of unseemly haste.

"You are very thoughtful," said Lorenzo, coming to sit beside her. He took her hand and kissed it. "You look sad, *piccola*."

"I feel sad," she admitted. "I don't want to go back on Saturday, Lorenzo."

"When do you start work?"

"Monday," she said gloomily.

"Then stay until Sunday. Once Emily's mother arrives you have no need to stay here at the villa." Lorenzo's eyes lit with the look which never failed to send heat rushing through her every vein. "We could leave here on Saturday morning, then stay in Firenze until it is time for you to leave."

Jess buried her face against his shoulder. "Yes, please," she said in a muffled voice. "I'd like that *very* much."

"Bene!" he said with satisfaction. "Because I have already asked my assistant to make the reservation for Sunday."

"You were so very sure I'd want to stay?"

Lorenzo gave his very Latin shrug. "Why should you be in London alone, I in Firenze alone, when we can be together for an extra day? Guido will fax me shortly with confirmation of your flight."

Jess looked after him with a wry little smile as Lorenzo strode into the house to wait for the fax. Lorenzo Forli was used to getting his own way. Though in this instance it was very much her own way, too. He was right. She wouldn't have time to get down to Friars Wood and back. And to spend Saturday night and Sunday on her own in London was madness when the alternative was extra time with Lorenzo. Alone with Lorenzo, she reminded herself, and gave an ecstatic little shiver at the thought of it.

Jess had fully expected her stay at the Villa Fortuna to be frustrating, since there would be little opportunity to be alone with Lorenzo, and even when they were the likelihood of interruption would prevent anything other than hand-holding and a kiss or two. But in some strange way she soon found she liked the arrangement very much. After rushing headlong into the ultimate intimacy with Lorenzo Forli it was strangely satisfying to back-track a little, just to be together, whether alone or not. It was a joy just to walk with him, to explore the property, or to sit and talk under the trees in the courtyard. He began teaching her a little basic Italian, but otherwise their time alone together was spent in a voyage of discovery.

"To make up for all the years before you came into my life," declared Lorenzo.

And at night, when Lorenzo escorted her upstairs to her room, long after Emily had retired to hers, he kissed Jess at length before they parted, but after the first day had never set foot in her room. Knowing he was in the bedroom next to hers, Jess had expected to spend restless, sleepless nights. Instead she slept soundly and woke early, eager to join Lorenzo for the breakfast Carla served them in the courtyard before the sun grew too fierce. Emily breakfasted in bed, happy to give Jess time alone with Lorenzo.

Late in the afternoon Jess was reading alone in the

courtyard while Emily had a rest, and Lorenzo was in his study dealing with hotel business over the phone. Jess looked up from her book at the sound of an approaching car, the sound growing louder in the stillness, indicating that the driver was heading for the Villa Fortuna, since the narrow track led only to the house.

When a car appeared through the cypresses Jess hesitated, wondering whether to go and find Lorenzo, or stand her ground and greet the visitor herself. In which case, she thought wryly, it was to be hoped that the visitor spoke English. The few words of Italian she'd learned so far were better suited to the bedroom than to welcoming guests.

A slim, bespectacled young man got out of the car, then reached inside it for a medical bag. Dr Tosti had obviously come to check on the patient.

"How do you do?" said Jess with a smile, holding out her hand. "I'm Jessamy Dysart."

"*Piacere*, Miss Dysart," he said, bowing over her hand. "Bruno Tosti. Anna has reported to me that your friend is improving, but Lorenzo wishes me to confirm this."

Lorenzo came hurrying from the house, his smile wide as he wrung his friend's hand. "*Come sta*, Bruno? But we are obliged to converse in English. Jessamy has very little Italian yet."

Bruno Tosti was a very pleasant man, and obviously much attached to Lorenzo. He admitted that it had been no hardship to leave the city to come to Villa Fortuna, and since he was not on duty that evening he would be very glad to accept Lorenzo's invitation to dinner.

"I'll go and call Anna," volunteered Jess. "Emily is reading on her bed, but I expect you'd like to talk to the nurse first."

"Thank you, Jessamy," said Lorenzo. "Will you ask Carla to bring coffee?"

Jess hurried off to embark on a funny little exchange with Carla, half-mime, have words, and a great deal of hand-waving. Afterwards she ran up the smooth stone stairs to Emily's room, and found Anna changing the sheets while her patient sat curled up in a chair with her book.

"Anna, Dottore Tosti's here," said Jess breathlessly. "He'd like to see you before he examines the patient."

The nurse hurried off at once, and Emily sprang rashly to her feet.

"At least I'm clean," she said, equally breathless as she brushed her hair. "Last time the doctor saw me I was covered in sweat and thoroughly unappetising. And he's rather nice in a quiet sort of way, isn't he?"

"Just as well you approve," said Jess, grinning. "He's staying to dinner."

This information threw the patient into some confusion. "Not that it matters what I wear," she groaned. "I'm not exactly at my best at the moment."

"Maybe the doctor won't let you stay up for dinner," teased Jess.

However, after a thorough examination of the patient, during which both the nurse and Jess were present, the doctor pronounced himself pleased with Emily's progress, but ordered a great deal of rest, and approved her decision to stay on at the villa for an extra week.

"This is good," he informed her. "It would be most unwise to fly home on Saturday, as Lorenzo told me you intended, *signorina*. But with your mother to look after you once Anna has gone, after another week of rest you should be fully recovered."

It was a quietly festive little party which gathered in

the courtyard before dinner. Emily and the rather serious young doctor got on very well, and Jess was left free to enjoy her proximity to Lorenzo, and contribute to the conversation now and then, but was mostly content just to sit near him, sipping her glass of wine sparingly, and savouring this new-found bliss she could hardly believe was hers.

When another car was heard approaching up the steep, winding bends to the villa, Lorenzo smiled with sudden pleasure as an Alfa Romeo Spider materialised through the cypresses, and came to a dramatic halt. A familiar figure jumped out and came striding towards them, a broad grin on his handsome face.

"*Buona sera!* I am in time for dinner?"

CHAPTER TEN

ROBERTO FORLI kissed Jess on both cheeks, hugged his brother, shook hands with the doctor, then turned the full wattage of his smile on Emily and demanded an introduction.

Jess felt sudden sympathy for the sober doctor. His animation diminished visibly as he witnessed his patient's reaction to the confident charm of Roberto Forli. Carla came bustling out of the house, stopped short dramatically, hand on heart, as she laid eyes on Roberto, and let forth a stream of scolding she responded to by taking her in his arms and hugging her until she relented at last and smiled lovingly on him.

Roberto excused himself to tidy up and went off with Carla, an arm slung round her shoulders as he offered extravagant apologies she responded to by patting his cheek as they went into the house.

"Did you know Roberto was back?" asked Jess.

"No." Lorenzo shrugged negligently. "But it is always so. He arrives unannounced. Carla gives him a furious lecture. Then she serves him food fit for a king."

"Does she ever scold you, Lorenzo?" asked Emily mischievously.

"Never," he said piously, eyes dancing. "I am much too virtuous!"

"Modest, too," said Jess, laughing, then turned to Bruno Tosti and drew him into the conversation.

When Roberto returned he helped Emily to her feet and escorted her into dinner, leaving the doctor to follow behind with Jess and Lorenzo. Roberto, thought Jess, amused, had obviously recovered his spirits since last seen leaving her sister's wedding in deep dejection.

While they enjoyed Carla's wild mushroom risotto Roberto Forli informed them he had just arrived from London that day.

"To find a message waiting for me from Isabella," he went on, with a significant look at his brother. "She arrived home today from her little holiday with her friend in Positano in much excitement, Lorenzo, because you told Andrea that Jess and her friend stay at the villa. So I decided to join you for dinner."

"Isabella did not insist on coming with you?" said Lorenzo dryly, pouring wine.

Roberto laughed. "After living without her for a week Andrea desires his wife's presence tonight. But tomorrow she will no doubt arrive before breakfast!" He explained to Emily that Isabella took a very keen interest in the lives of her brothers, her greatest ambition in life to see them both happily married.

"My sister's just the same with me," she said, smiling.

"You have no wish for this, Emily?" asked Bruno.

"Oh, yes," she said airily. "One day. But not yet."

He eyed the portion of risotto left on her plate. "You must eat, or you will not get well."

"If I eat any more I won't manage the next course," said Emily apologetically, and asked Lorenzo to explain to Carla. "She's so kind. I wouldn't hurt her for the world."

"You may eat as much, or as little, as you like," he assured her.

"Drink some wine instead," urged Roberto.

"No, she must not," said Bruno quickly. "Mineral water only, Roberto, because of her medication."

The evening had been convivial before Roberto's arrival, but his presence was a catalyst which changed the occasion into a party. He kept them entertained with tales of his stay in London while they ate thin slivers of pork grilled with lemon, rosemary and garlic, followed by a confection of chestnut purée and whipped cream. But at last Emily, though very obviously enjoying herself enormously, began to look tired. At which point Bruno Tosti took unconcealed satisfaction in scoring points off Roberto, even if it meant depriving himself of his patient's company.

"And now, Miss Emily," he said formally, once coffee had been served, "it is time you retired to your bed."

"At this hour?" protested Roberto, then caught the look Lorenzo gave him, and threw up his hands in surrender. "Emily is your patient, of course, Bruno."

"Esattamente," agreed the doctor stiffly. "And to recover sufficiently to fly home next week it is essential she takes much rest."

Emily got up at once. "You're right, doctor," she said, smiling as she held out her hand to him. "Thank you so much for coming to see me." She turned to Roberto. "It was very nice to meet you, too."

"Prego!" He kissed her hand, then straightened, smiling. "But you will do so again in the morning, Emily. I am staying the night."

After Emily's round of goodnights the two women went out together, leaving, Jess suspected, rather an awkward silence behind them.

"How are you feeling, really?" she asked, as she took Emily's arm to mount the stairs. "Are you up for this, or shall I call for some muscles from your rivals down there? Which do you fancy? Roberto's the hunkier of the two."

Emily laughed breathlessly, then regretted it as the familiar pain caught her. "I can make my own way tonight, thanks," she gasped at last. "If we—keep—to a crawl!"

Before they'd negotiated more than a couple of steps Anna came hurrying down towards them to take Emily's other arm.

"It is late," she scolded, "and you should be in bed, *cara*. I could not interrupt when Dottore Tosti was there, but I was most worried."

"Sorry, Anna." Emily smiled at the nurse apologetically. "I should have come earlier, but I was having such a good time." She turned to Jess. "Off you go, back to the fray."

Jess gave her a hug and a kiss, wished her a restful night, then went back downstairs to find Lorenzo and Roberto alone in the courtyard. They both got to their feet as she joined them, and Lorenzo informed her that Bruno sent his apologies, but had been obliged to leave.

"I think I spoil the evening for Bruno," said Roberto, without any noticeable penitence. "Let us be comfortable in the *salotto*. Will you have some grappa, Jess?"

"No, thanks." Jess sat down on a small sofa beside Lorenzo, who took her hand in his and held it there.

"Roberto," he said, lifting Jess's hand to his lips. "I have asked Jessamy to marry me."

Roberto looked stunned for a moment, then his eyes lit up with pure delight, and he got up to kiss Jess on both cheeks. "*Ottimo!* From the look of triumph on my brother's face, *cara*, I assume you have consented?"

She nodded. "You probably think this is all very sudden. Do you approve?" she added bluntly.

Roberto gave his brother a drink, then sat down opposite with his own, grinning as he raised his hand in blessing. "If Lorenzo is happy of course I approve. I think my brother is a fortunate man." He shrugged. "But it is no real surprise, Jess. After years of trying to interest him in various charming ladies, with no success at all, one day he saw your photograph and—" He snapped his fingers. "That was that."

The telephone rang in the hall and Lorenzo got up, excusing himself as he went to answer it. When they were alone, Robert leaned forward, his eyes bright with urgency.

"My brother was greatly affected by his wife's death, Jess," he said rapidly in an undertone. "He may not have told you this. He has never discussed it. But for a long time afterwards he was like a man turned to stone. It has taken him a very long time to recover, and I would not see him hurt again, you understand. You are sure of your feelings for him, Jess? In such a short time?"

"Utterly certain." Jess gave him a very straight look. "I never imagined something so wonderful would ever happen to me."

Eyes softened, Roberto sat back in undisguised relief. "*Bene!* Then I welcome you to our family with a glad heart." He paused, staring down into his drink. "Does your—your family know?"

Knowing he really meant Leonie, Jess shook her head. "No. I need time to get used to the idea myself first."

"Naturally." Roberto looked up with a smile as his brother returned. "Isabella?"

"No, the hotel. A small crisis which demands my presence for a while tomorrow." Lorenzo shrugged ruefully, and resumed his place by Jess. "I must leave you for a few hours in the morning, *carissima*. But I shall return to you as soon as I can."

* * *

After the excitement of the dinner party Emily was glad to stay in bed next morning, and sent her goodbyes via Jess, who breakfasted with the brothers before they drove off separately to Florence.

"You must also rest, *carissima*," said Lorenzo, once Roberto had gone. "I shall be home this afternoon, I promise."

"I'll miss you," she said huskily, as she walked with him to the car, and Lorenzo took her in his arms and held her tightly.

"I am very glad that you will miss me!" he said against her lips and kissed her, leaving Jess to wave forlornly as he drove off.

Anna came hurrying out into the courtyard to inform Jess that the invalid had gone back to sleep after her breakfast. "The evening exhausted her. She is not as strong yet as she believes," said the nurse darkly. "Dottore Tosti has asked me to stay until Emily's mother arrives to look after her."

Jess thanked her, then sat under the trees with a book, smiling to herself. Bruno Tosti obviously thought she couldn't be trusted to look after her friend herself, even though she'd done it before often enough, due to Emily's habit of catching any bug going the rounds during winter.

In some ways Jess felt glad to be alone for a while, just to sit and think over the past few days. Love at first sight was possible, she knew very well from Leo and Jonah, but she had never, in her wildest dreams, expected to experience it herself. On the rare occasions when marriage had actually figured in her thoughts, she'd visualised some steady, affectionate man who would make a good husband and father. But all that had changed the day she first set eyes on Lorenzo Forli. She stretched out on the couch she normally shared with him, so lost in daydreams she was startled when Carla touched her shoulder gently and mimed a telephone call.

"Lorenzo?" said Jess hopefully, jumping up.

Carla shook her head, smiling indulgently, and said very clearly, "Signora Moretti—Isabella!"

Jess went in the house and picked up the telephone from a marble table in the hall, clearing her throat a little nervously before she said a cautious hello.

"This is Isabella Moretti, sister of Lorenzo. You are Jessamy?" said an attractive voice more heavily accented than either of her brothers'.

"Yes, I am. How do you do?"

"*Piacere!* Carla says he has gone to Firenze, and you are alone. I hope I did not disturb you."

"No, indeed. How nice of you to ring. Roberto said you might come to the villa today."

"This is why I call, *cara.* I would so much like to meet you, but I know your friend has been ill. Would it disturb her if I come to lunch?"

"Not at all," said Jess with complete truth. Emily would be agog. "We'd both be delighted. Are you bringing your little boys?"

Isabella laughed, a husky, joyous sound very like Roberto's. "No, no. That would be much too much for everyone. They are in school. You shall meet them another time. Tell Carla I arrive at noon. *Ciao!*"

Jess went into the kitchen to inform Carla, with a great deal of hand-waving, that Isabella was coming to lunch, then went upstairs to find the invalid up and dressed.

Emily turned from the mirror to smile at her, hairbrush in hand. "Feeling blue without Lorenzo?"

"I was." Jess admitted, grinning. "But we'll soon have diversion, ducky. Signora Isabella Moretti is coming to lunch!"

Emily laughed. "Not breakfast, then?"

"No. And at least she warned us first. I'm off for a shower." Jess eyed herself in the mirror without pleasure. "Just look at my hair—I was mad to have it cut so short."

"Very stylish, dearie, as you well know, so go and do magic with a hot brush, and I'll creep downstairs to the courtyard to read." Emily grinned. "Don't worry, Anna's given permission!"

Jess eyed her friend's face closely. "You certainly look better than you did last night, Em. Too much excitement, obviously, especially when Roberto turned up."

"Probably—he's very different from big brother!"

"Of course," retorted Jess. "Lorenzo's unique."

Certain that Isabella Moretti would be the picture of Italian chic, Jess worked on her hair until it gleamed, and dressed in black linen trousers and a cream silk shirt, with a plaited black leather belt Leonie had once brought her from the shops near the Santa Croce in Florence.

"Very classy," said Emily, when Jess joined her in the courtyard. "None of the babes you hire for the agency could do better."

"Thank you for those kind words." Jess pulled a face. "Silly, I know, but I'm nervous."

"How old is this famous Isabella?"

"She's the youngest, so late twenties, I suppose." Jess looked round with a smile as young Gina came out, carrying a tray with a pitcher and glasses. "*Grazie*, Gina."

"I pleaded with Anna for a change from mineral water," said Emily, inspecting the ice-filled jug. "This, by the look of it, is fresh lemonade—bliss!"

When a car was heard soon afterwards Jess put down her glass and got to her feet, inwardly bracing herself as a sleek white roadster appeared through the cypresses. "You stay there, invalid. I'll do the necessary."

The driver slid from the car the moment it stopped, whipping off scarf and sunglasses to smile as she hurried forward, her dark eyes bright with animation.

"You are Jessamy," said the new arrival, and seized Jess by the shoulders and kissed her on both cheeks.

Isabella Moretti was a feminine, curvy version of her brother Roberto, her hair cut to hang in a skilful bell-shape about her face.

"How nice to meet you," said Jess, responding involuntarily to the visitor's unaffected warmth. Isabella Moretti was just as elegant as imagined, in a starkly plain beige linen dress, her matching shoes a miracle of Florentine craft, her jewellery limited to a pair of rings and a watch set in a gold bracelet which hung loose from her wrist. "Please come and meet my friend, Emily Shaw."

Emily got up to extend her hand in greeting, and said a rather shy hello.

"*Piacere!* Sit, please," said Isabella, and took the hand, but also kissed both of Emily's still-wan cheeks. "Such bad luck to be ill on holiday."

"I've been very fortunate to come here to get better, *signora*."

"Isabella, *per favore!*"

"Will you have some lemonade?" said Jess, wondering if she should offer coffee instead, but reluctant to sound too territorial in the house that had once been Isabella's home. And still was, in some ways.

Isabella was very happy to drink lemonade. She tossed her fabulously beautiful handbag on the table and took a chair next to Jess, leaving the sofa to Emily. "Lie there and rest, *cara*," she advised. "You look pale."

"We had rather a lively evening," Jess informed her,

and smiled at Emily. "Dr Tosti came to visit the invalid, then stayed on to dinner—"

"And Roberto joined you, of course." Isabella laughed. "He told me he would. But you, of course, Jessamy—" She paused. "Does everyone call you that?"

"No," said Emily. "Only Lorenzo. To the rest of the world she's known as Jess."

Isabella plainly found this bit of information fascination. "Then I shall call you this, also, and leave your special name to my brother. But, Jess, you know Roberto already, of course. Before you met Lorenzo."

"My sister and I had dinner with him when he came to England earlier in the year," agreed Jess.

Isabella cast her eyes skywards. "I know this! He was unbearable when he came home." She leaned nearer confidentially. "I was amazed when Roberto decided to attend her wedding. And now I find Lorenzo was there also. Is your sister happy, Jess?"

"Very. She's on her honeymoon, probably in the South of France by now."

"You approve of her husband?"

"Very much indeed." Jess smiled. "I've always been fond of Jonah."

"*Bene*! Tell Leonie I wish her well," said Isabella, and turned to Emily. "And you, *cara*, do you have a special man?"

Emily looked startled. "Er—no. No, I don't. Not at the moment."

Carla came hurrying out before there were more questions. Isabella jumped to her feet to embrace her, and embarked on a long, affectionate exchange before turning to the others in apology.

"Forgive me, but Carla always desires information

about my sons. Also she says lunch is ready inside. *An-diamo*.''

Over a lunch of salad and *frittata*, Carla's perfect asparagus omelette, Isabella was only too happy to talk about Antonio and Claudio.

"They are enchanting, also, exhausting," she said, chuckling, "but I have a very good girl who helps with them, and now they are in school life is easier." She looked at her watch. "I must return in time for them to come home today, because I was away all last week with my friend Angelica, listening to her woes. She is a lawyer, and very clever, but unlucky in love!" Isabella rolled her eyes. "I was very happy to return to Andrea. He also is a lawyer, but when it comes to love—" She smiled engagingly. "He says he is a fortunate man."

Jess could well believe it. Isabella Moretti was a young woman of great charm and vivacity, and after an entire week without her Andrea Moretti had no doubt welcomed his wife home with open arms.

The three of them spent a very pleasant time together over lunch, but when it was over Emily got to her feet.

"Please excuse me, Isabella. I'd better go up for a rest, or Anna will scold. I'm so glad to have met you."

Isabella professed herself equally pleased, invited Emily to visit her in Lucca whenever she wished, then went out to the courtyard with Jess to drink coffee under the trees.

"How long do you stay, Jess?" she said, as she filled their cups, automatically taking on the role of hostess.

"Until Sunday, if Lorenzo can arrange it. I should be flying back on Saturday, but I don't start work until Monday, so—"

"So Lorenzo persuaded you to spend every minute

you could with him before leaving him," said Isabella, nodding. "What is this work, *cara*?"

Jess described her job at the agency, finding it very easy to talk to someone so fascinated by insight into the life of the successful model.

At last, with much regret, Isabella announced it was time for her to drive home. "But before I go," she added, her vivid face suddenly sober, "there is something I must say to you."

Jess braced herself. "Yes?"

Isabella fiddled with her watch. "You know that Lorenzo has not had a—a real relationship with any woman since his wife died?"

"Yes. He told me." Jess smiled a little. "Roberto told me, too."

Isabella made a face. "And now I am repeating it." She threw out her hands in appeal. "I have no wish to intrude on private feelings, *cara*, but after the tragedy of Renata I so want Lorenzo to be happy. I love him very much, you understand."

"So do I," Jess assured her. "And to set your mind at rest, Isabella, I never, ever intend to cause him any hurt. In fact," she added, smiling radiantly, "Lorenzo has asked me to marry him and I've said yes."

Isabella gave a squeal of excitement and jumped up to kiss Jess with wild enthusiasm. "*Meravigliso!* I am so glad. I must hurry home right away to call Andrea. Lorenzo must bring you to dine with us tomorrow. I shall ring him tonight. *Dio*, I am so happy for him. And for you, *cara*!" She rushed into the house to say goodbye to Carla, then ran back out again to embrace Jess once again, gave good wishes for Emily's recovery, and drove away, waving until she was out of sight.

Jess sat alone for a long time afterwards, her eyes on

the rolling vine-clad hills. Isabella's reaction to her announcement had been gratifying in the extreme, Roberto's, too. But now it was time to ask for Dysart approval, which was something new for her parents. Jess had never taken any man home to Friars Wood, something they had found rather strange, she knew only too well. But they had taken very quickly to Lorenzo, which was a good start. Though perhaps they'd feel sad at losing another daughter to Italy, when the first had just returned home for good from Florence. But Jess was confident they would give her their blessing.

"You look very serious," teased a familiar voice, and Jess sprang to her feet and into Lorenzo's arms.

"You're early!" she exclaimed.

"Of course I am early," said Lorenzo at last, smiling down into her eyes. "This is a very special day."

"Every day since I've known you has been special." Jess rubbed her cheek against his. "What's different about today?"

Lorenzo held her away from him, frowning in mock indignation. "You have forgotten? This is our anniversary, *innamorata*, a whole week since I first saw you in the flesh!"

CHAPTER ELEVEN

"Ah, such beautiful flesh," he murmured in her ear, and kissed her again, then frowned when he discovered she was crying. "Tears, Jessamy. Why?"

"Because you're so wonderful and I'm so happy," she said thickly, and smiled at him through the tears clinging to her lashes. "I can hardly believe it's only a week since I first saw you. Everything in life before then seems unimportant."

Lorenzo drew her down to the couch and put his arm round her. "Those are very rewarding words for a man to hear, *carissima*."

"But the truth," she assured him, sniffing inelegantly.

He reached in his pocket. "I have a present for you to mark the occasion."

Jess gazed in awe at the ring he produced. It was modern, a heavy gold band with a plain shank widening into a raised mound encrusted with small diamonds. Lorenzo slid it on her ring finger, and kissed it.

"This is just a token, not an *anello di fidanzato*, because we are not yet officially engaged. You can wear it on the other hand, if you wish. When I have your father's approval I shall buy you another, which we shall choose together. Do you like it? *Dio*, you are crying again!"

Jess flung her arms round his neck and kissed him, careless of the tears streaming down her face. "Darling, I love it. And I love you. I've missed you so much today. Lorenzo, I wish you could fly back with me."

"I, too," he said, kissing away her tears. "But this is

not possible for a week or so. I shall join you the moment
I can, I swear.'' He looked up to smile at Emily, who
was hovering in the doorway.

''Come. Join us,'' he said at once, getting to his feet.

''I don't want to intrude,'' she said awkwardly, ''but
I heard Jess crying. Is anything wrong?''

Jess smiled, sniffing hard, blissfully ignorant of mas-
cara streaks under her eyes. ''Come and sit down.
Look!'' She held out her hand. ''Lorenzo just gave me
this.''

''And you're crying?'' Emily shook her head. ''I'd be
over the moon if someone gave *me* a ring like that!''

''I did not bring you a ring, Emily,'' said Lorenzo,
handing over a package. ''But I think you may like this.''

She gazed at him, horrified. ''After all you've done for
me I don't need presents!'' Recalling her manners hurriedly, she thanked him and undid the parcel, her embarrassment changing to laughter when she held up a packet
of Earl Grey tea. ''Wonderful! Just what I need,'' she
assured him.

Lorenzo went off to hand the tea over to Carla, and to
change his formal suit for something more comfortable,
and the three of them spent a relaxed afternoon together,
Jess telling him how much they'd enjoyed meeting the
vivacious Isabella.

''She's going to ring you tonight to invite us to dinner
tomorrow,'' said Jess, ''but it seems a shame to desert
Mrs Shaw on her first evening here, especially when I'm
leaving next day. Lorenzo, could you invite Isabella and
her husband to dine here instead? Roberto, too, of
course.''

''You mustn't change your plans on my account,'' said
Emily swiftly. ''Mother would hate it if she thought she
was causing any trouble.''

Lorenzo smiled at her in reassurance. "Jessamy is right. I shall ring Isabella myself to suggest a change of plan, and tell her I am to do as she wishes and get married again."

"I've already told her," said Jess quickly. "I hope you don't mind, Lorenzo."

"Mind? I am delighted!"

"I just hope another dinner party won't be too much work for Carla."

Lorenzo laughed indulgently. "When I tell her we celebrate not only the arrival of Emily's mother but our own betrothal, *carissima*, Carla will be very, very happy to make a special dinner."

He was right. After a conversation with his sister after dinner Lorenzo went off to talk with Carla in the kitchen. She came hurrying back with him to kiss Jess and embrace her with exuberance, tears in her eyes as she professed her joy in a spate of words which needed no translation before she rushed off to give her husband the official news.

Emily went to bed soon afterwards, insisting she was tired out by all the excitement. Blessing her friend's tact, Jess spent the rest of the evening in the small sitting room with Lorenzo, her head on his shoulder as they made plans.

"I hope your family will receive the news with equal joy," said Lorenzo huskily, his cheek on her hair.

"I'm sure they will." Jess turned her head to meet his eyes. "But even in the unlikely event that they don't, nothing will change my mind, Lorenzo."

"Carissima!" He kissed her at length to show his appreciation. "I am delighted to hear this, of course, but I would prefer to receive your parents' blessing. I like them

both very much. And little Fenella, at least, will be most pleased. She wishes to visit me here, remember.''

Jess chuckled. ''The moment she hears the news she'll want to be bridesmaid again, too—'' She frowned. ''But perhaps you'd rather not have a church ceremony this time.''

''Because of my first wedding?'' Lorenzo shook his head. ''This time it will be very different for me. I would like to marry in your charming little church, Jessamy. Your parents would prefer this, no?''

''Of course they would.'' She looked at him questioningly. ''What sort of date did you have in mind?''

''My choice would be tomorrow if we could!'' He kissed her hungrily and at once the urge to talk vanished, replaced by desire so swift and overwhelming Jess surrendered herself to his mouth and hands with a lack of inhibition which, in more private surroundings, would have swiftly brought them to the inevitable conclusion.

''This is torture,'' Lorenzo said hoarsely. ''If you love me, Jessamy, for the love of God marry me soon. I need you.''

Shaken to the core by his plea, Jess held his head against her breast, smoothing the dishevelled dark hair until they were calmer. ''Lorenzo,'' she whispered at last, and he raised his head to look at her.

''Yes, *tesoro*?''

''On Saturday, shall we stay at your apartment in the hotel?''

He sat up, his eyes narrowed to a triumphant gleam. ''No. We shall not.''

Jess raised an eyebrow. ''Where, then?''

''Isabella has offered us her house in Lucca for the night. Andrea is taking his wife and sons to visit his parents in Siena. They will return on Sunday morning, just before we leave for the airport.'' He raised an eyebrow. "You approve?"

Jess felt a tide of hot colour flood her face. "You know I do," she muttered, and buried the offending face against his shoulder.

Lorenzo heaved in a deep, unsteady breath. "Isabella takes pride in the room she keeps for visitors. I have slept there before. But always alone. This time—"

"This time you can hold me in your arms all night," said Jess in a muffled voice.

"My problem, *amore*, will be to let you go in the morning!"

Because Emily was still in no fit state to make the journey, next day Jess went with Lorenzo to fetch Mrs Shaw from the airport at Pisa, and sat in the back of the car with her to reassure her that Emily was improving fast. Janet Shaw looked tired and pale, but after expressing repeated thanks to Lorenzo grew very animated at the thought of her unexpected holiday to Italy, and exclaimed in delight at everything she saw on the journey. When they reached the Villa Fortuna Emily was sitting under the trees, waiting. Janet flew out of the car and rushed to embrace her daughter, and, leaving them to their tearful reunion, Lorenzo and Jess went inside the house to ask Carla to bring tea to refresh the weary traveller.

The evening was even livelier than the one before. To do justice to the occasion Jess wore a clinging black dress bought for her brother's twenty-first birthday party, with no jewellery other than the new ring, which she slid onto the appropriate finger, happy for the world to see Lorenzo's love token on her hand. When she found him alone in the *salone*, he said nothing at all for a moment as his eyes moved over her, then he seized her in his arms and slid a hand down her spine to hold her close against him.

"In future," he said against her mouth, "you will wear this dress only in private with me."

"Don't you like it?"

"I like it too much," he growled. "You can feel how much, no?"

"I can, yes!"

The sound of footsteps in the hall tore them apart, and when Janet Shaw came in with her daughter Lorenzo was pouring wine and Jess sitting demurely on one of the brocade armchairs. By the time Emily and her mother were provided with drinks cars were heard approaching outside, and shortly afterwards Isabella, stunning in a red dress, came rushing in with her husband, with Roberto bringing up the rear. Andrea Moretti was neither as tall as the Forli brothers nor as striking when it came to looks, but Jess met humorous blue eyes in a thin, clever face, and liked him on sight before she was engulfed in the flood of introductions and embraces which welcomed Lorenzo's visitors within the family circle.

Carla's dinner was a triumph, as expected. Roberto took the seat between Emily and her mother, and flirted so outrageously with both of them that by the time the first course was eaten Janet Shaw had forgotten any shyness and was enjoying herself as much as her daughter.

Later, after all the toasts had been drunk, grateful thanks expressed by the Shaws, and congratulations given to the happy pair, Jess managed a few private words with Isabella before the party broke up.

"Thank you so much for letting us stay at your house!"

Isabella's eyes danced. "My little betrothal gift to you, *cara*. I was sure you would prefer this to the hotel. And

Andrea was perfectly happy to make a surprise visit to
his parents.''

Laughter dawned in Jess's eyes. ''You mean—?''

''*Si*. A sudden inspiration of mine. When I suggested
it to him last night Andrea, being a man, was quick to
see the advantages for Lorenzo. For you, also, no?''
added Isabella with a wicked little smile. ''We shall leave
at ten in the morning, but Lorenzo has keys to our house,
so come to Lucca whenever you wish. We shall return
on Sunday morning to say goodbye before you leave.''

After the drive from Florence through the industry-
dominated Lucchese plain, Jess was delighted with the
historic centre of Lucca, where Lorenzo told her that only
taxis and residents were allowed to drive within the city
walls. He pointed out the Roman legacy still evident in
the grid pattern of its narrow streets, and the Piazza del
Mercato, which followed the shape of the original am-
phitheatre, then took her to the Moretti house, which was
situated just within the city walls, with a small garden
which backed onto the tree-crowned sixteenth-century
ramparts.

''I'm so grateful to your sister for taking such trouble
for us,'' said Jess, while Lorenzo showed her round the
house.

''Since Andrea was taking his family to Siena for the
night, it was no trouble. Though I, too, am grateful—*very*
grateful,'' added Lorenzo, ushering her into the guest
room.

''Andrea had no idea he was visiting his parents this
weekend. At least not until Isabella informed him on
Thursday after lunching at the Villa Fortuna,'' Jess informed him, much taken by the charm of curtains and

lampshades in pomegranate silk, the dark, carved furniture.

Lorenzo began to laugh. "So. My sister took delight in playing cupid. She must like you very much, *carissima*!"

Jess turned to him with a smile. "I hope she does, but actually her main aim is to please *you*, Lorenzo."

He took her by the shoulders, sudden heat replacing the laughter in his eyes. "Is your aim the same, Jessamy. Do you wish to please me?"

Jess nodded mutely, astonished to find she felt shy now that they were alone in the room where they would sleep together for the first time. "And I'm going to start right now by putting some lunch together," she said, brisk in her effort to disguise it. "Isabella said she would leave instructions about food."

Lorenzo's eyes softened. "Have no fear, *amore*. I will not rush you straight to bed, I promise!" He put his arm round her as they went downstairs. "But I must translate Isabella's instructions for you. She speaks English very well, but to write it is beyond her."

Jess gave him a challenging look. "I hope it's not beyond you, Lorenzo, because I want lots of letters from you after I go back."

He kissed her swiftly. "I can achieve reasonable English, yes, but I trust we will not be parted long enough for me to write *very* many letters! I want you with me here as soon as possible."

In some ways feeling like a little girl playing house, Jess found it strangely exciting to prepare lunch for Lorenzo in such unexpected privacy. Lorenzo, reading from his sister's instructions, informed her that Isabella apologised for the simplicity of the food provided, but was sure Jess had better things to do than spend her time in cooking. In the refrigerator there was ravioli stuffed with spinach and cheese, ready to cook and serve with a butter sauce flavoured with fresh sage. For dinner there was *arosto misto*, which Lorenzo explained was a selection of cold roasted meat.

"Chicken, pork and spiced sausage," he reported, after inspecting a covered platter. "But we can eat out if you prefer, *carissima*."

Jess slanted a look at him. "Is that what you want to do?"

"No," he said forcibly. "I do not."

"That's settled, then, because I'd rather spend every possible minute alone here with you."

"Grazie!" Lorenzo made an instinctive move towards her, then halted, smiling, and threw out his hands. "See how virtuous I am!"

The flushed cook smiled at him happily, then busied herself with the unfamiliar stove, while Lorenzo sliced bread and found the butter.

"I love the bread you have here," Jess told him, when they finally began on the simple, delicious meal.

"So you will be happy to live here in my country with me?" he asked, as he poured wine.

Jess smiled. "The last two words were the important bit, Lorenzo. I just want to be wherever you are."

He reached across to take her hand. "How I wish we had met sooner, Jessamy."

She nodded. "So do I. But now we have, let's celebrate the fact." She raised her glass. "To the future."

Lorenzo echoed her toast with fervour, then in response to Jess's questions about Isabella's sons began telling her about their exploits and the devilry they got up to.

"Would you like us to have a son?" Jess asked suddenly.

Lorenzo gazed at her in eloquent silence, his eyes giving her his answer. "A son or a daughter," he said at last. "Whatever God sends, *amore*."

They cleared away together, Jess amused by Lorenzo's very obvious lack of experience in the process, and afterwards they took their coffee to drink under an umbrella outside in the small, secluded garden.

"It's lovely here, but I prefer the Villa Fortuna," said Jess, and gave him a wry little smile. "I'll tell you a little secret. I was *very* relieved when we first arrived there, Lorenzo."

His eyebrows rose. "Relieved? You found the journey from Firenze tiring?"

"No, I don't mean that." Jess looked down at her new ring, twisting it on her finger. "You house is so very different from my imaginings. I was afraid it would be horribly grand, with Venetian windows, and vast, high-ceilinged rooms full of tapestries and antique furniture so valuable I would be afraid to go anywhere near it."

Lorenzo chuckled. "The Villa Fortuna must have been a great disappointment, then. It is quite old, it is true, and large enough, but just a simple country house, Jessamy, not a Medici *palazzo*."

"Which is why I love it," she assured him. "It's so warm and welcoming. Much nicer than your apartment at the hotel."

"I shall find another apartment for us, a private one, somewhere nearby in Firenze," he promised. "I know you will not like to live in the hotel. By the time we are married I shall arrange it, *carissima*." He smiled into her eyes. "As I have said before, I would do anything in the world for you." He got to his feet. "*Allora*. Shall we take a short walk along the walls? There are good views of the city, and an occasional glimpse of a private garden like this, and when you are tired we shall stop to eat ice cream. You cannot leave Lucca without tasting some of the local *gelati*."

Jess was delighted with the idea. The afternoon was hot, but her dark blue lawn dress was cool, and her feet were comfortable in the matching flat sandals. Lorenzo insisted she borrow a large straw hat Isabella wore in the garden, and found Jess looked so irresistible in it he promptly removed it so that he could kiss her, and Jess kissed him back, filled with a sudden desire to capture the moment and never let it go. And later, as they walked hand in hand through the double avenue of trees, she felt a fierce sense of possession when the man at her side attracted glances of open feminine admiration as they walked.

"What are you thinking, Jessamy?" asked Lorenzo.

"You might grow conceited if I tell you," she said, smiling demurely.

"Are you by any chance thinking that it is good to be here with me like this?"

"Yes, I am." Jess smiled at him under the hat-brim. "Do you want to know why it's so good?"

Lorenzo laughed, his grasp tightening on her hand. "Tell me!"

"Because you belong to me. And I belong to you."

He stopped dead to look down at her, sudden colour in his face. "You have a habit of choosing public places to say such things, *amore*."

They gazed at each other, oblivious of passers-by, in their absorption neither of them noticing the storm clouds beginning to gather. Suddenly it began to rain, and Lorenzo grinned, his teeth white in his dark face. He seized her hand and began to run back the way they'd come. People were running in all directions around them, there were screams as lightning flashed with a simultaneous crack of thunder, and Jess let out an excited laugh as the heavens opened in earnest, drenching them both in seconds. She ran like the wind with Lorenzo as they raced back along the ramparts, and by the time they reached the Moretti house she was panting and hot, but utterly exhilarated, her eyes glowing beneath the sodden hat-brim. Lorenzo pulled her inside and shut the door, then tossed the wrecked hat aside and pulled her into his arms to relieve her of what breath she had left by kissing her so passionately the effect of their headlong race through the storm, coupled with their utter and complete privacy in the silent house, set them both alight.

Lorenzo tore his mouth away at last and picked her up, and Jess wreathed her arms round his neck, kissing his taut, wet throat as he mounted the stairs to the guest room. The moment they were inside he set her on her feet and pulled her hard against him.

"You should have a hot bath," he panted as he drew her into the bathroom, and Jess reached behind her back for her zip with fingers too unsteady for the task.

"Help me," she said tersely, and Lorenzo spun her round, pulled the zip down and lifted her clear of the sodden dress. Jess began on Lorenzo's shirt, but he was before her, so impatient that shirt buttons went in all directions. Jess stripped herself of her wet underwear and the moment Lorenzo was equally naked he took her in his arms. Their bodies clung together, hot and wet and so taut with need that there was no more talk of a bath. Instead Lorenzo flung a large towel on the floor and they sank on it together, both of them so aroused their bodies fused without preliminaries of any kind, the savagery of the storm outside equalled by the frenzy of their love-making as they surged together towards the climax which broke over them at last like a tidal wave.

"I hurt you?" demanded Lorenzo hoarsely, when he had breath enough to speak.

Jess shook her head vehemently. "No." She heaved in a deep, quivering breath. "I had no idea it could be like that."

"I was too rough, too violent?"

"No." Jess looked up into his searching eyes, trying to find the right words. "It was—glorious!"

Lorenzo gave out a deep, relishing sigh, and pulled her up with him as he got to his feet. "I love you so much, Jessamy."

"I love you too, Signor Forli," she returned, smiling mischievously. "What shall we do now?"

"We take a shower—"

"And after that?"

The explicit gleam in Lorenzo's eyes sent shivers down her spine.

"After that, *diletta mia*, we enjoy the custom of the country. We take a siesta!"

Although they spent the major part of it in bed their time alone together passed far too quickly for Jess. She woke later that afternoon to meet Lorenzo's dark, caressing gaze, and exclaimed in dismay at wasting their time together in sleep.

"Even I," said Lorenzo modestly, "cannot make love continually, *carissima*—" He let out a howl as she gave him a very unlover-like dig in the ribs.

"I meant we could have been talking," Jess retorted, then pressed her lips and tongue on the place she'd hurt, which resulted in a very long delay before they finally went downstairs to eat the supper she was just as famished for as Lorenzo.

"This time tomorrow," said Jess, sighing, "I'll be back in London."

"Not for long," Lorenzo reminded her. "When shall I come to see your parents?"

"I'll go down next weekend. Perhaps you could come the weekend after?" Jess looked so downcast Lorenzo took her in his arms.

"You do not want me to come so soon?" he teased.

"Of course I do. But that's two whole weeks before I see you again!"

Lorenzo held her close, muttering a great many gratifying things to her, both in English and Italian. And before long they gave up any pretence of wanting to spend the evening in the Moretti *salone*, and went back upstairs to lie in each other's arms for the remainder of their time together.

By the time Isabella and Andrea arrived with their sons next morning Jess was packed and ready, dressed in the linen trousers and yellow halter top she'd worn at her first encounter with Lorenzo at the Chesterton in Pennington. There was much hugging and kissing from everyone, followed by delighted squeals of laughter as Lorenzo picked up each dark-haired little boy and spun him round, then introduced both his nephews to Jess, who was allowed a kiss from each of them.

"Thank you so much for inviting us here," said Jess later, smiling at her hosts.

"*Tante grazie*, Isabella. I am in your debt," added Lorenzo, grinning at his sister.

"Our pleasure," she assured him.

Andrea chuckled. "Once my wife ordered me to visit my parents I was most happy to oblige you, Lorenzo."

He smiled at a hectically flushed Jess. "You like our house, *cara*?"

"It's delightful," she said fervently. "It was so kind of you to give us time together like this before I go back." She pulled a face. "Something I'm not looking forward to very much."

"Nor I," said Lorenzo broodingly, then smiled as he warded off the two clamouring little boys. "*Basta*— enough! They want me to play football in the garden, Jessamy. Support me, Andrea, *per favore*. A few moments only; it grows late."

When they were alone Isabella smiled sympathetically at Jess. "You look tired, *cara*. Was the bed in my guest room not comfortable?" She clapped a hand to her mouth in distress when Jess blushed to the roots of her hair. "Forgive me—I did not mean to embarrass you. I speak before I think."

Jess laughed wryly. "The bed was very comfortable and the room is so charming we spent most of our time there."

Isabella put an arm round Jess's waist and kissed her affectionately. "I have never seen my brother look so happy and relaxed. It is so wonderful to see him like this. He looks tired," she added, eyes sparkling, "but years younger!"

Jess looked out of the window to watch Lorenzo dribbling the football down the garden like a Juventas striker, his nephews in hot pursuit. "Isabella," she said at last, "could I ask you something?"

"Anything, *cara*. What do you wish to know?"

"Would you mind telling me how Lorenzo's wife died? I don't like to ask. But I need to know just to avoid hurting him in any way."

Isabella sighed heavily, her face sombre. "I agree it is best you know, *cara*. Lorenzo never speaks of it because it is so painful to him. Poor Renata. After all those years without babies she died in childbirth."

CHAPTER TWELVE

THE ARRIVAL of the men put an abrupt end to the conversation, for which Jess, feeling as though she'd been dealt a mortal blow, was passionately grateful. In shocked silence she shrugged into her jacket and handed her luggage over to Lorenzo to take to the car, and hoped that if anyone noticed her lack of conversation they would put it down to her sadness at the coming parting. She hugged both Andrea and Isabella wordlessly by way of thanks, received more kisses from their small sons, and soon she was on her way from Lucca on the first leg of her journey home.

"You are very quiet, *carissima*," said Lorenzo, glancing at her fleetingly as he touched her hand in sympathy.

Jess nodded mutely, somehow controlling the urge to snatch her hand away.

To her relief Lorenzo took it for granted that thoughts of leaving him had rendered her silent with misery, and because the traffic was heavy and they ran into another storm there was not only little opportunity for conversation, they were late arriving at the airport, for which Jess was fiercely grateful. Lorenzo gave her a stream of urgent instruction which needed little more than a nod of acknowledgement, then her flight was called and he seized her in his arms and held her so close she thought her ribs would break.

"Ring me at the hotel the moment you arrive at your flat," he ordered. He kissed her cold lips, then held her away a little, his eyes questioning. "What is wrong? You feel ill, *amore*?"

She nodded. "Travel nerves," she choked, desperate to get away. "I've got to go. Goodbye, Lorenzo."

Jess hurried off without looking back, knowing that a last look at Lorenzo Forli would shatter her iron control into pieces. On the plane she huddled in her window seat as the plane filled, so numb with misery she hardly noticed when the plane took off to begin its steep ascent. The couple beside her were too engrossed in each other to pay any attention to her, and Jess, grateful for it, spent the entire journey in silence, staring blankly at the blue sky above the carpet of clouds.

When she arrived at Heathrow it was almost as hot in London as Italy, and, unable to bear the idea of a train, Jess waited in line for a taxi. When she reached the flat she dumped her luggage down, switched on the water heater for a bath, then picked up the telephone and got through to the hotel beside the Arno to ask for Signor Forli.

Lorenzo answered at once, his relief evident in his tone as Jess told him she was home.

"How are you feeling, Jessamy?" he asked urgently. "I have been mad with worry. You looked so ill when you left me—"

"You know I hate flying," she cut in. "And I still feel horribly sick. I really can't talk now, Lorenzo."

"*Poverina!* I will ring you later."

"Tomorrow, *please!*" Jess implored, suddenly at the end of her tether. "I'm going straight to bed now."

When she put the phone down she realised she was still wearing Lorenzo's ring. With an exclamation of disgust she wrenched it off her shaking hand and threw it across the room, then put the kettle on and made herself a cup of black coffee to drink while she rang Friars Wood to announce her arrival. Her mother answered, and, always alert to nuances of expression when it came to her young, demanded to know what was wrong. Jess pleaded travel sickness and fatigue, reported that Emily was on the mend, and promised to ring next day after her return from the agency.

"Should you be going to work tomorrow if you feel ill, darling?"

It was preferable to staring at the walls in the flat. "I'll be fine, Mother," said Jess firmly. "I really can't take any more time off." She asked after her siblings, sent her love to her father, then put the phone down before she could weaken and sob out her sorry tale to her perceptive parent.

Once she'd showered Jess slid into bed and stared at the ceiling of the small, functional bedroom which was so different from the room she'd slept in—or not slept in—the night before. And at last the numbing fog fell away, and a great wave of anguish and disillusion swept over her.

When the storm of weeping was over Jess mopped herself up and faced facts. Just like the other men in her life, in the end Lorenzo Forli had used all the means he possessed to seduce her into his bed. Admittedly his approach had been very different from the others. Not only fairy stories about love at first sight, but shameless lies about his relationship with Renata. A novel spin on the old 'my wife doesn't understand me' gambit, thought Jess, and ground her teeth in furious distaste. She had been so gullible, so full of compassion for him as Lorenzo had told her about his arid, loveless marriage. She'd listened with such sympathy, aching for him when he said he had never touched Renata again after their

wedding night. Yet the inescapable truth remained. To
die in childbirth Renata had to have been pregnant first.
Which meant that at a late stage in the relationship either
Lorenzo had resorted to force or Renata had experienced
some kind of epiphany and welcomed him into her bed
at last.

The thought acted on Jess like an emetic, and she
bolted to the bathroom, her fiction about nausea suddenly
the truth. Later she lay awake for hours in shivering misery, bitter as she remembered the way Roberto and
Isabella had pleaded with her not to hurt Lorenzo. Jess
buried her face in the pillow. In the end *she* was the one
who'd been hurt, not their beloved brother. And the worst
of it was she still loved Lorenzo passionately, and wanted
him here right now, in this bed beside her. She groaned
in despair, mortified by her own weakness. In the past
she'd been so scornful about sensible friends who
changed overnight into mooning idiots over men. She had
sworn it would never happen to Jess Dysart. Yet here she
was, for the first time in her life helplessly, hopelessly in
love. So much so she'd surrendered unconditionally to
the man who'd taught her just how breathtakingly wonderful love could be. Only to discover that the object of
her passion was not nearly as perfect as she—and everyone else who knew him—believed. Lorenzo Forli was as
capable of lying to gain his ends as any lesser mortal.

At some time in the night Jess fell into a troubled
sleep, but woke early to crawl out of bed and search the
floor on hands and knees until she found the ring. She
sat down at once to write a cool, dignified letter to
Lorenzo, telling him that their brief, passionate relationship had been a mistake. Too hot not to cool down and
all that. Not that this was true. She hadn't cooled down.
The merest thought of Lorenzo's lips and hands... Jess

groaned in anguish and went to stand under the shower again.

Her first day back at the agency was an unwelcome revelation to Jess. She had counted on using work as an opiate for the injury to her damaged heart. But to her consternation she found she no longer had any enthusiasm for her job. The work she had once found so interesting now seemed trivial and boring. And without Emily to come home to in the evening the small basement flat felt like a stuffy prison after the space and charm of Villa Fortuna.

Jess worked late that first, endless day, and returned home eventually to listen to several messages from Lorenzo demanding that she ring him back. Refusing to add expensive phone calls to the bill she shared with Emily, Jess took a shower, made a sandwich with the groceries she'd bought on the way home, then sat down with it to wait.

Before she was even half way through her sandwich Lorenzo rang again.

"You are there!" he said with relief when she answered. "I was so worried, *amore*. Where have you been?"

"Working. I had a lot of catching up to do."

"I hate to think of you working so hard. Do you feel better? he demanded.

"It all depends on what you mean by better."

"You are saying you miss me," he said, the triumphant note in his voice acting like a match on the fuse of her anger. "*Carissima*, I know how you feel. I miss you so very much already—"

"I'm afraid," she said coldly, "you'll have to get used to that, Lorenzo. And you have no idea how I feel."

"Cosa?" he said incredulously. There was a pause. "What do you mean?"

"I mean," said Jess with deliberate cruelty, "that I won't be seeing you again."

"What is this nonsense?" he demanded roughly. "You are saying you no longer want me?"

If she did she'd be lying. Jess gritted her teeth. "Let's just say I no longer want to marry you. It was a crazy idea anyway. I've written a letter to explain. You should receive it shortly—"

"Jessamy!" he said urgently. "What has happened? What has changed your mind? I cannot believe you mean this, not after the joy we shared—"

"You mean sex," she said scornfully. "Don't worry, Lorenzo. I'm sure you'll soon find another woman just as gullible as me, only too happy to pander to your needs. Goodbye."

Jess put the phone down and threw herself on the sofa, sobbing bitterly. As expected the phone rang again soon afterwards, and with clenched fists rammed against her quivering mouth she listened to Lorenzo's enraged voice ordering her to pick up the phone. Eventually, when it became clear to him she had no intention of obeying him, he rang off. Soon afterwards the phone rang again, but this time Frances Dysart's voice began leaving a message, and Jess picked up the receiver to assure her mother she was feeling better, though her first day at work had been hard going.

"You don't sound better. Are you coming down this weekend?" asked Frances. "We'd love to hear all about Lorenzo's home. Your father was very taken with him, darling. Are you seeing him again?"

"No," said Jess flatly. "I'm not."

There was a pause. "Something wrong?"

"No, not really." Jess managed a laugh. "Lorenzo's quite a charmer, I grant you. But not really my type."

"If you say so."

"I do. Have you heard from the honeymooners?"

Taking this as a plea for less emotive conversation, Frances gave news of Leo and Jonah, who were returning shortly, Kate, who had finished her exams, Adam, who was still awaiting the results of his, and Fenella, who had quarrelled with her best friend. Soothed by the minutiae of life at Friars Wood, Jess promised to travel down the following Saturday and returned to her sandwich. But, revolted by it, and every other form of food, she threw it away and made herself some tea, then tried to watch some television. But the programme could have been broadcast in Sanskrit for all the sense she made of it, as she sat waiting for the phone to ring again.

When it did, a long, endless hour later, Jess waited for Lorenzo's voice to start making demands again, but instead it was Emily, sounding very distressed, and Jess seized the phone to answer her.

"What's up, love?" she said breathlessly.

"You're asking *me* that?" said Emily, incensed. "What the devil are you playing at, Jess Dysart?"

"What do you mean?"

"What do I mean! Lorenzo drove here a short while ago, asking if I'd heard from you. And behind that controlled mask of his he was in a terrible state. When I said I hadn't spoken to you since you went back he apologised for disturbing Mother and me, and took off again. What's going on?"

"I've told him I don't want to see him again."

"*What?*" Emily said something her mother would have been horrified to hear. "Well, that's a lie for a start. Whatever happened to truly, madly, deeply?"

Jess sighed wearily. "I was given certain information about his past. Something I just can't cope with."

"Are you sure about this? Whoever told you could have got it wrong."

"Not likely. It was Isabella."

Emily breathed in sharply, then began to cough, and it was some time before she was able to speak again. "Sorry about that. Look, I must ring off. This is costing Lorenzo a fortune, and heaven knows he's shelled out enough already. On both of us," she added. "Look, Jess, are you sure you haven't got the wrong end of the stick somehow?"

"Very sure," said Jess desolately. "I wish I had."

As the week dragged on there were no more calls from Lorenzo. Which came as a mortifying surprise. Jess had been so sure he would persist until he knew the reason for her attitude. She had looked forward to throwing the truth in his face, daring him to deny that Renata had lost her life trying to give birth to his child. In her stilted, brief letter, which had taken sheet after sheet of rough drafts before she was satisfied, she'd said nothing about Renata. She wrote that it had been a mistake to agree to marry him after so short an acquaintance, and therefore she was returning the ring.

After years of trying to diet herself into something approaching her sisters' slenderness Jess found her weight diminishing by the day. Which was no surprise. Since her return from Italy the mere thought of food had sickened her. Lorenzo Forli was to blame, she thought in anguish. At last Jess gave up expecting a message from him whenever she got home, but couldn't control a wild leap of hope every time the phone rang, just the same. On one occasion it was Simon Hollister, her fellow juror, who rang up as he'd promised, suggesting a meal. Why not? thought Jess wearily, but arranged to meet him for a drink instead of putting him to the expense of food she couldn't eat. Simon was an amusing companion, and the evening passed pleasantly enough, but when he suggested a repeat Jess was vague, saying she'd give him a ring when she was free. Simon was nice. But he wasn't Lorenzo. No one was. Nor ever would be.

Lack of nutrition, sleep, and enthusiasm for life in general, made Jess very tired as the week wore on. After coping with the tantrums of a model whose success had gone to her undeniably beautiful head, she was late getting back to the flat on Friday evening, and when the doorbell rang soon afterwards she groaned in despair, in no mood to talk to anyone.

"Mr and Mrs Savage here, Jess," said her sister's voice over the intercom. "Let us in."

Leonie rushed in through the door Jess opened and gave her sister a hug, then stood back, eyeing her in frank, sisterly horror. "Good heavens above, Jess, what have you done to yourself?"

"Thanks!" said Jess dryly, then submitted herself to Jonah's embrace in turn. "Go on," she told him, resigned. "Get your bit over with as well. I know I look gruesome."

Like his wife, Jonah Savage looked the picture of health and happiness, but his eyes were full of concern. "Never gruesome, love," he assured her, "but something's obviously wrong, Jess. What's up? Your mother told us to come round and check on you the moment we reached London."

Leonie gave her husband a speaking look. "Pop out and buy some wine, darling. I think a drink is called for."

"I've got some wine," protested Jess.

"My beloved means she wants me to make myself scarce for a bit," said Jonah, grinning. "Though by the look of her, Leo, Jess could do with a double helping of fish and chips, not wine."

Jess shuddered, clapped a hand over her mouth and fled to the bathroom. When she emerged, ashen and shivering, Jonah had vanished and his bride was making tea.

"Better?" asked Leonie. "Come and sit down. Mother told me all about Emily and your mercy trip to Florence with Lorenzo, not to mention the stay at the Villa Fortuna. I gather you and Lorenzo hit it off to such an extent Mother can't understand why you don't want to see him any more. What went wrong?"

"Oh, you know me and men, Leo," said Jess flippantly. "I never get it right."

"Hmm." Leonie added milk to the steaming beakers and handed one to Jess. "Kate assured me that you and Lorenzo are—I quote—'madly in love'."

Jess scowled. "We hardly know each other."

"What difference does that make? I knew Jonah was the man for me the moment I met him."

"That's different."

"Why?"

"Jonah's a straight arrow."

"And Lorenzo isn't?" Leonie frowned. "Strange. Roberto—who is nobody's fool, Jess—has enormous respect for him."

"I don't want to talk about it," said Jess mulishly, then rushed off to throw up again, which was a painful process on an empty stomach. When she got back to the sitting room Leonie fixed her with a searching dark eye.

"Look, love, you're not—not in the same boat as me by any chance, are you?"

Jess flushed painfully. "No, I'm not," she said miserably, and burst into tears.

Leonie took her in her arms and let her cry for some time. At last Jess mastered herself and sat up, scrubbing at her eyes.

"For your ears only, I suppose I could have been pregnant," she admitted reluctantly. "But today I found I wasn't."

"But you wish you were!"

"Even if I was," flared Jess, "I wouldn't tell him."

"By 'him' I assume you mean Lorenzo Forli?"

"Of course I do."

"Mystery solved, then. You're throwing up because you're heartbroken. I remember the quarrel you had with some boy after a school dance," Leonie reminded her. "You were sick for days afterwards."

"Right." Jess pulled a face. "But this is in a different class from that, unfortunately. I can't eat, can't sleep, hate my job, and if this is love you can stuff it!"

Leonie smiled sympathetically. "I know how you feel. I've been there myself. But don't punish yourself if you do want Lorenzo, Jess. Life's too short. What on earth did he do to get you in this state?"

"He lied to me, Leo."

Leonie stared in astonishment. "Is that all? Haven't you ever lied to anyone?"

"Not about something as serious as this."

Leonie sighed, then got up as the doorbell rang. "That'll be Jonah."

Jonah, to Jess's relief, had not carried out his threat about fish and chips. Instead he presented her with a six-pack of mineral water and ordered her to eat something before she wasted away. Then Leonie, well aware that Jess needed to be alone, announced it was time to go.

"Jess, we're off to eat with my parents now," said Jonah as they left. "But we're going down to Friars Wood in time for dinner tomorrow night."

"I'll see you tomorrow, then," said Jess, smiling valiantly.

Leonie gave her a rather protracted hug, and smoothed the damp hair back from her sister's forehead. "Think about what I said," she instructed, and nodded towards the telephone. "Call him."

"Call who?" demanded Jonah.

"Tell you on the way home," promised Leonie, then smiled at Jess. "And tomorrow we'll bore you with tales of our stay in France."

Jess bit her lip in remorse. "Sorry! I forgot to ask how you enjoyed your honeymoon." She managed a smile. "Not that I need to. You both look wonderful."

When she was alone Jess sat staring at the telephone, wondering whether to follow her sister's advice. But it rang before she could make up her mind. To her disappointment it was Emily, saying she was flying back in the morning and would be staying with her mother until their own doctor pronounced her fit to return to work.

"How are you feeling?" asked Jess.

"Still a bit feeble, but definitely on the mend. I'm enormously grateful to Lorenzo," added Emily deliberately, "for providing me with such a marvellous place to convalesce in. And for inviting my mother here as the icing on the cake. It's been a great treat for her."

Jess fought with herself and lost. "Have you seen him?" she asked gruffly.

"Of course I've seen him. He looks terrible."

"Easy to see whose side you're on," said Jess bitterly.

"Must there be sides? I just want to see you both happy again, like you were before. Anyway," Emily went on quickly, "for heaven's sake don't wallow in gloom all weekend in the flat, Jess."

"Of course I won't! I'm off home to Friars Wood in the morning."

The conversation with Emily decided Jess to ring Lorenzo next day, and at least let him know her reason for ending things between them. Her empty stomach reacted to the sense of the decision by demanding food, and Jess made herself some toast, took it to bed with a mug of tea, and once she'd consumed her little feast fell fast asleep. She surfaced so late next morning it was time to drive immediately to Stavely, if she had any hope of arriving at Friars Wood for lunch. The phone call to Lorenzo was too important to be rushed, Jess decided. She would ring him when she got home.

The hot weather had broken, and the trip along the motorway was punctuated by heavy showers which made driving difficult. By the time the car was buffeted about by crosswinds on the Severn Bridge Jess was heartily glad she was almost home. The main door of Friars Wood opened the minute her car reached the terrace, and all four Dysarts in residence came rushing out with the dog to welcome her back.

"Adam's still in Edinburgh," said Frances Dysart over lunch. "Mrs Briggs is coming in later, to clean bathrooms and help with dinner and so on. Why not have a rest in Adam's bed in the Stables this afternoon, Jess?"

"Good idea!" Jess smiled brightly, secretly glad at the prospect as she helped herself to a modest portion of chicken salad.

"You've lost weight," accused her father, now he'd had time to look at her properly. "Didn't you eat anything in Italy?"

"Of course I did. The food was wonderful. But I've

been very busy since I got back." Jess kept the smile pinned on her face. "I soon worked the extra pounds off."

"And a few more while you were at it," said Kate with sibling bluntness.

"Is Lorenzo's house nice, Jess?" asked Fenny eagerly.

"Yes," said Jess casually, breaking an awkward little silence. "It's lovely. Right out in the countryside. My friend Emily soon got better once she arrived there."

"How is Emily?" said Frances quickly, to stave off more questions from Fenny.

"Much better. She should be home by now; she was flying back with her mother this morning."

After the strain of keeping a brave face in front of her family Jess was tired, and grateful to her mother for the unexpected privacy of the Stables. Once she'd had some coffee after the meal she smiled apologetically, and said she was off to Adam's bed.

"Pathetic, I know, but it was a nasty drive down, and I'm really tired. I promise I'll be more lively by the time the others arrive."

"I'll help you carry your things," said Kate.

Adam's room in the Stables was furnished entirely to his own taste, with a vast brass bed and tawny orange walls, and to Jess it felt like a warm, welcoming haven. Kate dumped her sister's holdall on the floor and took a change of clothes out of it, but made no attempt to ask questions Jess wasn't ready to answer.

"Get your things off and pop straight into bed," said Kate. "I'll take your holdall back and hang the rest of your stuff in your own room. Mother's put milk and things in the fridge downstairs, so you can make yourself some tea when you get up. In the meantime we shall all be frightfully tactful and refrain from asking what happened to make you look so—''

''Ghastly?''

''I was going to say fragile,'' said Kate, looking worried.

''Sounds good. No one's ever called me fragile before,'' added Jess with a genuine chuckle. ''How did the exams go?''

''All right, I think.''

''Which means brilliantly, of course, Miss Genius.''

Kate grimaced and crossed her fingers. ''Don't tempt fate, please!''

When Jess was alone she stretched out in the big bed, deciding to ring Lorenzo later. Right now she just couldn't face it. All she wanted to do was sleep and sleep, and wake up to find herself back at the moment before Isabella Moretti had innocently put an end to the fairy tale.

When Jess woke rain was lashing against the windows. As usual, ever since her flight from Italy, the first waking moment was the worst, but Jess lay quiet, weathering the pain as she tried to think of what to say if—when—she rang Lorenzo. Here at home she was her rational self again, with the courage to face the truth. She loved Lorenzo whether he'd lied or not.

Jess listened suddenly, aware that someone was in the house.

''Is that you, Kate?'' she called. She jumped out of bed and pulled on Adam's bathrobe, and went to the door, yawning. ''If so you can make some tea.'' She peered over the banisters on the small landing and looked down for a long, frozen moment into Lorenzo's haggard, upturned face. His hair was wet, and his eyes held a look which pierced Jess to the heart.

"Forgive if I startled you, Jessamy. Kate insisted I wait alone until you wake," said Lorenzo, his English less polished than usual.

"How—why are you here?" said Jess with difficulty.

"I flew to England last night. I stay at the Chesterton again." Lorenzo thrust a hand through his wet hair, his bleak, bloodshot eyes holding hers. "Please dress and come down. I wish to talk to you, Jessamy. After that—" He stopped, his mouth twisting. "After that, if you no longer desire my company I shall return to Firenze."

Jess looked at him for a long moment, then nodded. "Just give me five minutes."

"Grazie," he said tonelessly, and turned away.

Jess dressed at top speed in a faded pink sweatshirt and old jeans grown soft with washing, then went downstairs to Adam's sitting room. Lorenzo was standing in front of the fireplace, dressed informally in a blue chambray shirt and jeans very much like hers, though Jess had no doubt they bore a more exalted label. But he wore beautiful leather shoes, as usual, and a rain-marked suede jacket lay on the back of a chair.

"You look tired, Jessamy," he said quietly.

"So do you."

He nodded. "I have slept very little since you left. Even less after I received your letter."

She looked away, not ready, yet, to get to the heart of the matter. "You must be cold. Can I make you some coffee?"

"Grazie."

Jess went through to the kitchen to fill Adam's kettle, and Lorenzo followed her, watching silently while she spooned instant coffee into beakers and set out milk and sugar.

"How did you know I'd be here at Friars Wood?" she asked quietly.

"I rang your parents when I arrived."

She looked up in surprise. "They didn't tell me!"

He nodded soberly. "I requested their silence. I feared that if you knew I was here you would refuse to speak to me." He paused, but Jess remained silent, her eyes fixed on his. "Jessamy," he said at last, "you would give me no reason for your change of heart, but I have now discovered this."

So not much point in hurling accusations after all. Not that she wanted to any more, now they were face to face. "What exactly did you discover?" Jess asked gruffly, needing to establish the facts.

"Eventually I found that my sister told you how Renata died," said Lorenzo flatly.

Jess handed him a mug of coffee, then led the way back to the other room. Lorenzo followed her to the large chesterfield sofa, waited until Jess curled up in one corner, then seated himself at the other end to sit staring into the empty fireplace. And at last the silence between them grew so tense Jess could bear it no longer.

"If things had continued as planned. Before Isabella told me, I mean," she said carefully, "had you any intention of telling me the truth at some time?"

"Yes. Though the truth was not really mine to tell." Lorenzo set the mug down on a small table beside him, then turned weary eyes on her. "I have never lied to you, Jessamy."

"How do you expect me to believe that?" she demanded. "You told me you had never lived a normal married life with Renata. Yet she died in childbirth."

Lorenzo's jaw tightened. "This is true. I received

much sympathy, many, many condolences. They sickened me.''

Jess eyed him narrowly. "But in the circumstances surely it would have been odd if you'd received no sympathy at all, Lorenzo?''

"I would have preferred that,'' he said with force. "But how could I tell my family, my friends, that for the last few months of my marriage I had been forced to live an even greater lie than in all the years before? Roberto, Isabella, neither of them knew the truth. I have never told anyone until now.'' He met her eyes. "I was not the father of Renata's child.''

"Lorenzo!'' Jess stared at him in horror, then slid along the couch to take his hand. "You mean she had a *lover*?''

Lorenzo looked down at the hand grasping his. "I thought I would never feel your touch again,'' he said unevenly.

Jess's self-control, which had been notable by its absence since her return from Italy, abruptly deserted her. Tears streamed down her face, and with a smothered exclamation Lorenzo put his arms round her and held her close.

"*Piangi!*'' he commanded, smoothing her head against his shoulder, and Jess obeyed, letting the hot, salt tears wash away the misery of their parting.

"Sorry,'' she said thickly at last, and pulled away to fish in her pocket for the tissues she was lately never without. "I've cried more this last week than in my entire life.'' She smiled up at him damply, and almost started crying again when she saw a trace of moisture on Lorenzo's thick black lashes.

"I have been in torment,'' he said roughly. "I had even begun to wish we had never met.''

Jess managed a smile. "I never got as far as that. But—"

"But what, *amore*?" he whispered.

"Even if we'd never met again I couldn't be sorry that you'd made love to me, Lorenzo."

"To hear you say this—" He let out a deep, shaky breath. "You know that I have only to touch you to want to make love to you again, but it is not for this that I am here."

"You don't want to make love to me?"

Lorenzo tapped a reproving forefinger against her flushed cheek. "You know very well that I do. That I always will while there is breath in my body. But first we must talk, to remove this cloud from our lives."

"If you don't want to tell me about Renata I don't mind," said Jess quickly. "Now I know the truth we can never talk about it again, if you prefer."

Lorenzo shook his head vehemently. "I swore to her that I would never reveal her secret, but I feel a deep need to talk to *you*, Jessamy. To tell you what no other living person knows about my life. I want no secrets between us, *carissima*." He drew in a deep breath. "Renata begged me to pose as father of her child."

Jess breathed in sharply. "She asked too much of you, Lorenzo. What happened? Did Renata just fall in love with someone else?"

"When Renata was forced, at last, to tell me what happened," began Lorenzo, his arm tightening round Jess, "she was hysterical with shame, and—and incoherent. That is right?"

Jess nodded. "As well she might be." She looked up in sudden fear. "Don't tell me she was raped!"

"*Dio*, no," said Lorenzo swiftly. "Not that." His mouth twisted. "Though in some ways I believe she would have actually preferred this, so that the guilt was not hers.''

Renata, he began slowly, had been in the habit of staying for long periods in her family's country home near Perugia. Lorenzo had been grateful for solitude in the house in Oltrarno, and Renata, never suited to matrimony, had been happy to stay for weeks at a time with her widowed mother. When her mother died Renata had inherited the house and spent even more time there.

One summer, while the housekeeper was on holiday, Renata had been alone in the house during one of the violent storms which had always terrified her. The man who took care of the garden had just left, and when the bell rang at the gate Renata, thinking it was the old gardener, returning to shelter from the storm, had run through the rain to let him in, desperate for company. Instead of the gardener she had found a drenched young man with a backpack asking for shelter until the storm passed.

Jess moved closer. ''What happened then?''

''Renata grew even more hysterical at this point,'' said Lorenzo tonelessly. ''Eventually I learned that the man was a foreign tourist, young, and very beautiful, with long golden hair like an angel, she told me. Fortunately for Renata, who was no linguist, he spoke a little Italian. When the storm grew fiercer he asked to stay the night. She agreed, and gave him wine and food.'' His mouth twisted. ''She even gave him dry clothes that I had left there once.''

''So he was tall, this stranger,'' said Jess thoughtfully.

Lorenzo shrugged. ''More important than that, Renata confessed that for the first time in her life she was physically attracted to a man—''

"Even though she was married to you?" said Jess fiercely, and clutched his hand. "She was a fool!"

"Thank you, *carissima*. You are very good for my self-esteem." Lorenzo gave her a fleeting smile. "To end the story, in the night lightning struck a tree in the garden. Renata screamed, the stranger rushed to see what was wrong, and the rest you can imagine."

"How on earth did you feel when she told you that?" said Jess, outraged.

Lorenzo shrugged graphically. "I have no English words to describe this. I cared nothing that she had taken a lover at last. But I cursed the man who went on his way next morning without a thought for the woman who spent most of her life afterwards on her knees in penitence. Renata looked on the pregnancy as punishment for her sin. This must sound dramatic to you, I know well, but all her life she had been very devout. Her guilt was so great she lost the will to live." Lorenzo's arm tightened. "She would not eat, could not sleep, and spent hours every day in prayer. The result was inevitable. When Renata gave birth, months too early, she died with her child."

Jess shuddered, and held Lorenzo close. "I was such a fool," she said bitterly.

He turned her face up to his. "A fool, *innamorata*? Why?"

"Because I didn't trust you." Her eyes blazed into his beneath their swollen lids. "I once gave Leo a lecture for failing to trust Jonah, but I was no better where you're concerned. When Isabella told me how Renata died I should have confronted you with it right away. But my blind instinct was to run as far away from you as I could get." She smiled shakily. "I was so disillusioned, Lorenzo. To me you were unique. Not only because I was madly in love with you, but for being such a saint where Renata was concerned—''

"I am no saint," he said harshly, and pulled her close, his eyes boring into hers. "But I did not lie to you, Jessamy. And I never will. *Sempre la verità*, I promised. And I meant it.''

Jess flung her arms round his neck and kissed him with passionate remorse. Lorenzo's response was everything she'd dreamed of in the long, unbearable days since she'd left him. At last he held her away a little, breathing rapidly.

"Since you left me I suffered torment for another reason, also.''

"Why?"

Lorenzo took her face in his hands. "I desired you so much I did not take the necessary care. I feared you might be expecting my child and would never tell me.''

She shook her head. "I'm not.''

He sighed heavily. "In one way I hoped so much that you were.''

Jess smiled a little. "So did I.''

Lorenzo's answering smile transformed his face so completely she was dazzled. "You mean this?"

She nodded. "When I had time to think, alone in the flat, I realised that even if you weren't the prince in my fairy tale, but just a normal, mortal man after all, I still loved you, Lorenzo. Just like all the Dysart females I'm a one-man woman, it seems.'' Her mouth drooped. "I was heartbroken when I found I wasn't pregnant.''

Lorenzo's English deserted him completely. He held her close, saying a great many things that Jess needed no interpreter to translate, but eventually, with mutual reluctance, they agreed it was time to go over to the house.

"Before another minute passes," said Lorenzo, "I

must ask your parents' approval. Do you think they will agree to give me their daughter?''

Later that evening, when the newlyweds arrived, Leonie exclaimed in delight when she found Lorenzo with Jess, and after drinks had been served to mark the homecoming of the bride and groom the family gathered round the dining table for the celebration dinner Kate had been helping her mother prepare for most of the day.

Fenny, in all the glory of her bridesmaid dress, was allowed to stay up for dinner, and asked Lorenzo endless questions about his house, then turned on Jonah with equally relentless curiosity to ask when the baby would come.

''Fenella!'' said Frances in dismay.

''People always have babies when they get married,'' said Fenny, undeterred. ''My friend Laura told me.''

''Then of course it must be true,'' said Tom Dysart, chuckling, and smiled apologetically at Jonah. ''Sorry about that.''

''No problem,'' said Leonie, exchanging a glance with her jubilant bridegroom. ''Actually, we think about Christmas time, Fen.''

Jess felt Lorenzo's hand tighten on hers under the table, and smiled to herself.

Kate stared at the blushing bride in surprise. ''Which Christmas?'' she demanded.

''This one,'' said Jonah smugly.

Fenny frowned in disappointment. ''That's a long time yet.'' She stared, puzzled, as everyone laughed, and Jess relaxed, aware that her parents, at least, had known before the general announcement.

''You knew this?'' asked Lorenzo.

Jess nodded. ''You should be grateful for it, too.''

"I?" he demanded.

"If Leo hadn't wept all over me and confessed she was pregnant I wouldn't have come rushing to Pennington that night to collect her earrings."

"Then you are right," said Lorenzo fervently. "I am *very* grateful."

When the meal was over, and they were still sitting round the table over coffee, Tom Dysart opened two bottles of champagne and with Jonah's help refilled all the glasses. Then he held up his hand for silence, smiling at the expectant faces turned towards him. "This seems to be a night for important announcements! I'm sure everyone here will be happy to know that earlier today Lorenzo asked our permission to marry Jess. He doesn't need it, of course, but both Frances and I were very happy to give them our blessing." He raised his glass. "To Jess and Lorenzo."

After the expected rush of kisses and congratulations Lorenzo Forli, looking very different from the dishevelled, wild-eyed man Jess had found earlier in the Stables, stood up, his face eloquent with such happiness and pride Jess felt a great tide of love rise inside her as he replied to the toast.

"I am very grateful to all of you for your kindness and good wishes," he began, and smiled down at Jess. "I know it is a very short time since I met Jessamy, but I wanted her for my wife from the first moment I met her, and promise to take great care of her. I consider myself the most fortunate man alive to have won her love."

There was much applause and excitement, and eventually Kate elected to haul an excited Fenny off to bed.

"Can I be bridesmaid, Jess?" Fenny demanded as she kissed her goodnight.

"I'm counting on it!"

"Let's get that dress off, then," said Kate, laughing. "You may need it again."

Later, when they were all gathered in the drawing room, Leonie left her place by Jonah to join Lorenzo and Jess on the sofa they were sharing.

"I'm the only one in the family who has the least idea how things were for you in the past, Lorenzo," she said in an undertone. "This time I know you'll be happy."

"I cannot fail to be with Jessamy for my wife," he said with certainty. "You know from Roberto that life has not always been good for me, but all that is in the past, Leonie. The moment I met your sister my life changed."

"For the better, I hope," teased Jess, smiling up at him.

"You know this very well." Lorenzo kissed her swiftly, oblivious of indulgent onlookers. "As I have told you often before, *innamorata*, you are my reward!"

THE SECRET
THAT CHANGED
EVERYTHING

LUCY GORDON

Lucy Gordon cut her writing teeth on magazine journalism, interviewing many of the world's most interesting men, including Warren Beatty, Charlton Heston and Roger Moore. She also camped out with lions in Africa, and had many other unusual experiences, which have often provided the background for her books. Several years ago, while staying in Venice, she met a Venetian who proposed to her after two days. They have been married ever since. Naturally this has affected her writing, where romantic Italian men tend to feature strongly.

Two of her books have won a Romance Writers of America RITA® Award.

You can visit her website, www.lucy-gordon.com.

PROLOGUE

HE WAS there!

After such an anxious search it was hard to be sure at first; aged about thirty, tall, lean, fit, with black hair. Was it really him? But then he made a quick movement and Charlotte knew.

This was the man she'd come to find.

He'd looked different last time, elegantly dressed, smooth, sophisticated, perfectly at home in one of the most fashionable bars in Rome. Now, in the Tuscan countryside, he was equally at home in jeans and casual shirt, absorbed in the vines that streamed in long lines under the setting sun. So absorbed that he didn't look up to see her watching him from a distance.

Lucio Constello.

Quickly she pulled out a scrap of paper and checked his name. At the back of her mind a wry voice murmured that if you'd sought out a man to tell him devastating news it was useful to get his name right. On the other hand, if you'd only exchanged first names, and he'd left while you were still asleep, who could he blame but himself?

She tried to silence that voice. It spoke to her too often these days.

She began to walk the long path between the vines, trying to calm her thoughts. But they refused to be calmed.

They lingered rebelliously on the memory of his naked body against hers, the heat of his breath, the way he'd murmured her name.

There had been almost a question in his voice, as though he was asking her if she were certain. But there was no certainty left in her life. Her family, her boyfriend—these were the things she had clung to. But her boyfriend had rejected her and the foundations of her family had been shaken. So she'd invited Lucio to her bed because—what did it matter? What did anything matter?

He was looking up, suddenly very still as he saw her. What did that stillness mean? That he recognised her and guessed why she was here? Or that he'd forgotten a woman he'd known for a few hours several weeks ago?

When Lucio first looked up the sun was in his eyes, blinding him, so that for a moment he could make out no details. A woman was approaching him down the long avenue of vines, her attention fixed on him as though only he mattered in all the world.

That had happened so many times before. So often he'd seen Maria coming towards him from a great distance.

But Maria was dead.

The woman approaching him now was a stranger and yet mysteriously familiar. Her eyes were fixed on him even at a distance.

And he knew that nothing in the world was ever going to be the same again.

CHAPTER ONE

GOING to Italy had seemed a brilliant move for a language expert. She could improve her Italian, study the country and generally avoid recognising that she wasn't just leaving New York; she was fleeing it.

But the truth was still the truth. Charlotte knew she had to flee memories of an emotion that had once felt like love, but which had revealed itself as disappointingly hollow, casting a negative light on almost everything in her life. It was like wandering in a desert. She belonged to nobody and nobody belonged to her. Perhaps it was this thought that made her leave her laptop computer behind. It pleased her to be beyond the reach of anyone unless she herself decided otherwise.

For two months she wandered around Italy, seeking something she couldn't define. She made a point of visiting Naples, fascinated by the legendary Mount Vesuvius, whose eruptions had destroyed cities in the past. Disappointingly it was now considered so safe that she could wander up to the summit and stand there listening hopefully for a growl.

Silence.

Which was a bit like her life, she thought wryly. Waiting for something significant to happen. But nothing did. At twenty-seven, an age when many people had chosen their path in life, she still had no clue where hers was leading.

On the train from Naples to Rome she thought of Don, the man she'd briefly thought she loved. She'd wanted commitment and when Don didn't offer it she'd demanded to know where they were headed. His helpless shrug had told her the worst, and she'd hastened to put distance between them.

She had no regrets. Briefly she'd wondered if she might have been cleverer and perhaps drawn him closer instead of driving him away. But in her heart she knew things had never been quite right between them. It was time to move on.

But where?

As the train pulled into Roma Termini she reckoned it might be interesting to find the answer to that question.

She took a taxi to the Hotel Geranno on the Via Vittorio Veneto, one of the most elegant and expensive streets in Rome. The hotel boasted every facility, including its own internet café. She found it easily and slipped into a booth, full of plans to contact family and friends. She might even get in touch with Don on her social networking site, just to let him know there were no hard feelings, and they could be friends.

But the words that greeted her on Don's page were 'Thanks to everyone for your kind wishes on my engagement. Jenny and I want our wedding to be—'

She shut the file down.

Jenny! Charlotte remembered her always hanging around making eyes at Don. And he'd noticed her. Pretty, sexy, slightly voluptuous—she was made to be noticed.

Not like me, she thought.

Some women would have envied Charlotte's appearance. Tall, slender, dark-haired, dark-eyed; she wasn't a woman who faded into the background. She'd always had her share of male admiration; not the kind of gawping leer that Jenny could inspire, but satisfying enough. Or so she'd thought.

But Don hadn't wasted any time mourning her and that was just fine. The past was the past.

She touched a few more keys to access her email, and immediately saw one from her sister Alex, headlined, You'll never believe this!

Alex liked to make things sound exciting so, although mildly intrigued, Charlotte wasn't alarmed. But, reading the email, she grew still again as a family catastrophe un-folded before her eyes.

'Mom—' she murmured. 'You couldn't have—*it's not possible!*'

She had always known that her father, Cedric Patterson, was her mother's second husband. Before him Fenella had been married to Clay Calhoun, a Texas rancher. Only after their divorce had she married Cedric and lived with him in New York. There she'd borne four children—the twins Matt and Ellie, Charlotte and her younger sister Alexandra. Now it seems that Mom was already carrying Matt and Ellie when she left Clay, Alex wrote. She wrote and told him she was pregnant, but by that time he was with Sandra, who seems to have hidden the letter but, oddly enough, kept it. Nobody knew about it until both she and Clay were dead. He died last year, and the letter was found unopened, so I guess he never knew about Matt and Ellie.

What do you think of that? All these years we've thought they were our brother and sister, but now it seems we're only half-siblings! Same mother, different father. When Ellie told me what had happened I couldn't get my head around it, and I'm still in a spin.

Quickly Charlotte ran through her other emails, seeking one from Ellie that she was sure would be there. But she found nothing. Disbelieving, she ran through them again, but there was no word from Ellie.

Which meant that everyone in the family knew except her. Ellie hadn't bothered to tell her something so momentous. It had been left to Alex to send her the news as an afterthought, as though she was no more than a fringe member of the family. Which, right now, was how she felt.

Returning to the lobby she again knew the sensation of being lost in a desert. But this desert had doors, one leading to a restaurant known for its haute cuisine, the other leading to a bar. Right this minute a drink was what she needed.

The barman smiled as she approached. 'What can I get you?'

'A tequila,' she told him.

When it was served she looked around for a place to sit, but could see only one seat free, at the far end of the bar. She slipped into it and found that she could lean back comfortably against the wall, surveying her surroundings.

The room was divided into alcoves, some small, some large. The small ones were all taken up by couples, gazing at each other, revelling in the illusion of privacy. The larger ones were crowded with 'beautiful people' as though the cream of Roman society had gathered here tonight.

In the nearest alcove six people focused their attention on one man. He was king of all he surveyed, Charlotte thought with a touch of amusement. And with reason. In his early thirties, handsome, lean, athletic, he held centrestage without effort. When he laughed, they laughed. When he spoke they listened.

Nice if you can get it, Charlotte thought with a little sigh. *I'll bet his volcano never falls silent.*

Just then he glanced up and saw her watching him. For the briefest moment he turned his head to one side, a question in his eyes. Then one of the women claimed his attention and he turned to her with a perfectly calculated smile.

An expert, she thought. He knows exactly what he's doing to them, and what they can do for him.

Such certainly seemed enviable. Her own future looked depressing. Returning to New York smacked of defeat. She could stay in Italy for the year she'd promised herself, but that was less inviting now that things were happening at home; things from which she was excluded.

She thought of Don and Jenny, revelling in their love. All around her she saw people happy in each other's company, smiling, reaching out. And suddenly it seemed unbearable that there was nobody reaching out to her. She finished her drink and sat staring at the empty glass.

'Excuse me, can I just—?'

It was the man from the alcove, easing himself into the slight space between her and the next bar stool. She leaned back to make space for him but a slight unevenness in the floor made him wobble and slew to the side, colliding with her.

'Mi dispiace,' he apologised in Italian, steadying her with his hand.

'Va tutto bene,' she reassured him. 'Niente di male.' All is well. No harm done.

Still in Italian he said, 'But you'll let me buy you a drink to say sorry.'

'Thank you.'

'Another tequila?' asked the barman.

'Certainly not,' said the newcomer. 'Serve this lady a glass of the very best Chianti, then bring another round of drinks to me and my friends over there.'

He retreated and the barman placed a glass of red wine

in front of Charlotte. It was the most delicious she had ever tasted. Sipping it she glanced over at him, and it was no surprise to find him watching her. She raised her glass in salute and he raised his back. This seemed to disconcert the women sitting on either side of him, who asserted themselves to reclaim him, Charlotte was amused to notice.

Despite being in the heart of Rome they were speaking English. She was sitting close enough to overhear some of the remarks passing back and forth, half sentences, words that floated into the distance, but all telling the tale of people who lived expensive lives.

'You were on that cruise, weren't you? Wasn't it a gorgeous ship? Everything you wanted on demand...'

'I knew I'd met you before...you were at the opening of that new...'

'Look at her. If she's not wearing the latest fashion she thinks...'

Leaning back, Charlotte observed the little gathering with eyes that saw everything. Two of the women were watching Lucio like lions studying prey, but they were in alliance. She could have sworn that one murmured to the other, 'Me first'. She couldn't hear the words, but she could read their expressions: watchful, confident that each would have their turn with him.

She could understand their desires. It wasn't merely his striking looks and costly clothes, but his air of being in charge, directing his own life and that of others. This was a man who'd never known doubt or fear.

She envied him. It must be good to know so certainly who you were, what you were, how others saw you and where you belonged in the world, instead of being that saddest of creatures—a woman who drank alone.

As if to emphasise the point the seat beside her was occupied by a woman gazing devotedly at her male companion, who returned the compliment with interest, then slid an arm about her shoulders, drew her close and said fervently, 'Let's go now.'

'Yes, let's,' she breathed. And they were gone.

At once the man in the alcove rose, excused himself to his companions and swiftly claimed the empty seat before anyone else could try.

'Can I get you another drink?' he asked Charlotte.

'Well, just a small one. I should be leaving.'

'Going somewhere special?'

'No,' she said softly. 'Nowhere special.'

After a moment he said, 'Are you alone?'

'Yes.'

He grinned. 'Perhaps you'd be better off with someone to protect you from clumsy guys like me.'

'No need. I can protect myself.'

'I see. No man necessary, eh?'

'Absolutely.'

A voice called, 'Hey, Lucio! Let's get going!'

His companions in the alcove were preparing to leave, beckoning him towards the door.

'Afraid I can't,' he said. 'I'm meeting someone here in half an hour. It was nice to meet you.'

Reluctantly they bid him goodbye and drifted away. When the door was safely closed he breathed out in obvious relief.

'Hey, your friends are crazy about you,' she reproved him lightly. 'You might at least return the compliment.'

'They're not my friends. I only know them casually, and two I never met before today.'

'But you were dousing them with charm.'

'Of course. I'm planning to make money out of them.'

'Ah! Hence the charm!'

'What else is charm for?'

'So now you're girding up for your next "victim" in half an hour.'

He gave a slow smile. 'There's no one coming. That was just to get rid of them.'

She looked down into her glass, lest her face reveal how much this pleased her. He would be a welcome companion for a little while.

He read her exactly, offering his hand and saying, 'Lucio—'

His last name was drowned by a merry shout from further along the bar. She raised her voice to say, 'Charlotte.'

'Buona sera, Charlotte.'

'Buona sera, Lucio.'

'Are you really Italian?' he asked, his head slightly to one side.

'Why do you ask?'

'Because I can't quite pinpoint your accent. Venice? No, I don't think so. Milan? Hmm. Rome—Naples?'

'Sicily?' Charlotte teased.

'No, not Sicily. You sound nothing like.'

'You said that very quickly. You must know Sicily well.'

'Fairly well. But we were talking about you. Where do you come from?'

His bright smile was like a visor behind which he'd retreated at the mention of Sicily. Though intrigued, she was too wise to pursue the matter just yet. Later would be more interesting.

'I'm not Italian at all,' she said. 'I'm American.'

'You're kidding me!'

'No, I'm not. I come from New York.'

'And you speak my language like a native. I'm impressed.' Someone squeezed by them, forcing them to draw back uncomfortably. 'There's no room for us here,' he said, taking her arm and drawing her towards the door.

Several pairs of female eyes regarded her with frank envy. It was clear that the watching women had their own ideas about how the evening would end.

Well, you're wrong, Charlotte thought, slightly irritated. *He's a nice guy and I'll enjoy talking to him, but that's all. Not everything has to end in* amore, *even in Italy. OK, so he's suave, sophisticated, expensively dressed and fantastically good-looking, but I won't hold that against him.*

'So why Italian?' he asked as they began to stroll along the Via Vittorio Veneto.

'I was always fascinated by foreign languages. I studied several at school, but somehow it was always Italian that stood out and attracted me more than the others. So I learned it through and through. It's such a lovely language.'

'And in the end you got a job here, probably working at the U.S. Embassy, just up the street.'

'No, I don't work here. I'm a translator in New York. I do Italian editions of books, sometimes universities hire me to look over old manuscripts. And I suddenly thought, it's about time I actually saw the country and drank in what it's really like. So I caught the next plane out.'

'Literally?'

'Well, it took a couple of days to make arrangements, but that's all. Then I was free to go.'

'No ties? Family?'

'I've got parents, siblings, but nobody who can constrain my freedom.'

'Freedom,' he mused. 'That's what it's really about, huh?'

'One of the things. I've done some mad, stupid things in my life, and most of them have been about staying free.' She gave a wry laugh. 'It's practically my family nickname. Ellie's the beautiful one, Alex is the lovable one and I'm the crazy one.'

'That sounds fascinating. I'd really like to hear about your craziness.'

'Well, there's the time I set my heart on marrying this guy and my parents said no. We were only seventeen, which they thought was too young.'

He considered this with an air of seriousness that had a touch of humour. 'They could have had a point.'

'The way I saw it they were denying me my own way. Hell would freeze over before I admitted they could be right. So we eloped.'

'You married at seventeen?'

'No way. By the time we'd covered a few miles I could see what a juvenile twerp he was. To be fair I think he'd spotted the same about me. Anyway, I got all set to make a run for it, and bumped into him because *he* was making a run for it, too.'

Lucio roared with laughter. 'What happened when you got home?'

'My mother's a very clever woman. She knew better than to make a fuss. When she caught me sidling in she glanced up and said, "Oh, there you are. Don't make a noise, your father's asleep." We had a talk later but there were no hysterics. By then she was used to me doing stupid things.'

'But would getting married be the path to freedom? Husbands can be very restrictive.'

She chuckled. 'I didn't think of that at the time. I just pictured him doing things my way. Luckily I saw the truth before too late.'

'Yes, husbands have this maddening habit of wanting their own way.'

'Oh, I learnt the lesson.'

'So you still don't have a husband?'

'No husband, no nothing.' She added casually, 'These days it's the way to be.'

'You're a true woman of your age. At one time an un-married girl would wonder why no man wanted her. Now she wonders what's the best way to keep them off.'

'Right,' she responded in the same teasing voice. 'Sometimes you have to be really ingenious. And some-times just ruthless.'

'You talk like an expert. Or like a woman who's been kicked in the teeth and is going to do some kicking back.' He saw her wry face and said quickly, 'I'm sorry, I had no right to say that. None of my business.'

'It's all right. If we all minded our own business there'd be precious little of interest to talk about.'

'I've got a feeling I should be nervous about what you're going to say next.'

'I could ask about Sicily, couldn't I? Is that where you keep a secret wife, or perhaps two secret wives? Now that would really be interesting.'

'Sorry to disappoint you but there's no wife, secret or otherwise. I was born in Sicily, but I left it years ago, and I've never been back. The life just didn't suit me. Like you, I went exploring the world, and I ended up with a family who owned vineyards. Vines, wine-making, I loved it from the start. They were wonderful to me, practically adopted me, and finally left the vineyards to me.'

And he'd turned them into a top money-making busi-ness, she thought. That was clear from the way he dressed and the way others reacted to him.

They were reaching the end of the street. As they turned the corner Charlotte stopped, astonished and thrilled by the sight that met her eyes.

'The Trevi Fountain,' she breathed. 'I've always wanted to see it. It's so huge, so magnificent....'

This was no mere fountain. A highly decorated palace wall rose behind it, at the centre of which was a triumphal arch, framing the magnificent, half-naked figure of Oceanus, mythical god of water, ruling over the showers that cascaded into the pool below. Everywhere was flooded with light, giving the water a dazzling glitter against the night.

'I've read about it,' she murmured, 'and seen pictures, but—'

'But nothing prepares you,' he agreed. 'Some things have to be experienced before they become real.'

Nearby was a café with tables out on the street. Here they could sit and watch the humming life about them.

'Nice to see people having a good time,' she murmured.

'Does that mean your life is unhappy now?'

'Oh, no,' she said quickly. 'But it does tend to be a bit too serious. Legal documents, history books. Not exactly filled with fun. And sometimes you need to remind yourself about fun.'

He regarded her curiously, thinking that a woman with her looks could have all the fun she wanted with all the men she wanted. So there was a mystery here. But he was too astute to voice the thought.

'But Italy should remind you of fun,' he said. 'It's not all cathedrals and sober history.'

'I know. You've only got to stroll the streets of Rome in the twilight, and see—well, lots of things.'

His grin and the way he nodded spoke volumes about his own life. Doubtless it was full of 'twilight activities', she thought. And they would be fun. She didn't doubt that either.

'Anyway,' she went on, 'my favourite Italian was—'

She named a historical character with a legendary reputation for wickedness.

'He wasn't as bad as people think,' Lucio observed. 'He was actually quite a serious man who—'

'Don't say that,' she interrupted him quickly. 'You'll spoil him for me. If he's not wicked he's not interesting.'

He regarded her curiously. 'There aren't many people who'd see it that way.'

'But it's true.'

'Certainly it's true, but we're not supposed to say so.'

'Well, I'm always doing things I'm not supposed to. That's why I'm the black sheep of the family.'

'Because you eloped at seventeen?'

She chuckled. 'There were a few more things than that. There was the politician who came to hold a meeting in New York, all virtue and pomposity, except that he'd spent the previous night in a place where he shouldn't have been. I'd seen him leaving and I couldn't resist getting up at the meeting and asking him about it.'

'Shame on you!' he said theatrically.

'Yes, I have no sense of propriety, so I'm told.'

'So you're wicked and interesting, eh?'

'Certainly wicked. You know, everyone has their own talents. My sister Ellie is a talented dancer, my sister Alex is a talented vet—'

'And you're a talented linguist.'

'Oh, that! That's just earning a living. No, my real talent, the thing at which I'm practically a genius, is getting my own way.'

'Now you really interest me.'

'It can always be done, if you know how to go about it.'

'Cunning?'

'Certainly. Cunning, devious, manipulative, wicked—whatever it takes.'

'Is that the real reason you broke off your career to go travelling?'

'In one sense. I wanted to find another world, and I'm finding it. That's the way to live. Know what you want, and don't stop until you get it.' She raised her glass to him. 'I guess there's probably a lot of interesting wickedness in your own life.'

He assumed a shocked air.

'Me? No time for it. I'm far too busy earning a respectable living, I assure you.'

'Right. I'll believe you. Thousands wouldn't.'

He grinned. 'You do me an injustice.'

'No, I don't. Any man who proclaims himself respectable needs to be treated with suspicion.'

'I protest—'

'Don't bother because I won't believe a word you say.'

They plunged into a light-hearted argument with much vigour on both sides, but also much laughter. When she looked at her watch she was amazed to see how much time had passed. She had a strange sense of being mentally at one with him. Almost like a brother.

But the next moment he turned his head so that she saw his profile against the glittering light from the fountain. Not brotherly, she thought. Disconcertingly attractive in a way that eclipsed other men, even Don. Or perhaps especially Don. But definitely not brotherly.

She remembered the first time she and Don had ventured beyond kisses, both eager to explore. But something had been missing, she knew that now.

'Are you all right?' Lucio asked.

'Yes, fine.'

'Sure? You seemed as if something had disturbed you.'

'No, I guess I'm just a bit hungry.'

'They do great snacks here. I'll get the menu.'

'I'll just have whatever you're having.'

He ordered spicy rolls and they sat eating contentedly.

'Why are you looking at me like that?' she asked.

'Just trying to solve the mystery. You don't strike me as the kind of woman who goes along with whatever the man orders.'

'Dead right, I'm not. But this is new territory for me, and I'm learning something fresh all the time.'

'So I'm part of the exploration?'

'Definitely. I like to find something unexpected. Don't you?'

'I sometimes think my life has had too much that's unexpected. You need time to get used to things.'

She hoped he would expand on that. She was beginning to be intrigued by everything he said. But before she could speak there was an excited cry as more crowds surged into the piazza, eager to toss coins into the water. For a while they both sat watching them.

'It's the age of science,' she reflected. 'We're all supposed to be so reasonable. Yet people still come here to toss coins and make wishes.'

'Perhaps they're right,' he said. 'Being too reasonable can be dangerous. Making a wish might free you from that danger.'

'But there are always other dangers lurking,' she mused. 'What to do about them?'

'Then you have to decide which ones to confront and which to flee,' he said.

She nodded. 'That way lies wisdom. And freedom.'

'And freedom matters to you more than anything, doesn't it?' he asked.

'Yes, but you must know what it really means. You think you're free, but then something happens, and suddenly it looks more like isolation.'

A sudden bleakness in her voice on the last word caught his attention.

'Tell me,' he said gently.

'I thought I knew my family. An older brother and sister who were twins, a younger sister, but then it turns out that there's been a big family secret all along. It began to come out and—' she gave a sigh '—I was the last one to know. I've always been closest to Matt, even though he can be so distant sometimes, but now it's like I'm not really part of the family. Just an outsider, in nobody's confidence.'

'You spoke of nobody caring. Nobody at all? What about outside the family?'

She grimaced. 'Yes, there was someone. We were moving slowly but I thought we'd get there in time. Well, I'm an outsider there, too. It feels like wandering in a desert.'

She checked herself there. She hadn't meant to confide her desert fantasy, for fear of sounding paranoid, but he seemed to understand so much that it had come out naturally.

'I know the feeling,' he said, 'but a desert can be a friendly place. There's no one there to hurt you.'

'It's true there are no enemies there,' she said. 'But no friends either, nobody who cares about you.'

'You wouldn't want to be there for ever,' he agreed. 'But for a while it can be a place to rest and recruit your strength. Then one day you can come back and sock 'em on the jaw.'

She longed to ask him what events and instincts lay behind that thought. All around her doors and windows seemed to be flying open, revealing mysterious roads leading to mists and beyond, to more mysteries, tempting her forward.

But could it be right to indulge her confusions with a stranger?

Then she saw him looking at her, and something in his eyes was like a hand held out in understanding.

Why not?

What harm could come of it?

'I guess my real problem is that I'm no longer quite sure who I am,' she said.

He nodded. 'That can happen easily, and it's scary.'

'Yes, it is. With Don I always felt that I was the one in charge of our relationship, but then I found I wasn't. Oh, dear, I suppose that makes me sound like a managing female.'

'Sometimes that's what a man needs to bring out the best of him,' he said.

'Did that happen to you?'

'No, she wasn't "managing" enough. If she had been, she might have bound me to her in time to save us both.' He added quickly, 'Go on telling me about you.'

Now a connection had been established it was easy to talk. Neither of them went into much detail, but the sense of being two souls adrift was a bond. It was a good feeling and she was happy to yield to it.

'What happened to your gift for getting your own way?' he asked at last.

'I guess it failed me. I didn't say it worked all the time. You have to seize the chance, but sometimes the chance can't be seized.'

A cheer that went up from the fountain made them both look there.

'More coins, more wishes,' he said.

'Aren't they supposed to wish for a return to Rome?' she asked.

'Yes, but they always add another one, usually about a lover.'

'I'd like to go closer.'

As they neared the water they could see a man tossing

in coins by the dozen, then closing his eyes and muttering fiercely.

'What's he wishing for?' Charlotte asked.

'My guess is he wants his lady-love to appear out of the
blue, and tell him he's forgiven. When a guy's as desperate as that it's pretty bad.'

Then the incredible happened. A female hand tapped
the young man on the shoulder, he turned, gave a shout of
joy and embraced her.

'You came,' he bellowed. 'She came, everyone. She's
here.'

'You see, it works,' someone shouted. 'Everyone toss a
coin and make a wish.'

Laughing, Charlotte took two coins from her bag and
threw one in, crying, 'Bring me back to Rome.'

'That's not enough,' Lucio said. 'Now you must wish
that Don will come back.'

'Too late for that. We're not right for each other. I know
that now. But what about you? Your lady might arrive and
decide to "manage" you, after all, since it's so obviously
what you want.'

But he shook his head. 'She's gone to a place from
which she'll never return.'

'Oh, I'm so sorry. Did it happen very recently?'

'No,' he said softly. 'It was a hundred thousand years
ago.'

She nodded, understanding that time, whether long or
short, could make no difference to some situations. But
another thought danced through her mind so fleetingly
that she was barely aware of it. Another woman had stood
between them, but no longer. Suddenly she had vanished,
leaving only questions behind.

Impulsively she reached out and laid a hand on his
cheek.

'Hey, you two, that's not good enough,' came an exultant cry from nearby. 'This is the fountain of love. Look around you.'

Everywhere couples were in each other's arms, some hugging fondly, some kissing passionately. Lucio gazed into her face for only a moment before drawing her close.

'I guess they feel we're letting the side down,' he said.

'And we can't have that, can we?' she agreed.

The feel of his lips on hers was passionate yet comforting, confirming her sensation that she was in the right place with the right person.

'I'm glad I met you,' he whispered against her mouth.

'I'm glad, too.'

They walked slowly back along the Via Vittorio Veneto. Neither spoke until they reached the hotel and he said, 'Let me take you up to your room.'

She could have bid him goodnight there and then, but she didn't. She knew now that as the evening passed the decision had been slowly building inside her. What she was going to do was right, and whatever might come of it, she was resolved.

When they reached her room he waited while she opened the door. Then he took a step back, allowing her time to change her mind. But she had passed that point, and so had he. When she held out her hand he took it, followed her inside and closed the door, shutting out the world.

In the morning she awoke to find herself alone. By her bed was a scrap of paper, on which was written, 'Thank you with all my heart. Lucio.'

At breakfast she looked around but didn't see him. She realised that she didn't even know his last name.

Strangely the situation did not distress her. They had been ships that passed in the night because that was what both of them had chosen, both of them needed. He'd been passionate and at the same time a gentle, considerate lover, with a mysterious gift for making her feel as though her troubles were falling away. She could go on to whatever the future held, stronger and more confident.

But gradually, a few weeks later, she discovered what the future did hold, and she realised that nothing would ever be the same. Now it mattered that she didn't know his full name. It took several hours' online research to discover that he was Lucio Constello, one of the most notable men in the business, with vineyards all over the country. But the most famous one was in Tuscany.

She'd set out to confront him, wondering how this business could possibly end, and soon she would know.

There he was, far ahead. The moment of truth had arrived, and she had no choice but to go forward.

CHAPTER TWO

'I'M NOT imagining this, am I?' he asked slowly. 'It's really you?'

'Sure it's me,' she said lightly.

'You…here? In Tuscany? It's great but I can hardly believe it.'

'Why? There was always a chance we'd bump into each other again.'

The reference to chance was deliberate. She was determined to play it casual. There must be no hint of how frantically she'd searched for him, how much it mattered. She, who prided herself on fearing nothing, had been dreading this meeting, dreading the sight of his face when she told him her news.

She covered her feelings with a smile, a cheerful shrug. He mustn't suspect before she was ready.

'I'm flattered you even remember me,' she said.

'Oh, yes,' he murmured. 'I remember. We had a great evening. You made me laugh.'

She stayed calm, although it was hard. Was laughter all he remembered about that night?

'As you did me,' she returned brightly.

'Yes, we had a wonderful time. I'm sorry I had to leave so suddenly the next morning. You were deeply asleep and I didn't want to awaken you.'

That wasn't quite the truth. He'd been overtaken by a desire to keep that perfect night apart, separate from all other contacts, like a picture in a frame. It had made him slip silently out of the room, leaving behind only the note that gave no clue to his identity or whereabouts. Perhaps he should be ashamed of that, but he couldn't think of it now.

The sight of her approaching had filled him with an overwhelming gladness. The awareness of that night was there again, spectacular, intense. She was even more beautiful than he remembered, and for a moment he felt nothing but pleasure.

Then she destroyed it.

'I had to find you,' she said. 'There's something you need to know.' She took a deep breath. 'I'm pregnant.'

'Wh-what?'

'I'm pregnant. I'm carrying your child.'

To his own horror his mind went blank. The pleasure at seeing her, the joy at the beautiful memories, everything vanished. He had the sensation of being punched in the face.

'Are you…sure?' he asked, barely knowing what he said.

'Quite sure. And in case you're wondering, I don't make a habit of doing what I did that night, so there hasn't been anyone else. You're the father.'

'Look, I didn't mean…'

He could have cursed himself for his clumsiness but he couldn't help it. He didn't mean—what? And what *did* he mean? If anything.

Watching him intently, Charlotte saw the last thing in the world she'd wanted to see. Confusion. Blank. Nothing.

A desert.

In a blinding flash her courage collapsed. Don had rejected her, and although her heart hadn't been broken, rejection was still rejection. Now Lucio was working himself up to reject her, and she wasn't going to hang around for it.

'It's OK, it's OK,' she said with a good imitation of a cheerful laugh. 'There's no need to panic.'

'I'm not—'

'Oh, yes, you are. You're on the verge of a panic attack. Oh, poor Lucio! Did you think I was trying to trap you into marriage? Not a chance! You and me? Get real! It would never work. We'd always—well, never mind that. Just don't panic. You're completely safe from me, I promise you. I'm only here because you have the right to know. Fulfilling my citizenly duty. How about that?'

She even managed a teasing note in the last words, and had the bitter satisfaction of seeing uncertainty in his face. He was floundering. Good. Serve him right!

'So there it is,' she said. 'Now you know. If you want to talk about it you'll find me here.' She thrust a piece of paper into his hand. 'But if you don't want to, that's just fine. Goodbye, Lucio. It was nice knowing you.'

Turning on her heel she walked swiftly away, determined to escape before he could insult her with any more blank-faced confusion.

But she gave him a last chance. That was only fair. After hurrying a few hundred yards she looked back, expecting to find him watching her, even perhaps stretching out a hand. That would have made her pause to see if he followed.

But he was frozen where she'd left him, immobile, staring down at the paper in his hand. She waited for him to look up, see her, call her name.

Nothing! Damn him!

There was only one thing to do, and that was vanish. She managed this by moving sideways between the vines so that she slipped into the next alley. This she did again,

then again and again until she was several alleys away
from the one where she'd started. Then she began to run,
and didn't stop until she reached her car. A few moments
later she was speeding away from the estate.

As she fled she asked herself ironically what else she'd
expected. A man who shared a woman's bed and vanished
without a goodbye had sent her an unmistakable message.
The woman who chose to ignore that message had nobody
to blame but herself if she suffered rejection.

And it certainly was rejection. Lucio hadn't said the
actual words, but only because he'd been trying to phrase
them tactfully. She wouldn't hear from him again but it
didn't matter. She'd told him what he had a right to know
and her conscience was clear.

She thought of her family back home in the States.
She'd known of her pregnancy for several weeks, but so
far hadn't told them. How would they react?

Or did she know the answer, only too well? They would
accept it as no more than you'd expect from Charlotte—
the difficult one, unpredictable, awkward, never quite fitting in.

And the one-night stand? Well, that was just like her,
wasn't it? Always ready to explore new territory, even if
it might have been best left unexplored. Not that she was
exactly a bad girl...

But then again, maybe she was.

She wished her brother, Matt, was here right now.
Strange that they should be so close, when he was Ellie's
twin, not hers. But there was something in their natures
that clicked. She knew that he, too, sometimes felt adrift
in a desert, and he fought it the way she did herself, with
humour that was ironic and sometimes bitter. She could
almost hear him now. 'Why did you bother finding this

guy? He didn't even give you his last name. Doesn't that tell you something?'

Perhaps he did tell me the name, she thought, *I just can't remember it. It didn't matter. It was that sort of evening. All about having fun.*

But it hadn't been fun trying to track him down afterwards. The thought of applying to the hotel for information had made her shiver with shame. Instead she'd gone to an internet café and then ransacked the internet for Italian vintners until she found no less than five of them called 'Lucio.' Luckily there was a photograph that identified him, but the search had made her feel like some abandoned serving girl from a bygone era. Which didn't improve her temper any.

She'd finally identified him as Lucio Constello, one of the most successful men in the business. His wine was famous throughout the world, and he seemed to live a glamorous life, enjoying yacht trips, rubbing shoulders with celebrities, making money at every point. There were pictures of him with beautiful women, one of whom had recently ended a romance with a film producer.

'And perhaps we know why,' enthused the text. 'Just look at the way they're gazing at each other.'

But after that the starlet was never seen with him again.

One article declared that he was 'a man who really knew how to enjoy himself.' Which meant, Charlotte thought wryly, that one-night stands were a normal part of his life. Hence his disappearance and her feeling that he wouldn't be pleased to see her.

His vineyards were many, spread out over Italy, and all subject to his personal supervision. Crisis! He could be anywhere. But an article revealed that he usually spent May in Tuscany at the Vigneto Constanza. There was time to catch him.

At the same time a perverse inner voice argued that there was no need to contact him at all. What did this baby really have to do with Lucio? Forget him. He belonged in the past.

But her mother's voice seemed to flit through her mind. It was weeks since she'd learned the truth of how Fenella had led Cedric Patterson into accepting Clay Calhoun's twins as his own, yet still the deception haunted her. No matter how much she tried to defend her mother she knew that she herself must be honest. So she would write to Lucio.

But somehow the letter wouldn't get itself written. Whatever tone she adopted was the wrong one. Too needy. Too hopeful. Too chilly. Too indifferent.

So she'd headed for Tuscany, checking into a hotel in the picturesque old city of Florence, and hiring a car from the hotel for the rest of the journey. For part of the way a map was useful, but when she grew nearer she asked directions. Everyone could point the way. The Vigneto Constanza was known and respected for miles around, clearly a source of welcome employment which was probably why they called the house a *palazzo*, she thought.

But she changed her mind when she saw the building, which was certainly a palace, rearing up three floors, with an air of magnificence that suggested nobility rather than business.

As she approached a middle-aged woman came out and stood waiting on the step.

'Good morning,' she said as Charlotte got out of the car. 'I'm Elizabetta, the housekeeper. Can I help you?'

'I'm here to see Signor Constello.'

'I'm afraid he's not here,' Elizabetta said.

Charlotte gave a sharp breath. He'd vanished. She'd pursued him for nothing. Suddenly she was in the desert again.

But then Elizabetta added, 'Not just now anyway. He's gone out inspecting the vines on the far side of the estate.'

'But he is…coming back?'

'Well, it's a big estate. He won't be home until very late, and sometimes he stays the night with one of his workers who lives on the far side.'

'I need to see him today. Can you tell me where he'll be?'

A few minutes later she headed off in what she hoped was the right direction. The sheer size of the grape fields was stunning—acre after acre, filled with long straight lines that seemed to stretch into infinity. She wouldn't have been surprised to discover that she'd arrived on a strange planet, and Lucio wasn't here at all.

'Stop being fanciful,' she told herself sternly. 'There he is in the distance. Everything's going to be all right.'

Instead nothing was all right. His response had been so bleak that she'd fled after a few minutes, and was now back in Florence, pacing the floor of her hotel room.

The paper she'd left him had contained both the hotel details and the number of her cell phone. He would call her soon, and they would settle it. But as time passed with no call, she faced the fact that she was alone again.

Another desert.

As the light faded she sat at the window, looking out at the old city. Her room overlooked the beautiful river Arno, with a clear view of the Ponte Vecchio, 'the old bridge,' which had stood there for over a thousand years. It was lined with shops on both sides, at one time a common Italian habit. But that convention had faded, and now the Ponte Vecchio was almost unique in still having them. They were lit up, dazzling and golden against the night air, flooding the water with light.

On impulse she determined to go down and explore the

bridge. She would take her cell phone. Lucio could call that number if he wanted to contact her. But if he didn't, he needn't think she was going to languish here waiting for him to deign to give her his attention.

In a moment she was downstairs and out of the door, heading for the street that ran along the river. Despite the lateness of the hour she was far from alone. Couples strolled slowly, absorbed in each other or leaning over the wall to gaze at the water before turning to meet each other's eyes.

At last she reached the bridge and walked halfway across to where there was a gap in the shops and she could look out over the dazzling water. On either side of her couples murmured, pleading, suggesting, happy.

Happy, she thought. Was it really possible to be happy in love?

And what was love anyway?

Briefly she'd thought she'd discovered the answer with Don, but she knew differently now. Not just because he'd let her down, but because in one devastating night with Lucio she'd discovered something that had reduced all other experiences to nothing.

Gazing down into the shimmering water, she seemed to be back in the hotel room, hearing the sound of the door close, feeling him move close. How warm his breath had been on her face, how gladly she had drawn closer to him, raising her head to receive his kiss.

She could still feel his mouth on hers, silencing the last of her doubts. Until then the voice of reason had whispered that she mustn't do this with a man she'd only just met. It wasn't proper behaviour. But the gentle, skilful movements of his lips had conquered her. Propriety had never meant much to her. In his arms it meant nothing at all.

It was obvious that he was a ladies' man, but he'd undressed her with an air of reverent discovery that made her feel special. Of course this was merely part of his expertise, she'd guessed, but it was hard to be realistic when his eyes on her were full of astonished worship.

He'd removed her dress, but before stripping her completely he'd tossed aside his jacket and shirt. There were no lights on in the room but enough came through the window to reveal his smooth, well-shaped chest and arms. Lying beside her on the bed, he'd drawn away her slip and bra, leaving only her briefs.

Then he'd smiled.

Something in that smile had made her reach for him and begin pulling at his clothes until he wore no more than she did. Now she, too, was smiling. This man was going to prove a skilful lover. Every instinct she had told her that was true.

His body was marvellous, muscular but lean and taut, hinting at strength that could bring a woman joy. Almost tentatively she slipped her fingers beneath the edge of his briefs.

Incredibly there was a question in his eyes, almost as though he was asking her even now if she had any doubts. Her reply was to tighten her grip, silently ordering him to strip naked. He obeyed and did the same for her, then stayed looking down at her, letting his fingertips drift across her breasts.

His caress was so light that he could barely be said to be touching her at all, yet the thunderous pleasure that went through her was like a storm. How could so much result from so little? she wondered frantically. Then all thought was forgotten in the delight that possessed her.

No man touched a woman so subtly without first understanding her, not just her body but traces of her heart and mind. Instinct from deep inside told her so, and everything in her responded to him. She couldn't have prevented that response even if she'd wanted to, but she didn't want to. Nothing was further from her desire than to resist him. In that magical moment she was all his, and all she wanted was to make him all hers.

Afterwards, he kissed her tenderly, stroking her hair as sleep began to claim her, and she felt herself drifting away into the sweet, warm darkness.

At the very last moment he whispered, 'You're wonderful.'

The night descended totally before she could respond, but that soft tribute lingered with her in the mysterious other universe where there was rest, peace and joy.

But when she awoke, he was gone.

The memory of the murmured words tormented her. Had she imagined them, or had he really said such a thing before abandoning her? Again and again she went over the moment, racking her brain to know whether it was true memory or only fantasy born of wishful thinking. The search nearly drove her crazy, but she found no answer.

In the weeks that followed she'd known that she could have loved him if he'd given any sign of wanting her love. Instead he'd rejected her so brutally that she'd come close to hating him.

It was cruelly ironic that her two encounters with Lucio had both been under circumstances that suggested romance. First the Trevi Fountain where lovers laughingly gambled on their love, and where she'd been tempted to gamble beyond the boundaries of both love and sense. Now she was in another city so enchanting that it might have been designed for lovers. But instead of revelling in the company of a chosen man she was alone again. Unwanted. Looking in from the outside, as so many times before in her life.

But enough was enough. This was the last time she would stand outside the magic circle, longing for a signal from within; the last time she would wait for a man to make up his mind. *Her* mind was made up, and he could live with it.

She almost ran back to the hotel. At the desk she stopped just long enough to ask, 'Any message for me? No? Right. I'm checking out in half an hour. Kindly have my bill ready.'

In her room she hurled things into the suitcase, anxious to lose no time now the decision was made. Her next step was vague. A taxi from the hotel to the railway station, and jump on the next train to—? Anywhere would do, as long as it was away from here.

At the desk the bill was ready. It took only a moment to pay it, seize up her baggage and head for the door. Outside she raised her hand to a taxi on the far side of the road, which immediately headed for her.

'Where to?' the driver called.

'Railway station,' she called back.

'No,' said a voice close by. Then a hand came out of the darkness to take her arm, and the same voice said, 'Thank goodness I arrived in time.'

She jerked her head up to see Lucio.

'Let me go,' she demanded.

'Not yet. First we must talk. Charlotte, neither of us should make hasty decisions. Can't you see that?' He laid his other hand on her shoulder. His touch was gentle but firm. 'You're not being fair, vanishing like this,' he said. 'I trusted you. Perhaps I shouldn't have done.'

'Perhaps *I* shouldn't have trusted *you*. I gave you the chance. I told you what had happened. You could have done anything but you chose to do nothing. Fine! I get the message.'

'There's no message. I was confused, that's all. It took me a while to get my head around it, but I thought at least you'd stay one night—give me a few hours to think.'

'What is there to think about?' she demanded passionately. 'The baby's here, inside me, waiting to be born and change everything. You're either for that or against it.'

He made a wry face. 'You really don't understand much about human weakness, do you? I didn't jump to your command at once, so you thought you'd make me sorry.'

'That's nonsense,' she said, but she knew a moment's discomfort at how close he'd come.

'I don't think so. Look, let's put this behind us. We have too much at stake to risk it with a quarrel.' He addressed the driver. 'Leave the bags. Here.'

He held out a wad of cash which the driver pocketed and fled.

'You've got a cheek,' she said indignantly.

'Not really. I'm taking a big gamble. I didn't anticipate you leaving without giving me a fair chance. I thought you'd wait for me to pull my thoughts together.'

'All right, maybe I was a bit hasty,' she said reluctantly.

'I wonder if it will always be like that with us, each of us going in opposite directions.'

'I think that sounds an excellent idea,' she said. 'If I had any sense I'd go in another direction right this minute.'

'But if you had any sense,' he replied wryly, 'you wouldn't have wasted time on me in the first place.'

'I guess you're right.'

'But since you did, and since the world has changed, isn't it time we talked to each other properly. There's a little café just along there where we can have peace. Will you come with me?'

She hesitated only a moment before taking his hand and saying, 'Yes. I think perhaps I will.'

CHAPTER THREE

AFTER dumping her bags in his car Lucio indicated the road
that ran along the side of the river. 'It's not far. Just a quiet
little place where we can get things sorted.'

But when they reached the café Charlotte backed off.
Through the windows she could see tables occupied by
couples, all seemingly blissful in each other's company.

Not now, she thought. An air of romance wasn't right
for this discussion. She needed a businesslike atmosphere.

'It's a bit crowded,' she said. 'Let's find somewhere
else.'

'No, they won't bother us,' he said, which left her with
a curious feeling that he'd read her thoughts. 'This way.'

He led her to a table by a window, through which she
could see the golden glow of the water, and the little boats
all of which seemed to be full of adoring couples.

But this situation demanded efficiency, common sense.
The last thing it needed was emotion.

Her mood had calmed. She was even aware of a little
shame at how hastily she'd judged him. But it still irked
her that he'd taken control. She glanced up and found him
studying her with a faint smile.

'If looks could kill, I'd be a dead man,' he observed
lightly.

'Unless there was some quicker way,' she replied in the same tone.

'If there was, I'm sure you'd know it.'

'Well, you've got a nerve, just taking over like that.'

'But I asked if you'd come with me. You said yes.'

'And if I'd said no, what would have happened?'

He gave a smile that made her heart turn over. 'I'd probably have taken the advice you offered me in Rome.'

'I gave you advice?'

'As I recall your exact words were, "Know what you want and don't stop until you get it". Impressive advice. I know what I want and, well—' He spread his hands in an expressive gesture.

'So you think you can do what you like and I can't complain because I put you up to it.'

'That's a great way of putting it. I couldn't have done better myself.'

'I—you—'

'Ah, waiter, a bottle of my usual wine, and sparkling water for the lady.'

'And suppose I would have liked wine,' she demanded when they were alone.

'Not for the next few months. It wouldn't be good for you or the person you're carrying.'

His use of the word *person* startled her. How many men saw an unborn child as a person, still less when it had been conceived only a few weeks ago? She knew one woman whose husband referred to 'that thing inside you'. But to Lucio this was already a person. Instinctively she laid a hand over her stomach.

Then she looked up to find him watching her. He nodded. After a moment she nodded back.

Now she'd had a chance to get her thoughts in order

she found her brief hostility dying. She could even appreciate his methods.

When the waiter returned with the drinks Lucio ordered a snack, again without consulting her. But it was hard to take offence when he was ordering the same things she'd enjoyed in the outdoor café at the Trevi Fountain, a few weeks and a thousand lifetimes ago. How had he remembered her taste so perfectly? The discovery made him look slightly different.

Studying him, she discovered another change. The man in Rome had been a flamboyant playboy, handsome, elegantly dressed, ready to relish whatever pleasures came his way. The man in the vineyard that afternoon had worn dark jeans and a sweater, suitable for hard work on the land.

The man sitting here now wore the same clothes but his eyes were tense. His manner was calm, even apparently light-hearted, but there was something else behind it. She sensed apprehension in him, but why was he nervous? Of her? The situation? Himself?

When the waiter had gone he turned back to her.

'I'm sorry for the way this happened, but I never dreamed you'd just leave like that.'

'And I thought my leaving was what you wanted. Your silence seemed rather significant.'

'My silence was the silence of a man who's been knocked sideways and was trying to get his head together. You tell me something earth-shattering, then you vanish into thin air, and I'm supposed to just shrug?'

'I guess I thought you were more sophisticated than this.'

'What you thought was that this kind of thing happened to me every day, didn't you?'

'Nonsense,' she said uncomfortably.

'Be honest, admit it.'

'How can I? I don't know the first thing about you.'

'Nor I about you,' he said wryly. 'That's our problem, isn't it? We've done it all back to front. Most people get to know a little about each other before they—well, anyway, we skipped that bit and now everything's different.

'I didn't contact you earlier because I was in a state of shock. When I'd pulled myself together I picked up the phone. Then I put it down again. I didn't know what to say, but I had to see you. I had to know how you feel about what's happened. Tell me frankly, Charlotte, do you want this baby?'

Aghast, she glared at him. 'What are you saying? Of course I want it. Are you daring to suggest that I get rid of it? I'd never do that.'

'No, I didn't mean—it's just—' He seemed to struggle for the right words. 'Do you really want the child or are you merely making the best of it?'

She drew a slow breath. 'I don't know. I've never thought of it like that. From the moment I knew, it felt inevitable, as though the decision had been taken out of my hands.'

He nodded. 'That can be a strange feeling, sometimes bad but sometimes good. You get used to planning life, but then suddenly life makes the plans and orders you to follow them.'

'Oh, yes,' she murmured. 'I know exactly what you mean.'

'And maybe it can be better that way. It can save a lot of trouble.'

'You'll have me believing that you're a fatalist.'

'Perhaps,' he said quietly. 'Things happen, and when you think you've come to terms with it something else happens and you have to start the whole process again.'

'Yes,' she murmured. 'Nothing is ever really the way we thought it was, is it?'

'No,' he said. 'That's true, and somehow we have to find our way through the maze.'

She turned to meet his eyes and saw in them a confusion that matched her own.

'I can hardly believe you're pregnant,' he said. 'You look as slim as ever.'

'I'm two and a half months gone. That's too early for it to show, but it'll start soon.'

'When did you know?'

'A few weeks ago. I was late, and when I checked—' she shrugged '—that was it.'

She waited for him to demand why she hadn't approached him sooner, but he sat in silence. She was glad. It would have been hard for her to describe the turmoil of emotions that had stormed through her in the first days after the discovery. They had finally calmed, but she'd found herself in limbo, uncertain what to do next.

When she'd discovered his likely location she hadn't headed straight there. Her mind seemed to be in denial, refusing to believe she was really pregnant. Any day now it would turn out to be a mistake. She'd continued her trip around Italy, heading back south but avoiding Rome and going right down to Messina, then crossing the water to the island of Sicily, where she spent a month before returning north.

At last she faced the truth. She was carrying Lucio's child. So she went to find him, telling herself she was ready for anything. But his response, or lack of it, had stunned her. Now here she was, wishing she was anywhere else on earth.

From the river below came the sound of a young woman screaming with laughter. Glancing down Charlotte saw the girl fooling blissfully with her lover before they vanished under the bridge. Lucio watched her, noticing how the glittering yellow burnished her face, so that for a moment she looked not like a woman but like a golden figurine, enticing, mysterious, capable of being all things to all men, or nothing to any man.

'So tell me what you're thinking,' he said. 'Tell me how it looks to you, and where you see the path leading.'

'I can't answer that. I see a dozen paths leading in different directions, and I won't know which one is the right one until we've talked.'

'If I hadn't turned up just now where were you headed?'

She shrugged.

'Home?' he persisted. 'To New York?' He searched her face. 'You don't know, do you?'

'Does it matter?'

'What about your family? How do they feel about it?'

'I haven't told them yet.'

He stared. 'What, nothing?'

'Nothing.'

'I see.' He sat in silence for a moment and when he spoke again his tone was gentle.

'When we talked in Rome you said there was a secret that you'd been the last to know, and you felt as though you weren't really part of the family any more. You still feel like that?'

'I guess so.'

'All these weeks you've had nobody to confide in?'

'It wouldn't be a good time.'

The thought of her family had made her flinch. So much was going on there already—the truth about Matt and Ellie's paternity, her feeling of isolation, her uncertainty about what a family really meant—she couldn't confide in them until she'd made up her own mind. She didn't even tell Matt. She'd always felt close to him before, but not now.

'So there isn't anybody—?' Lucio ventured slowly.

'Don't you dare start feeling sorry for me,' she flashed. 'I can look after myself.'

'Will you stop taking offence at every word? You don't have to defend yourself against me. If you'd just given me a chance this afternoon—'

'All right, I shouldn't have dashed off the way I did,' she admitted. 'But you looked so horrified....'

'Not horrified,' he corrected her gently. 'Just taken by surprise. It's never happened to me before, and it was the last thing I expected.' He made a wry face. 'I just didn't feel I could cope. I guess my cowardly side came to the surface.'

'But there's no need for you to feel like that,' she said. 'You don't have to have anything to do with this baby. I told you because you had a right to know, but I'm not expecting anything from you—'

She stopped, dismayed at his sudden frozen expression.

'Thanks,' he said harshly. 'You couldn't have showed your contempt for me more clearly than that.'

'But I didn't—I don't know what you—'

'You're carrying my child but you don't expect anything from me. That says everything, doesn't it? In your eyes I'm incapable of rising to the occasion, fulfilling my obligations. In other words, a total zero.'

'I didn't mean it like that. I just didn't want you to feel I was putting pressure on you.'

'Doesn't it occur to you that there ought to be a certain amount of pressure on a man who's fathered a child?'

'Well, like you said, we don't know each other very well.'

The words *Except in one way* seemed to vibrate in the air around them.

Seeing this tense, sharp-tempered man, she found it strange to recall the charismatic lover who'd lured her into his arms that night in Rome. How he'd laughed as they stood by the fountain, tossing in coins, challenging her to make two wishes—the conventional one about returning to Rome, and another one from her heart. She'd laughed too, closing her eyes and moving her lips silently, refusing to tell him what she'd asked for.

'Let's see if I can guess,' he'd said.

'You never will.'

That was true, for there had been no second wish. She had so many things to wish for, and no time to think about them. So she'd merely moved her lips without meaning, as part of the game.

She'd teased him all the way into her bedroom and the merriment had lasted as they undressed each other. They didn't switch on the light, needing only the glow that came through the windows, with its mysterious half shadows. His body had been just as she'd expected, slim and vigorous, not heavily muscular but full of taut strength.

Everything about their encounter had been fun: it was scandalous, immoral, something no decent girl would ever do, but she enjoyed it all the more for the sense of thrilling rebellion it gave her. No pretence, no elaborate courtesy, no bowing to convention. Just sheer lusty pleasure.

His admiration had been half the enjoyment. In the glow of success she had soared above the world, but now had come the inevitable crash landing, and the two of them stranded together.

She looked around the café, trying to get her bearings. It was hard because there were lovers everywhere, as though this part of Florence had been made for them and nobody else. Glancing at Lucio she saw him watching the couples with an expression on his face that made her draw a sharp breath. Gone was the irony, the air of control that seemed to permeate everything else that he did. In its place was a haunted look, as though his heart was yearning back to a source of sadness from which he could never be entirely free.

She looked away quickly. Something warned her that he would hate to know she'd seen that revealing expression.

One couple in particular caught her attention. They were deep in conversation, with the girl urgently explaining something to the young man. Suddenly he burst into a loud crow of joy, pointing to her stomach. She nodded, seizing his hand and drawing it against her waist. Then they threw themselves into each other's arms.

That was how it should be, Charlotte thought. Not like this.

'No prizes for guessing what she told him,' Lucio observed wryly.

'I suppose not.'

He seemed to become suddenly decisive. 'All right, let's see if we can agree on something.'

Here it was, she thought. He was going to offer her a financial settlement, and she was going to hate him for it.

'I've been doing a lot of thinking since this afternoon,' he said. 'And one thing's clear to me. You mustn't be alone. I want you to come and stay with me.'

She frowned. 'You mean—?'

'At my home. I think you'll like it there.'

Seeing in her face that she was astonished he added, 'You don't have to decide now. Stay for a while, decide how you feel, then we'll talk and you'll make your decision.'

Dumbfounded, she stared at him. Whatever she'd expected it wasn't this.

'Please, Charlotte. You can't just go off into the distance and vanish. I want you where I can look after you
and our child.'

She drew a shaky breath. Of all he'd said, three words
stood out.

I want you.

To be wanted, looked after. When had that last happened to her?

'You surely understand that?' Lucio said.

'Yes, I—I guess I'm like you. I need time to get my
head round it.'

'But what's difficult? We're having a child together.
That makes us a family. At the very least we should give
it a try, see if it can be made to work.'

'Well, yes, I suppose so....'

'Good. Then we're agreed. Nice to get it settled. Shall
we go?'

'Yes,' she said slowly, taking the hand he held out to
her, and letting him draw her to her feet.

The die was cast. She had no intention of leaving him
now.

'Are you all right?' he asked as they stepped out into
the street.

'Yes—yes, everything's all right.'

He led her to where he'd parked the car and ushered
her into the front passenger seat. In a few moments they
were heading out of Florence and on the road that led the
twenty miles to the estate.

There was a full moon, casting its glow over the hills of
Tuscany, and holding her spellbound by the beauty. Lucio
didn't speak and she was glad because she needed time to
understand what had happened.

I want you.

Three simple words that had made it impossible for

her to leave, at least for the moment. Later, things might be different, but for now she had nowhere else to go, and nobody else who wanted her.

With a few miles to go Lucio pulled in at the side of the road and made a call on his cell phone.

'Mamma? We'll be there in a few minutes…. Fine…. Thank you!'

As he started up the engine and drove on he said, 'Fiorella isn't actually my mother. She and her husband, Roberto, were the owners of the estate when I arrived here twelve years ago. I worked for them, we grew close, and I nearly married their daughter, Maria. But she died, and Roberto followed her soon after, leaving the estate to me.'

'But shouldn't he have left it to his wife?' Charlotte asked.

'Don't worry, I didn't steal her inheritance. He left her a fortune in money. She could go anywhere, do anything, but she chooses to live here because it's where she was happy. She's been like a mother to me, and I'm glad to have her.'

Her head was in a whirl at these revelations. Lucio had been engaged to Fiorella's daughter. How would she feel at the arrival of a woman carrying Lucio's child, a child that in another life would have been her own grandchild? At the very least she would regard Charlotte as an interloper.

'You should have told me this before,' she said.

'Why? She wants to meet you.'

'But it's an impossible situation. Her daughter—you—however can this be happening?'

'Charlotte, please, I know it's difficult, but don't blame me. You've known about this pregnancy for weeks, but you sprang it on me without warning. I had to make decisions very quickly, and if I was clumsy I'm sorry. Don't look daggers at me.'

Since his eyes were fixed on the road he couldn't see the daggers, but he'd known by instinct. She ground her teeth.

What did Fiorella know about her? What had Lucio said? What had Elizabetta, the housekeeper, said after she'd arrived, asking for Lucio, earlier that day?

In the distance she could see a palatial house, standing high on a hill and well lit so that she could recognise it as the one she'd visited. As they neared she could see two women standing just outside the front door. One of them was Elizabetta and the other must be Fiorella.

The two women were totally still as the car drew up. Only when Lucio opened Charlotte's door and handed her out did they come forward.

'This is Charlotte,' he said. 'She's come to stay with us.'

Clearly neither of them needed to ask what he meant. Lucio had prepared the ground well. Elizabetta smiled and nodded, but Fiorella astonished Charlotte by opening her arms

'You are welcome in this house,' she said.

Charlotte's head spun. She'd been prepared for courtesy, but not this show of warmth from a woman whose daughter Lucio had once planned to marry. It was Maria who should have borne his children, which surely made her an interloper.

She managed to thank Fiorella calmly, and the two women ushered her into the house while Lucio returned to the car for her bags.

'A room has been prepared for you,' Fiorella said. 'And some food will be brought to you. Tomorrow we will all eat together, but tonight I think you are tired and need to sleep soon.'

She was right, and Charlotte thanked her for her consideration. Secretly she guessed that there was another reason. Now that she'd set eyes on her, Fiorella wanted to take Lucio aside and demand more answers. And she herself would be glad to talk to him privately.

He led the way up a flight of stairs, so grandiose that they confirmed her impression that this was more of a palace than a farmhouse. Then it was down a wide corridor lined with pictures, until they came to a door.

'This is your room,' Lucio said, leading the way in and standing back for her to see.

It was a splendid place, large and extravagantly furnished, with a double bed that had clearly been freshly made up, and a door that led to a private bathroom.

'This is kept for our most honoured guests,' Lucio said. 'I think you'll be comfortable here.'

'I'm sure I will be,' she said politely.

Fiorella appeared, followed by Elizabetta pushing a table on wheels, laden with a choice of food, fruit juice and coffee.

'Have a good night's sleep,' Fiorella said. 'And we will get to know each other tomorrow. Would you like Elizabetta to unpack your bags?'

'No, thank you,' Charlotte said quickly.

She wasn't sure why she refused. But while she was still learning about this place and the people in it some instinct warned her to stay on guard.

'Right, we'll leave you alone to get settled,' Lucio said. 'Go to bed soon. It's late.'

She would have preferred him to stay, but of course he must sort out final details with Fiorella. He would come to her later.

She ate the supper, which had clearly been created by someone who knew her tastes, meaning that Lucio had been at work here, too. Then she unpacked, hung up her clothes in the elegant wardrobes and took a shower. It felt wonderful. When she stepped out her flesh was singing and she felt better physically than she had for some time.

What to wear to greet Lucio when he came? Nothing seductive. That would send out too obvious a message. The nightdress she chose was silk but not seductively low-cut. Some women would have called it boring. Charlotte called it useful. They could talk again, but this time it would be different. She no longer felt the antagonism he'd provoked in her earlier. Tonight would decide the future, and suddenly that future looked brighter than it had for months.

It was only a few hours since she'd arrived at the estate, a confident woman, certain that she knew who and what she was. She would explain the facts to Lucio, they would make sensible arrangements and that would be that.

But nothing had worked out as she planned, and now here she was, in unknown territory. She knew there was much to make her grateful. Where she might have found hostility she was treated as an 'honoured guest'. Lucio wanted their child, and was set on being a good father, which made him better than many men. But he was focused on the baby, not herself. What would happen between the two of them was something only time would tell.

She threw herself down on the bed, staring into space. One question danced through her mind. How much had Maria meant to him? How much did her memory mean to him now? He'd spoken of her without apparent emotion, but that might have been mere courtesy towards herself. Or perhaps they had planned no more than a marriage of convenience.

Surely that wasn't important. How could it matter to her?

Yet, disconcertingly, it did.

Face it, she thought. *He's attractive. You thought so from the first moment in Rome, otherwise things wouldn't have happened as they did. What was it someone used to say to me? 'When you've made a decision, have the guts to live with the result.' I made a decision, and this is the result. Perhaps even a happy one.*

We could even fall in love. I'm not in love with him now, but I know I could be. But isn't that a kind of love already? Well, it'll be interesting finding out.

She smiled to herself.

And I could win him. Couldn't I?

I'll know when I see him tonight. He'll be here soon.

But hours passed and Lucio did not appear.

CHAPTER FOUR

FROM his bedroom window Lucio could see the window of Charlotte's room. The blinds were drawn but he could make out her shadow moving back and forth against the light, until finally the light was extinguished.

He went to bed, thinking about her, lying alone in the darkness, just as he was himself. Was she struggling with confusion? Did they have that, too, in common?

He wasn't proud of himself. His reaction to her news had been fear so intense that at first it had held him frozen. After she'd left he'd spent hours walking back and forth through the alleys of vines trying to believe it, trying not to believe it, trying to decide how he felt. Failing in everything.

But as the hours passed he'd come to a decision. Life had offered him something to hold on to, something that could have meaning. A drowning man who saw a life belt within his grasp might have felt as he did then.

Looking back to the start of the day he marvelled at how clear and settled his life had seemed, and how quickly that illusion had vanished into nothing.

But that was how it had always been.

His childhood in Sicily had been contented, even sometimes happy, although he'd always sensed that his parents meant more to each other than he meant to either of them.

This troubled him little at the time. It even gave him a sense of freedom. And if there was also a faint sense of loneliness he dealt with that by refusing to admit it.

But at last he became aware that the father he adored inspired fear in others, although Lucio couldn't understand why. Why should anyone be afraid of a lawyer, no matter how successful? But he'd come to realise that Mario Constello's clients were at best dubious, at worst criminal. They were used to getting their own way by threats, if necessary channelled through their lawyer.

The discovery caused something deep in Lucio to rebel in disgust. When he challenged his father, Mario was honestly bewildered. What could possibly be wrong with dishonesty and violence if it made you rich?

After that it was only a matter of time before Lucio fled. He begged his mother to come with him but she refused. She knew the worst of her husband, but even for the sake of her son she couldn't bear to leave him.

'Mamma, he's a monster,' Lucio had protested.

'Not to me, my son. Never to me. You're so young, only seventeen. One day you will understand. You'll learn that love isn't "reasonable". It doesn't obey the commands of the brain, but only of the heart.'

'But if your heart tells you to do something that could injure you?' the boy had demanded fiercely. 'Isn't that time to heed the brain and tell the heart to be silent?'

Her answering smile had contained a world of mysterious knowledge.

'If you can do that,' she said softly, 'then you do not really love. But you will, my darling. I know you will. You are warm-hearted and generous and one day you'll know what it is to love someone beyond reason. It will hit you like a lightning bolt and nothing will be the same again.

And you should be glad, for without it your life would be empty.'

To the last moment Lucio hoped that she would choose him over his father, but she had not. On the night he slipped away she'd watched him go. His last memory of his old home was her standing motionless at the window until he was out of sight.

He'd headed for the port of Messina and took a boat across the straits to the Italian mainland. From there he'd travelled north, taking jobs where he could, not earning much but living in reasonable comfort on the money his mother had given him. In Naples and Rome he spent some time simply enjoying himself, and when he reached Tuscany the last of his money had gone. Someone advised him to seek work in one of the local vineyards, and he slipped away to take a sneaky look at the Vigneto Constanza, to see what kind of work it was.

There he'd collapsed from hunger and exhaustion, and by good fortune had been discovered by Roberto Constanza, who'd taken him home.

He'd spent a week being nursed back to health by Signor Constanza's wife, Fiorella, and sixteen-year-old daughter, Maria. His abiding memory was of opening his eyes to see Maria's anxious face looking down at him.

When he'd recovered he'd gone to work in the vineyard and loved it from the first moment. Unlike the other employees he'd lived in the house, and it had become an open secret that he was regarded as the son the Constanzas had never had.

He stayed in touch with his mother, but his father cut him off. Lucio's departure, with its implied criticism, had offended him, and the only message from him said, 'You are no longer my son.' Lucio's response was, 'That suits me perfectly.'

His connection with his parents had been finally severed three years after he left them. Someone with a grudge against Mario had broken into his home and shot him. His mother, too, had died because, according to a witness, she had thrown herself between her husband and his killer.

'She could have escaped,' the witness had wept. 'Why didn't she do that?'

Because she didn't want to live without him, Lucio thought sadly. *Not even for my sake. In the end he was the one she chose.*

There was no inheritance. Despite his life of luxury Mario had been deeply in debt, and when everything was repaid there was nothing for his son.

'Perhaps that's really why your mother chose to die with him,' Roberto suggested gently. 'She faced a life of poverty.'

'She could have come to me,' Lucio suggested. 'I wouldn't have let my mother starve.'

'But she loved you too well to be a burden on you,' Roberto said.

But the truth, as Lucio knew in some place deep inside himself, was that she had not loved him enough. Life without her adored husband would never be worth living, even if she was cared for by a loving, generous son. For a second time she had rejected Lucio.

After that it was easier to accept Roberto and Fiorella as his parents. Looking back he sensed that that was the moment when his life here had truly begun.

The years that followed were happier than he had dared to hope. Everything about being a vintner appealed to him. He was a willing pupil, eager for whatever Roberto had to teach. From almost the beginning he had 'the eye', the mysterious instinct that told him which vines were outstanding, and which merely good. He sensed every stage of ripening, knew to the hour when the harvest should begin. Roberto, a vintner of long experience, began to listen to him.

Sweetest of all was the presence of Maria, her parents' pride and joy. A daughter so adored might have become spoiled and petulant. She was saved from that fate by the wicked, cheeky humour that infused her life, and which drew him to her.

From the first moment he'd thought her pretty and charming, but at sixteen she seemed little more than a child. For a while they were like brother and sister, scrapping, challenging each other. She was popular with the local young men and never seemed short of an escort.

Lucio, who was also popular with the opposite sex, studied her boyfriends cynically and warned her which ones to be wary of. But there was no emotion in their camaraderie.

He still relived the night when everything changed. Maria was getting ready for an evening out with a young man. He was handsome, exciting, known locally as a catch, and she was triumphant at having secured his attention.

Lucio had come home late after a hard day. He was tired, his clothes were grubby and he was looking forward to collapsing when he walked into the main room downstairs and found Maria preening herself at the mirror. Hearing him approach, she'd swung round.

'What do you think?' she demanded. 'Will I knock him sideways?'

For a moment he couldn't speak. The vision of beauty before him seemed to empty his brain. Gone was the jeans-clad kid sister with whom he shared laughter. Laughter died and enchantment took its place. It was the moment his mother had foreseen, the bolt of lightning, and everything in him rejoiced.

But she was unchanged, he was dismayed to notice. She teased and challenged him just like before, went on dates with other men and generally convinced Lucio that he'd be a fool to speak of his feelings.

And why should she want him? he asked himself bitterly. She was a rich girl and he was just one of her father's labourers, despite the privilege with which he was treated. Her escorts were similarly wealthy, arriving in expensive clothes and sweeping her off to luxurious restaurants.

He tried to cure himself. Why should he love a woman who would never love him? But nothing worked. He believed she was 'the one'.

Then one night, at a party, he'd rescued her from the unwanted attentions of the host's son, and his self-control had died. Seizing her in his arms he'd kissed her fervently, again and again.

When at last he released her he found her gazing at him with ironic amusement.

'I thought you were never going to do that,' she said.

'Maria, do you mean—?'

'Oh, you're so slow on the uptake. Come here.'

This time it was her kiss, full of the fierce urgency of a young woman who'd waited too long for this and had finally lost patience.

This time their embrace was so long that her parents came in and found them. Lucio prepared to beg them to understand, not to dismiss him from the estate. But then he saw that they were smiling with delight. They knew he was the right man for their child. Nothing else mattered.

Now Maria admitted that she'd loved him for months.

The next few months were sweet and gentle as they got to know each other on a new level. Long talks went on late into the night, leaving them both with a sense of a glorious future opening up. Nobody wanted to rush things, but, even without a definite proposal, it was taken for granted that they would be together forever.

One day, while they were guests at a friend's wedding, he said, 'Do you think we could—?'

'Yes,' she said quickly. 'I really think we could.'

They were engaged.

Fiorella and Roberto were overjoyed. They didn't care that he was poor.

'You're a great vintner,' Roberto told him, adding with a wicked chuckle, 'This way I can tie you to the estate. Now I don't have to worry that you'll leave me to work for someone else.'

Then he'd roared with laughter at his own joke, not fearing to be taken seriously. His and his wife's love for their foster son was too well known to be misunderstood. The only person who meant more was Maria, and the fact that they were giving her to him told him everything.

The time that followed was so joyful that, looking back, Lucio wondered why he hadn't guessed it was bound to end terribly. Fate didn't allow anyone to enjoy such happiness for more than a brief moment. He hadn't known it then but he'd learned it since.

The wedding was to take place in autumn, when the harvest was safely in. Maria and her mother had spent a long afternoon in Tuscany choosing a wedding dress, returning home in triumph. Mario had filmed her in it. Lucio had walked in while she was parading up and down for the camera. She'd laughed and displayed herself to him, but Fiorella had screamed.

'You mustn't see her in the dress before the wedding. It's bad luck.'

'Not for us, Mamma,' Maria had said blissfully.

'Not for us,' Lucio had agreed, taking her in his arms.

'We love each other too much. We will never have bad luck.'

How tragically ironic those words had become only a week later, when Maria had crashed the car she was driving, and died from her injuries. She'd lingered for two days before finally closing her eyes. Her funeral had been held in the church where the wedding should have taken place. Lucio and her parents had attended it together, bleak-eyed, devastated.

Roberto never recovered. A year later his heart gave out and he died within hours.

'He didn't want to live after we lost Maria,' Fiorella said as they sat together late into the night. 'Everything he did was a preparation for his death.' She placed a gentle hand over Lucio's. 'Including rewriting his will.'

'Mamma, I'm so sorry about that. I didn't know he meant to leave me the estate—'

'But I knew. We talked about it first and I told him I agreed. This place needs you. He's left me money and the right to live here, so there's no need for you to worry about me.'

He'd plunged into running the estate, making such a success that the profits soared and he was able to expand magnificently. Soon he owned several more vineyards and began to spend time travelling between them. The money increased even more. His life expanded into a routine of glamour.

Sometimes he felt like two people. There was the man who gladly returned home to where Fiorella, the mother of his heart, would care for him. And there was the other man who fled the estate with its memories, so achingly sweet, so beautiful, so unbearable.

There were plenty of female entanglements in his life, but none touched his heart. He steered clear of emotional

involvement, flirting with women who seemed as sophisticated and cynical as himself. Even so he sometimes blundered, and knew he'd inflicted much pain before he came
to realise that the part of him that loved had died with
Maria.

It was lucky that he'd met Charlotte, who seemed like
himself, taking life as it came, ready to make the best of
a situation. He could be honest with her. He wouldn't fall
in love but neither would she. Apart from the child they
would give each other strength, safety, comfortable affection, but no unrealistic dreams on either side.

The future was hopeful.

Next morning Charlotte was awoken by Elizabetta, with
coffee.

'Breakfast will be served downstairs when you are
ready,' she said respectfully.

'I won't keep them waiting.'

She bathed and dressed quickly. Her thoughts of the
previous night had shown her where the road led—devel-
oping love with Lucio and a future based on the certain-
ties of that love. A child. A family. A secure home. It was
a pity he hadn't come to her the night before. There was so
much they could have said. But she suppressed her disappointment. Time was on her side. She was singing as she
got out of the shower.

She chose a blue dress that was stylish, elegant, but
modest. Today was about making a good impression.

There was a knock on the door, and Lucio was standing there, smiling.

'You look wonderful,' he said.

'Thank you, kind sir,' she said, taking his arm.

'Fiorella has cooked a splendid breakfast for you,'

he said, leading her downstairs. 'She's the best cook in Tuscany.'

In fact, the meal was more elaborate that she normally chose, but she appreciated that Fiorella had gone to a lot of trouble to make her welcome, and expressed much appreciation.

'Your room is comfortable?' Fiorella asked. 'If the mattress is too hard or too soft it can be changed.'

'No, it's perfect. I slept so well.'

'Good. You need to build up your strength to prepare for what lies ahead. Pregnancy is exhausting. If there is anything you want, you simply tell me.'

Lucio regarded them with a pleased smile. This must be just what he'd hoped for, Charlotte thought. She returned his smile. Just looking at his handsome appearance was a pleasure.

He was dressed as she hadn't seen him before, not expensively fashionable as on the first night, nor in workman's clothes, as she'd seen him in the vineyard.

Had that only been yesterday? she wondered. The world had changed since then.

Today he looked like a businessman, plain and efficient.

'Got a meeting this afternoon,' he explained. 'Could be a big deal at stake. But we'll have this morning to ourselves and—'

His phone rang. He greeted the caller cheerfully.

'I'm looking forward to this afternoon. There's some interesting— What's that?...Damn! All right, I'm coming now.'

He hung up, scowling. 'He's got some crisis. He didn't go into details but he sounds in a bad way.' He laid a hand on Charlotte's arm. 'Sorry.'

'Don't be,' she said. 'Business comes first.'

'Bless you.'

'You can leave everything to me,' Fiorella said. 'I shall enjoy showing Charlotte around.'

When they were alone Fiorella said, 'Now, tell me how you are feeling. Is your pregnancy going well?'

'Very well.'

'Morning sickness?'

'Mostly no.'

'How lucky you are. But you will need to be registered with a doctor, and I should like to take you to the one we use. He's in Siena, only four miles away.'

She made the call at once, and a few minutes later they were heading down the hill. As the car turned Charlotte took the chance to look back for her first real view of the palace, rearing up against the sky, a magnificent building, but not at all like the farmhouse she'd been expecting.

As they neared Siena, Fiorella explained that the doctor was an old family friend, and very happy to hear her news.

In the surgery he listened to her heart, asked her questions and nodded.

'Excellent. You're in good health. About your diet—'

'You can leave that to me, Doctor,' Fiorella said.

Siena was a beautiful, historic city. As they strolled the short distance to the restaurant Fiorella had booked for lunch, Charlotte looked around her at the ancient buildings.

'I've always wanted to come here,' she murmured.

'You'll have plenty of time now. Soon it will be time for the Palio, which we never miss.'

Charlotte had heard of the Siena Palio, a horse race and pageant that was part of the town's colourful history. She asked Fiorella eager questions until they were settled in the restaurant, where, it was clear, the table had been booked in advance.

'This place is just as beautiful as I've heard,' Charlotte enthused. 'I can't believe that incredible...'

Fiorella let her talk while the food was served, occasionally joining in with an observation.

'You know this land so well,' she said at last. 'And you speak the language fluently. Lucio told me you were taking a long trip to study Italy.'

'This country has always been my passion,' she said. 'I translate for a living, and I thought I should see the reality for myself.'

'You are obviously a very independent young woman, who makes big decisions for herself. Now I am afraid I have offended you.'

'How could you possibly have done that?'

'I practically frog-marched you off to the doctor, I had this restaurant arranged without consulting you—'

'Considering how little I know about Siena restaurants, that's just as well,' Charlotte said cheerfully.

'True, but you might complain that my family had taken you over.'

'Well, perhaps I don't mind being taken over,' Charlotte mused. 'You've welcomed me, and I'm not foolish enough to object to that.'

'Then we are friends?' Fiorella asked.

'Friends,' she said warmly. Isolated from her family back home she was doubly grateful for this welcome.

'But there is still something troubling you,' Fiorella said gently.

'Not trouble exactly. I just wonder how this must be for you. You're very kind to me, but I think how painful it must be for you. Your daughter—Lucio was going to marry her, and she died....'

'And you think I must hate you because of that?'

'I couldn't blame you. I'm having the baby that should have been hers—your grandchild.'

'But it's not the same. Lucio has told me that what has

happened since Rome is a surprise to both of you. He needs the stability that you can give him. Maria was—' she hesitated '—she belonged in another life, lived in another world. Now a new world opens to both of you, and I hope to be part of it, because to me he is my son.'

It was pleasantly said, and there was kindness in the older woman's eyes as she squeezed Charlotte's hand. Charlotte supposed she should be glad, since this meant Fiorella could offer her friendship. But what if she won Lucio's heart—would there be trouble looming? And it was his heart that she was determined to win.

CHAPTER FIVE

ON THE way home Fiorella said, 'I wonder if he's finished with Enrico Miroza yet. That's the man who called this morning.'

'Enrico Miroza?' Charlotte echoed. 'Not *the* Enrico Miroza?'

'You know about him?'

'You hear his name everywhere. They say that where money's concerned he's the "big man", with a finger in every financial pie. I saw him once at a reception and he seemed so forbidding, grim and fearsome, like he ruled the world.'

'Yes, he strikes people like that, but there's another side to him. While his wife was alive he had a life of quite unnerving virtue and respectability. Then, a year after she died, he met Susanna, a greedy little gold-digger who set out to marry him for his money, and managed it. Any other man would have been wary of her, but he had very little experience of women, and he just collapsed.'

'Lucio mentioned a crisis.'

'Yes, and this is a bad time for it. Enrico is an important associate for Lucio. In a few days they'll be hosting a weekend house party in Enrico's home, for a lot of important guests. Bankers, investors, people like that. Also, they're buying a business together, and the owner will be there.'

A few minutes later they reached the palazzo, where they saw Lucio's car parked outside.

'Good.' Fiorella sighed.

Lucio appeared and came to them quickly.

'I've brought Enrico home with me,' he said. 'He's in a bad way, and I didn't like to leave him alone.'

'But what's happened?' Fiorella asked.

'His wife's walked out on him.'

'That terrible woman!' she exclaimed. 'He's better off without her.'

'I agree, but he doesn't see it that way. He's madly in love with her no matter how badly she behaves.'

Fiorella snorted and turned to Charlotte, saying, 'This is always happening. To Susanna he's just money, money, money, and if he doesn't hand over enough she throws a tantrum.'

'This time she set her heart on a lavish set of diamonds,' Lucio said. 'When he hesitated she walked out, and I don't think it's coincidence that she picked this moment, two days before the big "do", so that he'll be humiliated before his guests. But before we go in, tell me how the two of you managed?'

'Wonderfully,' Fiorella said. 'The doctor is very pleased with our Charlotte. Now, I must go and talk to Elizabetta.'

She hurried out of the room, leaving them alone.

'Our Charlotte,' she mused. 'Did you hear that?'

'Of course. You are "our Charlotte". You're mine, but you're also hers. It's all over the estate by now, that you're keeping the family going, so in a sense you're everybody's Charlotte.'

'All over the estate? You mean people already know?'

'Good news travels fast.'

'She's so kind to me.'

'Fiorella is a matriarch in the old-fashioned sense. What

counts is family. You're part of the family now. Both of you.' Smiling, he indicated her stomach.

'Yes, she as good as told me. It's so nice to be wanted and—' She checked herself, fearful of revealing too many of her innermost feelings.

'Did you notice how tactfully she left us alone?' Lucio asked. 'She knows we need time.'

He led her outside to where some seats overlooked the magnificent view down the hillside.

'I knew this was hilly country,' she said, 'but now I see it, it takes my breath away.'

'The slopes give the grapes more direct sunlight, which is one reason this area is so good for wines. At one time this part of the country housed a lot of nobility, but gradually the wine took over.'

'Is that why the house is so grand?'

'Yes, it used to belong to a count.' He grinned. 'But Enrico's home puts it in the shade. It's a real palace.'

'That's why you're having the big "do" there?'

'Right. And I'm not looking forward to it. I'll talk to some contacts and make my escape. How do you feel about coming with me? You don't have to if you think it's too soon to plunge into deep water.'

'I'd like to plunge in. Don't worry, I'll cope alone and not distract you from talking business.'

He grinned. 'Thanks.'

'Tell me about your other vineyards,' she said. 'What made you buy more?'

Lucio hesitated. To tell her that he'd been fleeing the pain of Maria's memory would have been unkind, so he merely said, 'I guess I wanted to prove myself independently, rather than just taking over another man's achievement.'

He began to describe the other estates, lingering over

details to forestall more questions, until the door opened and Fiorella beckoned them.

'Time to return to duty,' Lucio said, taking her hand.

Charlotte recognised Enrico from their brief, previous encounter. Tall, thin, reserved, with a lined face and white hair, he gave the impression of a man who would never yield an inch. But his manners were perfect.

'I do apologise for my intrusion,' he said, holding her hand between both of his and speaking English.

'You don't need to. I'm delighted to meet you.'

She spoke in Italian and saw his eyes brighten with surprise.

'You know my language?'

Now he, too, spoke in Italian, and launched into a speech. At first he spoke slowly, but when she replied, speaking fast, he responded in the same way. Lost in the mental excitement, Charlotte was barely aware of Lucio watching them with a look of astonished pleasure.

'This has been a pleasure,' he said at last. 'I look forward to seeing you at the party. My friends will appreciate you, and you will enjoy yourself.'

'I look forward to it.'

Enrico stayed the night and spent dinner telling her about his home and the planned celebration. It was clear that he knew her status as Lucio's 'official lady' and the mother of his child. As Lucio had prophesied, word had spread fast.

She asked many questions, all guaranteed to show that she was up to the task. Lucio watched in silence, but seemed pleased.

Later, when Enrico had gone to his room, Fiorella surprised Charlotte by saying in a censorious voice, 'Of course, you're not properly equipped for this occasion.'

'I think she's demonstrated that she's very well equipped,' Lucio said, astonished.

'Oh, you men! You never know what's important. So she's intelligent! So what? I'm talking about clothes. She'll need a glamorous wardrobe for this.' She took Charlotte's hand. 'Ignore him, my dear. Tomorrow we'll go into Florence and spend money.'

'Of course,' Lucio agreed. 'You must forgive my male ignorance. That hadn't occurred to me. I leave it in your hands, Mamma.'

When he'd gone Fiorella said, 'We're going to have a wonderful time tomorrow.'

Charlotte was glad, for her travelling wardrobe contained nothing that would suit such an elaborate occasion, but an imp of mischief made her say, 'Suppose I don't need any new clothes.'

'Nonsense! Of course you do!'

Laughing they went along the corridor together, and said an affectionate goodnight.

As Fiorella had prophesied, the following day was a delight. They headed for the Via de' Tornabuoni, lined with fashion boutiques. Fiorella declared that Lucio would pay for everything, and spent an amount of money that made Charlotte stare.

'The more, the better,' Fiorella declared. 'You must do him credit. There will be many such occasions, not just when you go visiting with him, but also when he brings important people home to dinner. Which reminds me that I need a couple of dresses myself for a dinner party next month.'

'Then let's start looking.' Charlotte chuckled.

They returned home in triumph, both sporting new clothes, which they displayed to Elizabetta and the maids. Lucio, attempting to enter the room, was firmly excluded.

Two days later they set off for the Palazzo Vidani, once the home of the Dukes of Vidani, now Enrico's pride and joy.

'What did you think of him?' Lucio asked as they travelled.

'Very interesting. He seems grim and chilly, but obviously there's another side to him.'

'Yes, he's spent his life putting money first. So when he reached sixty and a fortune hunter got him in her sights he was helpless. Now she treats him like dirt, but he can't bear to get rid of her. The closest he's ever come to making a firm stand is about these diamonds which would have cost him millions.'

When they arrived Enrico greeted them at the door and personally escorted them upstairs to the luxurious ducal apartments.

'Duke Renato built this for himself and his wife in the seventeenth century,' he said, showing them around the splendid bedroom. 'She was of royal blood, so he wanted to impress her. Normally I sleep here, but tonight it's yours. I'll be in the dressing room next door.'

It was truly a room from another age. Oak panels lined the walls, which were elaborately decorated with paintings. There was also a huge fireplace, although rendered unnecessary by a discreetly located radiator. Floor-length brocade curtains framed the tall windows, and matching curtains hung around the bed which, Charlotte realised with a slight disturbance, was a double.

Clearly Enrico had assumed they slept together. He would have been aghast to learn that they had separate rooms, and that Lucio came to hers only briefly to say a chaste goodnight.

The bed was large, so they could keep a certain distance, but it was still a slight shock to discover that she had no choice in the matter. She wondered how Lucio felt about it, but when she glanced at him his face revealed nothing.

'I'll leave you to get settled in,' Enrico said. 'Tonight's the big night.'

When she saw the multitude of cars that drew up in the next hour Charlotte knew he had been right. Excitement was rising in her. If she and Lucio were to work out a future she had to be able to fit in with occasions like this, and she was confident that she could do it.

He took the first shower while she unpacked with the help of two maids who gasped with admiration as they discovered her new clothes.

'Hang them in the wardrobe,' Charlotte said. 'I want them to be a secret until the last minute.'

They nodded, understanding perfectly and giggling.

She surveyed them, wondering which one would make Lucio catch his breath. That was the one that really mattered. She didn't try to deny it to herself.

The gown that attracted her most was deep gold silk. It was elegant, sophisticated, and the bosom was just low enough to be enticing without being outrageous. When it was time to dress for the evening she slipped into the bathroom while Lucio attired himself in the bedroom. When she emerged they were both fully dressed.

It was hilarious, she thought wryly, to take such trouble not to see each other in a state of undress, when they already knew each other naked. The memory danced through her brain: Lucio, as he'd been that night, lean, vigorous, delightful.

Tonight he wore a black dinner jacket and bow tie. His hair just touched his collar, and his face was handsome and intriguing. Somehow she must spend the evening with this man without revealing how much he disturbed her. But what about him? Didn't she cause him any disturbance? Surely she must. But if so he concealed it behind perfect control.

She had a partial answer at the astonishment on his face as he approached her, and nodded.

'You'll knock them all flat,' he said. Then he dropped a light kiss on her cheek and said, 'Let's go.'

They entered the great hall down a wide staircase, and Charlotte knew at once that word had gone ahead of her. Everyone here knew what this occasion was about, and who she was.

So many people to meet. So many successful men and beautiful women, and most of those women had eyes for Lucio. The looks they cast him were the same as she'd seen in the hotel in Rome, when almost every female seemed aiming to be first with him. He could have taken any one of them to bed.

And some of them he probably has, she thought. *But he's with me now, so the rest of you can just back off.*

She took a deep breath and raised her head. She was ready for anything.

From the first moment she was a success. As so often the Italians warmed towards a non-Italian who'd taken the trouble to become expert in their language. They were particularly impressed by her knowledge of dialects.

Most regions of Italy had dialects vastly different from Italian. This did not apply in Tuscany, where the dialect was so like standard Italian that it was reputed to be the basis of the main language. But it was certainly true of Venice, where the *lingua Veneto* was less a dialect than an independent language that defeated most non-Venetians.

But Charlotte had been fascinated by it and, during her visit, had managed to master a certain amount. So she was looking forward to meeting Franco Dillani, owner of the shop in Florence that Lucio and Enrico were aiming to buy.

When the moment came Signor Dillani greeted her in English.

'It is a pleasure to meet you, *signorina.*'

Beaming, she took his outstretched hand, saying, *'E mi so veramente contenta de far la vostra conoscensa, sior. Lucio me ge parla tanto de vu.'*

She had the pleasure of seeing both Lucio and Franco Dillani stare in amazement. She had spoken in Venetian, saying: 'And I am delighted to meet you, *signore.* Lucio has told me so much about you.'

'You speak all Italian languages?' he exclaimed, again in Venetian.

'No, I was just very attracted to yours,' she said.

'But that is wonderful. I am honoured.'

He immediately monopolised her, talking Venetian with great vigour until she had to protest, laughing, that he had exceeded her knowledge. Whereupon he proceeded to instruct her in *lingua Veneto,* which he enjoyed even more. By the time Lucio and Enrico converged on him for a business talk he was in the best of moods.

'How's it going?' she murmured to Lucio as the evening drew to an end.

'Wonderfully. A few more details to be settled, but the feeling is positive, thanks to you.'

'It can't be me. It must be a good deal in itself or he wouldn't be interested.'

'But tonight he's been listening as he never did before, and that's because you cast a spell on him.'

'Nonsense,' she protested, but her heart was soaring. This was what she'd hoped for, to find a niche in his life as well as his heart.

'No, it's not nonsense. Now, let's retire for the night. You need rest. I shall want you to do a lot of this kind of thing tomorrow.'

'Your wish is my command,' she said merrily.

'You should be careful. I might take you seriously.'

Laughing they ascended the stairs together, watched by several envious pairs of eyes.

Once in their room he collected his night attire and vanished into the bathroom. Charlotte guessed that this night, however triumphant so far, would end prosaically, however much they might each hope otherwise.

Did he hope so? she wondered wistfully. Was he so much in command of himself that he could resist the temptation that teased her?

Whatever the answer, self-respect demanded that she stay in control. Her thin silk nightdress was too revealing, too obviously enticing. She covered it with a matching wrap.

There was a knock on the door that connected them to Enrico's room, and his voice called, 'May I come in?'

'Yes, of course,' she said, opening the door.

'I just wanted to say goodnight,' Enrico said. 'And to ask if you have everything you want.'

'Everything,' she said. 'It's such a lovely place.'

Lucio emerged from the bathroom and the three of them exchanged friendly goodnights, before Enrico retreated, closing the door again.

'Oh, my goodness!' Charlotte exclaimed. 'Did you see where he's sleeping? That tiny narrow bed, how spare and dismal everything is.'

'It's only meant to be a dressing room. He's making do with it tonight so that we can have his room. Still, I know what you mean.' He yawned. 'It's been a long day. I'm really looking forward to a good night's sleep.'

'So am I,' she said untruthfully.

He laid a gentle hand on her shoulder.

'You did wonderfully tonight. They all admired you.'

The movement of his hand caused the wrap to slip away to the floor. He retrieved it and laid it around her bare shoulders. His fingers barely brushed against her but suddenly Charlotte was intensely aware of every inch of her body. Every day she studied it to see if her pregnancy was becoming noticeable, but for now there was only a slight increase in the voluptuousness of her breasts and hips. It was still the same beautiful body that had entranced Lucio on the night that had changed the world. Perhaps it was even more beautiful.

And he, too, realised that. The sudden rasping sound of his breath told her that he'd become aware of her in another way. This was no longer just the mother of his child. She was the woman who'd made his spirits soar and his body vibrate.

She knew she should try to get control of herself, to subdue the thrilling impulses that invaded her. But they had always been there, she now realised, lurking in the shadows, waiting to spring out and remind her that her freedom was an illusion. Lucio's presence, or even just the sound of his voice, was enough to bring them to life, teasing, troubling, tempting.

Now she couldn't deny that ever since the first incredible night, she had wanted him again. Not just for his body's power but also its subtlety—the instinctive understanding that had told him which caresses would most delight her, the gentleness and skill that he devoted to her.

And he, too, was filled with yearning. She knew it from the way he trembled, standing so close to her. In another moment he would yield to his desires, take her in his arms and claim her in the way they both wanted. She raised her head, searching his face, and finding in it everything she longed to see. She reached up to touch him—

Then he seized her hand, holding it away from him.

'It's late,' he said. 'We both need our sleep.'

She wanted to scream that what she needed wasn't sleep. It was him, his thrilling body, his power, his passion. But that would tell him that her desire for him was greater than anything he felt for her, and her pride revolted at the thought.

'You're right,' she said. 'After all, we're here to work. Which side do you prefer?'

'This one,' he said, walking away and getting into bed on the far side.

He settled on the extreme edge, so that when she'd climbed in on her own side there was still a clear distance between them. She lay still, her face turned towards him, her whole being tense for any movement from him. But there was nothing. Lucio stayed motionless, only a slight unevenness in his breathing revealing that he was less relaxed than he pretended.

At last the sound changed, becoming quieter, more regular, telling her that the impossible had happened. Lucio, lying a few feet from her half-clad body, had fallen asleep.

It was insulting.

Only the fact that she was tired prevented her seething with indignation.

At last she, too, sank into sleep, driven more by desolation than tiredness.

She was awoken by a heavy hand on her shoulder, shaking her. Opening her eyes she saw the face of a furiously angry woman.

'I should have known,' the stranger snapped. 'I haven't been gone five minutes and already he's got another woman in my bed.'

'In your—? Are you Signora Miroza?'

'Yes, I am and you're going to regret this. And he's going to regret it even more.'

She switched on the bedside light, pointing at the far side of the bed.

It was empty.

A light beneath the door of the bathroom showed where Lucio had vanished.

'So that's where he is,' Susanna grated.

'No,' Charlotte said, pushing the woman aside. 'You've got this all wrong.'

To her relief the bathroom door opened and Lucio appeared, seemingly relaxed, smiling.

'Susanna, how nice to see you. I'm sorry that Charlotte and I are in your room, but Enrico thought you wouldn't mind.' He slipped an arm around Charlotte's shoulders, a gesture designed to make matters plain.

It worked. Susanna's jaw dropped.

'Are you two—I mean—?'

'Charlotte and I are a couple,' Lucio said. 'Enrico thought it would be nice for us to be in here.'

'But where is he? No, don't tell me. He's off in some floozy's bed, making the most of my absence.'

Charlotte lost her temper.

'No, I'll tell you where he is,' she snapped. 'And then maybe you'll stop your nonsense. Here!'

In a flash she was at the door of the dressing room, wrenching it open and switching on the light, revealing Enrico, virtuously alone in the narrow little bed.

'Nobody else,' she said firmly. 'There isn't another door into this room and you can see he's completely alone.'

She wrenched open the wardrobe door, revealing clothes but nothing else.

Roused by the commotion Enrico had opened his eyes and was regarding them with sleepy surprise.

'Hallo,' he murmured. 'You're back.'

'I'll go now and leave you to it,' Charlotte said.

She marched out.

Lucio was waiting for her, watching her with a new light in his eyes.

'I'm beginning to realise that I've underestimated you. You can be so proper and serious when it suits you, but your other side is a cheeky imp and a warrior by turns.'

'And which one do you think is the real me?'

Slowly he shook his head.

'I'm not sure there is a real you. I think you produce whichever "you" it's useful for someone to see. You've already shown me several different faces, and I'm curious to know what surprises you still have in store for me.'

She stepped back and looked up at him, eyes bright with teasing humour.

'You'll find out—one day,' she said. 'In the meantime you'll just have to wonder.'

CHAPTER SIX

SHE spoke lightly, watching his reaction, and was pleased to find him regarding her with new interest.

'But how long will I have to wonder?' he mused. 'I'm not a patient man.'

'Well, I know that,' she agreed.

'But it doesn't worry you?'

'Not in the least.'

He grinned. 'Think you can get the better of me, huh?'

She laughed softly. 'Think I can't?'

'I'm not foolish enough to answer that question. Like I said, I don't know how many different personalities you have hiding, ready to pop out and knock me flying.'

'Maybe I don't even know that myself. Perhaps you're the man who'll bring them out. Why don't we just wait and see?'

'I'm up for it if you are.' He nodded. 'I think life is going to become very interesting.'

'Really?' she asked, wide-eyed. 'Whatever makes you think that?'

'Either interesting or alarming. Or both.'

Before she could answer there was a noise from Enrico's dressing room.

'I wonder what's happening in there right now,' she mused.

She had an answer with unexpected speed. The door opened, revealing Susanna and Enrico, arms about each other's waists.

'Goodnight,' Susanna said majestically. 'We shall not disturb you again.'

Heads high, they crossed the room and departed. Enrico, Charlotte was fascinated to notice, looked ecstatic.

'He's got a grandiose suite down the corridor,' Lucio observed. 'They'll head for there and—whatever they feel like doing.'

'He's won this one,' Charlotte said. 'Did you ever see a man look so pleased with himself.' She gave a choke of amusement. 'Oh, goodness! His face when he first saw her.'

Lucio joined in her merriment, placing his hands on her shoulders, and suddenly the laughter died. She was no longer wearing the wrap, and the feel of his fingers against her bare skin filled her with delicious tension. The nightdress seemed flimsier than ever and she realised that his pyjama jacket was no longer respectably buttoned up high, or even buttoned up at all. It had fallen open, showing the smooth, muscular chest that she remembered.

She sensed his tension equalling her own. Also his confusion. He'd dealt with this situation earlier in the evening, but it had refused to stay dealt with. Now it was taunting him again, and he was struggling with himself, with her, but most of all with his own desire.

Good, she thought with a surge of pleasure. It would be an enjoyable battle, the herald of many. And she would always be the victor. It was time he understood that.

She leaned forward, turning her head slightly so that her cheek rested against his chest. She felt the shock go through him and the thunder of his heart, a sensation so intense that she drew back to look at his face. It was haggard, tormented, the face of a man driven by demons, far beyond his own control.

She understood that feeling. It possessed her too, giving her a powerful urge to drive the demons on, cry out to them exultantly to do their worst, because their worst was what she desperately wanted.

His caresses intensified, the fingers slipping behind her head to draw her to him so that his mouth could touch hers softly, tentatively, then urgently. Her warm breath against his face drove him on to put his arms about her, exploring, rejoicing in the feel of her flesh through the thin nightdress. He kissed her repeatedly while his hands roved over her as though this was their first time together.

And perhaps that was true. Their night in Rome had been so different, so impossible to repeat, that now they were like two strangers knowing nothing of each other except that they were flooded with desire.

He took a step towards the bed, moving slowly as though giving her time to refuse. But she was far from refusing, clinging to him frantically. He was breathing heavily, his flesh rising and falling beneath her fingers.

Then they were lying down, he was stripping away her nightdress and tossing aside the rest of his own clothes. His eyes, looking down on her, were full of fervour and his lips were touched by a smile that she had never seen before.

'You're beautiful,' he whispered. 'More beautiful than ever.'

'I don't know what you mean by that,' she said provocatively.

His fingers drifted over her, causing a storm to go through her.

'I mean this,' he said softly. 'And this.' He laid his lips against her, moving them so skilfully that she trembled, holding him closer, whispering 'Yes, yes…'

Her hands seemed to act of their own accord, seeking, begging, demanding. Their only previous lovemaking had burned itself into her consciousness so deeply that she knew what he most enjoyed.

She closed her eyes, holding him tightly against her, desperate to relish every possible moment.

Now she could face the thought that she had never before dared to admit; that if she'd had to live the rest of her life without this man ever making love to her again, she would not have known how to endure it.

Inwardly she pleaded for this to last forever, pleasure unending, happiness without boundaries. Then, it was over, and yet not over. It would never be entirely over, she thought. Now she had everything to look forward to. Not just the sedate companionship of two people who were to have a child, but the blissful closeness of physical harmony, with its promise of a sweeter, more emotional union.

She searched his face, trying to meet his eyes for an exchange of feelings. But he turned away from her and she almost thought he shook his head. Then she saw that his eyes were closed, as though he'd retreated inside himself. With a convulsive movement he wrenched himself away from her, left the bed and strode to the window. Aghast, she followed him.

'Lucio, whatever's the matter.'

'I'm sorry,' he groaned. 'I shouldn't have done that.'

She pulled him around to face her. 'Why not?'

'Because you're carrying our child. Just the sight of you was too much for me…. Forgive me—it'll never happen again, I promise.'

She regarded him tenderly, astonished by his miserable self-blame which roused her protective instincts as nothing else in her life had ever done.

'Lucio, dear, it's all right,' she said. 'There's nothing

wrong in what we've just done. I've got friends who go on enjoying each other practically until the birth. One of them has four children, all perfectly healthy. The doctor says I'm in fine shape, and as long as that's true nothing else has to change.'

'It's not just the baby,' he said sombrely. 'We've got to be careful about you. We never know what might be going to happen.'

She was about to say that he was being overly dramatic when she remembered that Maria had died suddenly, leaving him devastated. Now he went through life alert for danger and heartbreak.

She forced her own feelings to abate. It was sad that he couldn't share her delight at their union, but they had a road to travel. It was too soon to say what awaited them at the end of that road, but to her hopeful eyes it looked increasingly bright and happy.

'Don't worry about me,' she said, touching his face softly. 'I'm strong, and I'm going to give you a healthy baby.'

'Thank you. And in future I'll take better care of you. I promise.'

He spoke fervently and she loved him for his concern. Now they would fall asleep tenderly in each other's arms, the perfect way for passion to end. And there would be other moments. He might mean to keep his distance, but she knew how to change his mind.

'Everything's going to be all right,' she assured him. 'Now, let's get some sleep.'

She took his hand and tried to lead him back to the bed. But he resisted her.

'No,' he said. 'I told you I'm going to care for you, and I meant it.'

'But—'

'I can't trust myself. I've just discovered that. But you must sleep. I've tired you, and I blame myself.'

He took up her nightdress, holding it out to her at a distance and waiting while she slipped into it. Then he pulled back the covers on her side of the bed and helped her in, pushing her gently back against the pillows.

As though I was a weakling, she thought desperately, *when I've never felt so strong as I have tonight.*

But this wasn't the moment to protest, so she lay down and let him draw the covers over her.

She waited for him to go around to his side of the bed. Once he was in he would fall asleep, and she would be able to move quietly across the space between, slide her arms about him, rest her head on his shoulder. When he awoke to find her there he would understand that this was the truth between them. She smiled to herself.

But her smile faded as he turned away from the bed, heading for a sofa on the far side of the room.

'Lucio—' she protested.

He lay down on the sofa, his head on a cushion.

'Goodnight, Charlotte. Sleep well. I won't disturb you.'

And he wouldn't, she thought bitterly.

As she'd feared, he kept to his resolve, breathing steadily until she reckoned he must be asleep. So that was how easily he could shrug off their glorious union, she thought bitterly. That was how little it meant to him. Damn him!

From the sofa, Lucio kept his eyes on the bed where he could just make out her shape in the darkness. She lay very still, he noticed. Was she stunned by what had overtaken them? As stunned as he was himself? Or did she feel triumphant at having exposed his weakness?

When he remembered how easily he'd yielded he groaned inwardly.

He waited a long time before leaving the sofa, crossing

the floor slowly and carefully to stand by the bed, watching her as she slept. At last she moved, turning over, throwing out her arms, then letting them fall back. She was murmuring something, but although he leaned closer he couldn't understand.

He reached out as if to touch her, but stayed his hand at the last minute, holding it still for several seconds before drawing it back.

He stood there for a while before returning to the sofa and lying down in the darkness.

Charlotte awoke to find herself alone. From the bathroom came the sound of Lucio singing cheerfully. After a moment he entered, fully dressed.

'Good, you're awake,' he said. 'I'll see you at breakfast.'

He departed, apparently not having noticed that the nightdress was slipping from her shoulders, revealing the beautiful swell of her breasts.

After a shower she donned a brown linen dress that was one of Fiorella's choices. It suited her perfectly, while projecting the air of sedate respectability that she guessed Fiorella had been aiming for.

She found Lucio deep in talk with Enrico, who immediately broke away to take her hand and speak warmly.

'Thank you so much, my dear Charlotte, for your help last night. I shall not forget your kind friendship.'

'I was glad to be of help. Did you and Susanna sort things out?'

'We've a way to travel yet, but we'll get there. Thanks to you. Excuse me a moment.'

Susanna had appeared, causing Enrico to hurry across to her. She was dressed in high fashion and clearly ready to flaunt herself as the hostess. She reached out to Enrico, accepting his hug as no more than her due.

'There's no fool like an old fool,' said a voice behind Charlotte.

Turning, they saw Piero, a young man-about-town they'd met the night before. He was handsome with the air of a man who would indulge himself at all costs.

'You'd think he'd have seen through her by now,' he added.

'Perhaps he doesn't want to,' Charlotte said.

'That's pretty certain. Like I say, he's a fool. Everyone knows she slept with him the night they met. That should have warned him. If a woman jumps into bed with a man she's only just met, well—we know what kind of woman she is, don't we?'

'Not necessarily,' Lucio said, clenching his hands.

'I suppose she might take you by surprise,' Charlotte mused.

'No way,' Piero declared. 'Sex on the first evening means she's after whatever she can get. Ah, I see someone I need to talk to. Bye!'

He vanished.

'Stop looking like that,' Charlotte muttered. 'Smile.'

'How can I?' Lucio ground out. 'Why aren't you insulted?'

'Why should I be? He wasn't talking about me. Unless of course you'd told him—'

'*No!*' He stared at her, incredulous and aghast. 'You're enjoying this, aren't you? How *can* you?'

'What I'm enjoying is the sight of your face. When he said it you didn't know where to look.'

'I was concerned for you. Evidently I didn't need to be.'

'That's right. My shoulders are broad. Come on, Lucio, enjoy the joke. Life's too short to get uptight about everything.'

'The sooner I get the serious business sorted out, the better,' Lucio growled. 'Then we can leave.'

'How close are you and Enrico to concluding your deal?'

'I'm not sure. He thinks the price is too high and he's holding out for a reduction.'

'Any chance that he's right?'

'None. It's a bargain because the seller wants to get rid of it quickly, and if we don't settle it now I'm afraid it'll be too late. So if Enrico delays again I'm calling it off.'

He had no need to. An hour later Enrico increased his offer, the seller accepted and the deal was concluded.

'Between you and me,' Enrico said, drawing Charlotte aside, 'I yielded out of gratitude. How could I obstruct Lucio when his wonderful lady has been such a good friend?' He added to Lucio, 'You're a lucky man. You've acquired a real asset. She'll bring you a big increase in profits.'

'That's what I'm there for.' Charlotte chuckled, and both men laughed with her.

'Now I think we'll leave,' Lucio said. 'I don't want Charlotte to get tired.'

'Of course you must look after her,' Enrico agreed.

They packed in record time and were soon on the road. Halfway home they stopped at a little village restaurant and relaxed over coffee and cakes.

'You didn't mind dashing away, did you?' Lucio asked.

'No, I think we needed to get out of there before there were any more dramas. Poor Enrico.'

'Yes, she's got him under her thumb again, and I bet she'll get her diamonds next. I don't understand how it can happen to a man like that, so powerful, so confident. He doesn't need anybody.'

'That's not true,' Charlotte mused. 'In a strange way he needs *her*.'

'How can any man need what she puts him through? You know why she came back, don't you? She was hoping to catch him with another woman, then she could divorce him and get a handsome settlement.'

'Or maybe just threaten divorce and keep him under her thumb. I think he'd pay up rather than lose her.'

'We need to rescue him from her.'

'You won't do that,' Charlotte predicted. 'She matters to him too much. And even if you could do it, it wouldn't be kind.'

'Not kind, to rescue him from a gold-digger?'

'From the only person he has to love. I heard a lot about him from other guests while we were there. He has no close family since his wife died. They had no children. He's alone in a—in a desert. And if you're stranded in a desert you often feel that you'd do anything to escape, even marry someone totally unsuitable and put up with the way they behave.'

'A desert,' he mused. 'You spoke to me of a desert on the night we met. You said you were living in one.'

'And you said it could be a good place to be,' she reminded him. 'A place to recruit your strength, and there was nobody to hurt you.'

'That's right,' he said wryly. 'It's a kind of safety.'

'Fine, if you want to be safe. But Enrico doesn't. He'd rather put up with Susanna than be safe and isolated.'

'Safe and isolated,' he murmured. 'Enrico's a brave man.'

'Yes, sometimes you have to take risks. Like we did, that night. Not that we thought of the consequences. If we had—'

'If we had you'd have run a mile from me,' he said, regarding her intently.

She gave him a faint smile. 'I'll let you know that another time.'

He had certainly never thought of the consequences, he recalled. The Charlotte he'd met in Rome had seemed so sophisticated, so adventurous and confident, that he'd simply assumed she was ready for anything.

Now he knew that what had happened that night had taken her by surprise. He, too, had been surprised, although not by the way the evening ended. That had happened to him before. What was new was the intensity of his enjoyment, not merely pleasure but a feeling of happiness as he lay in her arms.

She was wonderful. He wasn't sure if he'd told her so, although he hoped he hadn't. Safer that way.

But safe was one thing he couldn't feel in her company. She threatened his precious isolation, which he'd valued since everyone he loved had either died or betrayed him— the isolation that gave him strength and which he would cling to forever. In this mood he had fled her next morning.

But from some things there was no escape.

When they were on the road again he told her some more about his business with Enrico.

'It's just the one shop for the moment, but we'll eventually have a whole chain of wine shops in different cities. Now we've taken the first step, thanks to you.'

'Hey, I didn't do much.'

'You pulled a trigger, and it helped. And the fact that he likes you so much will also be useful in the future.'

'I'm going to be good for business, huh?' She chuckled.

'You'd better believe it. Enrico's right. Meeting you was a stroke of luck in more than one way.'

He didn't elaborate and it wasn't the time to press him,

but one day soon Charlotte promised herself that she would make him enlarge on that topic.

'Did you notice that he was delighted to see us leave?' she mused. 'He wants the room back for himself and Susanna.'

'That's very cynical.'

'Sometimes cynical is the right thing to be. Aren't you ever cynical?'

'There are times when you have to be.' After a moment he added, 'And there are times when you can't afford to be.'

'I wonder which we—'

'Hey, look at that idiot!'

He braked sharply to avoid a pedestrian, then continued on the way.

Nothing was said about the night before, and soon they were on the last stretch home.

Once there he told Fiorella about the successful deal, emphasising that Charlotte had helped by winning Enrico's goodwill.

When they were alone Fiorella said triumphantly, 'You see how well you fit in here? I knew it. I'm going to cook you a special meal to celebrate.'

Charlotte couldn't help but think that Fiorella was simply trying to secure her and the child for the family, but even thinking that, it was pleasant to be treated in such a way. When she looked back on the trip she felt she had much to make her glad. If only Lucio hadn't spoiled the memory of their lovemaking by regretting it. But they were still strangers in many ways. Things would get better.

Late that night he looked into her room to say goodnight.

'The deal is set up and I'll be signing papers at the lawyer's office in a couple of days. Care to come with me?'

'I'd love to.'

'Fine. Goodnight. Sleep well.'

He departed without having come anywhere near her.

He was as good as his word, taking her to the lawyer, where they found Franco Dillani, full of good cheer at having sold the shop. With all the papers safely signed he invited them to lunch. Enrico couldn't stay but Lucio and Charlotte accepted with pleasure. Over the meal Franco was open in his admiration of Charlotte, talking Venetian with her while making the occasional apology to Lucio, who waved him aside good-humouredly.

Charlotte leaned back and just enjoyed herself. It was good to feel that she'd established a position for herself in her new life, and actually been of some real use to Lucio.

But sweeter than anything else was the knowledge that Lucio was watching her with a knowing smile on his face. His eyes, too, were full of a message that made her heart beat faster. Pleasure, admiration, satisfaction—they were all there.

But she also sensed something else, something to which she couldn't yet put a name, but which she was determined to pursue and make her very own.

Brooding on the way home, she knew the task she'd set herself wasn't going to be easy. Lucio was passionately attracted to her, yet in a strange way he feared her. What she'd seen in his eyes was a secret that he wasn't ready to disclose. She would have to lure it from him, even against his will.

At the vineyard he immediately immersed himself in work. His manner was kind, gentle, considerate, but he came to her room only for a few moments to say goodnight. He would kiss her cheek when other people were there, but never when they were alone. Nor did he ever take her in his arms. He was a perfectly behaved gentleman, but not a lover.

She guessed that he kept his distance because he was determined not to be tempted again. But it hurt that he could resist so successfully. Within herself temptation raged. At night she would listen for the moment when he put his head around the door, longing for him to come right in, sit on the bed, talk to her, give her the chance to reach out to him. But he would smile and be gone. Recalling what she'd seen in his arms at her moment of triumph she even wondered if she'd imagined it.

No, I didn't imagine it, she told herself fiercely. *I won't believe that.*

Lying in the darkness, she would wonder about the future, and the many different ways it could turn out. Was Lucio restrained only because he dreaded to hurt her? Or was there another reason? Was he avoiding her emotionally? When he'd said that meeting her was a stroke of luck, had he only been talking about business?

Once he'd said she was wonderful.

Would he ever say it again?

CHAPTER SEVEN

Two days later Lucio set off to visit one of his other vineyards, accompanied by Charlotte. The place was fifty miles south, in Umbria, and she looked forward to visiting an area of Italy she hadn't seen before.

She found the trip interesting rather than enjoyable. As Lucio had warned, he would be working morning, noon and night, and there was no time for pleasure. She accompanied him whenever possible, learned all she could about the different varieties of grapes and listened to endless work discussions.

The trip was valuable for the insight it gave her into him. Before her eyes he turned into someone else. She'd known him first as an elegant man-about-town, then a skilful and imaginative lover, and then an efficient manager. Now that final aspect was growing harder, sharper, revealing a man who lived for nothing but business and shrewd, sometimes harsh dealing. For this he had the admiration of his tenants who ran the place, but not their affection. Nor did he apparently want it.

She remembered the night they'd spent in Enrico's palace, when he'd remarked how many different aspects there were to her personality.

'You've already shown me several different faces,' he'd

said, 'and I'm curious to know what surprises you still have in store for me.'

She was beginning to understand what he meant. Her view of him was exactly the same.

As they drove home he asked, 'What did you think?'

Receiving no answer he glanced at her briefly and saw that she was asleep. He nodded. He didn't blame her.

He had two more visits coming up, but she gently declined the chance to go with him. He didn't protest and she had the feeling he was glad of her decision.

At home she concentrated on learning about life there, and fitting in with it. Fiorella took her to meet the neighbours, most of whom were kindly and pleasant. One family surveyed her with suppressed hostility, which Fiorella explained thus.

'Those two daughters had set their sights on Lucio, and they're furious that you've snatched him from under their noses. Good for you. I prefer you to them any day.'

Three times Lucio called her, asking how she was, assuring her that he was thinking of her. But there were always distractions in the background that caused the call to end soon.

When he returned to the Vigneto Constanza he embraced Charlotte, then stood back with his hands on her shoulders and regarded her closely. 'How are you?'

'Doing fine,' she told him.

'That's good because I've brought a couple of guests home with me. We've got a lot of business to do, but they're anxious to meet you.'

The guests took up his attention through the meal and the rest of the evening, but as she was going to bed he came into her room and opened his arms to her. She threw herself in gladly, and felt him enclose her in a fierce hug. Her heart leapt.

'How are you? Are you really all right?'

'Ready for anything,' she said, hoping he would detect her real meaning.

But he only said, 'That's the best news I've had. I drove Fiorella crazy every night demanding to know how you were. But you look fine. Come here.'

He enfolded her in another hug. She held her breath, waiting for the sweet feel of his hands drifting over her, but they never moved until he said, 'Go to bed now. Sleep well.'

He put her to bed, pulled the covers up over her and departed.

She was left staring at the ceiling, coming to terms with the discovery that while he'd called her only three times, he'd checked on her by calling Fiorella every night.

For the next few days he was preoccupied with his guests, and she decided to spend some time looking around the area, especially Florence. Lucio arranged for Aldo, one of the workers to drive her there and wait for her. But when they reached the town she sent Aldo home. He looked uneasy and she guessed Lucio had told him to stay with her if possible.

'Tell your boss I'm all right,' she said, adding firmly, 'Goodbye.'

She had an enjoyable day in Florence. When it was time to get a taxi home she paused, considered, then made her way back to the hotel where she'd stayed when she first arrived here, and where she had hired a car. As she had hoped they willingly hired her another one.

This was better, she thought as she drove back to the estate. She was happy with the welcome she'd received from the family, but she also felt a little swallowed up by it. Now she would have some freedom and independence.

She had to admit that driving across the estate was a

little confusing. The roads were unlit and twice she lost her way. But at last she saw the house, high on the hill, gleaming with lights in the darkness, and heaved a sigh of relief.

As she drew closer she saw Lucio standing there, watching her until she halted, when he strode over and opened her door.

'Where have you been?' he demanded.

'What's the problem? I've spent the past few months finding my own way around Italy and I can manage these few miles. And I called to say I'd be late.'

'Yes, Fiorella told me, but I didn't expect you to be as late as this. Can't you understand that I—?'

He stopped, clearly searching for words and not finding them. The next moment he reached for her and pulled her fiercely against him, holding her in a grip of iron. His breath was hot against her cheek.

'Hours and hours and you didn't come home,' he growled. 'Anything could have happened to you.'

He drew back a little to look at her, and she was shocked at the torment she saw in his face.

'I'm here now,' she whispered. 'It's all right. Lucio, it's all right. *It's all right.*'

'Yes…yes—'

His mouth was fierce on hers, kissing her again and again while his arms grew even tighter.

'Let me breathe,' she gasped, laughing and delighted.

'You think it's funny to put me through the wringer?'

'No, I don't think it's funny. I'm sorry, Lucio, I never imagined you'd be like this.'

'Didn't imagine I'd want to protect you? Don't you understand that I—? I don't know…I can't explain…I can't—'

She was overwhelmed by a feeling of protectiveness. At first she'd thought he was angry, but he was distraught. Gently she took his face in her hands and kissed him.

'It's all right,' she repeated. 'And it's going to stay all right, I promise.'

'But you're not going to drive that old banger,' he said, indicating the hired car.

'Hey, you're not telling me what I can do, are you?'

'No, I'm telling you that I'm going to buy you a decent car. Think you can put up with that?'

'I guess I'll try.'

'I'm sorry, I didn't mean to upset you.'

'And I didn't mean to upset *you*.'

'When you didn't come back... These dark, unfamiliar roads—you could have had an accident. You could have—both of you.'

She nodded, touching her stomach. 'Yes, there are two of us, aren't there? I guess I wasn't thinking straight. I like my freedom, but I should have remembered that when you're pregnant you lose a lot of freedom.' She gave a rueful sigh. 'It's not just me any more. I did get lost, just for a little while.'

'Only because the roads are unfamiliar. When you've driven in and out of Florence a few times you'll know the way and have no more problems. Now come inside and have something to eat. You must be famished.'

He kept his word about the car, escorting her to the showroom next day, watching her reactions to vehicle after vehicle, until he saw her face light up with pleasure.

'That one?' he said.

'That one. Oh, no, look at the price!'

'Let me worry about that.'

The test drive confirmed her best hopes, and within an hour she was the owner.

'Now you can drive me home,' he said.

'But what about the car we came in?'

'Aldo can pick it up. Come on. This time I'm going to be the passenger.'

He did everything in his power to make her forget his agitation of the night before, and all seemed well.

But when she thought how distraught he'd been she knew there was something there that she didn't understand, something that suggested another, deeply mysterious man, tormented and troubled to the point of agony, lurking below the surface.

Who was he? How often did he emerge? And why?

Now her life was contented, even happy. Not only was Fiorella friendly but Elizabetta and all the servants combined to spoil her. They knew about the coming child, were delighted by it and would do anything to make sure she enjoyed living with them.

The only disturbances were tiny things, impossible to predict, such as the time she opened a cupboard door and found a picture of a young girl.

She knew at once that this must be Maria, and gazed, fascinated. Maria had been not merely pretty but glorious, vibrant with youth, seeming to sum up in one delicate person everything that would make life worth living.

She then saw Lucio in the photo, clasping Maria's waist and standing behind her. She couldn't see much of his face, but she could just make out that he was smiling ecstatically, and his attitude was one of triumph, the victor holding the trophy.

She put the picture carefully back and closed the door, guessing that it had been hidden away so that she should not see it. Doubtless it was kindly meant, but she couldn't help thinking that it had the perverse effect of warning her that Maria was still her rival for Lucio's heart: a rival who had no intention of giving up easily.

She lowered her head, her eyes closed, a prey to a sudden feeling of weariness, almost despair. Once again she was on the outside looking in. Her family, Don. They had all made her feel excluded. But recently things had changed. Here in Tuscany, at the vineyard, with Lucio, she had been made welcome. Or so she'd thought.

But the welcome was not complete. Suddenly the door was barred against her again, and the one who stood there, warning her that she would never get past the barrier into Lucio's heart, was Maria.

But she would refuse to yield to the treacherous feelings. Giving in was for weaklings. She was ready for the fight. If only Lucio was here, so that battle could commence.

One evening she came home to find he had arrived a day early. He greeted her cheerfully with a kiss on her cheek.

'Been exploring again?'

'Yes, but mostly the towns, which isn't what I want.'

'Surely towns are interesting. All those delightful fashion shops—'

'Yes, I've visited a few. And the shop that's going to be your wine store. But I haven't seen much of the place that interests me most.'

'And where would that be?'

'It's called the Vigneto Constanza,' she said, her head on one side as she reminded him of his own estate. 'You must have heard of it.'

He scratched his head. 'It seems vaguely familiar.'

'Everyone says it's the biggest and the best. I'd really like to explore it properly.'

He grinned. 'Then I guess I'll have to oblige.'

It was little more than a month since she'd come here to find him, but already she could see a new lushness in the grapes that would one day be Chianti wine. As they strolled down an alley he said, 'Do you remember this place?'

'Yes, this was where I told you I was pregnant. You were standing down there.'

'Watching you walk towards me from a great distance. I knew even then that you were going to cause an earthquake, but I had no idea how big it was going to be.'

'Neither had I. I knew I was pregnant but this—' She made a flourishing gesture, taking in the view for miles. 'This makes everything different.'

'Do you like it here?'

'Oh, yes, it's lovely. I've been learning as much as I can. I go online, and read books. I know that you'll harvest these grapes in October, and store them for two years before they can be wine. But that's just facts. Standing here amid all this beauty is different. But I suppose you see it more practically.'

'You think I can see only the money, but I can feel the beauty, too. When I first came here I spent a night sleeping under the stars in one of these fields. It was pure magic, and next morning I went to ask for a job because I knew I never wanted to leave. I'm glad it affects you, too.'

They strolled on, both enjoying their shared warmth and contentment. But, as often happened, it died in an argument only a moment later.

'There's been something I've been meaning to tell you,' he said. 'I don't know how you're fixed financially, but I don't want you to have any worries about that. So I've opened a bank account for you. Here.' He handed her a chequebook. 'It's all set up and I'll be making regular payments.'

But instead of eagerly taking the chequebook she stepped back and shook her head.

'No, thank you. I'd rather not.'

He stared. 'What did you say?'

'I've already opened an account for myself. I'm not in need of money, my family are fortunately very wealthy and I've saved quite a bit from my job back in New York. I wouldn't have started this trip if I couldn't finance it without help.'

'But you're carrying my child. It's my job to look after you.'

'And you're doing that. You've given me a home. I don't need any more. I appreciate you thinking of me, and I'm not ungrateful, but I won't take your money, Lucio.'

'But why?' he demanded.

'Why should I? Not all women want to take a man's money. Let's take it easy. There's a lot we still don't agree about.'

'Do we have to agree about everything?'

'Not about everything, but some things matter.'

'All right. Have it your way.' He sighed and thrust the papers back into his pocket, making a wry face. 'After all, why should I object? I can spend the money you've saved me on riotous living.'

'Naturally. That's what I hope you'll do.'

'You're the most maddening woman, do you know that?'

'Of course. I work at it.'

'Why work at it? You have a natural gift for awkwardness.'

'I'm not the only one. That's one of the things we still have to negotiate, whether my awkwardness and yours can live with each other.'

'Would you like to take bets on who'll be the winner?'

'No, that would be boring.'

He grinned. 'That's one thing I'm never afraid of with you. I'll let you win this time.'

'Coward,' she jeered.

'Whatever you say. Come on, there's a lot for you still to see.'

Charlotte wondered at herself. Lucio seemed to have offered her a gesture of acceptance, the very acceptance she was eager to find. Yet was it her he sought to bind to him, or only the child?

With all her heart she longed for him to want her for herself, and until she was certain of that she would retain some independence—however perverse and awkward she might seem, not only in his eyes but in her own.

These days she was often in contact with her family in the States, not just through email but with a video link on her new laptop.

Ellie had much to tell. She had been to see their Calhoun relatives in Larkville, Texas.

'Clay had four children,' she told Charlotte. 'Two daughters, Jess and Megan, and two sons, Holt and Nate. I haven't met all of them yet but that's going to be the next thing. Every year in October Larkville has a festival. This year it's going to include a celebration of Clay Calhoun's life, to mark the first anniversary of his death. His children really want us to be there, so I'm going to stay here for it, especially now I've met Jed, and you must come, too.' Ellie had travelled to Larkville earlier in the year wanting to know the truth about her father and had fallen in love with Larkville's sheriff, Jed Jackson.

'But I can't,' Charlotte said. 'My baby's due about then. I can't take a long flight so close to the birth. Just imagine Lucio's reaction to that idea.'

'And who's Lucio to tell you what you can and can't do?'

'He's the father. That gives him some rights.'

'But he can't tell you whether you can or can't come home.'

Home, she thought. How strange that word now sounded. Wasn't Tuscany her home now?

'What about marriage?' Ellie demanded.

'We haven't talked about it, but we get on well.'

'Charlotte, shouldn't you be facing facts now? Does he actually want to marry you? I mean, if he hasn't asked you—'

'I—'

'He hasn't, has he?'

'No, but that doesn't mean—'

'Doesn't it? Look, I care about you. I know you don't believe that after the trouble recently, but it's true. I want you to be happy, and I don't think you are. You're having his child, he's moved you into his house but he won't make it final. Doesn't that tell you something?'

Charlotte couldn't speak. Conflicting thoughts and emotions stormed through her. Her feelings were greater than Lucio's, but she'd told herself a thousand times that she could cope. Now Ellie was forcing her to face something she wanted to avoid, at least for the moment.

'What about you?' Ellie pursued remorselessly. 'Do *you* want to marry *him*?'

'Don't be so old-fashioned,' Charlotte said quickly. 'People don't have to marry these days.'

'No, but if things are right between them they want to get married. That's how you know. Does he say he loves you?'

'Look—'

'I guess that means he doesn't. For pity's sake, get yourself back here as soon as possible. He thinks he owns you but he won't commit to you. Come home, Charlotte.'

'Ellie, I've got to go. We'll talk again soon. Goodbye.'

She shut the call down and sat with her face buried in her hands, devastated. It was no use telling herself that Ellie didn't understand the situation. The words 'He thinks he owns you but he won't commit to you' rang in her ears despite her frantic attempts to shut them out.

'It's not true,' she whispered. 'He needs time. We're close, even if it's only as friends. I can build on that.'

But in her mind was another voice, saying cruelly, *'You're fooling yourself. He doesn't care for you in the way you want, and you just believe what you want to believe.'*

'But I'm not giving up yet,' she whispered.

As part of her desire to fit in with Lucio's life she asked him to show her the shop in Florence that he had bought with Enrico. It was in the luxurious Via della Vigna Nuova, which translated as the Street of the New Vineyard. Not surprisingly it was to be a wine store.

She met Vincente, who would be in charge, organising the shop, stocking it, arranging the grand opening. She found him pleasant and receptive to the ideas that were beginning to bubble in her mind. She wanted to be involved in this venture.

As they were just about to leave there was a new arrival, the last person they expected to see there.

'Franco,' Charlotte exclaimed, holding out her hands.

'I'm not selling this place back to you,' Lucio said at once.

'Don't worry, it's all yours. But I remember I left some stuff of mine in the cupboard under the stairs.'

They helped him fetch his things, and the three of them had lunch together.

Franco continued to happily talk away in Venetian with Charlotte, until at last he switched back to Italian to say,

'I suppose you'll make a bid for one of the Bantori vineyards now.'

'I've been thinking of it,' Lucio agreed, 'but why do
you say "now"?'

'Because now you have Charlotte, who speaks Venetian,
you'll find a lot of things easier.'

'Venetian?' Charlotte exclaimed. 'But surely you can't
grow grapes in Venice, with all those canals?'

'Not actually in Venice,' Lucio told her. 'But there are
vineyards in the surrounding countryside, and I've been
thinking of expanding.'

'I can put you in touch with several useful people,'
Franco said.

Charlotte grew very still. An idea was creeping up on
her, mischievous, delightful, a bit naughty but all the more
fun for that.

Assuming a tone of serious consideration she said, 'I
think we should go to Venice as soon as possible. There's
important business to be done. The next few days would
be a good idea.'

Lucio eyed her curiously. 'What are you up to?'

'Me?' she asked, eyes wide and innocent. 'I'm just trying to help you make money. Why would you suspect me
of an ulterior motive?'

'Because I'm beginning to know you, and an ulterior
motive is the first thing that comes into my head.' He
grinned. 'Come on. Own up. What am I being tricked
into?'

Franco began to laugh. 'Of course, I should have thought
of it. Where was my head?' He beamed at Charlotte. 'I
should have known that someone as knowledgeable about
Italy as you would have been alert to this.'

'It's something I've always wanted to see,' she said.
'And here's my chance.'

'When you two jokers have finished,' Lucio said ironically. 'Are you going to let me in on the secret?'

'Perhaps we ought to tell him,' Franco asked.

'I reckon we'd better,' she said solemnly. Her eyes met Lucio's, his wary, hers brimming with fun.

'If we go now we'll be in time for the festival. You know—the Festa della Sensa. You must have heard of it.'

'Of course I—is it now? Yes—' He slapped his forehead.

'And you're an Italian,' Charlotte mocked.

'I'm Tuscan not Venetian. I don't keep all their festivals in my head. But I've heard of this one and I agree it would be good to go.'

The Festa della Sensa was a glorious Venetian water pageant, whose peak was the moment when a ring was tossed into the water, symbolising Venice's marriage to the sea. By sheer lucky chance it was due to start in a few days, and they would have time to get there and join in.

'You're a conniving little so-and-so,' he said when they returned to the car.

'Nonsense. I'm doing my bit as your Venetian assistant. Just wait and see how useful I can be.'

'I think I'm going to enjoy this,' he said.

'I hope so. I know I am.'

That night, somewhere in her dreams, Charlotte heard Lucio's softly murmured, 'You're wonderful.' Then she awoke and lay awake listening, longing to hear again the whisper that would bring her to life.

He'd said it to her after their night of passion. Surely one day he would say it again.

Waiting—waiting…

Light was coming in around the gaps at the blinds, and she rose to go to the window, wanting to watch the dawn. Now she felt as though light was dawning in her life. Everything in her yearned towards the trip to Venice that she would take with Lucio, share work with him, and perhaps share even more.

Then she saw something that made her grow still. At a little distance on a hill there was a man, completely still, watching the dawn. As the light slowly engulfed him she could see that it was Lucio.

What had made him go out to that isolated place to stand against the sky, so alone that he might have been the only person alive in the world?

And she remembered what he'd said about a desert that very first night; that it could be a place of safety because there was nobody to hurt you. And he'd meant exactly that. She knew it now.

With all her heart she longed to go to him, open her arms and draw him against her heart, telling him that he didn't need to live in a desert. But at this moment he would turn away from her, because the desert was what he had chosen.

She stood watching him for a long time, hoping to see him move, to return home to her. But he stood there, imprisoned in a terrible, isolated stillness.

At last she returned to bed and lay down in her own desert.

CHAPTER EIGHT

THEY nearly didn't make the trip to Venice. With only two days to the festival every hotel for miles was booked. But a sudden cancellation came just in time.

'We're going to stay in the Tirani Hotel,' Lucio told her.

Charlotte's eyes widened. 'Wow!'

The Tirani was one of the most luxurious hotels in Venice. On her last visit she had stayed in a far more modest establishment, occasionally walking past the Tirani, just close enough to see that it was way out of her price range.

'I hope it lives up to your expectations,' Lucio said, grinning and correctly interpreting her amazement.

They travelled by train, boarding at Florence Station for the two-hour journey.

'I loved Venice when I was there before,' she said as they neared the magical city. 'But it was winter and everywhere was under snow, even the gondolas. I've always wanted to go back and see it in the sun.'

'And you managed it, by manipulating me like a puppet. Well done.'

'Oh, that's how you feel. Well, if the vineyards in the Veneto aren't worth fighting for, why don't we just go back?'

He eyed her with grimly humorous appreciation.

'If you think I'll fall for that, forget it. I know you well enough by now to reckon that you'll have researched the subject and know exactly how good they are.'

'Right! I did just that, and I know that the Bantori vine-yards are well known for their white grapes, which are used to make the very best prosecco wine. In Tuscany you grow Sangiovese grapes to make red wine, so you'd prob-ably enjoy branching out into a different area.'

'You really have been doing research,' he observed.

He wished he could have kept the touch of admiration out of his voice. It galled him to discover that he respected her brains, but he couldn't help it.

He'd never sought the company of intellectual women. Nor was that how she'd appeared on the first evening. True, she'd argued like someone whose brain was up to every trick, but soon other aspects of her had risen to distract him. Now he was discovering that to keep one step ahead of her he would need all his wits.

As she gazed out of the window he took the chance to study her, knowing that her combination of beauty and brains was likely to cause him even more trouble in the future than it had already. Pregnancy suited her, causing a glorious flowering. Yet the alertness was always there in her eyes, warning him to take nothing for granted.

He marvelled at the situation in which he found him-self. He, not she, was Italian, yet in thirty-two years he had never visited Venice. But she knew the city well and was revealing it to him. Something in the irony of that ap-pealed to his sense of humour.

Not that there had been much humour in his life. Once, briefly, he'd enjoyed a time of vibrant emotion, but when it was snatched from him he'd determined to banish feel-ings, clinging only to things that could be relied on. Work, money, philanthropy. He was known for his fine actions benefiting his neighbours, raising money for good causes and donating generously. Few could have guessed that this was actually another way of keeping people away. When they praised his noble generosity they did it at a distance, so there was little need to reach out to them.

Eventually he supposed a wife and child might have formed part of his schedule. To have them imposed on him out of the blue had been a shock, but one he had decided to accommodate. It was good to have an heir, and a woman who understood the kind of man he was had seemed ideal. Understanding her in return hadn't entered into his calculations. At least, not at first.

But being with her was like living with one of those legendary beings whose touch changed the world. There was no choice but to follow. Gradually he was getting into her mind, but her ability to catch him off guard was disconcerting. Sometimes even pleasant.

She turned and met his gaze.

'Nearly there,' she said, smiling.

They had reached Venice Mestre, the last railway station on the mainland before the Liberty Bridge, which stretched nearly two miles out across the lagoon to the Santa Lucia Station in Venice itself. As they crossed the water Charlotte gazed, riveted, at the view she had longed to see again ever since she had left the city.

When they got down from the train she almost ran out of the station to where it opened onto the Grand Canal, and stood, breathless with delight at the sight of the boats and the water.

'This was it,' she breathed. 'This was it! Oh, isn't it beautiful?'

Now Lucio found that she could wrong-foot him again. Charlotte the efficient researcher had vanished, replaced by Charlotte the eager child, ready to plunge into a delicious fantasy.

'This is where I have to rely on you,' he said. 'What do we do now?'

In a city where the roads were made of water there was no place for wheeled vehicles. To get to the hotel they must either walk through the multitude of little back alleys, or travel by motorboat.

'We could get onto a *vaporetto*,' she said, indicating a huge water bus that had just docked. 'But a taxi's better. Over there.'

She pointed to where a group of motorboats were moored, ready for passengers. In a moment they were aboard, gliding along the Grand Canal, between the palaces, beneath the great bridges, until they reached the hotel. The receptionist greeted Lucio with the awe due to a man who'd hired the most expensive suite.

The place lived up to all Charlotte's expectations. She had her own bedroom, next to Lucio's, with a view of the canal. Looking out she saw Lucio at his own window, just a few feet away. He nodded.

'I'm glad we came.'

'Hey!'

A cry from below made them look down to see Franco standing up in a boat, hailing them.

'You're here!' he yelled. 'That's wonderful! Tonight you will be my guests for dinner. I have important people for you to meet. I'll collect you in an hour.'

Charlotte sighed as she saw her dream of dinner alone with Lucio vanish. But there was no choice. Doubtless the 'important people' Franco mentioned would have something to do with vineyards. This trip was about business, and she mustn't let herself forget that.

While she was unpacking her cell phone rang. It was Ellie.

'Is he there with you?' she wanted to know.

'Not in the room, but we're in Venice together.'

'Has he mentioned any further commitment?'

'No, but—'

'Charlotte, you've done some pretty mad things in your time, but this is something that affects us all. We think you should come home. You can't cope alone.'

'I'm not alone. I'm living with nice people who are kind to me.'

'But you can't mean to stay there for good. You belong here, with your family.'

'Family? Belong? Ellie, do you know how hollow those words sound to me now?'

She heard her voice sounding sharper than she'd intended and checked herself.

'I can't talk now. I have to go out—'

'Can't it wait? This is important.'

'And my life here is important to me.'

'If we could just talk about—'

Suddenly Charlotte felt her temper rising.

'No. Not now. When I'm ready to talk I'll call you. Goodbye, I've got to go now.'

She hung up, wishing Ellie hadn't chosen this moment to make contact. The last thing she wanted to think about was her old life, not when her new one was so tempting.

For the evening she chose her attire with great care. Something suitable for a business meeting, yet which would attract Lucio. At last she chose a cocktail dress of black velvet. It would be the last time she could fit into it for a while, and she was going to make the best of what it could do for her. Lucio was determined to behave 'properly' as he saw it, making no sexual claims on her for fear of causing harm. But she knew there was no need to fear harm, and while she still had the chance she was going to get him to behave 'improperly,' no matter what it took.

She knew she was on the right track when she saw his face, eyes alight with admiration, a smile that he was trying to keep under control, and not entirely succeeding.

'Do I look like an efficient assistant?' she asked. 'All ready to do my duty?'

'Is that how you're trying to look?'

'Well, this is going to be a working meal, isn't it?'

'Is it?' He sounded baffled.

'Who do you think these "important people" are that Franco wants us to meet? They must be something to do with the vineyards. Obviously they're friends of his and he's helping them find a buyer. That's why he suggested you might want to buy a Veneto vineyard, and why he's bringing you together.' She met his gaze with well-contrived innocence. 'Surely that's obvious?'

'Yes—yes, of course,' he said hastily. He pulled himself together. 'I can see you're going to be an excellent assistant. I'm impressed.'

Franco was waiting downstairs, ready to lead them the short distance to the restaurant.

'There will be ten of us,' he said. 'My son has recently become engaged, and will be joining us with his fiancée, Ginevra. Also Ginevra's parents will be there. You'll have a lot in common with them, Lucio. They own several vineyards around here.'

Charlotte stole a sly glance at Lucio and found him looking right back at her. As their eyes met each knew the other was suppressing a smile.

'I think you must be psychic,' he whispered in her ear. 'You might find that a very useful gift in an assistant.'

'An assistant isn't exactly what I had in mind. Yes, Franco, we're just coming.'

Together they walked on, each wondering exactly what the other was thinking, and each thoroughly enjoying it.

In the restaurant they found the four people Franco had described, also his wife, who greeted them with a beaming smile. Charlotte found herself sitting next to Rico, owner of the vineyard, with Lucio on his other side, confirming her suspicions that this was a work meeting.

She did what was expected of her, speaking Venetian, making the occasional error and leading the laughter at her own expense. As the evening moved on the mood became increasingly friendly. Rico, in particular, was happy to talk to Charlotte. The subject was his vineyard but he seemed unable to take his eyes off her, as Lucio in particular noticed.

There was a brief, awkward moment when her cell phone rang and she answered it to find Alex.

'I've been talking to Ellie,' she said. 'She's worried about you, and we were both think—'

'I can't talk now,' she said hastily. 'I'll call back. Bye.'

She shut the phone down and switched it off, cursing herself for not doing so before. Everyone was looking at her with interest, as though speculating who her caller might be.

She turned her brightest smile on Rico. 'I really look forward to seeing your estate,' she said.

'And I hope you will come very soon, perhaps tomorrow,' he declared fervently.

'That would be excellent,' Lucio said before she could reply. 'May I suggest an early start?'

They all agreed on an early start.

'Then I think we won't stay out too late tonight,' Lucio

said. 'An early start tomorrow means an early night now. Are you ready, my dear?'

'Quite ready,' she said.

'Oh, surely, just a little longer—' Franco protested.

'I look forward to tomorrow,' Lucio interrupted him.

As they strolled back to the hotel she said, 'Were you wise to risk offending him? After all, if you're going to do business—'

'I'm the buyer. I make the terms. And if he rakes you with his eyes like that again I'll—I don't know…'

'Knock a few thousand off the price you offer?' she suggested.

'I had something else in mind,' he growled.

'Nonsense! Money's far more effective. He badly needs to sell that vineyard.'

'He told you that?'

'Not in so many words, but it came through. He's had a lot of "expenses" recently, by which I think he means gambling debts. His wife said the word *casino* in a certain tone that spoke volumes. They're planning a lavish wedding for their daughter and counting on the money from the vineyard. So you've got the advantage.'

'I'd still rather punch his lights out.'

'Only the money matters. Cling to that.'

'Yes, ma'am! You're really getting the hang of this.'

'Right. I think I missed my vocation. I should have gone into big business. Since I've been here I've seen a whole new future opening up, chief of a money-making enterprise, giving orders left, right and centre—' She stopped, glancing up at his face. 'All right, I'm only joking.'

'And I fall for it so easily, don't I?'

'You have your moments.'

'Fine, go ahead. Have fun. My time will come.'

My time will come. She'd said this to herself so often

that hearing it from Lucio caught her by surprise. Suddenly she glimpsed thoughts and feelings inside him that she had never suspected. Was he really holding his breath for what could happen between them? Just like herself?

'I suppose I shouldn't have dragged you away like that,' he mused.

'No, you shouldn't. I was still eating a lovely cake.'

'Then I'll buy you another one.'

'First you bought me a car, now a cake,' she teased. 'What next? You think money buys you out of any situation, don't you?'

'Of course it does. You just taught me that, and I'm learning. Let's go in there.'

He indicated a little café just up ahead, and soon they were sitting at a table, being served with cake and sparkling water.

'You can drink alcohol if you want,' Charlotte said. 'Are you afraid that I'll be tempted if I see a bottle of wine? No need. I'm quite grown up. Honestly.'

He made a face and ordered some wine. 'I was trying to be considerate.'

'Thank you for the thought but there's no need.' She gave a blissful sigh. 'Oh, I did enjoy today.'

'I'm glad to see you in a happier mood.'

'Whatever do you mean? I haven't been grumpy, have I?'

'Not with me, but whoever you were talking to on the phone earlier today. I heard you from the next room. You sounded ready to bite their head off.'

'Oh, that! Yes, I wasn't at my best.'

'This person did something to annoy you?'

She made a wry face. 'You could say she's been annoying me since the day we met, twenty-seven years ago.'

'Family?'

'Sister. Well, half-sister. I've always been fond of her but I can't help resenting her, too. She's so beautiful, so elegant. Men have always pursued her and she has to fend them off. Honestly, sometimes I could have murdered her for being so gorgeous.'

'Don't underestimate your own looks.'

'Oh, come on!' She turned to regard herself in the wall mirror, giving a disparaging flick to her long hair. 'I'm not beautiful.'

'You're striking,' he said, recalling how her hair had looked spread out over the pillow. 'I have no complaints.'

'That's because you're a gentleman with perfect manners.'

'Liar!' He grinned. 'Well, I had to say something. Was that her who called you during the meal?'

'No, that was my other sister Alex.'

'Is she gorgeous, too?'

'She's pretty, but she has something more important than looks. She has charm. And don't you dare tell me I'm charming.'

'I swear it never crossed my mind. I'm much too afraid of you.'

'Good. Keep it that way.'

'So how did Ellie offend you?'

'Nothing special,' she said quickly. 'She was just concerned about how I was managing.'

'But you sounded annoyed.'

'Yes, well—they have their own ideas but it doesn't concern them, and I don't want them interfering.'

'Is this what you hinted at the first night? You mentioned an older brother and sister who were twins and a younger sister. But you said there was a big family secret, and you were the last to know. It made you feel like an outsider.'

'Yes.' She sighed. 'My father is my mother's second husband. Before him she was married to a man called Clay Calhoun, but the marriage broke up, she left him and met Cedric Patterson soon after. They planned to marry, then she discovered that she was pregnant by Clay. But Cedric still wanted her. They married and she had twins, Ellie and Matt, which my father raised as his own.

'But recently we found out that my mother wrote to Clay telling him about her pregnancy. If he'd responded she might never have married my dad. But he didn't because he never got the letter. Sandra, the new woman in his life, kept it from him and then they got married.

'She died a couple of years ago, and Clay died last year. His daughter Jess was going through his things when she found a box belonging to Sandra, and the letter was in it. That's how she learned that her father had two other children.

'I think she had to search for them on the internet. At last she found Ellie and told her. So just a few months ago she and Matt discovered that they were Clay's children, and not our father's. She told Alex first, I guess because she's always been closer to her, but she delayed telling me.'

'Hell!' Lucio exclaimed.

'Yes, that's how I felt. You remember the hotel in Rome where we met?'

'The Hotel Geranno.'

'Right. I'd just been down to their internet café and found an email from Alex telling me all about it. From Alex, not from Ellie. She couldn't even be bothered to email me herself, not about that nor the fact that she seems to have found "Mr Right". I felt I'd come at the end of a long queue.'

Lucio took her hand and squeezed it. 'They shouldn't have done that to you.'

'I felt so unwanted, unnecessary, surplus to requirements, don't call us, we'll call you—or perhaps not.' She sighed. 'Until then I'd always felt so pleased about having a family—a "real family" as I called it. With a family you weren't alone. Only then I discovered I was wrong.'

'But Ellie and Matt are still your siblings even if you do only share one parent now. And Alex is your full sister.'

'Yes.' She sighed.

'But that doesn't help much, does it? Is there no one in the family who could help you? Your parents?'

'I can't talk to them about this. A while back my father's mind started to go. These days he's very confused and looking after him is my mother's priority. Nothing else really matters to her, so when I called her—'

'She wouldn't talk to you about it?' he asked, frowning.

'Not exactly. She confirmed it had happened, but she said it was all a long time ago, and why should I worry about it? Obviously it involves Matt and Ellie because they're Clay's children, but I'm not, and she didn't seem to think it concerned me.'

'But a family upheaval like that concerns everyone.'

'That's how I think, but my mother doesn't seem to understand. I used to feel close to her—well, sort of. The twins were special and Alex is gorgeous. I'm the middle one and I don't stand out like the others. I've always felt that, and sometimes I've acted a bit daft, trying to attract attention, I suppose. Some of them call me the rebel of the family, some call me the idiot—'

'Stop right there,' he interrupted her. 'You're going to put yourself down and I won't have it.'

She smiled. 'Well, I can't help remembering what that man at the party said about women who—'

'*That's enough!* He knows nothing.' Lucio laid his hand over hers. 'At least, he doesn't know what I know.'

'Thank you,' she choked.

'You'll sort it with your family one day.'

'Will I? I don't know. They've made me feel so shut out. You know that saying, "Home is the place where they have to let you in". Now it's as though they wouldn't let me in.'

'That feeling won't last. You need time to get over it, but it'll happen. After all, you have another home now.'

She studied him curiously, aware of the mysterious sensation that had overcome her before in his company, as though their minds were in harmony. Even Matt, the sibling to whom she'd always felt close, hadn't given her such a feeling.

Had he ever? she mused. His failure to tell her what the others knew had left her feeling distant from him. But even in the past, had she felt as she did now with Lucio, that she'd found a friend to confide in? In time he might be more, but best friend was the least she would settle for.

'Is something funny?' he asked, watching her.

'I was just thinking what a wonderful brother you'd make, which I suppose is a bit funny in the circumstances.'

'Not really. You and I need to be friends, allies, comrades.'

'That's true. We always could read each other's minds, couldn't we?'

'From the first moment,' he agreed. 'Remember that argument we had at that café near the Trevi Fountain? I kept having a weird sensation that I knew exactly what you were going to say next. And you usually did.'

'That must have made me very boring,' she said lightly.

He shook his head. 'No, you're never boring. Don't put yourself down. You were in a bad way that night, and you needed someone. I'm glad it was me.'

He raised her hand and laid his cheek against the back.

'So that's why I got lucky,' he said softly. 'I've always wondered.'

'What do you mean?'

'Well, I could tell that you're not the kind of girl who goes in for one-night stands. Even if you are the rebel of the family, it was the first time your rebellion had ever taken that particular form, wasn't it?'

She nodded.

'But it happened with me. I'm not conceited enough to think you fell for my "looks and charm". You felt sad and lonely and I just happened to be there.'

'It was a bit more than that,' she said huskily. 'You made me feel wanted.'

'I'm glad. And you know what I'm even more glad about? That it was me and nobody else. You were so vulnerable. You could have been hurt.'

'But not by you,' she said, smiling.

'No, not by me. You made me feel wanted, too, and I guess it filled a need, just at the right time. It's almost enough to make you believe in fate. You needed me, I needed you, fate brought us together.'

'You didn't need me,' she said. 'Don't forget I saw you in the hotel, surrounded by admirers. Or do I mean worshipers? There wasn't a woman there who wouldn't gladly have changed places with me.'

'And did you see me inviting them?'

'You wouldn't have had to try very hard,' she said wryly.

'If you mean that I lived a self-indulgent life in those days, I don't deny it.' He pulled a self-mocking face. 'But that's over. I haven't slept with another woman since I found you.'

'You mean since the day I told you about the baby?'

'No, I mean since that night in Rome. Yes, I don't blame you for looking cynical, but it's true.'

'But why should you? I mean, you didn't expect ever to see me again.'

'I know. But somehow you were still with me. There were times I was tempted but you always stepped in and made me back off. I found myself living like a monk.'

He saw her gazing at him in astonishment. 'It's the truth, I swear it. Say you believe me. But only if you mean it.'

For a moment she was lost for words. This was the last thing she'd expected to hear.

He made a wry face, misunderstanding her silence.

'I guess I can't blame you. I probably wouldn't believe me either.'

'But I do,' she murmured. 'I do believe you.'

Incredibly, she really did.

'Do you really mean that?' he persisted. 'Truly?'

'Truly.'

'Thank you. Not many people would, given the way I've lived, dashing around, enjoying a superficial life. But once there was you, something changed.'

'But suppose you hadn't made me pregnant, and I hadn't come to find you?'

'That doesn't bear thinking about.'

She knew a surge of pleasure so intense that she struggled to hide it. She managed by retreating into cynicism.

'Oh, come on!' she jeered lightly. 'If it hadn't been me it would have been one of those willing ladies.'

'Most of those "willing ladies" have husbands or make a career out of being available. And they're all the kind of people that I can't get close to—not as we've grown close. I can talk to you like nobody else. I'm close to Fiorella but there are things I can't confide in her about. She's been hurt too much, I have to protect her.'

'And that's my big advantage?' she teased. 'I don't need protection.'

'Hey! You've missed no opportunity to tell me that you can look after yourself. I've lost count of the number of times you've said it as a way of slapping me down.'

'Some men need slapping down, preferably as often as possible.'

'Duly noted.' He gave a mock salute.

'But I guess in future I'll have to find another way.'

'I'm sure you'll think of something.' He grasped her hand and gave it a squeeze. 'But seriously, of course you need my protection. As though I'd let you of all people run any risks. But I do know that you're strong and independent. If it came to a battle between us I'd back you against me.'

'So would I. Let's agree on that.'

'I guess we should be going,' he said. 'It's late and you should be in bed.'

'I'm not a child to be sent to bed.'

'I'm making sure you're all right. Isn't that what I'm supposed to do?'

'Just be careful not to push your luck.'

'Let's go.'

Together they strolled out. The street was narrow, and above it was a fine strip of sky, glittering with stars. Charlotte gazed up entranced.

'It's as though they're pointing the way home,' she said. 'Just a few yards and then— Whoops!'

'Careful!' he said, grasping her as she stumbled, nearly losing her balance. 'If you don't look where you're going I guess you do need someone to keep an eye on you, after all.'

'Well, perhaps you're right.'

His arm was now firmly around her shoulders, and it was natural to lean her head back against it.

'You're still not looking at the road,' he reproved her.

'With you to guide me I don't need to. I leave everything in your hands.'

'Hm! Why does that submissive act fill me with suspicion?'

'I can't think.'

She slipped her arm about his waist and, like this, laughing and holding on to each other, they drifted on their way.

CHAPTER NINE

EARLY next morning a motorboat collected them from the hotel and drove them to Piazzale Roma, the car park on the edge of town, beyond which no wheeled vehicle was allowed. Here they all loaded into Franco's palatial car to be driven over the Liberty Bridge onto the mainland, and from there another fifty miles to the vineyard.

There Rico met them and gave them a conducted tour through his magnificent fields. What little Charlotte had seen of vineyards was enough to tell her that this was a splendid place, and the greatest favour she could do for Lucio was stay in the shadows.

She could tell that he was impressed by what he saw and heard, although his outward response was muted, as befitted a man with money at stake. Occasionally Rico would address her in Venetian, but only as a courtesy. Serious business was conducted in Italian, and increasingly she sensed that all was going well.

She particularly liked the house; not a palace like the ones she saw in Tuscany, but sprawling with an air of warmth and friendliness. Children could live happily here, she thought, wandering through the rooms.

At last there were handshakes and smiles all round. It was settled, and everyone was pleased.

'Tonight we meet again in Venice, to celebrate,' Rico declared. 'You will all be my guests.'

On the journey back Lucio and Franco continued an animated discussion on the necessary arrangements. Charlotte stayed quiet, but made notes.

Back in the hotel she adjusted her attire a little more than last night, choosing a neckline just an inch lower to take advantage of her generous bosom. Lucio made no comment, but the way he nodded told her something she wanted to know. She was determined to believe that.

The evening was a triumph. There were the same guests as the night before, and everyone involved in the deal felt they had gained.

'I can't thank you enough,' Lucio murmured as he clinked glasses with Charlotte.

'For what? I've kept my mouth firmly shut all day.'

'I could say that a woman who knows when to do that is worth her weight in gold, but you'd probably accuse me of being a sexist beast, so I won't. It was clever of you not to get involved in the negotiations—'

'Since they would have been over my head.'

'Will you stop trying to trap me, you little fiend? And stop laughing.'

'No, why should I?'

'I meant that you made the negotiations happen. Without you I probably wouldn't be here, and I'd have lost a lot.'

'So if it turns into a disaster it'll be all my fault?'

'Of course. What else?'

She began to laugh and he joined in. Glancing at them Franco thought that he had never seen a couple who belonged together so completely. He turned away to make a discreet call on his cell phone.

The rest of the evening was spent discussing the festival next day. At last Franco rose to his feet.

'We shall all meet again tomorrow,' he said, 'to take part in the festival. But now I have something else to say. Work is important, but this is also an evening for couples. My son and his future wife are a couple, my friends Charlotte and Lucio are a couple. My wife and I recently celebrated our wedding anniversary, and you—' he indicated Ginevra's parents '—will celebrate yours next month. So tonight I've arranged something special. Ah, I think it's here now.'

He looked up at a man, dressed as a gondolier, signalling him from the doorway.

'They are waiting for us,' he said. 'Shall we go?'

One of the doors of the restaurant opened on to a little side canal. There they found five gondolas ready to receive them.

'A romantic journey for each of us,' Franco said. 'Goodnight until tomorrow.'

Hardly believing that this was happening, Charlotte took the hand that the gondolier held out to her, and climbed in carefully. When all the boats were full the procession glided away.

Looking around Charlotte saw the other three couples snuggled happily in each other's arms. Franco was clearly a master of show business—a gondola ride in Venice, the very essence of romance.

Cheers and jeers rose from the other three boats when the occupants saw that Lucio and Charlotte were the only couple not embracing.

'Go on, spoilsport!'

'Why don't you kiss her?'

From Rico came words in Venetian which made Charlotte laugh.

'What did he say?' Lucio demanded.

'Something rather rude about you.'

'Tell me.'

'No way.'

'I see. Then I'll just have to put him right.'

He tightened his arm, laying his mouth against hers in a theatrical manner that made their companions cheer even more raucously.

Charlotte restrained her impulse to pull him closer, knowing that this was just more showmanship. If only they could be alone. Then she could do everything she wanted to turn showmanship into reality.

It was the gondolier who came to her rescue, calling in Venetian, *'Dove voi andare?'*

'What was that?' Lucio murmured.

'He asked where we want to go.'

'Canale Grande?' the boatman called. *'Ponte di Rialto?'*

'Do you want to see the Grand Canal and the Rialto Bridge?' she translated.

Lucio shook his head. 'I'd prefer something a little quieter, more private.'

'We'll keep to the little back canals,' she called.

'Sì, signorina.'

Now it was like being in another universe, created from narrow alleys, gleaming water and darkness. The boatman made no intrusive comments and they could imagine they were alone in the whole world.

'Your night of triumph,' he murmured.

'Hardly,' she said, thinking of how much she still had to achieve. 'It doesn't feel like triumph. Not yet.'

His eyes met hers, seeking her true meaning.

'What would make it a triumph?' he asked softly.

'You,' she said, reaching for him. 'Only you.'

This was her kiss. She was the prime mover, and knew that her triumph was beginning. She slipped her arms above his head, determined that this time he would not escape, but he had no thought of escape. She could tell that with every fibre of her being.

She had dreamed of this ever since he'd fled from her at Enrico's home, making love to her and then setting a cruel distance between them. Now everything she longed for was being given back to her. Every movement of his lips was a promise, and she would reclaim that promise with interest. She assured herself that while her sense of triumph soared.

A slight bump announced that the gondola had arrived at the hotel. Dazed, they wandered into the hotel and up to their suite. But there he paused, and a little fear crept over her. To conquer it she drew him close again. He put his arms about her, gentle, almost tentative.

'Charlotte, I—'

'It's all right,' she whispered against his mouth. 'Everything's all right.'

'Is it? Can you be sure? I know myself. I can't be near you without wanting to do something selfish. Just touching you brings me to the edge of control.'

'Good. That's where I want you—until you leap over the edge completely.'

'Or until you lure me over.' He tightened his arms, speaking in a tense voice. 'I've tried to be strong but you're not going to let me, are you?'

'Not for a moment.'

'Charlotte, don't—don't— *Charlotte!*'

And then there was only the feeling of victory as he drew her into his bedroom, pulling at her clothes. She would have helped him but he moved too fast for her, so she ripped his off instead.

No doubts, no hesitation, no false modesty. Just the plain fact that her will was stronger than his.

'Charlotte...'

'Yes, yes...'

His eyes, looking down on her, were mysteriously fierce and tender at the same time. 'You're a wicked woman,' he whispered.

'You'd better get used to it.'

'In a thousand years I'll never get used to you.'

He laid his head down against her breast and she wrapped him lovingly in her arms. There was still a way to go yet, but they would get there. In time she would win everything she wanted. In time he would be all hers.

After a while she felt him move, raise his head and grow still again, looking down on her.

'Are you all right?' he whispered.

'Of course I am.'

'Are you sure?' Now he was backing away, leaving the bed, until she reached out and stopped him.

'Oh, Lucio, please—don't do this again.'

'What do you mean?'

'I mean that last time we made love you ran from me as fast as you could, as though it had been a traumatic experience for you. Am I really so terrible?'

'The terrible one is me, selfishly taking what I want when you—'

'Then you're not the only selfish one, because *I* want it, too.'

He gave a sigh that was part a groan, and sat on the edge of the bed, running his hands through his hair.

'You probably think I'm mad, being so paranoid. Perhaps I am.'

'Lucio, I do understand, honestly I do. But no harm will come to me because of what we've done. Or to our child.'

'But things happen so easily. Just when you think everything's going well it's all snatched away from you. And you start to feel it might be better to have nothing, than to have something precious and lose it.'

'Why don't you tell me everything?' she asked gently. 'I have the feeling that there's so much you're keeping from me. Can't you trust me?'

'I do trust you, but it can be so hard to— Do you remember the night we met, the life I was living then?'

'Yes, you seemed on top of the world. Everyone wanted your attention, everyone was out to attract you.'

'Huh!' He gave a bleak laugh. 'That may be how it looked but it was an empty life. I felt that all the time—bleak, meaningless—but I couldn't live any other way. There was nothing else for me in those days. I had no anchor, and I didn't want one.'

'Didn't want one? As bad as that?' she asked softly.

He nodded.

'Tell me how it happened.'

'It started so long ago that I can barely remember it—the place, the people, everything I once called home.'

'Before you came to Tuscany?'

He nodded.

Now she knew she must tread carefully. Seeking him online she had several times found him described as a man of mystery.

'He appeared from nowhere,' one article had said. 'Nobody seems to know where he came from, or, if they know, something—or someone—has persuaded them to keep silent.'

She sat in silence, refusing to ask any questions. What happened now must be his choice. At last he began to speak.

'Sometimes I feel so far away from that world that it's almost as though it never existed. But when I'm honest with myself I know that it shaped me, created the dark side of me.'

'The dark side?'

'The part of my nature that's capable of revenge, ruth-lessness—deliberate cruelty.'

She was about to protest but something held her silent. She'd never seen cruelty in Lucio, but instinct told her it was there. Driven too far he would be capable of the most terrible acts, the most coldly savage indifference.

Somewhere a warning voice whispered, *Leave him. Flee quickly while there's time. He's only using you because he wants the child and one day he'll break your heart. You know that. Don't you?*

Yes, she thought. *I know that. But I won't ever leave him. Because I can't.*

Because I'll never give up hope.

Because I love him.

The words seemed to leap out at her. She hadn't meant to admit the truth, even to herself. But it had crept up on her without warning and now there was no escape.

He was watching her, seemingly troubled by her silence.

'Now you know the worst of me,' he said. 'Don't tell me you never suspected.'

She shook her head. 'You're wrong. I won't know the worst until I discover it for myself. And perhaps I never will. Stop trying to blacken yourself. Just tell me about this "other world". You had to escape it, but you've never really left it behind, have you?'

'No, I guess that's true.'

'The night we met you told me you came from Sicily. Did you have a large family?'

'No, just three of us, my parents and me. My father was a lawyer, but a very particular kind of lawyer, as I came to realise. His clients were rich and powerful. At first all I saw was that he was powerful, too. I admired him, wanted to be like him. I'd have done anything for his good opinion, or even just his attention.'

'He ignored you?'

'Not exactly. In his way he was a good father, did everything correctly. But I never felt that I was important to him. He only really loved one person in the world, and that was my mother. She was the same. Only he existed. They had the sort of marriage that most people would say was charming and idyllic.'

'Not if you were the child looking in from the outside,' she said.

For a moment he didn't react. Then, very slowly, he smiled and nodded.

'Yes,' he said. 'Of course you understand. I suppose I knew you would.'

'If your parents really love each other, you're never going to come first with either of them.'

'That's true, although to be fair to them they were kind and affectionate, in their way. As long as things went well. It was just when it came to a crisis—' He stopped.

'And one day the crisis came?' she asked softly.

He nodded. 'My father wanted me to become a lawyer. When I'd finished my training he reckoned I could become his partner. He gave me a job fetching and carrying in his office, so that I could "get the feel". That's when I started to realise what his clients were like, what he was like. He made his living protecting men who used violence and cruelty to get their way. He didn't care what they were like or what they'd done, as long as they paid him well.

'What really hurt was that he didn't understand why I minded. He called me a weakling for "making a fuss about nothing". No son of his would be such a fool. I knew I had to leave but I stayed for a while, hoping to persuade my mother to come with me. I couldn't believe she knew the truth about him, and I was sure when she learned it she'd want to flee him, as well.

'But when I told her, all she said was, "I knew you'd find out one day. I told him he should explain carefully". She kept saying my father was a good man who did what he had to for the sake of his family. But I couldn't believe it. He didn't do it for us. He did it because he wanted money at any cost, and he got a kick out of associating with crooks, as long as they were successful crooks. I begged her to come with me, but she wouldn't. She gave me some money and stood at the window as I slipped away one night.

'That was the last time I ever saw her. Three years later they were both dead. Someone killed my father and she died trying to save him. She didn't have to die, but she preferred that to living without him. Then I remembered something she'd said just before we parted, when she was trying to explain why she chose him above everything else, good and bad.'

He fell silent, and there was such pain in his face that Charlotte reached out and touched his cheek.

'Don't talk about it if you can't bear to,' she said.

'No, I want to tell you. I know I can rely on you to—to know…to feel.'

'Yes,' she whispered.

'She said that one day I'd know what it was to love someone beyond reason.'

'That's what we all hope for,' Charlotte murmured.

'Yes. She said I should be glad, for without it life would be empty. And she was right.'

'You found that out yourself?'

He squeezed her hand. From somewhere she found the resolve to say, 'You found it with Maria?'

He nodded.

'Did you fall in love with her at once?'

'No, we used to squabble a lot, but not seriously. Her parents took me in and I just seemed to fit in at once. I loved the life. I belonged. As Maria and I grew up we became closer until at the end it was just what my mother had predicted. Love beyond reason. I began to understand why she'd chosen to die rather than live without my father.'

'That must have been...earth-shattering,' she said softly. 'And beautiful.'

'Yes,' he said in a husky voice. 'Yes.'

From outside came a roar of laughter. She rose quickly and went to close the window, determined to protect Lucio. His memories were tormenting him and the last thing he needed was disturbance from outside. At all costs she would prevent that.

Before returning to him she took a moment to sort out her thoughts, which were confused. She wanted his love, and it might seem unwise to talk with him about Maria, the woman he'd loved. Yet she needed to understand how deep that love had gone, for only then could she guess her own chance of winning his heart.

She turned back to him, then paused at what she saw.

Lucio was sitting with his head sunk so low it almost reached his knees. His whole being radiated pain and despair, and she felt as though her heart would break for him.

He looked up. The sight of her brought a tense smile to his face, and he stretched out his hand in a way that was almost a plea.

'I'm here,' she said, hurrying over and clasping his hand. 'I'll always be here.'

'Will you? *Will you?*'

'Of course. I promise.'

He lifted his head and she gasped at the tragedy and desolation in his eyes.

'It's easy to promise.' He groaned. 'But nobody is always there.'

'Did she promise?' Charlotte asked softly.

'Many times. She vowed she'd never leave me—never in life—and she didn't leave me in life. She left me in death. She was so young. Her death was the one thing we never thought of.'

'How did it happen?'

'She went to Florence one afternoon, to do some shopping. I saw her driving home and waved. The next minute the car swerved, hit a rock by the roadside and overturned. I managed to get her to hospital. She was terribly hurt, there seemed to be no hope, but still I—'

He choked into silence. His eyes were closed again, as though he'd chosen to retreat back into a private world. But his fingers clutched Charlotte's hand convulsively. She laid her other hand over his, sending him comfort in the only way that could reach him.

'She lived for two days,' Lucio said softly. 'Mostly she was unconscious. Sometimes she opened her eyes and seemed to look at me, but even then I'm not sure if she could see me. I begged her not to leave me, to forgive me—'

'Forgive you? Surely she had nothing to forgive?'

'I may have caused her accident, waving when I did. Perhaps I distracted her, perhaps she waved back and took her attention off the road—'

'Lucio, don't—'

'But for me she might not have died.'

'That's just your imagination—how could you be sure?'

'I can't,' he said with soft violence. 'That's what's so terrible. I'll never know but I'll believe it all my days. I did it. *I killed her.* How can I ever have peace?'

'By asking yourself what she would have wanted,'

Charlotte said. 'Maria loved you. Surely you know that, deep in your heart?'

'Yes, I—'

'If you let this idea wreck your life you're being unfair to her, to her memory. Did she manage to say anything to you before she died?'

'Yes, she said she loved me.'

'Of course she did. Her last message to you was love, so that you would always remember it. She was trying to give you peace. Don't refuse her the last thing she wanted.'

He didn't reply, and she wondered if he'd even heard her. But then he leaned towards her, resting his head on her shoulder so that his face was hidden. His clasp on her tightened, sending her a silent message, and she clasped him back.

Would she one day regret what she was doing? Instead of banishing Maria's ghost she was restoring her to him. But nothing mattered but to ease Lucio's suffering and perhaps even give him some happiness. If it meant that she herself was the loser, she would find a way to live with that.

'I'm sorry,' he said. 'I shouldn't really be talking to you about this.'

'Why not? Remember what we said? Friends, allies, comrades? I'm the best friend you have, and you can tell me anything, any time.'

'Thank you,' he said softly. 'You don't know what a comfort that is—what it's like never to be able to talk to anyone.'

'What about Fiorella?'

'I never could. Maria's death caused her such pain—how could I make it worse? And then her husband died only a year later. She's suffered such unbearable pain.'

'So you protected her,' Charlotte said.

He protected everyone, and they had all left him alone,

she thought, her heart aching for him. But he wasn't alone now, and she must let him know that.

'You're exhausted,' she said. 'Lie down and go to sleep.'

Gently she pulled him down onto the bed, drawing him across her so that his head rested on her chest. A mirror in the corner gave her a slight glimpse of his face, enough to show that his eyes were closed. Everything about him radiated contentment.

'That's it,' she whispered. 'Now you can do whatever you like. We can talk if you like, because there's nothing you can't tell me, and I promise never to do anything to make you regret it. Or you can sleep in my arms. And don't worry about anything, because your friend is here.'

He stirred, and she felt the warmth of his breath against her skin. She stroked his face, laying her lips against his hair, whispering, 'She's here, and she'll always be here, as long as you need her.'

CHAPTER TEN

SHE awoke to the sound of music from the canal below. It was the day of the glorious water parade, and the wedding to the sea, and all Venice was alive with pleasure and expectation.

'It's going to be wonderful,' she murmured, reaching for him.

He wasn't there.

In an instant she was back in the nightmare, alone, rejected, unwanted, first by her family, then by Lucio.

'No,' she groaned. 'No, *no, oh, please, no!*'

At once the door was flung open and Lucio hurried in.

'Charlotte, whatever's the matter?'

'Nothing,' she choked, 'nothing—I—'

He sat on the bed, placing his hands on her shoulders.

'Then why are you crying? Why were you calling out? What's upset you?'

'Just a nightmare,' she floundered frantically. 'I can't even remember....'

You vanished and all my demons began shrieking again.

But she couldn't tell him that.

'No time for nightmares,' he said merrily. 'Franco has just called to say he expects us on his boat at nine o'clock. So I've ordered breakfast up here and then we must be off.'

He kissed her cheek and retreated to the bathroom.

Left alone, she took some deep breaths, trying to focus her mind on the day ahead, but it was hard when dazzling memories still lived inside her. Last night they had achieved perfect physical union, and it had been beautiful. But just as beautiful had been the emotional and mental union that followed. He had called her his friend, and she had assured him that was what she would be.

But a friend could be a lover, too, and in time he would understand that. This was her promise to herself.

By nine o'clock a multitude of boats had gathered in the water next to St Mark's Square, and within fifteen minutes they had moved off in a colourful parade across the lagoon to the Lido island. Rowers in medieval costume hauled on the oars as they crossed the glittering water.

Franco had hired a magnificent vessel, big enough for thirty people; he leaned over the side enjoying the procession as it glided over the lagoon to the Lido island. There they were joined by an even more magnificent boat, known as the *Serenissima*.

Once the Doge of Venice had performed the ceremony of tossing a golden ring into the water, intoning in Latin, *'Desponsamus te, Mare, in signum veri perpetique dominii.'*

'I marry you, O sea, as a sign of permanent dominium.'

Now the ceremony was performed by the mayor. Cheers went up as he made the triumphant declaration.

A few feet away Charlotte could see Franco's son and his fiancée, gazing into each other's eyes.

'Presto,' he said joyously. *'Presto mi sposera.'*

'They were going to marry in autumn,' Franco confided. 'But now he's pressing her to marry him quickly. That's the effect this ceremony can have. It makes people long for their own marriage.'

He turned away, calling to his other guests.

'Perhaps he's got a point,' Lucio observed.

'How do you mean?'

'Maybe it's time we were talking about marriage. We agreed that when you'd been here for a while you'd make a decision about staying. I can't believe you want to go away. You've fitted in from the beginning. Everyone likes you and they're all eagerly waiting for the announcement of our forthcoming marriage. Perhaps we should give it to them.'

So that was his idea of a proposal, she thought. After the night they'd shared she'd expected something that at least acknowledged their shared passion. Instead there was reasoned logic and efficiency.

'Only if we actually decide to marry,' she said. 'I don't remember us doing that.'

'Sorry. Where are my manners? Charlotte, I want to marry you. I think we can have a good life together, not just because of our baby, but because you really belong here. You've felt that, too, haven't you?'

'It's true that I like it here. As you say, I've been made welcome and people are kind. But there's more to marriage than that.'

'Of course there is. A man and a woman have to go well together, and we do.'

'Yes, we're good friends,' she said wryly.

'That's important. The strongest couples can be the ones who started out knowing they could rely on each other. You know how deeply I trust you. We spoke of it last night. Surely you remember that?'

'Yes,' she murmured. 'I remember last night.'

'So do I, and there were things about it that mean the world to me. There's such freedom in being able to talk to you. You know things about me that nobody else knows, or ever will, and I'm so glad. And I hope you have the same feeling that you can rely on me.

'Do you think I won't work to make you happy? I promise that I will. Anything you want, if it's humanly possible I'll see that you get it.'

Anything I want, she thought wryly. *Your heart? Your love? But you're telling me they wouldn't be humanly possible.*

How had this happened? Only a little time ago she'd vowed to be satisfied with their close friendship and not ask for more until later. Simple common sense.

Common sense hurt more than she'd suspected, but now she realised sadly that it was all she had. And it wasn't enough.

'Don't rush me, Lucio,' she said. 'I know we've talked about where this road is leading, but I'm not sure yet.'

He looked astounded, and she understood. How could she refuse him after last night? She didn't comprehend it herself. She only knew that she wouldn't be rushed into handing over her life to a man whose feelings fell short of hers.

'We'll talk about it later,' she said.

'All right. When we get home tonight.'

'No, I meant in a few weeks.'

His face grew tense. 'Last night you promised to always to be there for me.'

She wished he hadn't said that. The memory was so painful that she winced. He saw it and misunderstood.

'I see,' he said with a touch of bitterness. 'You regret it already.'

'No, I don't, but we were talking of friendship. As a friend, and the mother of your child, I'll never entirely leave you but I still need some independence. Just how much I need I'm not sure.'

'Come along!' That was Franco, coming towards them

to sweep them back up into the festivities. 'We still have a wonderful day before us.'

'I'm not sure how long we can stay,' Charlotte faltered.

'But you must see the races,' Franco protested.

'And after that we must return,' Lucio said. 'We're grateful for your hospitality, but I have urgent things to attend to at home. I'll arrange matters through my lawyer, and come back soon to sign papers.'

For the rest of the day they smiled and said what was appropriate before travelling back across the lagoon. All around them Venice was enjoying colourful celebrations, but they could take no part. Hurrying back to the hotel they packed and prepared to leave. A motorboat was hired to take them to Piazzale Roma, and there they collected the car and drove across the bridge to the mainland.

As they drove back to Tuscany in the twilight Charlotte gazed out of the window and wondered at herself. She'd been offered so much that she longed for, yet without warning her old rebelliousness had come alive, saying that it wasn't good enough. Perhaps she had devastated the rest of her life. Maybe the day would dawn when she cursed herself for being unrealistic.

But it made no difference. The streak of sheer cussedness that had always intervened at inappropriate moments had cropped up now.

And, most incredible of all, she had no regrets.

For the next few weeks they saw little of each other. Lucio spent much time at distant vineyards and for once it was a relief to Charlotte that he wasn't there.

When he came home he behaved courteously, constantly asking after her health, patting her growing bulge protectively and accompanying her on a check-up visit to the doctor. Wryly she recalled a friend back home whose husband distanced himself from the details of her pregnancy. When she protested at his lack of emotional support he was astounded. He gave her plenty of money, didn't he? The rest was 'women's stuff'.

She would really envy me, Charlotte thought wryly. *Lucio is everything her husband isn't: kind, attentive, interested, concerned.*

And yet—and yet...

She tried to distract herself by going online to talk to her family, and found Matt putting a call through to her. It was good to see his face on the screen. In the past she had often found more comfort in his presence than with her sisters. They were alike in many ways, sharing jokes, standing back and taking the same ironic view of life. She could tell him what had happened, and count on him to be supportive.

But this time his support took a more detached stance than she had expected.

'Ellie told me she was worried that this guy hasn't proposed to you. Now you're telling me that he did propose and you turned him down. Are you nuts?'

'I didn't turn him down. I just said we could talk about it later.'

'Listen, there are ways and ways of rejecting someone, and saying you'll talk later is one of the best known. You're nuts about him, you admit that, yet you're taking the risk of losing him altogether. Why? Because he didn't say all the right words and you want to kick him in the teeth.'

'That wasn't it. Truly, Matt, I wasn't just being awkward—'

'Oh, I reckon you were. As long as I've known you, you've been famous for awkwardness. You could get a medal for it. How many times have I rescued you from your own foolishness?'

'About as often as I've rescued you.'

'OK. Check. But now it's *me* riding to *your* rescue. I don't want to see you break your heart because you're too stubborn to admit you're an idiot.'

'All right, all *right*! I admit it. But what can I do?'

'You'll have to work that out for yourself, but whatever it is, act fast. Time isn't on your side.'

'I know that,' she said, patting her stomach.

'I don't just mean the baby, although it's true your time for playing the seductress is running out.'

'Thanks!'

'I'm talking practicalities. You're not Italian, so if you want to marry in Italy you'll need to produce a mountain of paperwork, starting with your birth certificate.'

'Oh, heavens! I never thought of that.'

'Time to be practical, decide if you really want to marry him and, if so, get things organised.'

'Yes, I guess you're right.'

'Let me know what happens.'

However blunt his words she knew Matt had spoken out of concern for her. *He's right,* she thought. *If I lose Lucio it's all my own fault. I played it so stupidly but I couldn't help it. I gambled on all or nothing and it looks like I'm going to get nothing. It's going to take a miracle to bring us together, and miracles don't seem to happen any more.*

If only Lucio was here now and she could say everything she was feeling. But another two weeks passed while he stayed away. She used the time investigating the other part of Matt's warning, and found it to be alarmingly accurate.

On the day Lucio was expected home he was late. She stood at her window, desperately looking for him, and as soon as she saw him she realised that something was up.

He was driving faster than usual, and when he parked the car he leapt out, looked up at the window and ran inside.

'All right,' he said, coming into her room. 'Enough's enough. I've been doing a lot of thinking on the way home, and you've played too many games with me. I want an answer.'

'I'm not playing games—'

'Then give me an answer and make it yes.' He grasped her arm. 'Charlotte, I mean it. You've driven me to distraction and I can't take any more. I know I made a mess of the proposal. I'm not the kind of man who can go down on one knee, but I asked you because I really want you.'

'Lucio, I—*aargh!*' She broke off in a gasp.

'What is it?' he cried. 'Charlotte what happened? Did I hurt you? I didn't mean to—I barely touched you.'

'No, you didn't hurt me,' she said in a dazed voice. *'Aaah!'* She gasped again.

'What happened?' he demanded, in agony.

'The baby—it's moving. It kicked me. There! It's done it again.'

'You mean—?'

She looked down, running her fingers over her slight bulge. 'Just there. You can feel the movement from the outside.'

Tentatively, almost fearfully, he touched the bulge with his fingertips.

'Can you feel it?' she asked.

'No—yes—I think. But is it all right? Should that be happening?'

'Of course. I've felt movement before but not as much as this. It's good. It means our child is strong and healthy. It'll have a good start in the world.'

With a sigh that was almost a groan he knelt so that he could lay his head against her. He kept it there, not mov-

ing for a few moments. Then he raised his face far enough
for her to see his closed eyes and gentle, ecstatic smile.

'Yes,' he whispered ecstatically. 'I can feel it—*yes*.'

He opened his eyes to see her looking down at him.

'Yes,' he repeated. 'It's wonderful.'

'Yes,' she agreed, taking his face between her hands.

'Charlotte—please—'

'Yes,' she repeated.

'You don't understand what I'm saying….'

'But I do.' She held his gaze for a moment. 'And my
answer is yes.'

He rose, looking at her intently. 'You mean it?'

'Yes.'

'Marriage?'

'Yes.'

He put his arms around her, drawing her a little closer,
but giving her extra room for the bulge.

'We're going to have a child,' he said in a dazed voice.
'I already knew that but…suddenly it's more real.'

That was also how she felt. She'd longed for a miracle,
and it had been given to her. Now they had shared this moment no power on earth could have made her refuse him.
Filled with contentment she rested her head on his shoulder, then tensed as there was another kick.

'Ah!' she gasped.

'Does it hurt?' he asked, full of tender anxiety for her.

'No, it just means our offspring is establishing a personality already. It's probably a boy. With a kick like that
he's going to be a soccer player.'

'Or a politician,' Lucio said with a wry smile. 'He already knows how to get the better of people. Remember I
said I couldn't go down on one knee?'

'And he made you do just that,' she said. 'Your first trial
of strength and he won.'

He hugged her. 'I'm really looking forward to meeting this lad. Come on, let's tell everyone.'

He led her out of the bedroom and down the stairs, holding her gently but firmly.

'Be careful,' he said.

'Lucio I've used these stairs a hundred times without an accident.'

'I know but…it's different now.'

'Yes, it is,' she said, taking his hand and smiling happily.

Downstairs they told Fiorella, who went into ecstasies.

'We must arrange everything as soon as possible,' she said. 'Charlotte, my dear, have you told your family that you're getting married?'

'No, we wanted to tell you first. I'll email them, and later we'll go online and talk.'

'And then you can introduce us. We will all meet as one big happy family.'

'We can't do it all at once. My family live a long way apart, Ellie in Texas and my parents in New York, Matt in Boston and Alex in Australia. I could tell Matt and Ellie now. We're only five hours ahead of them.'

She fetched her laptop, set it up and connected to the program that provided the video link. A glance at her list of contacts showed that neither Matt nor Ellie was online.

'No problem,' she said. 'I'll email them, tell them the news and say let's talk face to face.'

'But if they live miles apart how can you get them together?' Fiorella asked.

'They won't really be together but I can put them on the screen at the same time,' Charlotte said. 'There, the emails are on their way. If they receive them soon they'll come online without delay.'

After a few moments an email arrived announcing that Alex was away today but would be back by evening.

'Her evening,' Charlotte said. 'We'll all be asleep by then. But I'll find a way to contact her soon. Ah, I think that's Matt.'

Sure enough a flashing light was announcing Matt's arrival on screen.

'Did you really write what I thought you wrote?' he demanded. 'You're getting married?'

'Yes, and this is Lucio, my fiancé,' Charlotte said, speaking quickly in case Matt should say something that would reveal his earlier advice.

But he was tact itself, congratulating them both. Everything went well. Courtesies were exchanged. Lucio introduced his mother. Then a bleep announced that Ellie had made contact and she, too, arrived on screen, smiling and pleasant.

When all the introductions had been made again Ellie said, 'So now you've got to come to Larkville, Charlotte, and of course Lucio will come with you.'

'They're celebrating Clay Calhoun's life in October,' Charlotte explained to Lucio.

'Matt and I are invited because he was our father,' Ellie said, 'but they want you and Alex there so we can all be together.'

'But I told you, I'll be giving birth about then,' Charlotte said. 'I'd love to come, but it won't be possible. Such a shame.'

'You might give birth early,' Ellie protested. 'Promise you'll come if you can.'

'If I can,' Charlotte agreed. She could sense that this conversation troubled Lucio and was eager to bring it to a close.

More smiles, congratulations, good wishes, and the links were closed down.

'It's nice that they want us to go over there,' Charlotte said. 'But I don't think it will be very practical.' She looked down at the bulge.

'It's not just that,' Lucio said. 'If you do go, it'll have to be without me. October is when we harvest the grapes. I couldn't possibly leave here.'

'Of course not,' she said. 'And I couldn't leave either, even if I'd already given birth. It would be too soon. Don't worry, it's not going to arise.'

His brow cleared. 'I hope not. I'd hate to refuse you the first thing you've asked me.'

'So now we have a lot of talking to do,' Fiorella declared. 'You must set the date, send out the invitations. How soon can we make it happen? How about the week after next.'

'I'm afraid not,' Lucio said. 'Because Charlotte wasn't born here we have to get a lot of paperwork—her birth certificate, a sworn declaration that she's free to marry which must be translated, annotated and taken round a load of offices. It can take a few weeks.'

Charlotte stared. This was what she'd been preparing to tell him, but he already knew.

'Oh, what a pity,' Fiorella mourned. 'Well, you'd better get to work on all those papers, and we'll have the wedding as soon as possible.'

She bustled away, full of plans.

'I know what you're thinking.' Lucio sighed. 'How do I know all this? I must have been checking up, which means I took it for granted that you'd say yes. Or I was planning to pressure you, which makes me all sorts of an undesirable character. It's not like that, Charlotte, truly. I just wanted to be ready for anything. Don't be angry with me.'

'Have you finished? Then listen to what I have to say. I know about all these formalities and how long they can take, and I've been doing something about it. Matt's already sent me the birth certificate and a sworn statement that I'd never been married.'

'You've been doing all that?' Lucio breathed.

'Yes. There's still some work left to do....'

'But you did this? So you meant to marry me?'

'I suppose I did. I've got as much ready as I can, but there's still some—'

She broke off as he seized her in his arms, and after that there were no more words.

Two days later he drove her into Florence.

'There's something I want to show you,' he said, leading her along the street until they reached a jewellery shop and pointing to a double-stranded pearl necklace in the window. 'What do you think of that?'

'It's really beautiful.'

'Would it make a beautiful wedding present?'

'Oh, yes.'

'Let's go in.'

In the shop she tried on the necklace and loved the way it looked on her. It was a wedding gift to make any bride happy.

'But what am I going to give you?' she asked as they left the shop.

He glanced down at her waist.

'You're already giving me the best gift in the world,' he said. 'I don't need anything else.'

She knew a burst of happiness. Everything was going to be all right, after all.

CHAPTER ELEVEN

FOR the next two weeks they were seldom out of each other's company, travelling from office to office, presenting documents, signing paperwork.

'So now everything's in order,' she said as they sat in a café, having just left the American consulate in Florence. 'Everything signed, every permission granted. The perfect business deal.'

'I wish I could say you were wrong—' he grinned '—but I've had commercial ventures that were less complex than this.'

'You can't blame them for being careful about foreigners,' she pointed out. 'I might have a dozen ex-husbands back in the States.'

'I'm not even going to ask you about that. I recognise one of your wicked moods. You'd enjoy freezing me with terror.'

'Well, anyway, we made it to the end, and we're all set for the business deal of the century. Shake?'

'Shake.' He took her extended hand.

She often teased him like this these days. It saved her from the embarrassment of making it obvious that her feelings were stronger and deeper than his.

It wasn't the kind of wedding a woman would dream of, especially with a man she loved. But it was better than parting from him. Inwardly she sent a silent message of gratitude to Matt, who had alerted her to danger in good time.

When everything was sorted they opted for a speedy marriage on the first available date. Instead of the huge array of business contacts that would normally have revelled in the public relations, only the very closest friends were invited.

Fiorella helped her choose a wedding gift for Lucio, using her knowledge of him to direct Charlotte to a valuable collection of books about the history of the wine industry. To add a more personal touch she bought a vest with the logo of the local soccer team, and wrote a note saying, 'You can give him this when he's ready.'

It was settled between them now that she was to bear a son who would make his name in some profession where his mighty kick would give him an advantage. When Lucio opened the parcel his delighted grin told her that he understood the joke. His hug was fierce and appreciative.

'We haven't discussed a honeymoon yet,' he reminded her.

'It's not really the right time, is it? Let's wait until after October when the harvest is in.'

He kissed her. 'You're going to be a great vintner's wife. But have a think about the honeymoon, too.'

In fact, she already knew where she wanted to go for their honeymoon, but she would wait for the right time to tell him.

The big disappointment was that none of her family could come to Tuscany for the wedding.

'Your father isn't well enough to make the journey,' her mother said. 'And I can't leave him alone.'

'Oh, I wish I could come,' Alex said.

'But Australia's so far away.' Charlotte sighed.

Ellie and Matt were also too tied up with events in their own lives. There was a triumphant video link during which they toasted Lucio and Charlotte, who raised their glasses in return.

'But it's not the same as seeing them,' Charlotte sighed to Lucio afterwards.

'No, it would have given you the chance to feel part of the family again,' he said. 'But there'll be another chance. There has to be.'

'I don't see how. Going to Larkville in October would have been a good chance because everyone will be there together, but that's out of the question. I'll be giving birth, and even if I'm not, *you'll* be giving birth.'

'Eh?'

'To a grape harvest.'

'Oh, I see. Yes, I suppose it is a bit like producing an offspring, being a proud father—'

'Telling the world that your creation is better than the next father's?' she suggested.

'Right. Or letting the world find out for itself.'

'Which it'll do at our wedding reception,' she said lightly.

But he wasn't fooled by her attempt to put a brave face on things.

'I'm really sorry your family can't be there. I wish there was something I could do.'

'But even you can't tell the grapes to wait another couple of weeks,' she said lightly. 'I'll get over it. Thanks anyway. Now get outta here. I'm going to put on my party dress and I don't want you to see it first.'

Although there would be no lavish reception there was a small party three nights before the wedding. Chief among the guests was Franco, who clearly felt he could take some credit for bringing the wedding about, and made a theatrical speech.

'What is life without love?' he demanded. 'There is no more beautiful sight in the world than two people deeply in love, vowing fidelity to each other. Together they will face the challenges that the world will throw at them, and because they are united they will be strong. Because they are one in heart they will achieve victory.

'My friends, a couple in love is an inspiration to us all.' He raised his glass. 'Let us toast them.'

Everybody rose, lifting their glasses and uttering congratulations. Lucio rose also, raising his glass to her. She responded in the same way, managing to look blissfully happy, and refusing to heed the irony in the speech. Lucio was her promised husband, as she was his promised wife. Together they would play the role of devoted lovers.

Somebody struck up on the piano, and there was dancing. The guests roared their appreciation as Lucio led her onto the floor and took her into his arms for a slow, dreamy waltz.

'You look beautiful,' he said. 'That's a lovely dress.'

'Thank you.'

'I'm wearing something special, too.'

'Yes, you look very handsome in that dinner jacket.'

'I don't mean that. I mean underneath. Look.'

He released her hand and slipped his fingers into the front of his shirt, pulling the edges apart just far enough for her to see—

'The soccer vest!' she exclaimed. 'You're wearing it.'

'It's the cleverest gift you could have bought me. I wear it in honour of you, and of him.'

'Oh, you—' She began to laugh. 'Of all the things to— honestly!'

Now he, too, was laughing, drawing her closer so that

she laid her head against him and together they shook with amusement. All around them their guests sighed with pleasure, for surely nobody had ever seen a couple so deeply in love.

'You don't mind if I vanish for a stag night?' Lucio had asked her.

Since he was already attired for an evening out the question was purely rhetorical.

'I'm tempted to say yes I mind a lot, just to see what you'd do,' she teased. 'Don't be silly, of course you must have a stag night. You don't want people to think you're henpecked, do you? Not yet anyway.'

'Yes, we'll wait a decent interval before you crack the whip,' he said, grinning.

'Oh, you think that's a joke, do you?' She pointed to the door and said theatrically, 'Get out of here at once!'

'Yes, ma'am, no, ma'am.' He saluted and hurried out to the car where his friends were waiting. She waved him off, thinking that these were the best moments between them, for now they were most completely in tune.

She was awoken in the early hours by the sound of the car arriving outside, and went hurriedly down to open the door. Having delivered him safely his friends said farewell and drove off.

For a man returning from a stag night he seemed relatively sober, although sleepy, and he regarded the stairs with dismay.

'I'll help you up them,' she said.

Together they managed to reach the top, but there he clutched the railing and murmured, 'I don't think I can go any farther.'

'Never mind. You can sleep in my room. It's just here. Come on.'

She got him as far as the bed where he dropped down with relief.

'Did you enjoy yourself?' she asked.

'Mmm!'

'Good. That's all that matters.'

He turned his head on the pillow. 'You're a very understanding woman.'

'If I'm going to marry you I'll need to be.'

'Mmm!'

'Go to sleep.' She chuckled.

His eyes were already closed, and he was breathing deeply. She watched him tenderly for a moment, then leaned down and kissed him on the mouth.

'Sleep well, and don't worry about anything,' she said.

Still without opening his eyes he moved his arms so that they enfolded her, drawing her close. Happily she snuggled up, her head on his shoulder.

'Mmm!' he said again.

'Mmm!' she agreed.

'I'm sorry,' he murmured.

'No need.'

'The baby.' He sighed. 'I feel guilty.'

'There's nothing to feel guilty about,' she assured him.

His next words came in such a soft whisper that she had to lean closer to hear it. What she heard made her tense, wondering if she'd misheard, for surely it wasn't possible—surely…?

'I wasn't fair,' he murmured. 'You wanted to wait until we were married…I wouldn't listen…forgive me—'

'But back then we weren't—'

'I begged and begged until you gave in…not fair…but when we're married, nobody will know that we…our secret…our secret. Say you forgive me.'

She took a deep breath, summoning her resolve. She

didn't want to do what she was about to, but there was no choice if he was to have peace.

'There's nothing to forgive, my darling,' she assured him. 'I want you as much as you want me. We love each other, and we'll be married soon.'

She had known about the burden he carried, blaming himself for Maria's death. Now she knew there had been another burden all along, one which haunted him, sleeping and waking.

They had been lovers, and Maria had conceived his child. Doubtless her pregnancy had been in the very early days, so nobody else suspected, and the truth could be hidden until after the wedding. But she had died, and the child had died with her. There had been nobody he could tell, and even now he staggered under a terrifying sense of guilt.

'Dead,' he was murmuring, 'my fault.'

'*No!*' she said fiercely. 'None of it is your fault.'

But she despaired of convincing him. She'd known that he was haunted by the fear that he had inadvertently killed Maria. Now she saw that his feeling of guilt and self-blame extended to the death of his first unborn child. It was wildly unlikely and illogical, but it shed a new light over his protectiveness towards her, his fear of making love.

The thought of his suffering made her weep, and she held him tenderly against her.

He stirred, clasping her more tightly. 'Are you there?'

'Yes, I'm here. Hold on to me, and go to sleep, my darling.'

He sighed and she felt the tension drain out of him. Now he was at peace, and all was well as long as she was there for him. She held him gently until they both fell asleep.

She awoke first, to find that neither of them had moved in two hours. His eyes were still closed, but as she watched they opened slowly. For a moment his expression was vague, but then he smiled as though something had eased his mind.

'So much for a macho stag night,' he said.

'As long as you enjoyed yourself, what else matters?'

He eased himself up, moving carefully.

'I'm sorry,' he said. 'I had no right to bother you while I was in that state.'

'What state? You didn't do anything objectionable. You just couldn't stay awake.'

'I probably talked a lot of nonsense.'

'Not a thing. Stop worrying.'

He made his way to the door, but looked back, seeming troubled.

'I didn't…say anything, did I?'

'Not that I remember. Bye.'

He hesitated a moment. 'Bye.'

He gave her a final look, and quietly departed.

The words were there in his mind, she thought, but he wasn't sure if it was a memory or a dream. Let him think of it as a dream. That would be easier for him.

In the beginning loving him had seemed simple. Now she knew it wasn't going to be simple at all.

But she had made her choice, and nothing was going to make her change it.

Franco was going to give the bride away. He arrived just as Lucio was about to leave for the church, slapped him on the shoulder and told him to be off. Then he ushered the bride out to his chauffeur-driven car, with Fiorella following.

'Have you got the ring?' he asked before they started.

For this marriage ceremony there were two matching rings, which the bride and groom exchanged.

'Here,' Fiorella said, holding it up. 'Everything has been taken care of.'

Everything taken care of, Charlotte mused as the car headed for Siena. But there were still so many questions unanswered, questions that might never be answered because they would never be asked.

As soon as she entered the church she could see down the aisle to where Lucio was waiting for her. Enrico gave her his arm, the organ struck up and she began to advance. As she grew closer to Lucio she could see that his eyes never left her for a moment. There was a contented look in them that filled her with pleasure, and as she neared he reached out to her, taking her hand and drawing her to his side.

The first part of the service was formal, but at last it was time to exchange rings. Slowly Lucio slid the ring on her finger, saying quietly, 'Take this ring as a sign of my love and fidelity.'

Then it was her turn. Raising his hand, she slid the ring onto it, murmuring, 'Take this ring as a sign of my love and fidelity.'

Love and fidelity.

She meant the words with all her heart. Looking up into his face she saw there an intensity of emotion that gave her a surge of joy.

The moment came. She felt his lips on hers, not passionate as she had known them, but firm and gentle. A brief trip to the sacristy to sign the register, then a return to the church where they were proclaimed husband and wife as they began the journey along the aisle, hand in hand.

He is my husband and I am his wife. Now I belong to him and he...perhaps he belongs to me—perhaps—or at least to our son.

The rest of the day was a triumph. To Charlotte it

seemed that almost everything she had wished for was coming true. Acceptance, a home, a new family.

At last it was time to retire to bed, now a shared room with Lucio. She climbed the stairs on his arm, followed him into their room and accepted his help undressing.

'I'm worn out,' she said sleepily. 'Who'd have thought getting married was so exhausting?'

'True,' he said, yawning. 'And I've got to be up early tomorrow to talk to Toni, my head steward. He's got some ideas for next year that we'll have to plan for now.'

'Goodnight,' she said.

His kissed her forehead. 'Goodnight, my dear.'

This was their wedding night.

The months moved on. Now she was glad to live a slower, more relaxed life, her thoughts always focused on the future. Eight weeks until the birth, seven, six—

'Oh, I can't bear this,' Fiorella squealed. 'We want to welcome him into the world and he keeps us waiting.'

'No, he doesn't,' Charlotte said with mock indignation. 'He's not late, it's just us that's impatient.'

'We are all impatient,' Elizabetta chimed in.

Charlotte regarded her fondly. By now she knew Elizabetta's history. As a young woman she had been married, and pregnant. But the child had been born early, at only seven months. Within a few hours it was dead, and Elizabeth, too, had nearly died. Charlotte felt that many a woman in her position would have felt resentful of another woman's luck. But Elizabetta was too generous and warm-hearted to feel bitterness towards her.

As autumn gradually appeared it was a pleasure to sit on the terrace, watching the setting sun, drinking in the warmth.

One evening she was sitting there feeling at one with

life, with the world and everyone in it. In the distance she could see a car that she recognised as Toni's. Doubtless he was on his way to make a report to Lucio. She would go inside and arrange with the kitchen staff to have his favourite coffee ready.

Exactly what happened next she was never sure, but as she passed across the tops of the steps that led down from the terrace to the ground, she felt her foot turn underneath her. She tried to grasp something to save herself but it was too late. She felt a bang as her head hit the stone railings, and the next moment she was tumbling down the stairs.

From somewhere far above she heard a scream. Then she blacked out.

CHAPTER TWELVE

THE pain was everywhere, sweeping through her in waves. She had the strange sensation of sleeping while being racked by gusts of agony. She tried to reach out, pleading for help, but it was hard to move.

From a great distance came voices: Fiorella screaming, 'Call an ambulance!' Then Lucio crying, 'Charlotte—oh, my God, what happened? Charlotte, speak to me, please. Charlotte! *Charlotte!*'

She tried to respond but his voice faded as she blacked out. But after a while she managed to open her eyes a little, and see strangers, wearing uniforms. One of them, a woman, was saying, 'Lift her this way—careful, easy now. How did this happen? Did anyone see it?'

'She fell down the steps of the terrace and hit her head.' That was Enrico's voice. 'I saw it from a distance but, oh, heavens! I was too far away to help her.'

'My baby,' she whispered.

The strange woman's voice replied, 'We'll soon have you in the hospital. Hold on.'

She was being carried. From somewhere came the sound of doors opening, then being slammed shut, engines roaring.

'Lucio?' she cried.

'I'm here,' he said, close to her ear. His hand grasped hers. 'Can you feel me?'

'Yes, yes…'

'Can't this ambulance go any faster?' he shouted.

The woman's voice said, 'I've alerted the hospital. They're ready for her. They'll do their best to save the baby.'

'They've got to save *her*.' Lucio's cry was almost a scream. 'Don't you understand? *Her!*'

She tried to open her eyes but the blackness was sweeping over her again. It blended with the roar of the engine to create a world in which there was only fear, pain, uncertainty.

Then she was being hurried along a hospital corridor on a trolley, lifted onto a bed. A doctor and nurse regarded her anxiously, and a fierce pain convulsed her.

'The baby,' she gasped. 'I think it's coming.'

'No,' Lucio groaned. 'Please, Doctor, don't let that happen. She's so weak and hurt, it'll be too much for her.'

'If it's really started,' the doctor said, 'then there's not a lot— Stand back please.'

He leaned over Charlotte, asking her urgent questions, which she found it hard to answer with her consciousness coming and going.

'Save my baby,' she begged. '*Please*—save my baby— *Aaah!*'

Now there was no doubt that her labour had started, nearly six weeks early. The focus of her life, the child that was to unite her and Lucio on the road ahead, was in danger.

Nothing was in her control. The urge to push possessed her and she bore down, struggling against the pain, groaning.

'No,' she whispered. 'No, please—I can't do this….'

'I'm afraid you must,' the doctor said. 'But we'll do everything we can to make it easier.'

'What can *I* do?' Lucio demanded harshly.

'Be here and support her—that is, if you feel you can. Some fathers can't bear to be present during childbirth.'

'Then they ought to be shot,' Lucio snapped. 'Just try to get rid of me.'

He dropped to his knees beside Charlotte so that his face was close to hers.

'Did you hear that? I'm staying here. We're going to do this together—no, that's not really true. You're going to be doing all the hard work, I'm afraid. But I'll be here, cheering you on.'

'And him,' she whispered. 'Our little soccer star?'

'And him. Right into the goal.'

'Always on the winning side. *Aaah!*'

'That's it,' said the doctor. 'Push. Excellent.'

To brace herself against the pain she clenched her hand tighter than ever, so that Lucio gave a sharp groan at the fierceness of her grip.

'Sorry,' she gasped.

'Never mind me,' he said. 'You just worry about yourself—and him.'

Her head was aching badly. A nurse tended it, wiping away a trickle of blood. In her confusion she believed that there could be no way out of this. She was trapped in a desert of agony and dread, and there seemed no escape. She had sworn to help Lucio in every way, and if the child died it would destroy him.

But then she felt Lucio holding her, sending a message of comfort and love that seemed to reach her down the corridors of eternity. She yearned towards him, not with her hands but with her heart and soul, knowing that now he was all she had in the world.

She had no idea how long the birth took. She only knew that nothing else existed in the world. Then, after a while, the pain ceased to attack her and faded to a constant ache. Swamped by exhaustion she vaguely sensed that something was gone from inside her.

'My baby,' she whispered. 'Please—'

Lucio leaned close.

'Our daughter was born safely,' he murmured. 'She's been put into an incubator, and she'll be there for several days.'

'She's…going to live?'

'It's too soon to be certain, but they're hopeful.'

'You said…daughter.'

'Yes,' he told her gently. 'We have a little girl.'

She wanted to say something but the world faded again. Surely Lucio had wanted a son, and she had disappointed him? What would he say? What would he feel?

Now she was on fire. Heat was all around her, inside her, destroying thought and consciousness. Destroying her. Voices again, talking about fever. But one voice dominated them all.

'Charlotte, listen to me. Can you hear me, wherever you are? You must, *you must hear me.*'

'Yes, yes…'

He seemed to become more agitated.

'You've got to hang on. You've got a fever but they're giving you something for it, and you're going to be all right. You understand that? You're going to be all right, but you've got to fight. I'm here. We'll fight together. You can't go off anywhere now, not when you've made me love you so much. That would be really inconsiderate, wouldn't it? And I know you'd never do that.'

His voice grew more gentle.

'Or perhaps you don't know how much I love you. I've

never said it but you're clever enough to understand without words. Mostly I didn't understand it myself. I don't think I really knew until now, but you knew. Sure you did, because you know everything. You saw through me from the start, and let's face it, you've had me dancing to your tune.

'But you can't do that and then just vanish. You can't just abandon me. Charlotte, my love, can you hear me? *Can you hear me?*'

His voice seemed to follow her into the engulfing darkness, holding on to her, never leaving her, so that at last she felt the darkness yield and give her back to him.

'Open your eyes, darling. That's it! Look, everyone, she's awake!' Lucio's face, haggard and unshaven but full of joy, hovered above her. 'Can you see me?'

'Yes, I knew you were there,' she murmured.

'I'm still here. I always will be.'

'Our baby—?'

'She's fine. She's beautiful. The doctors say you're both doing well, but if you knew how scared I've been.'

She could believe it. He looked terrible, like a man who hadn't slept for a year.

Suddenly she remembered him as he'd been at their first meeting in Rome, just over seven months ago; wickedly handsome, vibrant, sophisticated, dominating the company with the power of his looks and personality, alive to every challenge, in control of every situation.

Now, even through several days' growth of beard, she could see lines that hadn't been there before. And his eyes told a story of agony. It was like looking at a totally different man. Who had done this cruel thing to him?

She had.

'There was no need to be scared,' she told him.

'How can you know that? If you could have seen how you looked—as though you'd already gone far ahead to a place where I couldn't reach you.'

'It's all right,' she whispered. 'That was never going to happen.'

'You can't be sure—'

'Yes, I can. I would never have left you.'

Fiorella came forward, her eyes warm and loving.

'Bless you, dearest Charlotte! Oh, it's so good to see you getting better! We were all so worried.'

Lucio had turned away to say something to a nurse. Fiorella lowered her voice.

'I thought he was going to go crazy. He's been here for days, refusing to leave you, except for a moment to see the baby. I had to bring food in to him because he wouldn't even go to the canteen.'

'Poor Lucio. He looks terrible.'

'Yes, but he'll be all right now his mind can be at rest about you.'

'He's seen the baby?'

'Yes, they couldn't bring her in here because she's in an incubator, but she's strong enough to leave it now so they'll bring her to you. If only you could have seen his face when he saw her for the first time. He wanted to take her in his arms but she had to stay in the incubator, and he was so upset. Lucio, tell Charlotte—oh, he's gone.'

While they were talking Lucio had left the room. They discovered why a moment later when he returned carrying a small bundle close to his chest. Fiorella slid out of the way so that he could sit on the bed, and discreetly glided out of the door, leaving them alone.

'Here she is,' he said. 'Our child.'

Gently he laid the tiny being against her mother's bosom, then turned his body, putting his arm behind her shoulders, supporting mother and child. Charlotte gazed down, entranced, at the tiny face. The baby's eyes were closed and she was deeply asleep, blissfully oblivious of the outside world and the anguish that her arrival had caused.

So we meet at last, Charlotte thought. *You're going to make everything different.*

Lucio's arms were keeping her safe. His rough, unshaven face was scratching her cheek. She turned her head to share a smile with him, receiving his answering glow before they both returned their gazes to the baby.

'Thank you,' he murmured. 'Thank you with all my heart.'

'No, thank you,' she whispered. 'You and she have given me something I never thought I'd have. Now I know I'll have it forever.'

Fiorella appeared in the doorway.

'I left because I thought you three would like to be alone for a while,' she said. 'But I must just see her.' She came over to the bed. 'She's so beautiful.'

'All this time,' Charlotte reflected, 'we were wrong about it being a son.'

'Only because we assumed that a strong baby must be male,' Lucio said. 'That was very old-fashioned of us. We forgot that females can be strong, too. The doctor says she's fit and vigorous, and she's come through that premature birth with all flags flying.' He grinned. 'You never know. She might grow up to play soccer yet. Or maybe she'll settle for ruling the world, the way she already rules ours.'

'But didn't you really want a son?'

'I told you, I didn't mind either way.'

'Yes, but I thought—'

'I know what you thought, that I was just being polite about it. You kept telling me I wanted a boy and I just accepted what you said.' He laid a finger against the baby's cheek. 'I guess I'll just have to get used to being bossed around by my womenfolk.' He gave Fiorella a wicked grin. 'After all, I've had lots of practice.'

'It'll come in useful.' Fiorella chuckled. 'And what are you going to call your little girl?'

'We haven't thought about it yet,' Lucio said. He laid a hand on Charlotte's shoulder. 'Do you have any ideas?'

'Yes,' she said. 'I want to call her Maria.'

Fiorella made a sudden movement, pleased but uncertain.

'You will name her after my girl?' she breathed. 'That is wonderful but, Charlotte, are you sure? Why do you do this? If it is kindness for me, I thank you, but please do not force yourself.'

'I'm not forcing myself,' she said. 'It's what I want to do.'

She looked at Lucio, who was watching her in stunned silence. Fiorella also saw his expression, understood it and slipped quietly out of the room.

'Forgive me if I don't know what to say,' he murmured. 'This is the last thing I expected. I don't know why you— but is Fiorella right? Is this an act of generosity because, if it is, you can't think I'd ever ask you to—'

'I know you wouldn't,' she said when he stumbled to a halt. 'This is what I want.'

'But why? Are you afraid of her? Do you think I love her and not you?'

'My darling, you've got it all wrong. I don't fear Maria as a rival. I did once, but now I know that she was one part of your life, and I'm another. Keep her in your heart. Go on loving her. She doesn't threaten me. I don't want to get rid of her, either from your life or mine.'

He was staring at her as though he couldn't believe what

he heard. Far back in his eyes she saw joy warring with something that was almost fear.

'And my love for you,' he stammered, 'tell me you believe in it, I beg you.'

'I didn't believe it for a long time. I knew you wanted to be a father, have the family we can make together.' She touched his face. 'I knew she was pregnant when she died. You told me when you came back from your stag night. You weren't in your right mind and you thought you were talking to her. Gradually I realised what you meant.'

He groaned and hung his head. 'I wondered next day—I couldn't be sure.'

'You could always have told me.'

'I meant to. I just didn't want to have any secrets from you, and I longed to tell you everything, but I was afraid you'd take it the wrong way. You might have felt insulted, or thought I was making you second best.'

'That was true once. There was a time when I felt you were just "making do" with me.'

'And you didn't sock me on the jaw? Why not? I deserved it.'

'I loved you. I didn't feel I had the right to blame you for not being in love with me. You can't love to order. I hoped we'd grow closer in time and then—who knows?'

'Yes, it took me too long to understand my own heart,' he said sombrely. 'It might have taken longer if you hadn't been in danger during the birth. Then it became hideously clear to me that if you died my own life was over. Nothing mattered but you.'

'And our baby,' she said softly.

He met her eyes and shook his head slightly. 'You,' he said. 'Just you.'

Without waiting for her reply he laid his head down on the pillow beside her.

'You make me complete and you keep me safe,' he murmured. 'I never knew before how much I needed that. But now I know, and I'll never let you go. I warn you, I'll be possessive, domineering, practically making a prisoner of you. Don't think I'll ever let you escape me, because I won't. You'll probably get very fed up with my behaviour.'

She enfolded him in her arms and he buried his face against her.

'I think I can just about manage to put up with you,' she whispered.

A week later mother and baby returned home and Charlotte entered a stage of life more beautiful than anything she could have imagined. Her strength returned quickly, her relationship with her child flowered.

She had the pleasure of seeing Lucio completely happy now that both his personal and professional lives were reaching a triumphant peak. Harvest time was approaching, and everyone was studying the grapes intently to pick exactly the right moment. Testing was under way to determine the levels of sugar, acid and tannin.

'At one time there was only one way to find out,' Lucio told her. 'And that was to put the grapes in your mouth. Nowadays there are machines that will do some of it, but there's still no substitute for what your own taste buds tell you. Mine tell me it'll need a few more days, but then I'll unleash my workers on the vines.'

While many vintners used machines for the harvest Lucio still preferred to have his grapes picked by humans. It made him popular in the area where the employment he offered was a godsend to many. Already the temporary workers were appearing on the estate, waiting for the signal to start.

Charlotte's other great pleasure came from the delight

of her family over the birth of their newest member. They squealed with delight when she held up baby Maria so that she could be seen via the video link.

'Oh, I do wish you were coming to Larkville,' Ellie sighed one night. 'You and Lucio and Maria. We're all so miserable at not being able to get over there for your wedding or the christening, and if you all came to Larkville it would really bind the family together.'

'I know,' Charlotte said, supressing a sigh. 'I really wish I could come, Ellie, honestly I do. But the harvest is about to start.'

'But why do you have to be there for the harvest?' Ellie asked. 'Surely they can do it without you?'

'Well, I won't actually be picking grapes,' she agreed. 'But I won't leave Lucio for the first harvest of our marriage. It's a great moment for him, and I must share it with him.'

'Would he really stop you coming here?'

'No, he wouldn't. He's too generous. But I wouldn't be so unfair as to ask him. I want to be here to share the harvest with him. It'll mean the world to me.'

'More than your family?'

'Lucio is my family now.'

'All right, you do what you think right. We'll be able to talk again tomorrow, then I have to be off to the airport.'

Charlotte shut down the link and sat for a moment thinking about what she had just done. It was a final choice, she knew that. Nor did she regret it for a moment. In Lucio she had gained more than she could have hoped for in a thousand years.

Smiling, she raised Maria in her arms and went to find him. Only to discover that he had just left the house.

'I don't know what got into him,' Fiorella said. 'I thought he was home for the day but he suddenly remembered something he had to do, and took off. Look, you can see his car in the distance. Men can be so annoying!'

Lucio returned a couple of hours later, coming upon Charlotte just as she was putting Maria to bed. Despite Maria being only a few weeks old there was no doubt that her eyes brightened at the sight of her father.

'It's lucky I'm not easily jealous,' Charlotte said. 'Or I might object to having to struggle for her attention.'

'Yes, Fiorella does try to come first with her.' Lucio grinned.

'Actually, I meant you. It's supposed to be the mother who gets up to look after her at night.'

'You mean last night? Well, I brought her to you, didn't I?'

'Only because I'm breastfeeding her. That's one thing you haven't been able to take over. It's lucky the harvest will be starting soon, and that will take up your attention.'

'Actually, it won't,' he said slowly. 'I'm going to let Toni take over the harvest, because I won't be here.'

'Won't—? But where will you be?'

He positioned himself to get a good look at her face before saying, 'I'll be in Larkville, with you and Maria.'

'But I—'

'I've checked with the doctor. He says it's OK for both of you to travel. And I know you want to go because I eavesdropped on the video link you had with Ellie yesterday.'

'You what?'

'And I'm glad I did. I learned a lot from listening to you, and it was very clear to me what I had to do. I've spent this afternoon talking to Toni, my overseer, and some of the others, about what to do while I'm away. They're delighted. They're all too experienced to need me.'

'But the harvest—I know what it means to you to be here.'

'And I know what it means to you to reconcile with your family and to meet your other family. There'll never be another chance as perfect as this, and you simply have to take it.'

He grasped her in urgent hands.

'Listen to me, Charlotte. I've told you that I love you, but I haven't proved it. They were just words, easy to say.'

'But I believe them.'

'And you're right. But the time will come when you'll ask yourself what I ever gave up for you, and I don't want the answer to be "nothing". So far all I've done is take. Now it's time for you to take and me to give.'

'Oh, Lucio—Lucio…'

'Come here.'

His mouth on hers was firm and gentle, assertive but pleading—a mixture of the feelings and attitudes around which their love was built.

'Now,' he said when he'd released her, 'get on to the computer and tell them we're coming. All of us. You, me and Maria.'

'Lucio, are you sure?'

'I was never more sure of anything in my life.'

With all her heart she longed to believe that he meant it, but still a little doubt remained. At the last minute he would realise the size of the undertaking he'd committed himself to, and realise that it was impossible.

These thoughts went through her head as they travelled to the Florence airport, to board the plane to Texas, accompanied by Fiorella. Every moment Charlotte expected him to say something, to back off, count on her understanding. But nothing happened.

It's down to me, she thought at last. *I must tell him that there's no need for this. I'll release him. I must.*

As they neared Passport Control she took a deep breath. 'Lucio—'

'Just a minute,' he said. 'There's my cell phone. *Toni!*'

So that was it, she thought. Toni had called to tell him they couldn't manage without him, and he must return at once. She listened to what Lucio was saying.

'Right.... Good.... So that's fine then. Thanks for telling me. Now I can really enjoy myself in the States. See you in a few days.' He hung up. 'Right now, are we ready? Goodbye, Mamma. I'll call you when we get there. Darling, is something the matter? You look strange.'

'No, I—I can hardly believe this is happening.'

'You'd better believe it. Off we go!'

And suddenly all the questions were answered. They were going through Passport Control, down the corridor into the departure lounge and onto the plane. Then it was time for take-off.

Lucio had prepared for the long flight by buying the best seats, and urging Charlotte to sit by the window.

Lying back, her child in her arms, her beloved at her side, Charlotte was able to look out on the clouds that separated her from the earth, and relish the sensation of being in another universe, one where everything was perfect.

'Maria's getting restless,' Lucio said at last. 'I think she wants to be fed.'

He moved, turning his body so that it formed a protective barrier between Charlotte and anyone who might pass down the aisle.

'Thank you,' she said happily. 'And we've got the seats in two rows all to ourselves, haven't we? What a lucky chance that nobody else wanted them. Why are you laughing like that?'

'It's not chance. I bought eight seats.'

'You—you did what? You bought all these seats?'

'So that you'd have privacy when you needed it.'

'You thought of that?' she whispered.

'I think of you every moment. I long for you to ask me for something, so that I can have the pleasure of giving it to you and showing you what you are to me.'

'Well…there is something.'

'Yes?' And the eagerness in his face told her that he spoke truly when he said he wanted to please her.

'That vineyard in Veneto, I loved the house. Now you've bought it, could it be our home? I know you'll still have to spend some time in Tuscany for Fiorella's sake—'

'But that place will be our main home. Yours and mine. You're right. In fact, you've given me an idea.'

'What?'

'Wait and see.'

They sat in silence, watching the child take nourishment from her mother, looking up at her with eyes filled with contentment.

'She feels safe,' Lucio said. 'Everyone who knows you feels safe.'

'But not only safe, surely?' she asked.

'We'll talk about that later, when you've completely recovered.'

She smiled. Lucio's protective side had been in full flood since the birth, for both herself and Maria.

'I still can't believe you let me make this trip,' she said.

'I didn't *let* you do it,' he corrected her gently. 'I *made* you do it, because you needed to. And whatever you need is what I want.'

He was right in everything, she reflected. Because of his sacrifice she could believe in his love as never before.

And he had understood that. It was the final proof of all that she needed to know.

Looking out of the window she saw that the clouds were clearing, and the world was full of sunshine.

Rome: four months later

Against the darkness the lights glittered on the rushing water. Everywhere there was music, people laughing and singing as they crowded around the Trevi Fountain. Coins were spun into the water, and a thousand wishes rose into the air.

'Have you guessed why I wanted to return to Rome for our honeymoon?' Charlotte asked as they made their way into the square.

'I thought it might have something to do with the last time we were here,' Lucio replied. 'Exactly one year ago today.'

'Yes, we sat at that little café over there, and we talked. Oh, how we talked!'

'And then we went to the fountain. You threw in a coin and cried, "Bring me back to Rome".'

'And I got my wish,' she said. 'Because here I am, with you. That was what I wanted then, what I want now, what I'll always want for the rest of our lives.'

'Who could have foreseen what lay ahead of us?' he marvelled. 'We thought we'd know each other for just a few hours. But that night, our whole futures were decided by a kindly fate.'

'Kindly?' she asked with just a hint of teasing. 'Are you sure?'

'You know better than to ask me that.'

She chuckled. 'You weren't so certain when Maria's

milk landed all over your shirt when you'd just got dressed for the evening.'

'She can do anything she likes and it's fine by me. You have to expect the unexpected.'

'And it's certainly been unexpected,' she mused.

'Right. That first night, who'd have thought that a year later you'd have her and me.'

'Not to mention finding myself the owner of a Veneto vineyard,' she mused.

'A man should give his wife a nice wedding present. Like you said, that will always be our real home. I'm glad you like it.'

'If I listed all the things about you that I like we'd be here forever.'

He held out his hand. 'Come on, let's go and tell Oceanus that he got it right.'

There was the stone deity, dominating the fountain, arrogantly accepting all the coins that were tossed at his feet.

'What happens to the coins?' Charlotte wondered.

'They're regularly gathered up and put into a fund for the needy,' Lucio explained. 'So it's a good way of saying thank-you for a thousand blessings.'

From his pocket he pulled out a bag, heavy with high-value coins, which he shared with her. Together they tossed coin after coin into the water.

'Bring us back to Rome,' he cried.

'Next year,' she added, 'and the year after.'

'And again and again,' he called. 'Do you hear that? Bring us back.'

'Bring us back,' she echoed.

Lucio put his arm about her, looking down at her with adoration.

'But it must be together,' he said. 'Because together is what we always want to be.'

Slowly she nodded. 'Yes,' she murmured. 'Yes.'

There was no need to say more. Everything had been said, enough for the rest of their lives. In the shining light of the fountain he laid his lips on hers for a kiss that was a herald of the night to come, and the years to come. Then, arms about each other, they walked away.

* * * * *

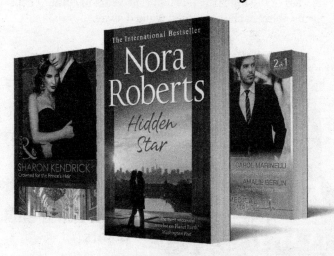
6